GHOSTS OF GREENGLASS HOUSE

GHOSTS OF GREENGLASS HOUSE

BY
KATE MILFORD

WITH ILLUSTRATIONS BY
JAIME ZOLLARS

CLARION BOOKS
HOUGHTON MIFFLIN HARCOURT   BOSTON   NEW YORK

Clarion Books
3 Park Avenue
New York, New York 10016

Clarion Books is an imprint of Houghton Mifflin Harcourt Publishing Company.

www.hmhco.com

The text was set in Bulmer MT.

Library of Congress Cataloging-in-Publication Data
Names: Milford, Kate, author.
Title: Ghosts of Greenglass House / by Kate Milford.
Description: Boston ; New York : Clarion Books, Houghton Mifflin Harcourt, [2017] |
Summary: "Twelve-year-old Milo is stuck spending the winter holidays
in a house full of strange guests who are not what they seem–again! He will have to
work with friends old and new to uncover clues in search of a mysterious map and
a famous smuggler's lost haul" — Provided by publisher.
Identifiers: LCCN 2016049761 | ISBN 9780544991460 (hardcover)
Subjects: | CYAC: Mystery and detective stories. | Hotels, motels, etc. — Fiction. |
Smuggling — Fiction. | Identity—Fiction. | Ghosts—Fiction. | Adoption — Fiction. | BISAC:
JUVENILE FICTION / Mysteries & Detective Stories. | JUVENILE FICTION / Family /
Adoption. | JUVENILE FICTION / Fairy Tales & Folklore / General. | JUVENILE FICTION
/ Holidays & Celebrations / Christmas & Advent. | JUVENILE FICTION / Legends, Myths,
Fables / General. | JUVENILE FICTION / Social Issues / Friendship.
Classification: LCC PZ7.M594845 Gho 2017 | DDC [Fic] — dc23
LC record available at https://lccn.loc.gov/2016049761

Manufactured in the United States of America
DOC 10 9 8 7 6 5 4 3 2 1
4500671559

❄

To Tess, Evy Lou, and Zoey,
at the start of their adventures,
with love

Contents

one

FROST

F ROST WAS PRETTY MUCH the worst. It was like a promise with nothing behind it. It was like not enough icing on a cookie, not enough butter on toast. It was like the big gilt-framed antique mirror in his parents' bedroom: from a distance it was shiny and beautiful, but once you got close enough, you could see the plain old everyday wood peeking through the gold paint. Frost, at least when you wanted snow, was about as disappointing as anything in this world had a right to be — assuming you figured things had a right to be disappointing. Milo Pine wasn't feeling that generous at the moment.

He knelt and leaned on the sill of one of the house's two big bow windows, examining the yard critically through a circle of clear glass in the middle of one white-rimed pane. An English-Mandarin dictionary and a notebook lay forgotten by one knee. Admittedly, the current spectacle was pretty impressive. The frost perfectly mimicked a dusting of snow, and because the temperature outside was so frigid, it had lasted through the day. It had crunched satisfyingly underfoot, too, which was a nice complement to the clouds that had puffed into the air with each breath as he'd crossed the lawn after his last day of school, headed back to the big old inn he and his parents called home. But it *wasn't* snow, which made it almost worse than nothing at all.

This was good. Being cranky about the weather was just what he needed to keep from thinking about the other things he didn't want to let up from the mental depths at which he could just barely manage to ignore them.

His mom sat down on the loveseat behind him and held out a steaming cup. "Want to talk about it?"

"I hate frost," Milo said in a tone that he hoped would signal to his mother to please not dare to suggest that the weather wasn't what was really bothering him.

Twilight was coming on, and he could sort of see her reflection in the glass. She had a look on her face that was both unimpressed and thoughtful, as if she had gotten the message and was debating whether or not to call him on it. But then, the glass was old, wavy and uneven, so maybe it was just twisting up her reflection funny. He reached back to take the cup.

On top of the hot chocolate was a float of unreasonably thick whipped cream that he'd heard Mrs. Caraway, the inn's cook, making about ten minutes ago. The cream was dusted with smashed candy cane bits, which was probably his mother's touch. He hazarded a look at her . . . she definitely knew he was upset about something other than weather. She was just waiting him out. Well, he could play that game too.

"Thanks," he said, and turned resolutely back to the window.

"First hot chocolate of winter vacation." Mrs. Pine raised her own cup. "Cheers."

"Cheers." As they sipped, footsteps approached on the stairs. Reluctantly, Milo pivoted to look over his mom's shoulder, following the sound. The ground level of the inn was big and open, with one room flowing into the next, and from where he was, Milo could see pretty much the entire floor. "When's he leaving?" he asked, watching the bottom of the staircase on the other side of the dining room.

"Tomorrow at some point. Supposedly," Mrs. Pine said quietly. Then she turned to the young man who appeared at the bottom of the stairs, a pencil behind one ear and glasses askew on his nose. "Drinks on the stove if you're done for the day, Mr. Syebuck."

Emmett Syebuck, their only guest, sighed happily. "I could just stay here forever. This place is amazing."

"Well, we're so glad you've enjoyed your visit."

"Hey, about that, Mrs. P."

Oh, no. Milo stifled a groan. His mom patted his shoulder.

The young man crossed the dining room and came to lean on the back of the loveseat. "I was thinking," he said. "One more day and I'll have every window at least sketched. Would it be a huge pain in the neck if I checked out day after tomorrow?"

Milo slurped in a huge mouthful to keep himself from answering. *Yes, yes, it would, actually. I, personally, would find it a huge pain in the neck.*

His mother, of course, said what Milo had known she'd say. "That's no problem, Mr. Syebuck."

Their guest beamed. "Thanks, ma'am. And I wish you all would just call me Emmett."

"You're welcome, and I'll try, Emmett, but you know, old habits die hard." Mrs. Pine glanced into the kitchen. "Mrs. Caraway leaves tonight, though, so just be aware that meals will be a little less fancy tomorrow."

"It could be toast and instant noodle soup and I'd be perfectly content," Emmett assured her. "I'm a simple fellow at heart. And in a pinch, some of my colored pencils are kind of tasty — not that I've tried them or anything."

Milo's mother laughed. "It won't come to that."

"Well, thanks again. And hey, thank you, too, Milo."

Milo turned, surprised. "What for?"

"For letting me impose on your holidays. I promise I'll be out of your hair before Christmas Eve. I know how it is."

"It's okay," Milo said gruffly.

"Well, I appreciate it. And now that I don't have to pack tonight, I think I'll relax and just stare at the fire awhile." He drummed a short *ba-da-ba-bump* on the back of the loveseat with his palms, then straightened and went into the kitchen.

"You think he's really an art student?" Mrs. Pine asked in an undertone.

"Probably," Milo said. "That or he's Skellansen in disguise, wanting to make sure his precious chandelier's being looked after properly." They'd been amusing themselves with speculations like this since the day Emmett had showed up.

"He's too young for Skellansen."

Milo eyed the guest's back critically. "Lots of makeup. And super-thin rubber prosthetics, like in the movies. You can do miracles with that stuff."

"Hmm. Maybe."

Among the many occurrences that had made last year's winter break about the strangest time in Milo's life was the discovery at Greenglass House of a cartoon: a valuable drawing of a stained-glass window by a mysterious artist named Lowell Skellansen. One of the inn's guests at the time, Dr. Wilbur Gowervine, had presented the cartoon along with a lecture at Nagspeake's City University over the summer. A couple months after that, Emmett Syebuck — student, artist, and Skellansen fanboy — had turned up toting enough art and photography supplies to open a store, eager to learn more about the house and its collection of stained glass.

It wasn't Dr. Gowervine's fault. After much discussion with Milo's parents, he'd promised to keep the location of the find between himself and his department chair. Still, when you took into account that not only Dr. Gowervine but five other guests had made their way to the inn last December by following different bits of the house's history to its doorstep, maybe the only surprising thing was that more curiosity seekers hadn't worked out where the mysterious Skellansen artwork had come from.

Not that the Pines had admitted to anything when Emmett had turned up, other than to confirm that yes, they had also attended the lecture, and yes, they suspected that the chandelier over the dining room table was a piece of Skellansen glass. But that had been enough for Emmett. The guy acted like a kid on Christmas morning. Every single day. And he'd been here a week already.

Of course, the other notable thing about last year was that none of the strangers who'd come to the inn that Christmas had been there for the reasons they'd claimed they were. Hence the *Is Syebuck who he says he is?* game, even though Milo was pretty sure that was all it was — a game. And really, Emmett's presence was fine, as long as he did what he said he would and got the heck out before Christmas Eve.

The door swung open, letting in a gust of wind but — naturally — no accompanying swirl of snow. Stupid frost. Didn't even blow around in the wind. Instead, the gust swept Milo's father inside with an armful of firewood. Mrs. Pine got up. "Ben, Mr. Syebuck — Emmett — is going to stay on an extra night."

"If that's okay," Emmett called from the kitchen, where Mrs. Caraway was busy ladling hot chocolate into his mug.

"Not a problem," Mr. Pine called back as he kicked off his boots on his way to the fireplace.

Mrs. Caraway joined Milo's parents in the living room. "Nora, Ben, you guys want me to stay on an extra night too?"

"No, no," Mrs. Pine said immediately. "Isn't Lizzie already coming to pick you up?"

"Probably, but she was out running errands anyway. I don't think she'll mind having made the trip. I might invite her to stay for dinner."

"Of course."

Mrs. Caraway turned to Milo. "Any requests? Grilled cheese and tomato soup? I have chili fixings . . ." She glanced at the dictionary on the floor. "Or I have some surprisingly good tomatoes that would be amazing in the egg-and-tomato stir-fry dish you like whose name I always mangle."

"*Xīhóngshì chǎo jīdàn,*" Milo said promptly. There weren't a ton of Chinese dishes he confidently knew the names of, but this one he'd made sure to memorize. "Yes, please. And maybe grilled cheese, too?" It wasn't the kind of dinner she usually made when there were guests, but then Milo didn't usually get asked for his input.

"Grilled cheese is my actual favorite sandwich," Emmett said as he dropped contentedly onto the sofa in the living room. "And I'm generally a fan of tomatoes and eggs. This is great."

"Well, good." Milo dropped his chin into his hands, waiting for that special relief that usually came with getting home from school at the start of vacation. It hadn't come yet, and the more he looked for it, the further away it seemed. Instead, he was tense and tight. And frustrated. And *angry*. And he wasn't sure whether it was Emmett's presence that was keeping him from feeling good or all the other stuff. Unfortunately, that uncertainty made all those worries he'd tried to cover with a layer of disappointing frost come bubbling back up.

You don't have to feel this way, he told himself. *Negret wouldn't feel this way.*

It didn't help. Not even remotely. That was maybe the most frustrating thing of all.

His father sat down on the floor next to him. "Hey, pal."

"Hey."

"So your mom said when you first got home you mentioned that something happened at school today."

"It was yesterday. I just didn't want to talk about it." *Still don't,* he added silently.

"Do you—" His father stopped mid-question and shifted gears. "Was it social studies again?"

Milo scowled at the window and nodded stiffly.

His father started to speak, paused, then said, "I think if you could tell me what happened so Mom and I can talk to the teacher, it's possible you might feel a little better."

"Why?" Milo asked. "It won't change that it happened."

"That's true, but would any part of you feel better knowing it won't happen again?"

"You don't know that," Milo grumbled. "Even if you and Mom talk to him, you don't know that."

"I submit that it's worth a shot," Mr. Pine said. "If we don't try, then we can be almost sure it *will* happen again, don't you think?

Or did you explain to him afterward, like you said you would last time he upset you?"

"No," Milo admitted in a very small voice.

"Wasn't that our agreement, though?" his dad asked gently. "You said you didn't need Mom and me to do it because you wanted to try yourself."

Milo nodded.

Mr. Pine nodded too. "Okay, well, how about this: how about we just start with you telling me what happened so you can get it off your chest?"

Getting it off your chest never did any good. That was a parent thing, thinking that talking about stuff helped. Because—and why did no one understand this?—nothing could change that the awful thing had already happened. That was why you felt crummy afterward, obviously—because it *happened,* not because you needed to talk about it and live through it all over again. But Milo didn't have any better ideas, and his dad didn't look as if he was going to leave.

"All right." He took a deep breath. "We're still studying Nagspeake history in the nineteenth century."

"I remember."

"Well, I guess after I said the thing last week about how our house was built during the War of 1812 and Mr. Chancelor said what he said"—here Milo forced himself to soldier on and not think about the previous week's debacle—"I guess after that, he must've gone home and done some research, because yesterday he came in and said some Nagspeake historian he knew had found something about a Chinese crew that came to the city much later, and Mr. Chancelor showed the whole class some written characters that I guess made up the name of the ship, and he asked me to translate them for everybody." His voice had gone shaky. "And I didn't know them. So then he read the Mandarin pronunciation out loud, and asked me to translate *that*." He gulped air. "And I still didn't know."

His father sighed. "That is utter crap, Milo. I'm so sorry."

It was three kinds of utter crap, if you wanted to get technical. In the first place, when Milo had raised his hand while they were discussing the War of 1812 to mention that Greenglass House — Lansdegown House, as it had been called then — had been built by a seafaring family with a Chinese child in it just before the war, Mr. Chancelor had said that in fact, there hadn't been any Chinese crews to visit Nagspeake until much later in the century. Milo had started to explain that it hadn't been a Chinese *crew*, it had been a British and Chinese blended family called Bluecrowne, but Mr. Chancelor had already moved on, as if he'd proved Milo wrong and that was that. This had been the cause of last week's breakdown.

Then yesterday had been crummy for two separate reasons. First, Mr. Chancelor had acted as though finding a Chinese crew arriving in Nagspeake in 1835 proved for sure that Milo was wrong about the Bluecrownes and their Chinese family members getting there earlier. That alone would've been untenable, because Milo *wasn't* wrong. Then the teacher had produced those characters and assumed Milo would be able to translate them just because he was Chinese, which had embarrassed him in front of his whole class. And that had been *awful*, not to mention unfair.

It was unfair because Milo *did* know a number of characters. He and his parents had been learning together for a while now, only they were learning *Simplified* Chinese characters, and from the looks of it, whatever writing system the ship's name had been composed in two hundred years ago was vastly more complicated than what Milo was studying. It was doubly unfair because he and his parents were learning Mandarin, too — but he wasn't a native speaker, in part because he'd grown up in Nagspeake, where the Chinese population still wasn't that big, and in part because he'd grown up with a mom and dad who not only weren't native speakers either, they were white. Plus there were a ton of distinct dialects used in China, so even if Milo *had* been a native speaker, Mr. Chancelor still shouldn't have assumed he'd necessarily speak Mandarin. There was really no way to know whether even Milo's own birth family had spoken it; he and his parents had chosen Mandarin to learn because it had been easiest for Milo's school to find him a Mandarin tutor. And it was extra-super *really* unfair because Milo was pretty sure there were plenty of actual Chinese people who wouldn't recognize every single Chinese character there was and plenty who couldn't read them at all.

But none of that was the truly awful part. The truly awful part was that all of these things, taken together, made Milo feel as if the phrase "actual Chinese person" didn't actually apply to him.

Mr. Pine leaned his elbows on his knees. "I'm guessing after that, it didn't feel like you could explain to him why it was upsetting."

No. After that, it had been all Milo could do not to burst into tears, and he'd gotten out of the classroom as fast as possible the minute it was time to go to lunch, where he'd worked hard to tamp down the panic attack he could feel coming on.

He shook his head. "I couldn't think of anything to say." Also: tears. Also: panic attack.

"I think I'd have felt the same way." His dad glanced at the dictionary and notebook on the floor. "I guess that explains those. Getting some vocabulary work in?"

"Yeah." They sat together for a moment, watching the twilight darken across the glittering lawn. In the living room behind them, the new wood crackled in the fireplace, and the smell tugged at Milo's heart. *It's vacation,* that smell said. *It's almost Christmas. You can be happy. Just let yourself be happy.*

Mr. Pine put an arm around him, and Milo leaned into his shoulder. "Hey, speaking of vocabulary, I have some new words I looked up this week. I need to double-check pronunciation, but here goes." Milo's dad held up his index finger. "First: *bridge.* Either *qiáo* or *qiáoliáng,* although I think *qiáoliáng* might mean a metaphorical bridge. Second: *broken,* meaning falling apart — that's *cánpò.* Then there's *ferry,* meaning the boat, which I think is *dùchùan.* Lastly: *late. Wǎn.*"

Milo grinned. "So what you're telling me here is that you didn't make it on time to that meeting you were going to today."

"I did not," Mr. Pine confirmed, "but let's focus on the fact that I can almost explain why in Mandarin. What've you got?"

Milo picked up his notebook. "*Winter* is *dōngtiān.* A *covering of snow* is *jīxuě. Frost* is *shuāng. Annoying* is *nǎorén.* That's as far as I got."

Mr. Pine chuckled. "Tell me how you really feel." Then his expression sobered. "Listen, you don't have to make a decision now, but I want you to think something over. It sounds to me like Mr. Chancelor thinks he's finding interesting things about the Chinese in Nagspeake, and he's just excited to share them. He doesn't realize how uncomfortable it makes you to be singled out, and he doesn't understand that he shouldn't make assumptions about you based on how you look. I think most people know they shouldn't make *bad* assumptions about people, but they don't always get that making *any* assumptions is probably not a good idea. And he probably knows you have a language tutor. Teachers do talk with each other. That could be why he thought you might know the Mandarin, anyway."

"I guess." It might've been logical, but it wasn't precisely comforting. Milo could barely even deal with the idea of being talked about by people he loved and trusted, and Mr. Chancelor definitely fell outside that category.

His dad made a sympathetic face. He knew. "I think it's time your mom and I talk to him and just explain things. I bet you anything we can straighten it out, and then you won't have to worry anymore." He held out his right pinkie. "But we won't do it unless you say it's okay."

Milo linked his pinkie with his dad's. Pinkie-swears were unbreakable vows. "If I say yes, you have to make him understand that I'm right about the Bluecrownes who built Greenglass House."

"Well, obviously. Are you kidding?" They shook their linked fingers. "Now maybe, if you can, try not to think about it anymore for a while. Because when you think about this kind of thing, you worry, and worrying just makes you feel worse."

That much was true, even if it was easier to *say* you were going to stop worrying than to actually *do* it. "I'll try."

"All right. We'll revisit this closer to New Year's, and in the meantime, if you want to talk more, you can come to Mom and me anytime. Deal?"

"Deal."

"Great. And may I also compliment you on your choice of dinner menu?"

"You may."

Milo's dad got up and went off to do whatever parents did to keep themselves from bugging you when you plainly wanted space. And while Milo was trying to decide whether he felt better or not, the unthinkable happened.

The bell rang.

two

THE BACHELORETTE PARTY

EVERYBODY FROZE. There was a distinct rattle of dishes in the kitchen: Mrs. Caraway had dropped something in shock. Milo turned slowly to look warily at his parents.

"Was that what I think it was?" Mrs. Pine asked.

The bell rang again. It had a slightly tinny, buzzing edge to its tone. "I believe it was," Mr. Pine said, setting down the coffee he'd just brought to the dining table. "I guess I'd better go."

"Does that mean someone wants to come up?" Emmett asked.

"Not up," Milo's father said as he headed for the door. "That's not the railcar bell."

"I'll come too," Milo said, darting for his boots and coat.

Greenglass House had two bells these days. There was the big old one that had hung on the porch almost since the house had been built, which was connected by a series of cords to a pull way down at the dock at the bottom of the hill. Usually this was the bell that announced guests, since most of them arrived by boat. But there was a second, newer bell, one that Milo's father had put in only this year. It, too, was an antique, but it was electric, and instead of connecting to the dock, its lines ran up the hill and into the woods. It hadn't been used since the Pines had tested it back when it had first been installed.

Milo and his father bundled up and marched out into the cold. "You know what this means," Mr. Pine said thoughtfully.

"Yeah," Milo replied. "I wonder who's with him."

They crossed the crunchy, frosty lawn and headed into the trees that covered the slope of the hill, all blue-green firs and bare bone-colored birches, passing the assorted red stone outbuildings scattered throughout the woods until they came to one that looked like a small, ramshackle house. In actuality, it was a train station. The doors were open, and a familiar tall, thin figure stood in the entrance: Brandon Levi, the sole conductor on Nagspeake's all-but-defunct and mostly secret Belowground Transit System.

"Oy, Ben. Hey, Milo," he said as they approached. "Bell worked, I take it."

"Like a charm," Mr. Pine said, shaking Brandon's gloved hand. "Was this a test?"

"Nope. Got a couple dubious characters looking for a place to lie low. Wanted to make sure the coast was clear."

More guests. Milo sighed.

And yet, he thought with a glimmer of excitement twitching to life in his gut, *this is how it started last year.* And last year had actually turned out to be more than just frustration and a bunch of changes to his beloved holiday routine. Last year he had discovered Odd Trails, a role-playing game that had helped him find a more heroic version of himself in the form of a character called Negret. Negret was an escaladeur, a kind of blackjack or trickster who specialized in reconnaissance and stealth—a nimble, capable, less anxious Milo-and-yet-not-Milo that he'd been able to turn to for a while when things got unpredictable or began to feel out of control. As Negret, he had played a sort of real-world version of Odd Trails last year, a campaign waged within Greenglass House itself, and in the course of that campaign he'd worked out the secrets that had brought eight unexpected guests to his home.

But all of that had been because last year, among those strangers that had turned up, there had been one special stranger in particular, the one who had introduced him to Odd Trails and Negret. He had waited and waited all year for her to turn up again, but she had never come back.

Meddy.

Meanwhile, Mr. Pine made a face. "We've got one guest—a Skellansen enthusiast, a student of some kind—and I'd say he seems pretty nonthreatening, for whatever that's worth. He's leaving day after tomorrow." He craned his neck to peer over Brandon's shoulder. "Who's with you? Anyone we know?"

"It's a surprise," Brandon said drily. He leaned back into the station. "You guys catch all that? Want to chance it?"

"Like we have anywhere else to go, Brandon."

"Can we just go in? I'm freezing my tail off here!"

Milo hadn't heard those voices in a long time, but he knew them both right away, and he felt his face break into a wide smile.

Milo's dad recognized them too. "Come on out, the pair of you," he laughed.

Brandon stood aside, and two women in their twenties burst out of the station. "Ta-da!" sang the one with a fringe of red curling out from under her black stocking cap.

"Merry Christmas," said the other, who wore a black beret over bright blue hair. "With apologies for the lack of notice."

Despite how little Milo relished the idea of more guests, these two were different. They'd been part of the bizarre and unexpected group of strangers who'd shown up last winter break, although back then they'd come as adversaries. Now, it seemed, they'd come as friends.

"Hi, Clem. Hi, Georgie," Milo said, waving. "It's nice to see you."

"What's this waving stuff?" red-haired Clem Candler demanded. "Next you're going to try and shake hands. Get over here." She wrapped him in a big hug.

"I'd hug you too," said blue-haired Georgie Moselle, "but I'm going to die of hypothermia if we don't get inside fast."

It was cold, but not *that* cold. Milo took a closer look at Georgie and realized she was practically swimming in a coverall suit that had to have been made for somebody over six feet tall. Someone like Brandon. Who, Milo realized (now that he was paying attention), wasn't wearing anything over his jeans and shirt and looked plenty cold too.

"Is your hair wet?" Mr. Pine asked.

"And my shoes," Georgie grumbled. "And my clothes, which is why I'm drowning in Brandon's. For which I am extremely grateful," she added as they all started walking toward the house.

"*Why* is your hair wet?" Milo inquired.

"And what are you doing here?" Mr. Pine added. "Not that we aren't delighted to see you, obviously."

"Obviously," Clem said, grinning. Then her usual good humor faded. "These two questions are not unrelated."

"We're on the lam," Georgie said grimly. "But if anyone asks, this is Clem's bachelorette weekend and I'm treating her to a cozy winter getaway."

"Bachelorette weekend?" Mr. Pine repeated dubiously. "Is this just a clever cover, or is there some truth to it?"

"The best covers always have some truth to them," Clem said. "Yes, Owen and I are getting married. Just before New Year's. That is . . ." Her voice trailed off.

"If I didn't just go and screw it all up beyond repair," Georgie finished.

Clem touched her shoulder. "I wasn't going to say that."

"I know you weren't. That's why *I* said it. But it's true."

"It's *not* true, and if I *were* going to say anything like that, I would have said if *I* didn't just go and screw it up."

Milo glanced at his father. Mr. Pine caught his eye, winced, and glanced at Brandon, who put both hands up in a *Don't ask me* gesture.

They had reached the lawn. "Clearly there's more to this than we're going to have time to hear just now," Mr. Pine said. "Like I was telling Brandon, I'm pretty sure the guy at the house is as advertised, just a fellow who's way into windows. But he's staying until day after tomorrow, so for the moment, what do we call you?"

Georgie and Clem glanced at each other. "Real names are fine," Georgie said. "Aliases aren't going to help us out of this one. They know who we are and what we look like."

Before anyone could ask what that ominous comment was all about, Mrs. Pine opened the front door. Georgie and Clem shouted hellos and took off at a trot for the warmth of the indoors. Then, just as everyone was crowding up the stairs, there was the sound of car tires on gravel behind them, and Lizzie Caraway honked and leaned out the window of her battered blue car.

Apparently it was going to be a full house for a while. Milo couldn't decide if he was about to freak out or not. *Come on, Meddy,* he begged silently. *Where are you?*

After a quick flurry of hellos and hugs, with introductions for Emmett Syebuck's benefit, Mrs. Pine took Georgie's plastic bag full of wet clothes to throw in the dryer and Milo led her and Clem upstairs to the guest rooms. Neither had much in the way of luggage. Clem had a smallish backpack and a short document tube, and Georgie had a messenger satchel. Halfway up the stairs, Milo remembered his manners. "Want me to take those?"

"Thanks, Milo, but there's glass in mine again," Georgie said with a half smile. Milo blushed. Last year he'd smashed a bottle of perfume while helping with Georgie's luggage.

"I'm fine," Clem said. "Thanks anyway."

"Okay. Any preference?" he asked as they reached the third-floor landing.

"Where's the civilian?" Georgie asked.

"This floor. Three E."

"Let's go up to five," Clem said tiredly.

"So you can get your runs in again?" Milo asked. When she'd been a guest here last year, Clem had spent a lot of time running the stairs.

But she shook her head. "Just looking for privacy. I don't know if I'm going to feel much like running."

Milo frowned. This was totally unlike the Clem Candler he knew.

They trooped up to the fifth floor, above which there was nothing but attic. Clem chose 5W, the same room she'd picked last year, and Georgie took the one next to it. Just as they were about to close their respective doors, footsteps drummed in the stairwell and Emmett Syebuck appeared from around the corner with his camera bouncing against his hip.

"Wait," he huffed. Both Clem and Georgie leaned warily out into the hall, still holding their bags. "Can I just—there are two windows on this floor I haven't sketched yet. Can I take some pictures before you settle in?"

The two girls looked at each other, then, with similar curious expressions, considered the art student still trying to get his wind back.

"Which ones do you still need to get?" Milo asked.

Emmett took one last deep breath and pointed at Clem's room. "The enameled window's in there, right? I need that one. And the one in five E, I think."

Clem stepped aside and waved an arm. "Go for it. I picked a different room anyway. I was just having a look at the enameled glass myself."

"Oh. Thanks." Emmett glanced at Georgie. "What about you? Will I be in your way if I take some pictures?"

"Nope," Georgie replied breezily. "We're both staying on four, but Milo said we shouldn't miss the windows up here." And without waiting to hear his reply, they headed back downstairs again.

Emmett watched them go, looking a little confused. "Guess you don't have to rush after all," Milo said.

"Yeah," Emmett agreed. "It's pretty dark already anyway. Still, as long as I'm up here . . ." He shrugged and disappeared into 5W.

Milo descended to the fourth floor and walked down the hall until he heard movement in one of the rooms. He knocked on the door of 4W. "What was that all about?" he asked when Georgie peered out.

"Job-related instincts," she said as the door to the adjacent room opened and Clem came out to join them. "Probably unnecessary, but just in case." She glanced at Clem. "What do you think?"

"About young Mr. Syebuck?" Clem considered, then gave Milo a gentle push into 4W. She followed him and closed the door behind her. She looked at Milo, then *around* him, as if there might be someone else in the room. Milo turned to see if somebody had somehow managed to follow him without his noticing. "Is it just you, Milo?" she asked.

Oh. Milo slumped. "Yeah, it's just me."

"Too bad. It would've been useful to have extra eyes and ears on things right about now." Clem perched on the desk and clapped her hands on her knees. "So. Syebuck. I don't get any particular vibe from him." She glanced at Georgie, who sat cross-legged on the bed, still engulfed in Brandon's coveralls. "You?"

Georgie made a noncommittal noise. "What else do you know about him, Milo?"

"Not much. He's a student at City University, and he's been sketching and photographing everything glass in the house. He's nice enough. Super enthusiastic."

"If he's at the university, then Gowervine would know him, right?" Clem asked. "I mean, since he studies glass and whatnot. How many stained-glass nerds could there be at one institution?"

"I'll try to get hold of the professor," Georgie said. "I'll feel a lot better if we can verify that this guy is who he says he is."

Clem nodded. She stood and started to pace.

Milo looked from one to the other. They both seemed so troubled. Georgie was clearly worried, and Clem . . . Clem looked concerned too, but mainly she seemed sad. Sadness looked totally wrong on her face.

"What's going on?" he asked. The two girls hesitated. "Don't you trust me?" Milo demanded, indignant.

"Of course we do, Milo." Clem sighed. "It's just that . . . well, you know what we do for a living."

"Yeees," Milo said slowly.

"And that it's not always legal, strictly speaking?"

"You're *thieves,*" Milo said pointedly. "When is that ever legal?"

"The point is, we don't want to get you in trouble. Or your parents, either. We just need a place to hide out for a while, and the less you know, the better. Isn't that how it usually works around here?"

"Usually," Milo admitted. Greenglass House's clientele was, to be accurate, mostly made up of smugglers. Generally smugglers on shore leave, but every once in a while, there were guests who the Pines suspected were not so much on vacation as hiding out. Everybody involved knew not to ask questions. Milo knew it. And yet . . . Clem and Georgie were their friends. And they were obviously in trouble.

"If there's anything we can do to help, Mom and Dad would want to know about it," Milo said. "Me too."

"I know, Milo," Clem said, ruffling his hair. She looked to Georgie. "And Milo did figure pretty much everything out last time we were here. Nobody would've found what they were looking for if not for him."

"That's the truth," Georgie admitted. "Let me think about it." She looked at Milo for a long minute. "Milo? Where's Meddy these days?"

"I don't know," Milo said, his frustration about his friend's absence bubbling right up to the surface. "I haven't seen her since last Christmas Eve!"

"But is she . . . is she here?" Georgie persisted.

Milo shook his head. "If she is, she isn't showing herself. I don't know why. But if she *isn't* here, maybe that means Emmett Syebuck is who he says he is. Last year she said she felt a wrongness in the house once the guests started showing up, and that's part of what brought her to us."

"Ghosts," Clem said, shaking her head. "Who can figure 'em?"

True enough.

three

TO CLEM AND GEORGIE

ILO LEFT GEORGIE AND CLEM to settle in — whatever that meant to a pair of nervous thieves without any actual luggage to unpack — and went down to the second floor, which was his family's private living space. There, in his parents' study, he found the keys to 4W and 4S, which he delivered to Georgie's room, where the two women were still camped out, talking in hushed voices that went silent the moment he knocked.

"Thanks," Clem said, whisking the keys out of his palm. She started to close the door, then sighed and looked back at Georgie. "I'd better just do it, hadn't I?"

"Unless you want me to," Georgie said listlessly. "*Mea culpa* and so forth."

"No, the longer I don't call, the weirder it'll seem." Clem turned to Milo. "Think I could use your phone?"

Milo looked at the phone on the table next to Georgie's bed. "Well, yeah, of course."

"No," she said apologetically, "I mean your family's private phone. Just since we know that Syebuck character wanders the guest floors. Should I ask your mom and dad?"

"No, that's okay. They won't mind. I'll show you."

He led Clem down to the second floor. This, at least, was familiar — if he hadn't known Clem was there, Milo would never have guessed he was being followed. She was utterly soundless as she walked, like a cat.

"Hey, Clem?" he asked. "Think while you're here you can show me how to use the lockpicks you gave me last year?"

"Sure, Milo," she said, sounding preoccupied. "Hey, would you do me a favor too? Would you be a lookout for me while I make this call? Just in case."

"Sure." Milo opened the study door and pointed to the phone on the drop-front desk. "I'll be right outside."

Clem slipped in and closed the door. Milo sat cross-legged outside the study. A moment later, on the other side of the wall, Clem began speaking. It sounded as if she was leaving a message for Dr. Gowervine — there were no pauses for anyone else to reply. Then came a brief silence. When Clem spoke again, it was in a completely different tone of voice. "Hey, love. Just wanted to let you know where I am." It had to be Owen on the other end of the line now.

There was a pause. "I know, I know, but Georgie arranged a

weekend away as a surprise. I would have called earlier, but I assumed you were in on it." Silence for a moment; then Clem spoke again. "That's not fair. I said I would, didn't I?" Silence. "We'll be back Monday." Pause. A short laugh, then: "Greenglass House, of course."

After that came the *I love you, goodbye* business. Milo stared hard at the ceiling and tried not to listen to anything other than the creaks of the house. Finally Clem emerged, closed the door behind her, and dropped to a seat next to Milo. She sat in silence for a minute; then she rolled her head against the wall to look his way. "Never lie to the people you love, Milo. It's so crummy, and it takes so much energy."

"Um. Okay," Milo said helplessly. "Everything's all right?"

"For the moment." She smiled weakly and got to her feet. "Thanks." Then she left, soundlessly as ever.

Since the inn now had three guests to feed (plus Brandon, who volunteered to stay for dinner if no one minded), Lizzie headed back into town for groceries. She and her mother had offered to stay the night to help prep meals for the next day. By the time she got back and they all sat down to eat, it was nearly seven—which wasn't that much past their usual dinnertime, but after all the comings and goings and the early nightfall, it felt a lot later to Milo.

The table was full: Milo and his parents, Mrs. Caraway and Lizzie, Brandon and Emmett and Clem and Georgie, who was looking a bit more comfortable now that she had her own dry clothes back. And although both girls were still acting not quite like themselves, it was a fairly companionable meal. Plus Mrs. Caraway was getting really good at the stir-fried tomatoes and eggs. Milo had two helpings.

"I hear we have cause for celebration," Lizzie said, throwing an arm around Clem's shoulders.

"Yes, it's true," Clem said, putting on a wide but definitely forced smile. "Owen and I are getting married right before the New Year."

"I picked up some champagne in town," Lizzie told her. "We can have a toast tonight."

"That's super, Lizzie. Thanks."

"You know they got together right here," Brandon said to Emmett. "Last year at Christmas."

"Sure did," Clem said. "That's why Georgie decided to bring me back to Greenglass House for a getaway before Owen and I tie the knot."

"I was wondering," Emmett said. "Seems a little low-key for a bachelorette party."

"I'm a low-key sort of girl," Clem told him.

"Then you must've met Dr. Gowervine," the art student went on. He glanced at Mrs. Pine. "Wasn't it last Christmas that he was here?"

Milo looked up at his parents. Nobody had confirmed that. Fortunately, the Pines had their answers worked out already—probably had since the day Emmett had turned up on their doorstep. "I'm sure you can understand that we don't talk about our guests to anyone else," Mrs. Pine said smoothly. "Privacy."

Emmett nodded, chastened. "Of course."

"So what brings *you* here, Mr. Syebuck?" Georgie asked.

Milo thought there was a bit of an inquisitorial edge to her voice, but if so, it went right over Emmett's head. Instantly his embarrassment melted away, and the brightness of the smile he turned on Georgie was enough to make her sit back in her seat a little. "Are you kidding? This place is a work of art!" He pointed to the chandelier over the table, a sort of minimalist imagining of a ship with curling triangular pieces of frosted glass for sails. "An actual work of Skellansen glass, just hanging up in an inn! It's like being invited to someone's place for Thanksgiving and discovering they live in a Frank Lloyd Wright house. Or going for a sail with a friend and his boat's an original Clinkervell clipper." He sighed happily. "It's extraordinary. Not to mention all the other glass. Eighteenth-century pieces in the stairwells. The enameled window on the fifth floor! Do you know, I think that's a Wellshowe window? As far as I'm aware, there are no other Wellshowe windows in Nagspeake that aren't in museums. And she painted them *in situ,* to be complimented by the particular light in that location at a particular time on a particular day of the year. If this is the original home of that piece, it's an unprecedented opportunity to see the window as the artist truly intended it to be seen. Plus," he added, turning to Milo's folks, "it would mean that Ellamae Wellshowe was once *literally here,* actually *in your home!*" He looked around the table, radiating delight.

"That's really something," Clem replied, amused.

"Hmm" was all Georgie said.

"And I don't know which rooms you picked on the fourth

floor," Emmett continued, "but I've been obsessing over one of the windows up there. It's a smallish window, copper foil holding the pieces, and it has four round medallions with images of people in them. It looks like gilded glass . . ." He scratched his head thoughtfully. "Maybe some artist's take on *verre églomisé*? It might even be very thin gold sandwich glass, although ordinarily it's not hard to tell the difference." Abruptly he seemed to remember he'd been talking to other people, and glanced expectantly from Georgie to Clem and back. "You know the one?"

"I think that's in my room," Georgie said warily.

He grinned. "Lucky. Also, I wish you would call me Emmett. Everybody, I mean," he added hastily.

"I'll try," Georgie said drily. She stood and picked up her plate. "Anybody else done? I'll clear the table."

Milo handed his plate over and turned to his mom. "May I be excused?"

"Sure, pal."

He ran up to his room and rifled through his desk for a spiral pad and pen he'd found in the attic a year ago. He slipped these in one of his back pockets, and in the other he tucked a rolled cylinder of leather tied closed with a cord: his lockpick kit. Then he dashed back down the stairs and into the living room and crawled into the space between the tree and the corner in which it sat beside the crackling fire. It was a spot that he looked forward to making his own every year, and usually it was a place he loved for its privacy. This year, though, it felt a little lonely.

He opened the pad and looked at a blank page for a long time.

Then he closed it again and sat back against the wall, letting his eyes go out of focus as he stared into the tree so that it became a blur of twinkles and gleams against a deep green canvas. There was something going on with Clem and Georgie for sure, but that wasn't so much a puzzle to crack as a thing they hadn't chosen to share. Somehow it didn't seem right to try to uncover the secrets of his friends. Especially since, whatever was up, Clem hadn't even told her fiancé about it.

"Another half-hour to cake," Mrs. Caraway announced in the dining room. "Shall I open the champagne? Who'd like a glass?"

Emmett was the only one to decline. "No need for me to be an interloper for your toast. Plus, there's an outrageous moon out there. Maybe I'll go check out that fifth-floor window again and see how it looks in moonlight."

A few minutes later Mr. Pine sat down at the edge of the hearth and passed Milo a tumbler of reddish punch with a cherry on a little silver toothpick in it.

"Fancy," Milo said. "Thank you."

"You're welcome. You have to have something for the toast. Come on."

Milo took his punch and followed Mr. Pine back to the dining room, where Lizzie popped the cork from a fat green bottle and poured champagne into seven low, saucer-shaped glasses. When everyone had been served, Mrs. Pine lifted her glass. "There will be so many toasts to the bride- and groom-to-be that I don't think the world will miss one if I change things up." She looked at Georgie and Clem, who each stood with her non-champagne-holding arm around the other. "Let's make this a toast to these two young ladies, who first came here as rivals but returned as true friends."

As Mrs. Pine spoke, Georgie's face fell. But Clem's, which had been pulled tight into an expression approximating happiness, relaxed into something real. For an instant, *true* happiness shone through, and it was in that moment that Georgie happened to glance at her friend. What she saw there made her own pained expression melt away too, and for a brief spell, the room was full of actual, unfeigned gladness.

Milo lifted his punch cup. "To Clem and Georgie."

"To Clem and Georgie," everyone else echoed. They clinked glasses all around.

Mrs. Pine came around to Milo and his dad. She linked her arm through Mr. Pine's and gave Milo a gentle nudge with the hand holding her glass. "Come on, you two."

She led them away from the others and into the living room, and the three of them sat on the hearth. "While we have a moment's peace, merry almost-Christmas, guys. Happy first day of vacation." They clinked glasses again.

Then someone cleared her throat, and the momentary peace splintered just like that. "I'm so sorry to interrupt," said Georgie. Clem stood a few paces behind her. "But while Emmett's up paying homage to the Wellshowe, we thought we'd better fill you in, since who knows when we might get another chance."

Mrs. Pine shook her head. "You don't have to tell us anything."

"I know," Georgie said. "And we thought at first that probably you'd rather we didn't. But we think you should have the whole story. In case, once you do, you'd rather we didn't stay. I'm not sure where else we'd go and feel as safe as we feel here, but we certainly have other options, and we would never in a million years want to put you in an awkward position."

"I can't imagine—" Mr. Pine began.

Georgie held up a hand. "I get it, I get it. But maybe, since we aren't sure how much privacy we'll have, we should just lay our cards on the table." She glanced over her shoulder to where Brandon was leaning on the back of the loveseat with his arms crossed. From there, he'd have a clear view all the way across the dining room to the stairs. "Brandon already knows—we told him on the Belowground. He'll warn us if Syebuck comes back."

"Okay." Mrs. Pine glanced briefly at Milo. "Would you rather talk on the screened porch?" Meaning, Milo guessed, *Would you rather Milo doesn't hear?* He gave her a sour look, got up, and climbed into the space behind the tree. His mom made an apologetic face in his direction.

"I think it might look less suspicious if we're all in here," Clem said with a wink at Milo.

His dad nodded. "All right, then. What's the story?"

Georgie sat on the floor with her back against the coffee table and her knees drawn up to her chest and rubbed her face hard with both hands. "I guess the summary is: I'm an idiot, and this whole thing is my fault, but basically Clem and I did our first and possibly only job together, and it went very, very wrong."

four

THE HEIST

A . . . JOB?" Mrs. Pine repeated cautiously.

"A job," Georgie confirmed. "The kind of job at which Clem and I are consummate professionals. *That* kind of job."

"Understood."

"Define 'very, very wrong,'" Mr. Pine suggested. "As in, you failed to complete the . . . the *work* involved in this job? Didn't . . . leave with a paycheck, or whatever?"

Over by the loveseat, Brandon snorted. "What am I standing lookout for if you're going to dance around everything? Worried Lizzie and Mrs. C. are going to squeal?" He leaned toward the kitchen. "You two going to squeal?"

"Yes," came Lizzie's disembodied voice.

"Absolutely," Mrs. Caraway replied.

Mr. Pine rolled his eyes. "So you didn't manage to take whatever it was?"

"Oh, we definitely did," Clem told him, dropping onto the couch. "Walked away with the entire haul."

"Then what's the problem?"

"There are two." Georgie held up her thumb. "One: We had to involve a third person, and we strongly suspect this third person tried—maybe hasn't finished trying—to double-cross us. Two." She held up her pointer finger. "We think we weren't the only ones after the haul, and it's possible the other thief isn't going to give up on it just because we stole it first."

"So two people are potentially after you. Who's the double-crosser?" Mrs. Pine asked. "Anybody we know? Not that we keep company with double-crossers, generally. Or thieves, present company excepted."

"Actually, you might have heard of him," Georgie admitted. "He's primarily a fence. Guy who acts as a middleman for moving stolen or illegal goods," she said to Milo.

"I know what a fence is," he said grouchily.

"Sorry. Anyway, his name's Gilawfer. Toby Gilawfer."

Milo's parents looked at each other. "Is that the guy Fenster was so mad at this fall?" Mrs. Pine asked her husband. "The thing with the flooded warehouse, where he lost all those really rare plants?"

"That's him," Clem confirmed. "Poor Fenster. I'm sorry to hear he lost cargo, but that flood gave us the clue we needed to find the cache we were after."

"To be fair to the jerk, the flood wasn't his fault," Georgie said grudgingly. "Gilawfer's warehouse was damaged by a much older structure buried right underneath it. There's lots of that kind of stuff in the Quayside Harbors — old, weird iron constructions hidden underground. Nobody knows much about them, but if you believe the stories, they're constantly shifting around. Something to do with erosion on the riverbank, maybe? Or just one of those oddball unexplainable things? Who knows. But I guess there's some truth to it, because Gilawfer had no idea there was anything under his foundations until these huge pieces of iron started working their way up from beneath his floor, and a ton of river water rushed in through the places the iron breached."

"Meanwhile, we were after this particular score," Clem explained. "All our information seemed to hint that it had been stashed in a subterranean hidey-hole somewhere on the Skidwrack just outside the Quayside Harbors, but we weren't making any headway on finding the right spot until Gilawfer's flood happened."

"And you realized that older building beneath Gilawfer's warehouse must've been the hidey-hole you were looking for," Mrs. Pine guessed.

Georgie nodded. "But there was no way in except through the warehouse, and, idiots that we were, we decided to offer him a piece of the haul in exchange for access to the structure below it. Long story short, he agreed, we went in . . . and the main score, the point of the whole job, the one thing that mattered . . . it just wasn't there."

"We assumed Gilawfer had hoodwinked us somehow," Clem said. "He was the only other person who knew there might be anything of value under his warehouse, but we hadn't told him exactly what we expected to find."

"The reason we hadn't told him, by the way," Georgie put in, "was that we had no intention of sharing that main thing. We'd have given him anything else in the cache — everything else, even — but not that. So yeah, our initial thought was that somehow he found out and got his hooks on it first. But then when he saw what we did find, he demanded we hand over the Big Thing, the thing that clearly wasn't there. So he *did* already know about it, and he *was* planning to cheat us, but he was as surprised as we were that it wasn't there."

"And he doesn't believe us that we don't have it, which hardly matters when you consider that we weren't going to give it to him anyway. But that's not the point." Clem sniffed. "We aren't liars. Or, well." She glanced at Milo, probably remembering their earlier conversation. "I mean, sometimes we are, but we weren't lying about *that*."

"And then there's the other guy." Georgie glanced at Brandon, who shook his head: no Syebuck yet. She leaned back against the coffee table. "Remember last year I told you about how Clem and I first got to know each other?"

Milo spoke up. "You were both trying to steal the same thing." *Someone's heart,* he thought, but didn't say. Owen's heart. The same Owen who'd turned out to have been in love with Clem all along, and who Clem had been speaking to upstairs in the study.

"Right." A little flash of emotion appeared in Georgie's eyes and faded away again just as quickly. "And remember I said it was virtually impossible for two elite thieves to make a play for the same prize without finding out about each other? Well, Clem and I quickly became aware of another thief at work. We suspect we were being watched from the moment we approached Gilawfer, and that the other guy decided to sit back, wait until we had the loot, and then come after us."

"And we aren't sure, but we think we know who it is, and if we're right, then we have a *huge* problem," Clem added. "There's a master thief called Cantlebone who sometimes turns up in Nagspeake, though you hear stories about incredible heists in other places that people think are his work." She threw up her hands. "Or hers. We don't know. *Nobody* knows who Cantlebone is or what Cantlebone looks like."

"It's a weird thing, when you suddenly think your personal hero might be out to get you," Georgie muttered.

"So that's why all this concern about Emmett," Mr. Pine said.

Clem shrugged. "He's the only unknown quantity here. He certainly could be Cantlebone."

"But he's been here for a week," Milo put in.

"If you can tell me he's never left the house in that time, I might feel better," Georgie said. "But even then I don't know if it matters. We don't know if Cantlebone works alone or with a crew."

Milo's mom shook her head. "He's been in and out. Library trips and research, supposedly. Mostly by boat, by way of the Harbors. When was your job?"

"Yesterday," Georgie said. "Although today's been fairly eventful too, frankly. Hence my turning up looking like a drowned rat. A small matter of a bridge that had to be sacrificed in the name of a good escape."

Mr. Pine chuckled. "So you're who I have to thank for the change in my commute today."

"Probably," Georgie admitted. "Sorry."

Milo's parents looked at each other. "Syebuck was definitely out of the house all day yesterday and for a decent chunk of the afternoon today," Mr. Pine said. "We shared a boat across at about midday, and he didn't come back until a little after Milo got home from school."

"Not to mention he was supposed to leave tomorrow, but this afternoon he asked to extend his stay through Sunday," Mrs. Pine added.

"So we definitely can't rule him out," Georgie muttered.

Milo raised his hand to ask the obvious question. "What were you looking for? What's the Big Thing?"

At this, both Georgie and Clem cracked real smiles at last. Another glance at Brandon, who gave a bored all clear; then Georgie said slowly, dramatically, "Have you ever heard of a *derrotero*?"

"*Derrotero?*" Milo repeated. He shook his head. He looked to his mother, whose face was blank.

"I don't think I know that word," she said.

Mr. Pine scratched his head. "Huh. You know, I think I *do* know it." He stared at the fire for a minute. "It's an atlas or something, right? A book of charts?"

"Essentially," Clem confirmed. "But very secret charts. Back in the age of exploration, European navigators would map the various bits of *terra incognita* they encountered. Coastlines in particular. They'd collect the charts in books, and because geographic knowledge was power in those days, these books were carefully guarded. Spanish mariners called them derroteros."

"Now think about our own waterways," Georgie put in. "The Skidwrack is notoriously difficult to map. Even people who know it well generally only know parts of it, and everybody who works on the river talks about how untrustworthy the available maps are."

"That's true," Mr. Pine agreed. "My father used to gripe about that all the time. Or he'd gripe about green navigators who trusted the maps too much and wound up running their vessels onto shoals that weren't marked, or who insisted there wasn't a channel or even an entire inlet where everyone else knew there was one, just because it wasn't on his chart."

"Right. So now imagine a derrotero of the Skidwrack. A truly accurate collection of charts of the river and all the inlets." Georgie's eyes glittered. "Can you imagine what a book like that would be worth?"

"Yeah," Mr. Pine said a little warily. "Smugglers would die for a resource like that. The customs department or the folks from Deacon and Morvengarde would kill for it."

"But is such a thing even possible?" Mrs. Pine asked. "I thought it was sort of accepted that the Skidwrack shifts too much for any map to stay accurate for long, and that's why the city had more or less given up on charting it."

"And people have claimed to have true charts before, you know," Mr. Pine added. "They always turn out to be frauds." The two thieves said nothing, but the glint in Georgie's eyes got even brighter. "Yet you clearly already know that," Milo's dad said suspiciously. "What else do you know that makes this different from any of those times?"

"What makes it different," Georgie said with the teensiest hint of a smirk, "is whose derrotero it was." She looked at each of them in turn: Mrs. Pine, Mr. Pine, Milo. "It belonged," she said at last, lifting her champagne in a salute, "to Violet Cross." She took a sip, waggling her eyebrows over the rim of the glass.

Milo's father's jaw literally dropped. "You're kidding," Mrs. Pine said, aghast.

Georgie shook her head. "Not in the slightest."

Milo sat back in his space under the tree and considered. He knew the name, of course. Violet Cross was one of Nagspeake's most famous smugglers, maybe the greatest runner the city had ever seen. In a relatively short time, she'd built one of the most impressive careers in city history, running circles around both the customs agency and the mail-order empire, Deacon and Morvengarde, which most of Nagspeake believed (with plenty of justification) essentially ran customs as its own private enforcement division. Violet Cross was a true legend.

"Okay," Mrs. Pine said. "I think . . . well, I don't know *what* I think, except *wow*."

"So you're telling us you two found a stash belonging to *Violet Cross?*" Mr. Pine's voice dropped nearly to a whisper at the end.

"Hand to God," Clem said. "Well, Georgie found it. It would've been the heist of a lifetime for anybody else. For Georgie, this was a weekend project. I mean, I'm good, and I have no problem saying so, but this was next level. I basically just tagged along."

"Quit flattering me," Georgie grumbled. "I couldn't have pulled it off without you. Not to mention, it was only *potentially* next level until it went wrong."

"Not your fault," Clem argued. "Jobs go wrong all the time. It's an occupational hazard."

Georgie ignored this and addressed the Pines. "If you're wondering why I'm taking it so personally that things went awry, the reason is this: the job was supposed to be a wedding present for Clem. It was our first job together, and it was going to be a last hurrah for her. A truly epic score before . . ."

Clem finished the sentence a bit sourly. "Before I give it up for good." She drained what was left of her champagne and stared grimly into the empty glass. "Is there more?"

Now they all looked at her. All except Georgie, who got up, left the room, and returned with an unopened bottle. She peeled away the foil at the top and popped the cork with as little noise as she could manage.

"You're going straight?" Milo asked, shocked. "Why?"

Clem sighed. "Because, Milo, I fell in love, which, in retrospect, I'm not sure I recommend." She held out her glass for Georgie to refill. "Or at least, thieves shouldn't fall in love with anyone who's not also a crook."

"You're quitting for Owen?" Now Milo felt a little indignant. "Is he making you? Why does he want you to be somebody else?"

"No, Milo, it's not like that." Clem shook her head. "He only asked me to give it up until after the honeymoon. And that's how I look at it: *giving something up,* like giving up candy or smoking or cursing. I don't think it means changing who I am. I'm not *only* a thief. I'm lots of other things too."

Georgie silently refilled her own glass. Judging from her expression, she didn't totally agree with Clem's interpretation of the situation.

"I figure law-abiding citizens generally would rather their spouses weren't going out at night to commit crimes," Clem continued quietly. "And I don't want it to come to Owen asking me to quit for good. That would . . . that would make me angry."

"So you decided to preempt his asking," Milo's mom said sadly. "All right, I see why this job was so important to you both."

Brandon coughed a low, deliberate cough. Then he straightened and sauntered into the dining room. Emmett was coming down.

"Now you know the whole thing," Clem said quickly, getting to her feet. "If you'd rather we leave, we'll understand. Brandon offered to run us back into town, or out to the end of the line if we want."

Mrs. Pine rolled her eyes. "Don't be ridiculous, Clem. I appreciate your honesty, but stay." She stood, squeezed Georgie's arm, rubbed Clem's shoulder, and headed for the kitchen.

"Really?" Georgie said to Milo's father. "You sure?"

"Absolutely," he said without hesitation. "Drink your champagne."

Emmett bounded into the living room. "What's everybody

looking so glum for? I saw Mrs. Caraway cutting the cake." He smiled at Georgie. "Can I get a piece for you?"

"Sure," Georgie said suspiciously. "Thanks."

"Welcome!" Out he went again, grinning like an idiot.

"There is definitely something weird about that guy," Georgie said, watching him leave the room through narrowed eyes. Then she turned back to Milo. "What do you say? We almost ruined your Christmas last year."

Milo shook his head. "No, you didn't. Not really."

"Okay, in that case, I guess we'll stick around for a bit. Thank you." She glanced down at her hands. "I'm going to need something to keep me busy, though." She thought for a minute, reached into her pocket, and pulled out a coin. Then she turned to Milo's dad. "Do you by chance have a Dremel tool? Or no, I can do it with sandpaper. Do you have sandpaper? Really fine grain would be best."

"Probably," Mr. Pine said, looking at the coin warily.

"Excellent. Could I have a piece? A whole sheet, ideally. In the meantime, I'll help pass out cake." Then she, too, left the living room.

Clem dropped onto the hearth. "Milo, why don't you go get those lockpicks now? I need something to take my mind off things too."

"What about Emmett?" Milo whispered.

She shrugged and lowered her voice. "If he's anyone to worry about, he already knows what I am. If he's not, who cares? Thieves aren't the only ones who need to know how to open locks. Also,

Georgie's about to attack a coin with a piece of sandpaper. Who's going to care what we're up to?" She winked. "But if he asks, you found the picks in your attic."

Milo climbed out from behind the tree, took the rolled cylinder from his back pocket, and sat next to her. "I was hoping you'd say something like that."

Clem whistled. "Way to be ready for anything, my young apprentice."

five

PICKS AND LOCKS

CLEM UNROLLED THE PACK between them, revealing a collection of picks and a couple of the bent-metal pieces she called torsion wrenches. "We're going to need something to work on that isn't currently attached to a door."

"Like a padlock?" Milo racked his brains. "I think there's one on the garage door, maybe."

"I might actually have something. Hang tight." Clem darted out of the room. Milo straightened the picks in their little pockets while he waited for her to come back.

Meanwhile, one by one, Brandon, Georgie, and Emmett drifted in with plates and cups of punch. Georgie spotted the picks, and her eyes flicked toward Emmett, who was headed right for Milo.

She opened her mouth, then changed her mind as Mr. Pine came in and held out two sheets of sandpaper. Georgie set down her plate and tested the grain with her fingers. "Perfect. Cake first, then crafts." She dropped onto the couch and started eating.

Emmett sat next to Milo. "Wow, what've you got there?" he asked, squinting down at the picks. "Tools of some kind?"

"Lockpicks," Clem said, returning without a sound. She waved a hand at Emmett. "Scoot over. Milo found them in his attic. We're going to try them out."

"Cool!" Emmett obeyed, scooting down to the other end of the hearth. "You know how to work those?"

"Sure," Clem replied. "Picked up the basics kicking around my dad's hardware store when I was a kid. You rotate the keyhole bit with the wrench and work the little toothy things with a pick. It's not hard."

"Can't be all that easy, or everyone would do it," Emmett mumbled through a mouthful of cake.

"I guess we'll find out." Clem reached into her pocket, took out a brass padlock, and handed it to Milo. "Let's try this one. Owen and I are going to leave it locked on a bridge on our honeymoon," she explained to the room at large.

"Wow." Milo turned the lock over, examining both sides. It was about the size of a nectarine, and it was engraved all over with eyes from the top of the curved hasp to the bottom edge. "That is the coolest thing I've ever seen." No way she was going to just leave it on some random bridge.

"It looks outrageous, but it's a pretty ordinary mechanism. A good one to learn on." She plucked it out of his palm and laid it flat on her own. "So here's what I know. The curvy bit that pops open and closed is called the *shank*. The main chunk is called the *body*. This part's called the *keyway*," she said, pointing to the keyhole in a circular inset in the bottom of the body, "and the circle it's in is the end of a cylinder called the *plug* that sticks up into the body. The locking mechanism's inside the plug, and that's what we're going to manipulate."

"So you know a lot, in fact," Emmett observed.

"My father's hardware store was a full-service shop." Clem took one of the torsion wrenches, a plain bit of metal bent into a ninety-degree angle at one end, from its pocket. From another pocket, she took a pick with a flattened tip curved into a sort of comma shape. She cupped the lock in one palm so that the keyway was facing her. Then she slid the bent end of the wrench into the bottom of the keyway and turned it. The wrench didn't move much—just the tiniest bit. But Milo could see that now the keyway was angled slightly to one side instead of straight up and down.

Then, holding the wrench in place with the fourth and pinkie fingers of the same hand that cupped the lock, Clem slid the pick into the top of the keyway and began twitching it gently. The movements were too small for Milo to guess at what she was doing, but after only a few seconds, the curved shank at the top of the lock popped open and swung loose.

"Wow!" Milo clapped. "That was fast!"

Clem made a face that seemed to mean both *Why, thank you* and *Not really, it wasn't*. She passed him the lock and the pick.

"Reach in there at the top of the keyway and dig around with the end, just to see what the mechanism feels like."

Milo did. "Bumpy," he said. "Like teeth poking down." Moving the pick along these bumps reminded Milo of sitting in the dentist's chair and feeling a pick moving over his own teeth.

"Right. Those are the *pins*. When you slide a key into a lock, the teeth on the key are meant to push each pin up and out of the way, which allows the keyway to turn and open the lock. But of course, we don't have the key. If you try, you'll find you can push each pin up with the tip of the pick. You'll also find they'll bounce right back down, which is a problem. We need them to stay out of the way so we can turn the plug and open the lock. This is what you need the torsion wrench for. With the wrench, you can tilt the plug just enough to keep the pins from popping right back down again when you push them up with the pick." Clem took the pick from his fingers and handed him the wrench. "Start by tilting the keyway. Remember, it doesn't go far."

Obediently, Milo inserted the bent piece of metal into the bottom of the keyway and gave it a turn. The plug moved so little that he had to try a second time to convince himself that he'd managed to shift it at all.

"Perfect," Clem said, adjusting his fingers so that he could hold the wrench in place with the same hand that held the lock, the way she had. "Now the pick. Start pushing the pins up and out of the way, one by one."

"How many pins are there?" Milo asked as he tried to do what she was describing. The pins bounced up a little with a springy sort of feeling, but they didn't seem to be staying out of the way once he pushed them. "Feels like a million of them."

"Four, in this lock. But different locks have different numbers of pins. Try starting all the way in the back and counting them as you move the pick forward."

Milo obeyed. "But they're not staying out of the way."

"Remember to keep a little pressure on the wrench." Clem adjusted his fingers again, and he realized he'd relaxed them, which had allowed the plug and keyway to move back into their normal up-and-down position.

With Clem's fingers gently reminding him to hold the wrench steady, Milo poked at the pins one by one. Then — wait! *There!* Suddenly something was different — he'd pushed a pin up with the pick and it had stayed put.

"Think I got one," he whispered.

"Great. Try another one."

He did, and after only two tries, that one stayed up as well. Two out of four . . . and then he got a third, and then suddenly the shank clicked open in his palm. Clem sat back and applauded. "Nice work, Milo! You did it!"

Milo looked at the open lock in his hand, then turned it over in wonderment. For the briefest second, a flicker of someone he had been searching for came to life in his heart: *Negret*. When Clem had given him the picks, she'd said that every blackjack needed a lock-pick kit. Maybe, if he could master this, he could get Negret back. He just needed something to help find his way to the blackjack he'd been. Surely learning a true escaladeur's skill would do the job.

"That's so cool," he said aloud. "Let me see if I can do it by myself."

"Sure thing. But don't get frustrated if you can't get it open again right away." Clem tossed her head in the direction of Emmett, who was now deep in conversation with Brandon. "Like the man said, if it was easy, everyone would do it. Just remember to keep pressure on the wrench while you work. I think that's going to be the hardest part for you. I know it was for me when I learned."

"How old were you?" Milo asked. "When you first learned, I mean?"

Clem considered. "Your age, I think. Maybe a little younger."

Milo felt his eyes pop. "Seriously? How did that happen?"

"Kinda like this, actually," she admitted. "Not quite, though." She gave a small nod toward the guest at the other end of the hearth. "Tale for another time. Now I believe I'll have some more cake. You?"

"No, thanks. I'm going to practice."

"Okey-doke." She got up, leaving Milo to try again. He looked down at the lock they'd just opened. The twinkling of the tree lights and the flickering of the fire made the collection of engraved eyes seem to flutter and blink. He clicked the shank closed again, then took a deep breath and slipped the torsion wrench into the bottom of the keyway. "Come on, Negret," he murmured under his breath. He gave the wrench a little twist, secured it in his fourth and pinkie fingers, slid the pick in above it, and started working on the pins.

Georgie, meanwhile, got up from the sofa and took up a spot on the floor not far from where Milo sat on the hearth. "Don't want to shake the couch," she explained as she tore a piece off the sheet of sandpaper. She folded it around her thumb, tucked the silver coin into her opposite palm, and started sanding one face.

"Dare I ask what this is for?" Mrs. Pine asked, looking down at her.

"Hollow coin," Georgie said without looking up. "Hey, Clem?" she called. "Could you bring me some water?"

"Is that legal?" Emmett asked as he watched Georgie sanding. Everyone was watching. The rhythmic scraping noise was impossible to ignore.

"Yes, it's legal," she replied. "Somebody gave me a U.S. quarter with my change today. Pretty sure you can do whatever you want with foreign currency." Georgie paused as Clem came back and passed her a cup of water; then she shook a drop onto the coin and started sanding again.

Emmett watched, fascinated. "That'll take forever with just sandpaper, won't it?"

"A few hours, yes, but it'll keep my hands busy. It's kind of a meditative—" Georgie stopped sanding and looked up sharply. "Know much about making hollow coins, do you?"

"I loved making stuff like that as a kid, with my dad," Emmett explained sheepishly. "Except we used a Dremel tool, so it went quicker, and nickels because they're thicker. Also, won't you need two quarters? One for the front and one for the back?"

Georgie's eyelids lowered dangerously. "The thing about meditating is that it works best if people don't tell you you're doing it wrong."

Milo snickered and refocused his attention on his picks.

The hours passed, almost without his noticing. The ding of the clock on the mantelpiece was meaningless background noise. He was dimly aware of Clem coming to sit by him again at one point, but when he didn't look up and ask for help, she took the hint and went elsewhere. Georgie kept sanding, and the noise became almost hypnotic.

Once, one more glorious time, the hasp of the lock popped open — and Milo had no idea how he'd done it. Still, success was success. Now all he had to do was replicate it. He looked up in delight and saw Clem doing a little golf clap from the sofa.

And then, suddenly, the clock was striking eleven, and Milo nodded forward into a tree branch with the torsion wrench dangling from one hand, forgotten. "Come on, kiddo," Mrs. Pine said as she tugged him gently to his feet. "All the time in the world tomorrow."

six

THE GAME OF MAPS

MILO WOKE to that delicious feeling that comes only on the first morning of vacation, which is somehow subtly different from an ordinary waking-up-on-a-weekend feeling. He swung out of bed and opened his curtains. Still no snow, but at least there was a satisfying crust of frozen condensation on the window. It made him feel as if he were looking through the starfish arms of a giant snowflake.

He stood there for a while, thinking about the story Clem and Georgie had told the night before of their heist-gone-wrong and the impossible book of maps, the derrotero they had been after. Had Clem and Georgie, two incredibly capable thieves, made a mistake and looked in the wrong place? Or maybe it was true that the

Skidwrack was, for one reason or another, impossible to map accurately, and the derrotero really didn't exist to be found at all.

Something jogged Milo's memory. *Impossible to map.* He left the window and went to his desk, where someone, probably his mother, had deposited his dictionary, vocabulary notebook, spiral pad, pen, and lockpicks. He took a moment to stack them neatly, one on top of the other; then he reached for a slim paperback with a plain red cover that stood between a pair of bookends shaped like anchors along with a small leather folder and a few other favorite books. He opened it to the second chapter, which was titled "The Game of Maps."

The Raconteur's Commonplace Book was a collection of Nagspeake folklore structured as a single tale in which a group of travelers find themselves stuck at a remote inn during a massive flood. The strangers take turns sharing stories, starting with "The Game of Maps." Georgie had given him the book last year, and she had opened it to this page to entice Milo to give it a try. It began, *There was a city that could not be mapped, and inside it a house that could not be drawn.*

Milo took the book to his bed and got back under the covers.

There was a city that could not be mapped, and inside it a house that could not be drawn. It stood at the bottom of a hill on a street called Fellwool, a lane with broken pavement that had been overgrown and mostly hidden by ancient, knotty pines. It was the kind of house that, in simpler times, might have been called enchanted or haunted or cursed. These houses appear now and then in towns and cities that will tolerate them. Sometimes they survive. Sometimes they do not.

This house had survived for many, many years. It had cop-per pipes that reached down into the earth like roots, its woodwork had taught its stonework how to breathe in exchange for lessons in strength, and the ironwork that chased the eaves and climbed the walls and curled along the windows danced in the sunset. It allowed its rooms to roam like cats. It had permitted residents now and then, when the endless march of the years got lonely, but it never kept them long. It was a crafty dwelling, and it had ways of regaining its soli-tude when visitors overstayed their welcome.

In the story, a boy called Pantin spends the night in the house in question. To pass the time while he's inside, he goes in search of a miraculous object he believes to be hidden there. His explora-tions, however, are complicated by two factors: the constant shift-ing of some of the rooms, and the fact that some of the rooms have malevolent natures. But ultimately, Pantin learns how to listen to the house itself. Then — this was the thing Milo had vaguely remem-bered, and he sat up straighter when he got to it — Pantin figures out how to construct a movable map, one that can be modified and adjusted and that helps him to see the patterns behind the seem-ingly chaotic shiftings of the house.

"A movable map," Milo said thoughtfully. How else would you undertake to chart waters that didn't stay put but with a map that could be changed accordingly? Of course, in the book, Pantin's map was aided by a few bits of magical hardware that presumably

Violet Cross, living in the real world, hadn't had access to. Still, there was something there he couldn't quite let go of.

He climbed out of bed again and put *The Raconteur's Commonplace Book* on his desk, under the notebooks in the carefully lined-up stack. Then he got dressed, tucked his lockpicks in his pocket, and went downstairs, where Lizzie Caraway and Mrs. Pine were in the kitchen. From the smell of things, there would be bacon this morning. Possibly Lizzie was making the kind her mother sometimes made that was brushed with maple syrup and dusted with cracked pepper. Milo let his nose drag him straight to the stove to stare hungrily down into the cast-iron pan. "Too close," Lizzie laughed, gently elbowing him back to a safer distance. "I'll let you know when I'm ready for a little quality-assurance testing."

Mrs. Pine put an arm around him and kissed his head. "Sleep okay?"

"Yeah. Anybody else up yet?"

"Emmett's painting out on the screened porch. I haven't seen either of the girls. Brandon slept over too. I imagine he'll be down right about when breakfast hits the table. That's usually his MO. And I told your dad to sleep in."

"Told Mom the same thing," Lizzie added, lifting a crispy brown slice out of the pan and depositing it on a plate lined with paper towels. "Don't touch that until it cools a little. I think I have the heat up too high."

Milo waited for a count of ten, then scooped up the bacon and ate it in three bites. It was so worth a burned tongue. "It's perfect," he managed through the blistering mouthful. Then he poured himself a glass of orange juice and headed for the living room. His mom hadn't started a fire yet, so he took his juice to the loveseat and sipped it there, staring thoughtfully out at the frosted lawn while he mulled over the idea of a map that could be manipulated and changed.

How might that work? His first thought was something like origami. Paper, after all, could be folded, torn, reshaped into pretty much any form you wanted. Milo knew nothing about making origami, but it didn't take a huge leap of imagination to picture a paper map of a waterway being endlessly changed in subtle ways by folds and creases. Heck, you could keep on messing with it until the paper itself gave out. He thought briefly of a map Georgie had given him that he kept in the little leather folder between the bookends on his desk, one that had been drawn on very old paper. Some paper could stand up to a surprising amount of folding and use.

How else could you make a map adjustable? Sliding panels? Pop-up bits? Or maybe it wasn't that complicated after all. Maybe Violet Cross, or her mapmaker, had discovered some set of underlying permanent features of the river and its inlets. An unvarying pattern upon which water and sediment and rock and driftwood and flora were overlaid like muscle and nerves and skin on a skeleton. Maybe if you knew about that skeleton, there was a way to make sense of the manner in which the Skidwrack changed, to predict it and plan for it.

The others drifted downstairs over the next half-hour or so as the smells of bacon and French toast and oatmeal and coffee reached their particular corners of the house. By nine, everyone was filling plates and bowls and cups and finding seats at either the big dining table or the little round ones by the dining room's bow window.

All except Emmett Syebuck. "Milo, would you just stick your head out and let Mr. Syebuck know breakfast's ready if he's hungry?" Lizzie called as she took her own plate and joined Georgie and Clem at one end of the big table.

With his empty orange juice glass in one hand, Milo leaned through the door in the living room that led to the enclosed porch. They didn't spend a lot of time out there in winter. Not that you couldn't—they called it the screened porch, but all the big windows that lined the long room had proper glass in them too. It was still drafty, though, and the chill came right up through the flagstone floor and penetrated even the thickest of socks in a matter of minutes.

The temperature didn't seem to have bothered Emmett. He was fast asleep in the chair he'd pulled up to the wood-and-iron worktable along one wall. The picture he was painting was taped to a board on a little tabletop easel: the beginnings of a watercolor of the fourth-floor stairwell window on a piece of heavy paper. To one side, two water cups were lined up by a battered metal paint box. To the other, a small assortment of brushes lay on a bunch of paper towels. The brushes and paint looked untouched, and so did the cup of coffee that hung precariously from his left hand.

Carefully, Milo extracted the cup from Emmett's fingers, which was enough to shake the guy from his snooze. "Oh, hey, Milo. Did I drift off?"

"Looks that way. Your coffee's cold. But breakfast is ready, if you're hungry."

"Is that what I'm smelling?" Emmett bounced to his feet. "I find I'm suddenly famished."

"Well, you better hurry, then, because the bacon's going fast."

As Milo turned to leave, Emmett tapped his shoulder. "Before you go." He lowered his voice. "What's the deal with the girls?"

Milo frowned. "What do you mean, what's the deal with them?"

"I mean . . ." He hesitated, then gave Milo a goofy half smile. "Okay, look, I know you're not supposed to share information about your guests. But do you happen to know if . . ."

"If what?" Milo asked warily. *If they're criminals? If, say, I happened to be a criminal too, might I be interested in what they're up to? If your parents would flip out if I battled them over stolen goods after breakfast?*

"If Georgie's single?" Emmett finished, looking embarrassed.

Milo hadn't realized he'd been standing so stiffly until all the tension left him. He gave Emmett a disbelieving look. "If she's *single?* What is this, the school cafeteria?"

"Just wondering if you know," Emmett said hurriedly, turning red.

"No, I don't know if she's *single.* Eww."

"Okay, okay. Well, don't say anything to her, for heaven's sake. I mean, don't tell her I *asked.*"

"I won't," Milo retorted. "How would that even come up?"

"I mean, unless *she* were to ask about *me.* Then obviously you could maybe mention that *I* asked about *her*—"

"I'm on vacation," Milo said firmly. "And if I miss out on more bacon because of you, you'll be sorry." With that, he departed the screened porch and went for a breakfast plate.

The rest of the day passed fairly uneventfully. Brandon departed after the meal, with a quiet promise to keep an ear out for any useful information. Milo's parents and the Caraways had a brief conference during which it was decided that Mrs. Caraway and Lizzie would stay at least until Emmett left. Mrs. Caraway's youngest daughter, Madeleine, went to school in another city near her dad and wouldn't get home to Nagspeake until Christmas Eve. So they needed to be home by then, but not necessarily before.

Milo practiced with the lockpicks and amused himself by watching Emmett try to start conversations with Georgie, who responded with suspicion and at least one rapid, temporary escape, ostensibly to wash away the black dust that accumulated in her palm as she continued to sand the coin. Since Milo wasn't about to explain to Emmett why Georgie was being weird when he tried to talk to her, pretty much all he could do was enjoy the spectacle for the comedy it was. Of course, Milo reflected, he could have told Georgie about the conversation on the porch so she didn't have to be so suspicious. But for the moment—as long as Emmett didn't try to drag him into it again—it was just too funny.

Since it was obvious to everyone that Emmett was, for whatever reason, keeping a close eye on Georgie, it was Clem who snuck away to the Pines' second-floor study to try again to get hold of Dr. Gowervine. But the only phone number anyone had for him was for his office at the university, and the university was on winter break too, so all Clem could do was leave another message and slip back downstairs looking frustrated.

At one point after lunch, Mrs. Caraway pulled the two girls and Lizzie aside and explained quietly that if Georgie and Clem were trying to look as if they were having a girls' weekend, they were doing a lame job of it. "Give me that," she demanded, holding out her hand for Georgie's quarter. "You can have it back after class." She tucked it in the pocket of her apron; then she handed Georgie a tray of fancy-looking drinks, passed an assortment of nail polishes from Mrs. Pine's medicine cabinet to Clem, and gave Lizzie a bowl full of something green that Milo was ninety percent sure contained an avocado he'd seen Mrs. Caraway peel and chop not long before. "Leave the mask on for fifteen minutes," she ordered, pointing at the bowl of avocado goop. "And I don't want to see any of you downstairs again until the varnish has dried on all thirty fingers and all thirty toes. Base coat, two coats of color, and topcoat. I'll come up with another round of cocktails in a bit."

The green stuff was supposed to go on their *faces?* Milo slunk away, trying not to gag.

Against all odds, spending the better part of an hour in relative solitude letting mashed food dry on their cheeks seemed to do the two nervous girls some good, and by the time they came back down, they seemed significantly more relaxed, although Georgie still went immediately to Mrs. Caraway to demand her quarter back. The hypnotic scratching of sandpaper commenced anew. Outside, the sun was painting the grounds, overlaying rosy gold on the glittering greenish sepia of the lawn and licking the west-facing sides of the birches with warm tones despite the cold. Milo had gotten the engraved padlock open a total of two more times, and though he still wasn't sure how he'd done it, the successes felt good. All in all, it hadn't been a bad day.

After dinner, Milo headed back to the space behind the tree to continue his lockpicking practice. On his way there, he paused by the loveseat, where Georgie sat with her feet up on the windowsill. She stopped sanding, wiped her dust-blackened hand on her jeans, and held up the quarter for Milo's inspection. "Getting there."

He took the coin. It was totally smooth and blank on both sides. "Cool. Now what?"

She sighed. "Well, Emmett was right. I'd actually have needed two of these to make a hollow coin. And honestly, the sandpaper was only going to get me so far. So I changed my mind. Now I think it's a bird." She reached into her back pocket and produced a compact multi-tool from which she unfolded a tiny but serious-looking pair of short-bladed shears. "Essential traveling gear," she said with a wink. "Now get. I'll show you when I'm done. I can't work with people hovering over me."

As Milo turned to leave, Emmett appeared at his side and leaned over the high back of the loveseat. "So did you check out the medallion window? Because I'm not sure, but those medallions might actually be recycled grave markers."

That was enough to make even Georgie glance up. "Glass grave markers?"

Emmett nodded. "The Romans sometimes marked bodies in catacombs with the decorated cut-off bottoms of drinking cups.

There's a church in Shantytown that does it too." He grinned expectantly, as if no one could possibly resist the coolness of discovering she'd been sleeping in a room with a window full of grave markers in it.

Something resembling a flash of interest actually did cross Georgie's face for a fleeting moment. Then it vanished. "I haven't, as a matter of fact," she said pointedly. "And you're blocking my light."

The wattage of Emmett's smile flickered, but only for a second. Then he spotted the shears. "Hey, what are you going to do with those?" The guy really was clueless. Milo shook his head and got out of there before Georgie's inevitable explosion.

As he crossed the living room, his ears picked out a sound, separating it from the various adult voices in the common areas and the clink of china and glasses and cutlery in the kitchen. This sound was coming from the same direction as the creaking of the bare trees scraping against each other in the woods and the wind that rattled the windowpanes. But those noises were well-known, even friendly ones at Greenglass House in the wintertime. This other sound . . . it was the oddest thing. Milo couldn't place it, and yet he had the feeling he'd heard it before.

"Hey, do you hear that?" He went to the big bow window by the loveseat and looked out into the night. Nothing there but the lawn, with its frosty grass glittering in the spill of light from the house all the way up to the dark line of trees that covered the slope of the hill down to the river. But here the familiar-yet-not-familiar noise was just a little louder, almost loud enough for Milo to make sense of it.

There was a jangling, and something else. Something like . . . was it *music?* He hurried to the bow window on the dining room side of the house, and peered out across that side of the lawn and into the woods that swept up the side of Whilforber Hill.

There were lights in the trees. Lights and bodies, and they were coming this way. "Mom . . . ?" Milo called warily. "I think someone's coming."

He couldn't have shushed the house faster if he'd screamed bloody murder at the top of his lungs, but only two sets of footsteps came to join him at the window. He didn't have to look to know it was his mom and dad. Which was good, because he couldn't tear his eyes away from what was coming through the trees.

The lights bobbed and dodged, golden and rose and oyster-colored, through the firs and the skeletal birches. Milo counted four big lights that seemed to come from lanterns, and two sets of much smaller luminosities that, from their erratic flickering, he thought must somehow be candles guttering in the breeze. There were also tiny flashes, like glitter, that shone briefly and roughly in time with the jingling that accompanied the spectacle. Bells, maybe, catching the light and tossing it back as they rang.

And now the music was clearer too: a handful of singing voices, some powerful and some less so, accompanied by those jangling bells and, now and then, the hallooing of some kind of horn. All of it taken together — the lights, the bells and horn, the singing, and the trees that hid the singers from view — created such an otherworldly effect that Milo almost didn't notice that he recognized the song. It was "Good King Wenceslas." And then he realized he knew who was singing it.

"Hey, everybody?" Mr. Pine called. "You probably want to see this. A real Nagspeake Christmas tradition. I think we're about to get a visit from the Waits."

seven

THE WAITS

HERE WAS A RUSH of footsteps as everyone else came to join them at the window. "Well, will you look at that," Mrs. Caraway breathed. "I don't remember the last time I saw the Waits."

"Well, you've usually gone home for the holidays by the time they show up," Mrs. Pine said. "And then, they don't come every year either. Last Christmas, for instance, there was too much snow. I think it's been two or three years since they've visited us." She put a hand on Milo's shoulder and lowered her voice. "Are you going to be okay? I think you were a little unnerved by them. But then, you were much younger. You might not remember."

"I'll be fine," Milo said with more courage than he felt.

He did remember. He remembered one thing in particular, the

thing that had sent him screaming up the stairs. He steeled himself for it now.

"Isn't it early for carolers?" Emmett asked. "It's the twenty-second, isn't it?"

"They only go to a couple houses a night," Mr. Pine said. "Takes a few days to visit even the handful of folks who live at the top of the hill."

As the lights emerged from the woods at last, so did the people who carried them. There were seven altogether: two with lanterns in their hands and two with lanterns dangling from long poles, and three who bore the smaller flickering candles. One of these three wore a ring of them around its head like a crown, and another carried a small forking branch hung with candles and other objects that glittered and glowed in their quivering radiance.

And then there was the final figure, the one that had given Milo nightmares for about a week after he'd seen it last time: a ghostly horse, its body shrouded in layers of white that caught the moon- and fire-glow in strange ways, like ice that had frozen and refrozen, been snowed on and windblown into wild arrays. Its head was a grinning skull with candles in the eye sockets and stags' antlers glowing patchily gold on its brow. Ribbons hung from the antlers and from the jaw of the skull, and they fluttered in the breeze. Milo swallowed. The head tossed and the jaw clacked open and shut as the creature walked along, led by one of the others, a black man in a blue cloak and a floppy, wide-brimmed hat.

"Wow," Georgie said quietly. "I've heard of the Waits, but that isn't at all what I pictured."

"The group is different every year," Mr. Pine said. "There's always a hobby horse and a chimney sweep, though it can be different people playing those parts." He glanced toward the living room. "Guess I'd better put out the fire."

"Why?" Clem asked.

"You'll find out," Mr. Pine replied. "Tradition. To bring good luck for the coming year."

"That thing is good luck?" Emmett asked darkly. Nobody had to wonder what he meant by *that thing*. It could only be the hobby horse, although Milo thought that was far too tame a moniker for something so creepy.

"Yup," his dad said cheerily. "Everybody get your coats on."

"Where did they come from?" Emmett asked as they all started dressing for the cold. "I didn't think there were any other houses around here. Not close enough to walk to in this weather, anyway."

"There are, just not many," Milo said. "And there's the monastery and the Liberty, too."

"Oh, right," the artist said, pulling on his stocking cap. "I think I did know there was a monastery up there. But what's the Liberty? I've never heard of that."

"Yes, you have," Mrs. Pine told him. "You just know it by a different name. Only people who live on Whilforber Hill call it the Liberty of Gammerbund — which, by the way, is also what its residents call it. Everybody else knows it as Saint Whit Gammerbund's Rest Home for the Mentally Chaotic."

Emmett's eyes widened. "The *madhouse?*"

Mrs. Pine winced. "And sometimes people call it that. It isn't, though, you know. It isn't a madhouse. Or at least, that's a very narrow way of looking at it." She gave him an apologetic look. "Not that I'm saying you're a narrow-minded person, Emmett. But the truth is, everyone who lives in the Liberty chose to be there for one reason or another. Some of them might seem eccentric if you ran into them on the street, but it doesn't mean there's anything *wrong* with them, or that they're dangerous. They just prefer to live apart."

"I don't know," Emmett said as Milo's dad opened the door to reveal the assemblage of unlikely figures making their slow, jangling, clacking way toward the house. "They look kind of crazy to me."

"Of course they do," Georgie said. "They're in costume. That's all part of the tradition." She finished lacing up her boots and stood. "I can't believe I'm going to see this at last."

Milo zipped his coat and followed her outside. He stood on the porch between Georgie and his father as the Waits crossed the lawn. The louder, deeper voices had dropped out of the song, and two, maybe three higher women's voices were singing.

> *"Sire, the night is darker now,*
> *and the wind blows stronger.*
> *Fails my heart, I know not how;*
> *I can go no longer . . ."*

Before the deeper voices could chime in again, though, a single high voice spiraled upward into a screech as one of the carolers, the woman with the branch, went up in flames.

Frankly, it was hard to see how it hadn't happened sooner — the candles that decorated her forked branch were totally unprotected from the wind. In any case, now the branch was crawling with fire. She tossed it to the ground and started stamping on it, apparently unaware of the flames that had already spread to the hood of her red cloak.

The other carolers saw, though, and they didn't hesitate. The man in the floppy hat shepherded the hobby horse to one side to keep its shroud clear, and the singer wearing the glossy green-leafed and candle-studded crown leapt in the opposite direction. The three remaining figures dropped their lanterns unceremoniously to the frosty ground. One, a pointy-bearded young man in a cape, old-fashioned tails, and a top hat, came forward with a bucket he'd been carrying in his other hand. The other two — a wiry guy with a wild mane of hair and bells hanging from his elbows and knees and a bigger man in a belted fur coat and some kind of carved wooden mask — tackled the red-cloaked woman just as she realized that her head had basically caught fire. They picked her up, turned her upside down, and dunked her headfirst into the bucket.

Water splashed up around her shoulders. Her cloak and dress flopped down to reveal a pair of furiously kicking blue-jean-clad legs, one of which connected squarely with the masked face of the guy in the fur coat. He howled in pain and let go, shoving up the mask and clutching his nose. The skinny wild-haired guy, suddenly off-balance and still holding one kicking leg, lost control, and he and the woman went down in a flailing, scrambling, jingling pile. The hobby horse and the other lady looked at each other. The lady sighed, took off her crown, and started blowing out her own candles.

"I guess I'd better get a towel . . . ?" Mrs. Pine said dubiously.

But the seven carolers got themselves back in order somehow, and they reassembled into a rough semicircle with the one lantern that hadn't gone out twinkling merrily on a pole overhead. A few glares went around the group, the lady with the now-darkened crown counted, "One, two, three," and the Waits launched into the final verse. By the time they got to the last lines — *Ye who now will bless the poor shall yourselves find blessing* — they had fully recovered and even managed some pretty fancy harmonizing.

Everyone on the porch broke into applause, and the Waits bowed.

The fur-clad man who'd been kicked in the face stepped forward and spoke through the hand that was still applying pressure to his injured nose under his mask. "Habe you roob at your hearth for weary trabelers to cub in frub the cold?"

"You want to answer?" Mr. Pine asked Milo.

It was his way of asking Milo if he wanted to invite the Waits in. There were two traditional responses, one if you wanted company and one if you didn't. Last time the carolers had come to Greenglass House, Milo had been so scared by the hobby horse that Mrs. Pine had given the *Thanks, but no, thanks* answer.

Milo considered. The hobby horse was still unnerving, but somehow this time — maybe because the fire incident had skated so close to slapstick — he got a pleasant, shivery feeling from the idea of inviting the group in. "Okay. What do I tell them if I want to say come in?" he asked. Mr. Pine whispered in his ear, and Milo stepped forward, raised his voice, and called out, "Come you all, and your good fortunes, too."

"Thank heavens!" the red-cloaked lady with the wet head exploded, and she started stalking toward the house. "I'm freezing."

A shrouded, arm-shaped protuberance popped up from the vicinity of the hobby horse's chest and a distinctly human, female voice shouted, *"Stop her!"*

The crowned lady and the fellow with the wild hair burst into motion and, accompanied by a chaos of ringing bells, tackled the red-cloaked caroler to the ground again just before she reached the first porch step.

"Oh my Lord, *WHAT NOW?*" the woman's muffled voice demanded from the bottom of the pile.

"Should we . . . ?" Mrs. Pine fretted quietly.

"No, it's okay, it's just that the sweep's the first-footer. He has to go up before anyone else," the wild-haired guy explained, helping the lady he'd felled get upright again. "Sorry," he said, patting her shoulder awkwardly.

The crowned woman, meanwhile, shook her head in disgust. "Noobs. Rupert! Get a move on. You're up."

At this, the man in the top hat gave a start. "Oh, darn, right. I forgot." He picked up his bucket, shouldered a long bundle he'd tossed aside with his lantern during the fire debacle, and started for the porch.

Before he could step off the grass, at least three of the Waits screamed, "Right foot!"

He gave an irritated noise, looked down at the foot—his left —that he'd been about to put down on the first stair, and whirled on them all. "Yes, I know, but it's the right foot *going through the front door,* no?" he demanded. "I'm just going up the steps! It doesn't have to be my right foot now, for crying out loud, does it?" He looked to the nearest of his companions: the wild-haired guy, the lady in the leafy green crown, and the sodden woman in the red cloak. They looked at each other uncertainly. Hair Guy and Green Crown hurried back to the hobby horse, its floppy-hatted handler, and Fur-Coat Man.

"Would you just make a decision?" the lady in red groaned, wrapping her arms around herself. "I am honest-to-God frozen here."

The other five huddled together like a football team discussing a play; then Green Crown turned and shouted back, "Could you do your right foot first up the stairs, too? Just to be safe?"

"What, you want me to hop or something?" the chimney sweep in the top hat asked, exasperated.

The others considered. "That would work," Green Crown said.

"Make way," Mr. Pine said in a voice that told Milo he was trying to keep it together. The group on the porch parted down the middle.

Meanwhile, the sweep muttered something under his breath, sighed, and proceeded to hop on his right foot all the way up the stairs. The others followed, coming to stand at the bottom of the steps to watch this performance with critical eyes. When he'd reached the top, the guy in the hat turned, made a face at his companions, then proceeded to walk very deliberately through the parted crowd of Pines, Caraways, and guests. He paused at the door, bowed to the folks on either side, and raised a foot to step over the threshold.

"RIGHT FOOT!"

The sweep clenched his fists, lowered his left foot, and stepped inside with his right. Just inside, he turned, and, framed by the doorway, swept the top hat from his head and gave a deep bow. Then he straightened and screamed, "RIGHT FOOT!" at the other Waits, who had begun to file up the stairs.

The soaking lady in red, who took this shriek right in the face, put a warning finger practically up his nose. "Stand between me and warmth and see what happens."

The next caroler, Green Crown, shook her head again. "You are such a child," she sniffed, and shoved past.

Chastened, the sweep caught Milo's eye and gave him a martyred look before following them inside.

The rest of the Waits trailed up the stairs, until only the man in the floppy hat and the hobby horse remained. Milo stood with the rest of his family and guests, waiting for them to enter too, but the man stopped just before the door and looked down at Milo. "Have you any grain or sugar for the hobby horse?" His voice was deep and musical. It sounded as if he had been born to sing the king's lines in the song they'd just finished.

Milo stared up into the glowing eyes of the ribbon-strewn horse under its patchily glittering antlers. *There's a person under there,* he reminded himself, but even knowing this, even having seen and heard the evidence only moments before, he couldn't look away from the ghastly bone face.

Mrs. Pine nudged Milo's arm and held out the sugar bowl, which she must have brought with her for exactly this purpose. Milo swallowed, reached in, and removed a single sugar cube. The hobby horse lowered its head until its candlelit eyes were level with Milo's. It opened its mouth. Milo hesitated. *I'm supposed to put my hand in there?*

He glanced back at his mother, who gave him an encouraging wink. Milo reached shakily past the yellowed teeth and the ribbons caught between them to place the sugar cube inside. Then he yanked his hand out of the way, certain the only behavior possible from a jaw like that was to snap shut on any hand foolish enough to be inside it. But it didn't. The skull closed its mouth delicately, and the jaws worked for a moment in a perfect mimicry of chewing. Then the hobby horse dipped its head in thanks and shuffled back a step or two.

"Well done," said the man with the floppy hat. "Now I will see to the beast and join you inside momentarily."

"Come on, everyone." Mr. Pine shepherded the guests, the Caraways, and Milo inside, closing the door behind them. The last thing Milo saw was the hobby horse watching him through the narrowing gap between door and jamb.

eight

THE RAW NIGHTS

𝕿HE INN WAS suddenly a full house. "Who can I get drinks for?" Mrs. Caraway called over the hubbub. A chorus of voices answered, and she and Lizzie laughed and headed for the kitchen. There was a cheerful swirl of activity as everyone, guests and residents and Waits alike, took off their coats and boots and began to offer introductions. It was clear, though, that there were two groups here, and one of those groups (and at least half of the other group, really) was made up of real characters. *Meddy would love this,* Milo thought a little sadly as he perched on the chair at the head of the dining table.

Mr. Pine followed the sweep into the living room before Milo got much of a look at him. As for the others — well, it was hard work, keeping himself from staring.

The woman who'd caught fire hung up her red cloak. Underneath, she wore a blue dress the color of robins' eggs. The cuffs of her jeans poked out from under the hem. She had dark hair, which was long and loose (and wet), but her face was lined, and despite the jeans and the lack of gray in her mane, Milo figured she was maybe fifty or sixty. She picked up her charred branch from the corner by the door and handed it to Mrs. Pine. There were tiny candles affixed to the branches, and even tinier glittering glass bits hung from them like ornaments. "Sorry about the burns, but you're supposed to put this in water and keep it inside. If it blooms, you'll have good luck."

"Thank you," Mrs. Pine said as she took the branch. "I don't think we've met before. I'm Nora Pine."

"Barbara Kirkegrim," the woman replied. And then, muttering, "Someone said something about drinks," she wandered into the kitchen.

Under his coat, the bell-clad fellow wore a getup that was somewhere between the mismatched ensemble of a ragpicker and a jester's motley. Arrays of assorted bells bounced at the ends of ribbons and scraps of leather and velvet that hung from braided garters at his knees. More bits of jewel-toned ribbon were braided into random chunks of his wild reddish-blond hair, and under that mane, his face was painted a pale blue-green. "Sylvester Alforn," he said. "Sorry about the bells. They drive me crazy, but it's tradition, and you don't mess with tradition."

"Yeah," Milo agreed warily. "I'm Milo. Hi."

Sylvester winced as another of the Waits sent up a jingling: the lady with the greens-and-candle-crown, who was shrugging out of her olive-colored, calf-length overcoat. She wore a white dress—it reminded Milo a lot of a wedding dress, except for the bright red ribbon at her waist and the white-berried greens around the neckline. The jingling came from a row of little silver bells sewn into the hem and cuffs of her coat.

"Let me help you with that, Lucky," Sylvester Alforn offered. They both looked youngish, Milo thought, maybe about the same age as Clem and Georgie.

The lady gave him a wary look, then caught Milo watching and switched her expression to a sweet smile. "Thanks." Sylvester stepped up behind her, helped her out of her coat, then, with a wink at Milo, ducked in fast, aiming his lips at her cheek.

But the lady in white was faster. She pivoted like a boxer and batted his face aside in an effortless gesture that was half slap, half shove. "Try it again, Sylvester," she snarled. "See what happens. It's a costume, not an invitation." With an aggravated noise, she shoved past her would-be kisser, leaving him to hang up her coat, which he did with a look that was more resigned than embarrassed—although not even the blue-green paint on his face could hide the fact that he was blushing.

"Thank you for inviting us in," she said to Milo. She glanced from him to Mrs. Pine, who was putting Barbara Kirkegrim's branch into a tall vase on the dining table. "I'm Lucia Julnissen. Lucky to my friends, among whom *you*"—she pointed at Sylvester—

"are not necessarily counted. You'll excuse me if I take this off, won't you?" she asked, turning back to Milo's mom and indicating the crown. "Spoils the effect a little not to wear it, but evidently *some people* can't handle being around a girl wearing mistletoe."

Mrs. Pine laughed. "Be my guest."

"Thanks." Lucky plucked off the crown and a wet handkerchief that had been sitting under it, on top of her blond head. "To keep from catching fire," she explained, setting the green ring on the countertop of the bar.

"Smart," Milo said.

"Well, some of us have done this before," she said with a quick but pointed glance at Barbara Kirkegrim.

"But not all of you?" Lizzie asked, reaching across the bar to hand her a mug.

"No, every year there are a few newbies," Lucky replied.

The remaining stranger in the room hung up his big fur coat and the carved wooden mask. He was a tall, older man of not-quite-grandparent age in a perfectly tailored green velvet suit and riding boots, with a little mustache that curled up on either side. Although the overall effect was plenty costumey, Milo suspected this guy might go around looking like that all the time. "Nicholas Larven," he announced. "Merry Christmas. Did I hear something about drinks, and would the options include anything in the vein of, say, a toddy of some sort?"

"We can manage that," Lizzie said. "I can do a pretty solid hot buttered rum. Or maybe another bowl of punch is the way to go. Let me see what we've got."

Mr. Larven's mustache curled up even further. "Well, if punch is in order and you don't mind swearing an oath of silence on the matter forevermore afterward, I don't mind telling you I happen to know the recipe for the very famous and very secret Shutter Club Punch." He rolled up the sleeves of his velvet jacket and swept into the kitchen, taking Lizzie's arm in a gentlemanly fashion as he passed. "Allow me. If you've got one of those handy little tea balls, it'll do nicely for steeping the spices."

The goatee-wearing, top-hatted sweep emerged from the living room, followed by a slightly nervous-looking Mr. Pine. "Coals are a bit too hot to start quite yet," the sweep announced, gratefully accepting a cup from Lizzie. He'd shed his cloak, but the old-fashioned tailcoat was still in place, along with his hat, which had a little sprig of holly tucked into the satin band around the crown. Whether from Milo's fireplace or someone else's, he already had sooty smudges on his nose and forehead. "Rupert Gandreider. Rob for short." He looked around. "Where are the others?"

Milo glanced around. Then he remembered the two Waits who'd stayed outside. As if on cue — and maybe it was — the door opened again and the man in the floppy hat entered, followed by a girl.

The man swirled off his long blue cloak. Underneath he was dressed like a huntsman from a fairy tale: tall boots, lots of leather, laced arm guards, and heavy gloves. "Happy Christmas," he said. "Thank you for your hospitality. My name is Peter Hakelbarend. This is Marzana."

The girl said nothing, just took off her coat and hung it up next to the rest. She was taller than Milo and probably older too, but he didn't think by much. She had dark hair in a single short braid, and dark circles around her eyes. She wasn't thin and she wasn't pale, but those dark circles somehow made her seem gaunt and pallid. She didn't seem big enough physically to have been the human inside the hobby horse, but there was no one else.

And where was the horse itself? The skull and the layered shroud were nowhere to be seen. Milo slipped off his chair and through the foyer as unobtrusively as he could, edging around the two newcomers. He opened the door and peeked outside. There was nothing in sight that looked at all like the trappings of the hobby horse, just the trampled frost that showed the path of the Waits to his home.

For a while it was all hot drinks and leftover cake as the carolers, the guests, and the denizens of Greenglass House mingled. It was a more-than-slightly-awkward process. Despite the relatively normal introductions, there was no getting past the fact that the newcomers to the house were visiting from a part of Nagspeake that was very different from the rest of the city. Not only that, but ordinarily Milo took it as a depressing given that, whenever he found himself in a group that included strangers, someone was going to ask him something uncomfortable, something that directly or indirectly referenced the visible difference between himself and his parents. He'd been waiting for it, steeling himself. But tonight, so far at least, no unpleasant questions had come.

After handing her branch off to Mrs. Pine and scoring a beverage, Barbara Kirkegrim went to stand by the window in front of the loveseat and alternated between blowing on her drink and chewing delicately on her fingernails. She didn't seem interested in chatting with anyone now that she'd played her part in the tradition; she looked ready to head back out into the night as soon as possible. Similarly, once he had his cup of punch, Nicholas Larven seemed to forget how to be social. He went to another of the windows, the big stained-glass one at the end of the dining room table. From his posture and bearing, if you didn't know better, you could've mistaken him for the lord of the manor rather than a random caroler who'd come in from the cold. Peter Hakelbarend stood self-consciously in the foyer, looking as if he couldn't quite decide whether he wanted to come in any farther. Marzana, as far as Milo could tell, had not moved from where she'd landed when she first entered. She stood against the wall by the dining table, her eyes flitting around the room like a pair of dark-haloed moths.

It wasn't all awkwardness, though. Georgie found her way almost immediately to Lucky, probably because Lucky seemed to be one of the non-newbie carolers, and from all the talk about traditions, there had to be some interesting lore behind the customs of the Waits. The two fell promptly into easy conversation. Rob the sweep and Sylvester (now with the unmistakable shape of a handprint marring his blue-green face) sat on the stools at the bar that separated the kitchen and dining room and set to devouring some cake. Emmett darted out to the screened porch and returned with a sketchbook and pencil. He looked around the room as if he couldn't decide who among the wild personalities to draw first, then settled on Sylvester and Rob. "You guys mind?" he asked, holding up his pencil.

"Fine by me," Sylvester said without looking up from his plate.

"Me too, if you go and get me a piece of that pie over there." Rob pointed with a fork still loaded with cake. Emmett nearly fell over himself to comply.

Clem sat at the opposite end of the dining table from the window where Mr. Larven had taken up residence. Milo knew immediately why she'd chosen that spot: from there she had a view of most of the open first floor.

He got himself a plate and cup and sat next to her. "Hey."

"Hey, Milo. This is something, huh?"

"Yeah." It was something, all right. The presence of all these bizarre strangers in his house acting as if it were perfectly normal for a guy with a blue face and bells around his knees to be eating cake next to a guy in an old-fashioned tailcoat and top hat gave Milo a sort of otherworldly feeling, as if one of the imaginary realms from the role-playing games he and his dad loved had begun to leak through into his own reality.

"Hey, Peter and Spookypants," Rob called. "If we're not going anywhere until I've done my job, you might as well get comfortable. It'll be a while."

Peter Hakelbarend gave him a narrow-eyed glare. "In the meantime, we are not, perhaps, projecting the right air of gravity and mystery," he said, folding his arms. He didn't move to sit down.

"I'm being as grave and mysterious as I can," Mr. Larven

protested from the window. "Though if we're staying a bit longer, perhaps I'll help myself to a jot more of this sterling punch."

Marzana glided at last from her spot by the wall to one of the little round tables by the dining room's bow window. "My name isn't Spookypants."

"Should be," Rob said under his breath.

Marzana stared at his back with those dark-rimmed eyes, then turned wordlessly toward the window.

Clem pivoted in her chair and beamed her thousand-watt smile on Mr. Hakelbarend. "So how does it work?" she asked. "What's the program of events? Singing, invitation . . . then what?"

Rob turned with a frown. "Are you in a hurry for us to leave?"

"No, no, I'm just curious. I've never seen"—Clem waved a hand—"all this before."

Rob mouthed a silent *Oh* and turned back to his pie. Mr. Hakelbarend answered instead, stepping a little farther into the house at last and raising his voice as if he were an actor about to start a monologue. "The days between the solstice and the second day of the New Year—"

"Or the fifth," Lucky put in from the sofa in the living room.

"—or the fifth day of the New Year," the huntsman amended. "The days between the twenty-first and the second or fifth day of the New Year—"

"It can be the twenty-first or the twenty-fourth," Lucky interrupted. "The twenty-first is the *astronomical* solstice, but the twenty-fourth is—"

"Depending on how you count," Mr. Hakelbarend interrupted loudly and patiently, "the days between either the twenty-first and the second day of the New Year or the twenty-fourth and the fifth of the New Year are the Raw Nights. They are uncertain nights, nights when it is said spirits and haunts come out to walk. But also they are oracle nights, augury nights, lot nights—nights when fortunes can be told, and good luck can be assured . . . or the opposite," he added. "So the Waits venture out during the Raw Nights, chasing away unkind spirits from the houses we visit and bringing good fortune with us in as many ways as we can. With songs, and bells, and candles." He pointed to the branch in the vase on the dining table. "With Barbara's branch, and with the sweep." He pointed to Rob, who raised his top hat with one hand while he forked pie into his mouth with the other. "Chimney sweeps are good luck, especially when they step over the threshold right foot first and then proceed to clean the chimney."

"Ideally," Lucky added, "you want a first-footer every morning between Christmas Eve and New Year's Day. Somebody outside the household who comes in and stirs up the coals in the morning. Always *right foot first*," she added loudly.

Rob made a loud scraping noise with his fork against his plate. "Didn't catch that, Lucky."

"RIGHT FOOT!" Lucky yelled. "WHY CAN'T YOU REMEMBER THAT?"

"Because I'm left-footed!" Rob shouted back. "It's hard to remember to do things opposite of how I always do them!"

"Left-footed," Lucky scoffed.

"Remember, Lucky, you were the one who insisted on Rob for the sweep this year," Sylvester put in.

"Yes, and why was that again?" Rob asked smugly.

Lucky grumbled something and looked down into her mug.

Rob got up and leaned around the dividing wall between the kitchen and the living room for a better look at Lucky. "Excuse me, Lucky, what was that?"

"Because Peter's too big to fit up a chimney, Sylvester's got red hair, and Nicholas is . . . less than spry," Lucky said defiantly.

"I will have you know that I am thoroughly spry, thank you very much," Mr. Larven said mildly. "I'll arm-wrestle any one of you right now."

Lucky dragged both palms down her face, exasperated. "No, we are not *arm-wrestling*."

Rob nodded along with all this. "I'm hearing you say, 'Because the sweep is supposed to be tall, dark, and handsome, and the only person here that fits that bill is Rob.'"

"That is *not* what I said."

"Just what I'm hearing," he said airily, returning to his pie.

"Enough," Mr. Hakelbarend barked. "The point is, we come, we sing, and one of us cleans the chimney, assuring you good luck for the coming year."

"The Waits come from a British tradition, originally," Lucky added. "At first, the Waits were bands of town watchmen who marked the hours by playing instruments through the night, and then the name came to refer to amateur bands that performed throughout the Christmas season. As for the sweep and the first footer and the hobby horse—"

"*I'm* tall, dark, and handsome," Barbara Kirkegrim interrupted. "Unless a female just can't be a suitable sweep."

"You're tall, dark, and lovely indeed, Mrs. Kirkegrim," Mr. Larven agreed as he returned to the window with his refilled cup of punch. "And I think we'd all concur that being female is no issue."

"I've gone caroling with girl sweeps on two occasions," Lucky volunteered.

"But," Mr. Larven continued, examining the bloom on a nearby poinsettia very carefully, "this morning you set a table on fire, to say nothing of what happened out there tonight. I think we can be forgiven for not wanting to mix you with an actual fireplace. Even letting you carry the branch was a bit of a stretch." Mrs. Kirkegrim rolled her eyes and turned back to her own window.

"So that's the program of events," Mr. Hakelbarend finished, sounding a bit as though maybe he, too, was ready to be done with the evening. He glanced into the kitchen. "Maybe I will have some coffee."

Clem turned to Marzana, who was still staring out and away. "The hobby horse is pretty amazing," she said. "How did you wind up in that role? What's it all about?"

Marzana gave her only the briefest glance. "I do the hobby horse so I won't have to talk to people."

"Oh," Clem said helplessly.

Conversation effectively died then for a minute or two. The occasional fork scraped on a plate. Mrs. Caraway asked if anybody needed refills, and Mr. Larven sang out a cheerful affirmative, waving his cup at her with a little more wiggliness in his arms than Milo thought he'd had before. That punch must've been strong. So far Mr. Larven was the only one who'd braved drinking it, though.

Rob stretched and swiveled off of his barstool. "Guess I'll investigate the state of the fireplace. Where'd I leave my stuff?"

"I think it's all on the hearth," Mr. Pine said, sounding a little strained. He didn't look all that excited about the ceremonial chimney cleaning.

"Can I maybe get some dust cloths or something?" Mrs. Pine offered.

"Nope, I have oilcloth," Rob called back as he headed into the living room.

Mrs. Kirkegrim addressed Mrs. Pine as she attempted to follow. "Where's your restroom, Mrs. Pine?"

"It's in the kitchen. I'll show you."

"Mom," Milo whispered, "I think Emmett's in there." The door was shut, anyway, and the artist was nowhere in sight.

"Oh." She paused. "If you'd rather not wait and you don't mind a flight of stairs, you're welcome to use ours on the second floor. Milo, could you . . . ?"

"Yeah, sure." Milo got to his feet and headed for the steps. "This way, Mrs. Kirkegrim." Behind them, Marzana rose and followed. Milo gave her a confused look. "You coming too? There's only one bathroom on our floor."

Marzana reddened. "I need a minute," she said in a low,

defensive voice. Her chin shook a little and her voice dropped even further. "There are too many people."

Too many people—Milo could certainly understand that. He still had places for hiding when the guests in his house became too much. For someone who had a real problem with people—and he was getting the sense that Marzana might fit into that category—this situation must be agonizing.

"Yeah, got it," he muttered back. "This way."

Milo led them up to the second-floor landing, where both the older lady and the girl paused for a look at the first of what Milo thought of as the Gate Windows. There was one at the landing on each floor. They were the oldest of the inn's collection of stained glass, and each had a warped gate worked into the metal that held the colored pieces. This one was done in shades of red and green, and Marzana in particular seemed fascinated by it. She glanced at Milo and looked as if she might want to say something, but before she could speak, quick footsteps sounded on the stairs and Georgie appeared.

"Excuse me," Georgie said, squeezing around the three of them. "Just heading up for a sweater." And she disappeared around the bend in the staircase.

"Bathroom's this way." Milo hurried the two carolers on down the hallway and forced himself not to glance over his shoulder. Georgie's light footsteps had been perfectly audible on her way up to the second floor, but he hadn't heard them start up to the third.

The bathroom was just beyond the second-floor living room.

He pointed out the door to Mrs. Kirkegrim, then dropped onto the couch under the biggest of the stained-glass windows in the house, which looked out onto the grounds from right over the front door. He reached for the lamp on the end table.

"Don't do that," Marzana said with an embarrassed look. "I mean, if you don't mind. It'll put a glare on the window."

"Oh. Okay, no problem." There was plenty of light in the room from the hallway.

She went to the opposite end of the couch, knelt on it facing the window, and put out a hand to touch a trapezoidal bit of violet. She said something, but her voice was so quiet Milo didn't catch it. "Sorry?"

"I've always been curious about your windows," she said shyly.

"Oh," Milo said, surprised. "Can you — can you see Greenglass House from the Liberty?"

Her face reddened again. "Well —"

She stopped speaking as the sounds of flushing and running water from the bathroom interrupted her. The door opened. "All yours, Marzie," Mrs. Kirkegrim said. Marzana made a sour face, then ducked past her and slammed the bathroom door.

"I don't think that nickname's going to stick, actually." Mrs. Kirkegrim glanced at Milo. "Guess I'd better apologize. This is the second time I've accidentally upset her tonight." She hesitated. "Can you give us a minute, Milo? You don't have to wait for us at all, but my feelings won't be hurt if you'd rather not leave strangers alone in your space."

Milo considered suggesting that Marzana would probably

prefer a couple minutes' privacy to an apology but decided against it. Mrs. Kirkegrim knew her better than he did. "Sure thing. I have to get something from my room anyway." And he headed down the hallway.

Milo heartily preferred not leaving strangers alone in his space. On the other hand, he was ninety percent sure that at that very moment Georgie was crouched in the stairwell to make sure neither of these two tried to slip up to the guest floors without her knowing. Even though she appeared to be delighted by the Waits, Georgie was a professional thief, and at present, she was a *paranoid* professional thief. Having seven strangers turn up had to have ratcheted her instincts up a notch. She'd hear anything that went on between the living room and the staircase. Milo could keep an ear on the rest of the floor from his room.

He flopped on his bed and stared up at the string of onion-shaped red silk lanterns that hung from the ceiling. The wind rattled his window, and he turned to look out. Darkness and frost. Milo raised a fist and shook it at the glass. *Darn you, frost.* He took a deep breath, inhaling the tiniest nip of orange and cinnamon from some cheerful Christmas candle his mother had probably left burning somewhere, and felt himself relax just a little. Marzana had had the right idea; momentary peace and quiet was just what he needed too.

And then his peaceful moment came to an abrupt end, ripped in two by a strangled yelp from the living room.

nine

THE INVISIBLE ASSAILANT

ILO BARRELED INTO the living room, arriving on the scene just as Georgie came sprinting in from the other direction. They stared in consternation as Mrs. Kirkegrim and Marzana picked themselves painfully up from the floor.

"What the heck happened?" Georgie demanded.

"I have no idea," Mrs. Kirkegrim groaned, rocking back on her heels and clutching the spot where her neck met her shoulder. "Something hit me."

"Who yelled?" Milo asked. He glanced from the older woman to the girl. "Should I get help?"

Marzana pulled herself up to sit cross-legged, rubbing the back of her head. "I don't think I yelled, but something hit me, too."

She pointed to Mrs. Kirkegrim with a confused frown. "It must've been you."

"Me?" Mrs. Kirkegrim protested. "It most certainly was not!"

Marzana shook her head, then winced and clutched it tighter. "No, I mean you must've been the one who yelled."

"But what hit you?" Milo glanced around the room. There was nothing out of place. They had both said "some*thing*," he thought uneasily, but maybe that was the wrong word.

He eyed Georgie. Under a forehead wrinkled in concentration, her eyes were flitting around the room too. "Milo, how about I'll stay with these two and you go get your mom and a couple ice packs?"

"Yeah, okay." On his way downstairs, he wondered why Mrs. Kirkegrim's cry hadn't brought more help already. When he got to the first floor, that mystery solved itself.

The first thing he noticed was a distinct haze in the air, as if he were seeing his home through a grayish filter. He spotted Mrs. Caraway in the kitchen, keeping resolutely busy with dishes. At the dining room table, Clem and Lizzie sat with expressions that seemed to be wavering between amusement and horror, watching whatever was happening in the living room like spectators at a circus being performed without a safety net.

And what was happening in the living room was — a puff of soot caught Milo in the face and he burst into a fit of coughing. "Boy oh boy," Rob's voice said cheerfully through the fug, "not a minute too soon, am I right? This chimney is filthy!"

It really didn't seem possible that one chimney could spew so much ash and fume into a space as big as this one. Milo squinted into the cloud of grime, searching for his parents among the indistinct figures moving around. "I don't know, do you think maybe we should just let this all settle?" Mr. Pine's disembodied voice suggested.

"Nope, nope, worst thing possible," Rob replied. "Can't stop halfway. Got to power through it."

Milo gave up looking. "Mom?" he called.

"Here." She emerged from the miasma, holding a tissue over her nose. "Thank God. Save me, Milo."

"Sorry, Mom. Bad news." He led her into the kitchen and whispered, "We need ice packs upstairs. Two of them."

Mrs. Pine frowned. "Ice packs?" Her voice dropped and took on a dangerous tone. "What for?" Mrs. Caraway looked up from the sink, sighed, wiped her hands, unearthed a pair of tea towels from a drawer, and headed for the freezer.

Milo glanced around. "There's been . . . an accident. Maybe."

"Oh, for the love of . . ." Milo's mom accepted the two tea-towel ice packs from Mrs. Caraway. "Fine. Let's see what fresh hell the evening has brought us."

When they got upstairs, they found Georgie pacing in the entry to the living room, eyeing the space beyond as if there might be someone hiding in a corner. Marzana and Mrs. Kirkegrim had managed to relocate themselves to the couch. "What on earth happened?" Mrs. Pine blurted.

"That's what we're trying to figure out," Mrs. Kirkegrim said. "One minute we were having a perfectly normal conversation, and the next—*bam!* We're both on the ground. Pummeled!" She took a lump of plaid towel from Milo's mom and settled it against her neck. "I hate to be needy, but do you have any aspirin? I think I'm getting a migraine."

Marzana said nothing, just leaned back, wedged the second ice pack between her head and a cushion, and stared at the ceiling. Milo wondered if she was trying not to cry. "Are you in a lot of pain?" he asked.

"It's not bleeding" was all Marzana said, blinking hard.

Mrs. Pine looked worriedly from one to the other. "Would you like to lie down? You can stretch out there, or if you want to brave one flight of stairs, you can each have a quiet room and a real bed to yourself for a rest." There were two spare rooms on the second floor, but Mrs. Caraway and Lizzie had already taken those.

Marzana nodded, still staring at the ceiling. "I can handle stairs. My head just hurts. But I think lying down might be nice."

"Georgie, you don't mind coming along, with us, do you?" Mrs. Pine asked. "I'm sure Mrs. Kirkegrim and Marzana are fine, but just to be sure nobody slips and falls while she's still recovering."

"Of course not."

"And Milo can rustle up some aspirin while we get you both settled. Milo, you know where it is, right? In the cabinet over the stove."

"I know where it is." He trudged to the kitchen, pulled a chair over to the stove, climbed up, opened the cabinet door, and ducked as a small landslide of pills, bandages, tape dispensers, and half-empty battery packets cascaded out. He located the aspirin bottle, shoved everything else back in, then poured a tumbler of water and followed the slowly moving procession to the stairs.

Georgie, who was last in line, reached for the aspirin and the water glass. "I'll take those, Milo. Could you wait here for your mom and me?"

"Sure." Milo sat on the stairs to wait. Overhead he heard muffled voices, mostly his mom's and Mrs. Kirkegrim's, then doors creaking and closing. Finally two pairs of footsteps descended again, and Georgie and Mrs. Pine rejoined him on the second floor.

They filed into the living room, and Mrs. Pine immediately began to pace. "How on earth does this happen? Two people just get —get *clobbered* completely at random in my living room?"

"I don't know." Georgie didn't pace, but the quarter she'd been clipping flashed through her fingers. "One thing's obvious, though —it wasn't a some*thing* that hit them."

"It was a some*one*," Milo finished.

Georgie pointed one index finger at him and tapped her nose with the other. "I don't know why neither of them put it that way —and I don't know how it could've happened without one of them seeing the attacker—but it had to be a person."

"But there was nobody else up here," Mrs. Pine protested. "Just you and Milo, and we know it wasn't either of you."

Georgie shrugged. "Milo and I were both in here practically before Mrs. Kirkegrim finished yelling, and nothing was out of place. Not that I'd know, but Milo would." She glanced at him. "Am I right?"

Milo nodded. "Everything was where it always is."

"And even if I could bring myself to believe a clock or whatever could have fallen off the wall and done this, I don't see how anything smaller than a chandelier or a roof beam could manage to coldcock both Marzana and Mrs. Kirkegrim within seconds of each other and without either of them noticing it happening until after the fact. There was a person. There *had* to be. Somebody hit them, one after the other, and did it on purpose."

Something different was nagging at Milo's brain. "I don't understand how neither of them saw the other one get hit. I wonder if one or the other *did* see the attacker, but she doesn't want to tell for some reason." He glanced at Georgie. "Did you hear whoever it was?"

She blew out a mouthful of air, annoyed. "Nope. Anyone could've come up."

"But weren't you on the steps listening?" Milo asked. "I thought for sure you were . . . I don't know, standing guard right around the bend in the stairs."

Georgie shook her head and plucked at the collar of the turtleneck she was wearing. "Against all probability, I was telling the truth: I went up to my room and got a sweater. After that, you're right—I came back down and sat on the steps to listen. But in the time it took me to get up to the fourth floor, open my door, find my sweater, lock up, and come back down, anybody could've snuck up on those two. And somebody must have."

Milo scratched his head. "Who was missing from downstairs, then, Mom?"

Mrs. Pine threw up her hands. "Are you kidding me? Once that

Rob guy started conjuring the ash demon in the living room, anybody could've slipped out. Nobody was paying attention to what anyone else was doing because we were all dying of air pollution. You could barely see your own hand in front of your face down there by the time Milo came to get me." They all looked at each other for a moment. "There'd better be some of that Larven guy's punch left," Mrs. Pine added through gritted teeth.

They started toward the stairs again; then Georgie stopped and turned slowly. "You know, there is a potentially simple explanation for how someone or something could have hit both of them, one after the other, without being seen and without leaving anything out of place in the room."

"What?" Abruptly, Milo realized she was looking at him. *"Me?"*

"Not you. A friend of yours."

Meddy. "No way." He shook his head emphatically. "You think *Meddy* attacked someone? *Two* someones? Two *strangers,* for absolutely no reason? Not possible. She might be a ghost, but she's not a loose cannon."

"But what if she thought there *was* a reason?" Georgie insisted. "What if she thought she was protecting you, or someone else in the house?"

Milo looked to his mother for backup. "Mom."

Mrs. Pine hesitated. "I don't know, Georgie. I think Milo's right. Although, since we know there's at least one haunt in Greenglass House, I guess it's not impossible that there could be more. Still . . ." She tilted her head, thinking, then shook it decisively. "I can't quite bring myself to believe a ghost is the answer here. That opens up a whole can of worms I'm just not ready to deal with in my life right now."

Georgie nodded. "Just a thought. Let's go see about that punch."

ten

IRRESISTIBLE BLANDISHMENT

THE CLOCK ON THE MANTELPIECE began chiming the half hour as Milo, Georgie, and Mrs. Pine arrived on the first floor. The air quality hadn't improved all that much. Milo coughed and wiped his eyes, trying to make a note of where everyone was. It wasn't easy.

Rob the Sweep and Mr. Pine were at the epicenter of the ashes, in the living room. Lucky and Sylvester were there too, Lucky offering suggestions (or maybe giving orders) to Rob as he worked and Sylvester sprawled on the couch. Mr. Larven was perched somewhat unsteadily on the back of the loveseat, making observations and gesturing grandly with his punch cup.

Everyone else was at the dining table. "Hey." Emmett popped up from his seat. "Everything all right?"

"In a manner of speaking." Mrs. Pine glanced at Mr. Hakelbarend. "Could I have a word, Mr. Hakelbarend? The others seem a little . . . preoccupied."

Milo figured that was a nice way of saying *You seem slightly less loopy than the rest of your party*. Mr. Hakelbarend appeared to have the same idea. He gave Mrs. Pine a *Let's not kid each other* look. But then his expression sharpened. "What's happened?"

Aha. There was something about the way he said those two words that sent a little prickle up Milo's neck. If Meddy had been there listening too, he was dead certain she would've given him an elbow to the ribs and some kind of Significant Look, and Milo would've whispered back, *Yes, he knows something. He knew — or suspected, or worried — that something might happen while the Waits were here.*

Mrs. Pine sat down. "Mrs. Kirkegrim and Marzana have had some kind of accident. They say that something hit them in the heads, but they didn't see what, or who. They're upstairs having a little lie-down now, and I have a suspicion that Mrs. Kirkegrim, at least, might sleep before she's ready to start back."

"Something hit them *both?*" Mr. Hakelbarend asked curiously. "I don't understand. Did something fall?"

"I have no idea," Mrs. Pine admitted. "It doesn't *look* like anything fell. But Milo and Georgie were both up there too, and none of the four of them saw anyone who could've done it, whether accidentally or on purpose."

Mr. Hakelbarend made a humphing noise. "All right. Thank you." He glanced over his shoulder toward Mr. Larven. "Nick there is a doctor, but in his current state I'm not sure he's likely to be much help. If they're both comfortable, it's probably good to just let them rest. I'm sorry to impose on you with all this"—he waved an arm to include the ashy haze—"when we're supposed to be bringing good luck."

Mrs. Pine shook her head. "Nonsense. We're honored to have you. I don't like people getting hurt in the inn, is all. Makes me feel like a bad host."

Now the huntsman smiled for the first time. "No one who could invite us into her home and remain cheerful even in the midst of this mess could possibly be thought a bad host."

For a few minutes the room was almost peaceful, except it felt to Milo as if everyone was waiting uncomfortably for the next unexpected, out-of-control thing to happen. Something was definitely going on here. If Milo hadn't quite been certain before, Mr. Hakelbarend's wary *What's happened?* had cemented it. Fortunately, Milo knew what to do to get a bunch of weirdoes talking when he needed information.

Negret the blackjack had had the ability to perform an exploit called Irresistible Blandishment, which allowed him, through sheer force of charisma and will, to convince someone to do what he wanted. Inspired by *The Raconteur's Commonplace Book,* he had used the Irresistible Blandishment exploit last year to entice the guests at Greenglass House to tell stories each night, and from those stories he and Sirin—a scholiast, Meddy's alter ego—had gotten the clues they'd needed to piece together the truth of why the guests had all come to the inn.

Well, Milo thought, looking around the room, *it worked before. Why wouldn't it work again?*

He walked to a spot near the foyer where he could see into each room, summoned up every shred of charisma he possessed, and said, "You know what's always fun? Telling stories." His voice sounded a bit wobbly, even to his own ears.

The folks who knew him well gave him an assortment of thoughtful looks. Mr. Hakelbarend glanced blankly at him. "Stories?" Sylvester repeated skeptically.

"Sure, stories." Milo looked hopefully to Georgie, who was sanding the clipped edges of her quarter at the dining table, and willed her to play along. *You know what I'm doing. Throw me a bone.* "Like in *The Raconteur's Commonplace Book.* Hasn't anyone else read it?"

Georgie paused in her work. "Oh, sure," she said brightly. "That's the one where a bunch of people are snowed in and they tell stories to pass the time, right?"

Lucky spoke up from the living room. "They're *flooded* in," she corrected Georgie. "They can't leave because the roads are washed out."

Milo fell on her words and tried not to sound desperate. "Exactly! Want to start us off?"

"I'll tell a story!" Rob appeared around the corner and shoved the brim of his top hat back on his forehead with the end of his brush. "It starts out, 'It was a dark and stormy —'"

"A dark and stormy night?" Lucky cut in sarcastically. "Really? You're *really* going to rip off that line to start your —"

"I was *referring* to the mixed drink," Rob retorted. "Ginger beer, rum, and bitters. But if you don't want to hear the story—"

"I *want* you to fix this *mess* you've made!"

"You know," said Mr. Larven, waving an unsteady finger in the air, "I happen to know a smashing recipe for a fancy dark and stormy. Shall I mix us up a pitcher?"

"As a matter of fact," Clem said, getting up and guiding him to a chair, "I'm kind of interested in any story that starts out with a cocktail, Rob."

Rob and Lucky were glaring fiercely at each other. "I don't think I remember the rest," Rob said coldly. He pushed his hat forward again so that it slanted low over his eyes and stalked away. Lucky gave an exasperated sigh and dropped onto the loveseat with folded arms.

"Come on, Lucky," Milo said with forced cheer. "I'm sure you know some great stories. You could tell us more about the Waits. You know, the traditions and stuff."

"I have a headache," she growled, and slumped lower in the seat.

"Let's go, people," Georgie said, her voice warm with encouragement. "Somebody's got to have a story they can start us off with. Mr. Larven?"

"Oh, certainly!" The man in the green coat stood grandly and gave an affected harrumph. "I shall tell you a story of Jackanory," he intoned, "and now my story's begun."

Mrs. Pine groaned. "Not that one."

"Oh, you know it?" Mr. Larven said, delighted.

"It's the one my father used to tell me every time I asked for a bedtime story and he didn't feel like telling one," she grumbled.

"Well, then I hardly have to tell *you* the rest, but perhaps Milo would like to hear it." He leaned down so that he was nose to nose with Milo. "I shall tell you a story of Jackanory, and now my story's begun. I shall tell you another, of John, his brother . . ." He straightened with a flourish and beamed. "And now my story's done." He bowed deeply, then looked around the room as if expecting applause.

Milo wilted. "That's all?"

"Yeah, I can see how that would be annoying if you wanted a real story," Georgie agreed with a scowl.

"I'm sure I can think of one," Emmett said. "It can be anything, right?"

Georgie turned to him with renewed interest. "Absolutely," she said, leaning on one elbow and looking across the table at him as she spun the clipped quarter between fingers already gone blackish again from her sanding.

Emmett beamed, and Milo thought his cheeks might've gone a shade pinker, too. "Oh. Well, then let me think." This was encouraging.

"All right, and while you do that, Mrs. Pine and I have decided to try this much-vaunted punch of Mr. Larven's. I'm sure you'll come up with something good." Georgie pocketed the coin. "Come on, Mrs. P. We'll let the man consider his tale."

"Good luck about that punch," Clem scoffed. "If there's any left, you can get me a cup too, but at the rate Mr. Larven's been going through it, I'm not gonna hold my breath."

"Did I hear my name being taken in vain?" Mr. Larven ambled over, waving a sloshing glass. "Up the revels!" He did a maneuver that looked as though it might've started out as a toast but finished with most of the contents of the cup running down the front of the crisp white shirt under his green jacket. "Who's with me?"

Mr. Hakelbarend plucked the cup from the mustachioed man's fingers. "You have had so much more than enough, Nicholas."

"Have I?" Mr. Larven asked. He glanced into the kitchen, leaning at a dangerously off-balance angle that made Clem put up a hand in case he fell on her. Miraculously, he didn't. "But there appears to be punch left," he protested.

"Don't worry, we'll take care of it," Georgie said, neatly maneuvering the older man onto one of the long benches that served as seats on either side of the dining table. "I promise it won't go to waste." She took Milo's mom's arm and steered her into the kitchen.

"Oh, well, that's just fine, then." Mr. Larven leaned his chin on his palm and stared at Lizzie for a long and awkward minute. "You, young lady, look a bit like a pepper grinder with arms and legs. The skinny kind you click to operate." He held up one hand in a thumbs-up, then proceeded to move his thumb up and down as if he were pressing a button. "Click, click. You know the sort I'm talking about? Click."

Lizzie considered him seriously, frowning. "A pepper grinder."

"I imagine it's the way you're wearing your hair. The bun is the clicker?" Mr. Hakelbarend sighed. "I can't believe I willingly joined this conversation."

Mr. Larven beamed, sat back, and looked around the table. "This fellow knows what I mean." Then, without warning, he tumbled forward directly onto his face on the table. And with that, Milo realized with a sinking heart, any chance his story plan had for success fell right to pieces.

Mr. Hakelbarend, Mrs. Caraway, and Lizzie lurched into motion toward the collapsed man. Clem was faster, but she was going in the opposite direction. Not only could Clem be silent when she wanted, she could move like a ninja, and she was barely more than a blur as she sprinted past Milo and into the kitchen to — *Holy cow!* — actually *kick the cut-glass punch cup out of Mrs. Pine's hand* with surgical precision just as Milo's mom was about to take her first sip.

The cup shattered against the cabinets over the stove. Georgie looked down at the cup in her own hand, set it carefully on the counter, and backed away from it with her hands raised in surrender.

"Oops," Clem said as several heads turned in the direction of the kitchen.

Mrs. Pine stared at the fragments scattered across the stovetop, then stared at Clem. Clem nodded over her shoulder at the dining table. By now, the folks there had Mr. Larven upright, but he was still unconscious.

"You don't think he's just drunk?" Georgie asked Clem quietly as Mrs. Pine rushed over to him.

Clem shrugged. "You don't think those two upstairs got knocked out by some random, unexplained accident?"

Milo looked at the two thieves, then at his frantic mother. A minute later his dad rushed in, his skin a shade of cindery gray that Milo didn't think happened in nature. Then Rob peered around the corner, his face blackened almost to the same shade as his facial hair and one hand clutching a giant, saucer-shaped brush on a pole. "Hey, what's going on?" he inquired. Then from the room behind him came a muted *poot,* and a fresh puff of black smoke engulfed him so completely that nothing was visible but his top hat and the bristles of his brush. The sweep swore.

Milo leaned against the wall, felt his hands curl involuntarily into fists, and knew a yell was building in his gut, a yell that would take some work to get under control again once it started on its way up his throat. He also knew that in the middle of an evening like this, the worst possible thing he could do was have a meltdown. His parents would probably lose it for real.

He took a deep breath, straightened, and headed for the foyer. Lizzie was the most available known-quantity adult just then, so on his way past, Milo plucked her sleeve and tugged her away from the rest. "I'm going outside," he informed her in a low, tight voice. Lizzie frowned. "If I don't get out of here I'm going to scream," he warned before she could argue. "And I don't think that'll help things."

Lizzie considered. "Nope. Don't stay out long or whatever a responsible adult would say. Wear a hat and whatnot."

"Yeah, I'll tie my shoes and everything." Milo yanked on all his outdoor gear and slipped out onto the porch.

Immediately he felt a weight lift from his shoulders as the sharp, cold, blessedly clean and clear air spiked into his lungs. Even the frost looked good after the haze from the fireplace.

He walked carefully down the steps and onto the wide-open lawn and stared up at the sky. It was diamond-clear in that way that only winter nights ever manage to be, with a perfect field of stars overhead. Milo gulped the air, then made himself slow down and breathe more evenly. The yell curled in his gut started to loosen, and Milo imagined picking it apart like a knot of yarn. It loosened a little more.

Milo wandered the lawn in circles for a few minutes, breathing in the cold and stomping down the crunchy, frosted grass. There was something amiss in the house. That much was plain. All right, maybe it didn't make sense to blame the mess Rob was making on anything but the fact that the Waits' sweep had been chosen because he was "tall, dark, and handsome" rather than because he knew anything at all about how to clean a chimney. And maybe Clem was mistaken about the punch and Nicholas Larven was just very, very drunk. But there was still the puzzle of what had happened to Mrs. Kirkegrim and Marzana, and there was still the matter of the adventure-gone-wrong that had driven Georgie and Clem to the inn to lie low. Whether those two events had anything to do with each other was another question entirely, but all things considered, Milo decided it wasn't totally outrageous to think maybe there was something serious going on at Greenglass House.

Again.

"This is a Negret problem," he said aloud. But to become the blackjack Negret again — there was just no other conclusion to come to — he needed Meddy.

Something moved at the periphery of the lawn.

Milo turned and scanned the timberline where the grass ended and the woods beyond hid the slope that led down to the Skidwrack. In particular he eyed the treeless space that marked the upper landing of the incline railway. On evenings when the Pines thought the railcar might get some use, the platform there was illuminated by strings of tiny Christmas lights. They'd been lit when Milo had come home from school, but at some point that evening either his mom or his dad must've come out and unplugged them, because now there was nothing but darkness there.

Nothing, that is, until someone stepped out of the shadows.

Milo's heart leapt into his throat. But only for a single beat, and then it slunk back down to its proper place. Because of course this figure was far too tall to be Meddy. This figure was adult-sized, and male. *Another guest?* Milo thought immediately. *Unbelievable.*

It was a logical first thought, but before he could take it a step further and call out, Milo realized this couldn't be a guest. The railcar hadn't brought anyone up since he had gotten home — it was still at the top of the hill where he'd left it. And while Milo *had* seen someone climb the more than three hundred incredibly steep steps from river to platform without practically dying at the top, he'd only seen it once — and from no less an athlete than Clem Candler, so he didn't expect to ever see it again. If this fellow had used the steps, he'd taken plenty of time to hang out in the woods and recover, which was not generally how potential guests behaved. Nor was it normal behavior for a guest to do what the man was doing at the moment: waiting patiently at the edge of the woods to see what Milo would do now that the stranger had been seen.

But mainly, Milo knew this couldn't be a guest because he knew who it was. He had seen this man before. Not in person, though — no, that would've been impossible. But he *had* seen him, and dressed exactly as he was now, down to the tarpaulin hat decorated with a gold pin that caught the starlight.

The man raised one hand in greeting. Milo raised his own, not quite able to believe what was happening — although he knew of two other people who had waved to this man when he had appeared from out of the woods at the cliff's edge on another occasion, many years before. One was a smuggler who was a regular at the inn. The other was Meddy.

Milo gathered his courage and walked across the lawn to where one of the most famous smugglers the city of Nagspeake had ever seen was waiting for him: Meddy's father, Michael Whitcher, who had gone by the moniker Doc Holystone. When he had been alive.

eleven

DOC HOLYSTONE

DOC HOLYSTONE'S IDENTITY had been a big secret until his death almost forty years ago, but by the time Milo was old enough to hear about it, almost everyone knew he'd been a man named Michael Whitcher. Not quite as well-known was that Greenglass House had once belonged to him, and that he'd had a daughter who'd died after falling from the fire escape on the same night her father had met his end.

Milo had seen pictures of Doc Holystone before — smuggling ran deep in the culture of Nagspeake in general and of the Pines' neck of the woods in particular, not to mention the fact that most of their clientele was made up of runners of some stripe or another. But the best picture, the most important one, the most meaningful and truest image of Michael Whitcher that Milo had ever seen was the one that had been found at Greenglass House a year ago. It was the cartoon that Dr. Wilbur Gowervine had displayed at City University and that had brought Emmett Syebuck to the inn for his sketching vacation. And it had shown Doc Holystone exactly as he now stood before Milo.

As Milo approached, the man in the tarpaulin hat lifted his chin and his face became visible for the first time. It, too, was exactly as Milo remembered, minus the mosaic-like colored shapes in the cartoon, which had approximated what the final stained-glass work made from it would look like. Doc was tall and clean-shaven, with reddish sideburns, and he looked older than he had in the cartoon, definitely older than Milo's parents; but then, presumably if you were making a portrait in stained glass you weren't going to bother putting lines in around the eyes. And just as his daughter, Meddy, had when she'd appeared to Milo, he looked solid and real, as real as any of the living back in the house. He beckoned. Milo hesitated a moment. Then he followed.

When they were both standing under the cover of the trees, the ghost spoke. "You must be Milo."

His voice perfectly matched everything else. It took exactly zero imagination to picture this guy giving orders on a clipper and having the complete and loyal trust of everyone aboard.

"Yes, sir." Milo hesitated again, not sure how to proceed. There was a smell of woodsmoke in the air. The familiarity of it helped to put him at ease. "It's nice to finally meet you."

Doc Holystone smiled. "I've watched your family, when I could. It's nice to meet you, too."

"Um . . ." What did you say to the ghost of one of the most famous people in local history? Milo went with the only questions that really mattered just then. "Why are you here? And where's Meddy?"

The ghost frowned. "Meddy?"

Oh, right. Doc would know his daughter by her real name, not the one she'd used when she'd been pretending to be a living person and Milo had mistaken her for Madeleine Caraway. "Addie, I mean. Your daughter." He lifted an arm, intending to point to the stone bench that hid her gravestone, then dropped it again. Maybe Doc didn't know she was buried there. Maybe he did, but pointing it out would be insensitive, a reminder of her death. Or did that even matter when you were talking with one ghost about another?

But Doc seemed to understand. "It's okay, Milo. It was a long time ago." His smile faded. "What do you mean, where is she?"

"She showed herself to us last year, Mr. . . . . sir. She's my friend. But I haven't seen her since then, and I . . ." Milo swallowed and told the truth. "I miss her. I kind of need her right now, and I don't know how to find her."

Doc's expression sobered even further. He put a hand to his face and drew it down his chin as he stared up through the trees and into the cold, clear sky. The ring on his fourth finger caught the starlight just as his hatpin had. At last he looked at Milo again. "I'm so happy to know she has a friend. But I don't know how to contact her, Milo. We haven't spoken since . . ."

"Since you both died," Milo finished tentatively.

Doc nodded. "I can't even come into the house. I can't go any farther than where I'm standing now. I've tried."

"I don't know if she can leave the house, either, but I know she saw you wave," Milo told him. "At least once. Did you see her wave back?"

The ghost put a hand to his forehead. "I think so, but . . ." He frowned. "It's hard to explain."

"I think I know what you mean," Milo told him. "Meddy — Addie — told me, *Time passes strangely*. She said she only remembers snippets, and not always clearly."

"That's it exactly."

"So if you're not here looking for Addie," Milo asked after a moment, "then what brought you back?"

Doc Holystone turned the full force of those piercing eyes on Milo, which was almost enough to make him squirm. "Do you really not know?"

I knew it. "There's something wrong in the house," Milo guessed in a breathless rush. "Can you feel it?" When Meddy/Addie had wandered into his life the year before, that was what had brought her out of whatever ghostly plane she inhabited — she'd sensed a wrongness at the inn, had been able to feel the seeking of all the secretive strangers who'd come to the inn.

Doc nodded again, slowly. "And I know what it is, though I think you do too."

"Violet Cross's derrotero," Milo said in a whisper.

The ghost whistled, impressed. "Then it's true. Trust Violet to do the impossible. That woman was the kind of genius the world only sees once or twice in a hundred years. Tell me the rest."

As Milo did, the smuggler's expression hardened by slow degrees. Doc listened in silence until Milo was finished, then scratched his chin and said, "What was the name of the third man in your friends' heist? The fence."

"I can't remember. Something with a *G*. Gilmore or Gillyflower or something like that."

"Gilawfer," Doc said darkly.

"That's it. And there's another thief they think might be after them. Some kind of master of disguise. He's got a name that sounds like part of a skeleton. Cantlebone, I think."

"Huh. Well, I've never heard of this Cantlebone, but Gilawfer, now — *him* I know, and he's a problem. Back in my day, he was already a fence as a teenager, but he was also known to many of us runners to be an informant for the customs department. His handler was the same fellow who . . ." Doc paused, and a flicker of fury crossed his face. "His handler was a man named Vinge. De Cary Vinge."

Milo stiffened. De Cary Vinge: the only person who'd come to Greenglass House last year for nefarious purposes. Even though the last time he'd seen Mr. Vinge, the old man had been running away in terror after being tackled by his own overcoat, Milo shifted uncomfortably. "I've met him."

Doc's face was grave. "If he's involved, Milo, the reality is, it isn't just these other thieves you have to be concerned about. It's customs. Because if Gilawfer doesn't think he can get the derrotero on his own, he can make serious money by turning evidence over to the department and letting them go after it."

"Georgie and Clem don't even think they have the derrotero," Milo protested. "It wasn't there."

"Hmm. Well, supposedly she left caches all around the river. I suppose if she did manage to create a derrotero, it could be somewhere else. Or," he said thoughtfully, "maybe it just doesn't look like a book, or a map. We're talking about charting the Skidwrack —something most people don't believe is even possible, after all. If she did it, she'd have had to think outside the box. Your friends should probably consider that, too."

Milo thought back to his idea of a movable map. You'd definitely have to think outside the box to create something like that. "I'll tell them," he said. "And I'll give them the warning, too."

Doc held up a cautious palm. "Find a way to do it without mentioning me, if you can, Milo. But I'll be here if you need." He extended his hand.

"Okay," Milo said, and shook it.

The ghost looked over Milo's shoulder. "You'd better get back before anyone comes looking for you. And if you see my daughter . . ." He smiled again. "Tell her to come and wave."

"I will," Milo promised. And, hardly able to believe what had just taken place, he sprinted out of the woods and across the lawn to the house. The ghost of Doc Holystone was on the grounds! "Where are you, Meddy?" Milo muttered as he ran.

The last remnants of that pleasant woodsmoke aroma he'd smelled under the trees evaporated as he opened the door. Milo waved one hand in front of his face as he stepped into the very different, not-at-all-warm-and-cozy smell of old, cold ash.

"Good breather?" Lizzie asked as he kicked off his boots.

"Did the trick," Milo said, glancing around the first floor. The group around the dining table had dwindled to just the Caraways and Emmett. Rob was literally *in* the fireplace — all that was visible were his legs from the knees down, and then only between drifts of soot. Mr. Hakelbarend stood by the hearth with arms folded. Sylvester, still lying across the couch, now had a pillow over his face. Hopefully he'd wiped off the blue first. Milo's mom would be super annoyed if he was getting makeup all over everything.

"So," Milo said hopefully, turning to Emmett. "Did you think of a story?"

"Sorry to say I didn't." Emmett stretched and stood. "But I'm too tired anyway, I think. I'm going to clean up my paints and call it a night."

Milo slumped. "Anybody else?" There was a general noise of demurral. Why were they so unhelpful? All he needed was a little cooperation.

"It was a good effort, Milo." Mrs. Pine was at the liquor cabinet pouring herself a glass of her favorite bourbon. She took both bottle and glass to the dining table and wiped her forehead with one arm, leaving a broad swipe of cleaner skin above her eyebrows. "Who else needs a little fortification?"

"Me," Mr. Pine replied as he and Lucky came down the stairs. "Mr. Larven's out, but I think now he's just sleeping." He smiled weakly as Milo's mom passed him her own glass and got up for another.

"So he's all right, then?" Mrs. Caraway asked. "Was it just too much punch?"

"He roused himself long enough to vomit," Lucky said in a voice full of carefully controlled annoyance, "but he made it to the bathroom first. Then he muttered something about physicians healing themselves and fell right asleep again."

"But he's stable," Mr. Pine said. "And he seems to be sleeping peacefully." He snapped his fingers and glanced at Lucky. "We should have checked on the two head cases while we were—" He blanched and put a hand to his mouth. "Oh, for the love of—I'm so sorry. That's not what I meant. I meant the two who got *hit* in the head, not—"

"We all knew what you meant." Lucky gave him a strained smile. "Sometimes things just slip out."

"I can't believe I said that," Mr. Pine said. "Please excuse me." He joined Milo, who was still standing grouchily by himself near the foyer. "I don't know about you," Mr. Pine said quietly, "But I'm officially about done."

"Yeah, me too. I thought the story thing might work again, but it didn't, and now . . ." Milo looked around helplessly. "I just don't know where to be, Dad." There were too many people, and all his usual escape spaces—the loveseat by the living room window, the corner behind the tree—were compromised by the chimney cleaning. If you could even call it that. He looked around, figured out who was missing. "Where'd Georgie and Clem go?"

"I've been a little preoccupied, but I think they called it a night." He glanced at the coat Milo had just put on the rack. "Did you go for a walk?"

"Yup. Needed a break." Should he tell his father now about what had just happened on the railcar landing, or wait?

"I can absolutely relate." Mr. Pine downed the rest of his drink. "Can I get you anything that's legal for me to get you?"

Doc had asked Milo not to mention his presence—or at least, to try not to. But it felt weird to keep something so significant from his parents. Negret would know how to manage this situation. "No, I'm okay, but . . ." Milo lowered his voice. "Do you think there's something weird going on in the house?"

"Milo, there is nothing *but* weird going on in the house tonight," Mr. Pine replied. "Whether it's something more than just a bunch of random incidents, though . . . I honestly don't know." He looked down at Milo. "What are your thoughts?"

"I definitely think it's more than just random stuff. What I can't figure is whether it has anything to do with Georgie and Clem."

"I guess that's the question."

"Because nobody could be in the house without our knowing about it, right?"

His father debated this, then shook his head. "Our friendly household haunt excepted, I truly doubt it. On the grounds, sure, but in the house . . . not a chance."

"Yeah, that's what I figured."

Mr. Pine studied Milo for a moment. "You okay?"

"Yeah." That was stretching the truth, but there was no way he was getting into it any further, not there and then. "I'm going up to bed too."

"Okay. See you in the a.m." Mr. Pine put an arm around him and kissed the top of his head. "Give your mom a hug first. She needs it." He glanced down, winced, and brushed at Milo's now-sooty sleeve. "Only maybe not with that arm."

"Oh, hey. Excuse me."

Milo and his dad both turned as Lucky approached. She held out a hand to Milo, glanced down at it, then looked at her once-white dress. "This is . . . just . . ." She sighed, rubbed her palm on her hip, and held it out again (now marginally cleaner) to Milo.

"You've got to be kicking yourself for inviting us in," she said, clasping his hand. "And all I can say is I'm really, really sorry. I swear to you it isn't usually this way. I've done this walk every year since I was your age, except when we couldn't do it at all because of weather or whatever, and I'm not saying things always go like clockwork, but this . . ." She shook her head in disgust. "This is just. It's. I can't."

"It's okay," Milo said, wondering how to get his hand back.

Lucky glanced at Mr. Pine. "I didn't think of it until just now, but I probably should go back up and check on Marzana. Babs, too, I guess, but I convinced Marzana to come this year. I feel responsible. I always carry aspirin with me. I could take some up."

"I'll get some water for you to take," Milo offered. "Mrs.

Kirkegrim had some aspirin earlier, but I don't know if Marzana had any." He pointed at the hand still clutched in hers. "I'm going to need that."

"Oh." She chuckled and let go. "Of course."

Milo headed into the kitchen to pour himself a cup of hot chocolate in addition to the promised glass of water. The remnants of Mr. Larven's punch were gone—the shattered cup had been cleaned away and the matching punch bowl now sat, sparkling clean, in the drying rack. Then he hugged his mother, careful not to spill anything on her or to use his sooty arm. "Lucky's going up to see Marzana and Mrs. Kirkegrim, and I'm going to bed."

Mrs. Pine kissed his cheek. "I'll come check on you before I turn in."

"'Kay." Milo waved to the Caraways, handed Lucky the glass of water, and mounted the stairs.

"So you've always lived here?" she asked, following.

"Yup." He didn't elaborate. Instead he stifled a sigh of resignation. Just when he'd started to think it wasn't going to happen this time . . . This was familiar territory, one of the seemingly innocuous questions people started with before they worked up to asking something about his adoption. Milo always knew that was where the conversation was going when he heard *Have you always lived here?* or *Did you grow up in Nagspeake?*—but that didn't mean he felt obligated to help the askers get there. The next question would probably be one of about five he could recite by rote. He figured Lucky was smart enough not to ask the worst of them (any question involving the phrase *real parents* where the asker clearly wasn't referring to Nora and Ben Pine), but the equally obvious *Are you adopted?* wasn't impossible. Milo braced himself as they reached the landing.

Instead, though, Lucky paused for a look at the stained-glass window. "Must be nice, having so many pretty things around you all the time." Her voice had a hint of wistfulness to it.

Surprised, Milo watched her examine the glass. "Yeah, I guess so. Do you not have . . . pretty views or whatever in the Liberty?" It wasn't exactly what he wanted to ask. What he wanted to know was *Why do you live in the Liberty?* But it didn't seem right to just come out with it. *I'm doing the same thing,* he realized. *Asking less offensive questions while I work up to what I really want to know, which is probably — definitely — none of my business.*

But if Lucky saw through that, she covered it like a pro. "Oh, sure, there's plenty of beauty in the Liberty. You've never been there, have you?"

"Me? No way." The words were out before he'd thought about them, and he certainly hadn't meant to speak in such a defensive tone of voice. "I mean —"

But Lucky just laughed. "Don't worry about it, Milo. I know what most people think of the Liberty, but I also know you don't really think that way, because if you did, you wouldn't have invited us into your home. Anyway, the Liberty is like any town — there are lovely parts and ugly parts, good people and not-so-good people. But *this* place is beautiful. Especially now that I can actually see what's in front of my face," she added. "I should warn you that if Rob Gandreider turns up dead, it will be me who offed him. Just call the police and tell them I confessed in advance."

Despite the situation, Milo laughed. "Okay."

"And poor Marzana." Lucky sighed. "I feel so awful. I thought she'd have a good time if I could just get her to come. Now this."

"She doesn't like people, huh? Is that why . . ." He was doing it again. Milo pursed his lips shut.

"Why she lives in the Liberty?" Lucky finished.

"Never mind," Milo said, embarrassed. "It's not my business."

Lucky gave him a thoughtful look. "No, it's not, but I like that you had the courage to ask. You should ask Marzana, though. I could tell you what *I* think the reason is, but it would just be an assumption, and probably inaccurate." She smiled briefly. "And I imagine you know something about how obnoxious it is when people assume things about other folks — or would that be another false assumption?"

"It is not," Milo said decisively.

Lucky nodded. "Good talk," she said. "You're relieved of duty."

Milo gave her an awkward mock salute. "Okay. I hope they're feeling better." He hesitated. "Will you guys be here in the morning, do you think?"

Lucky slumped. "What time is it, like ten thirty?" She rubbed her sooty face. "It's an hour's hike back up the hill and through the woods to the Liberty, but if your parents don't kick us out on our tails the second Marzana and Babs and Nick can walk, they're flipping saints. It's a miracle they haven't kicked us out already. So . . . I don't know."

This was about what he'd figured the situation to be. Milo worked up another smile. "See you tomorrow, then, maybe."

Lucky nodded and rounded the bend in the stairs. Milo decamped to his room at last. There he set his hot chocolate carefully on a tile coaster on his desk, turned, and flopped onto his bed. "This is ridiculous," he grumbled. Negret would already be working through it all, trying to piece together what was going on. Of course, ideally, Negret would've had Sirin by his side.

Milo turned his head to look at the three miniature figurines that stood on his bedside table: a little curled ivory dragon that had been a gift from Clem's fiancé, Owen, who was also Chinese and had also been adopted as a child; a crouching boy holding two short swords that was a character from the Odd Trails role-playing game universe and that had once belonged to his father; and a little owl with the face of a girl that had been made specially for Meddy. Painted across the base that supported the branch upon which the owl perched was the name *Sirin*.

Milo discovered it was a little harder to breathe than it had been before. His eyes began to prickle. He rolled over onto his side and gave in to everything — the confusion, the frustration, the anger, the loneliness. Everything, from the unpleasantness in Mr. Chancelor's classroom to Emmett Syebuck's failure to leave on time to the chaos that had descended upon the house with the arrival of the Waits to Meddy's refusal to return and help him find his way back to Negret.

Negret, the part of himself that would've managed to keep it to-gether even in the face of that entire laundry list of Crummy Stuff. Negret, for whom this would've been an adventure rather than a hardship.

"Where are you?" He buried his face in his blanket to let the knitted squares soak up the moisture seeping out of his eyes. "Why can't I find you?"

He lay there letting his misery wash over him until his clock showed that it was nearing eleven. Then he pushed himself upright, wiped his face, sniffled once, and looked around his room.

A pair of black cotton slippers with woven fabric soles were lined up neatly on the floor. He tugged off his socks and pulled the shoes on, trying hard to ignore the fact that they felt a little small, then reached for his dad's old City Scout rucksack, which hung from his chair. He emptied his schoolbooks onto his desk, plucked his spiral pad, pen, and lockpicks from under the jettisoned books, and tossed those in. He added a pair of brown leather gloves from his drawer, and, on impulse, he hunted in the pile on the desktop again for *The Raconteur's Commonplace Book* and tucked that in there too. Then he slung the strap resolutely over his shoulder. It was time to quit waiting around for Negret and Sirin. He opened his bedroom door and nearly jumped out of the almost-too-small shoes.

In the hallway stood a girl in a yellow silk robe that had been christened with the unlikely name of the Cloak of Golden Indis-cernibility. She was about his height, with reddish hair peeking out from under a fur-lined aviator's cap—the Helm of Revelations

—and eyes that were currently giving him a highly dubious look through a pair of blue-lensed, wire-framed glasses grandly called the Eyes of True and Aching Clarity.

"Excuse me, but were you about to go somewhere without your adventuring partner?" Meddy asked.

twelve

MEDDY

WHERE HAVE YOU *BEEN?*" Milo demanded. He grabbed her by the sleeve, yanked her into the room, and slammed the door. "I have been looking for you for . . . for you have no idea how long!"

Meddy took off her glasses and looked curiously at him. "Have you been crying, Milo?"

He swiped at his eyes. "Don't change the subject! Do you even know how long you've been gone?"

She looked from Milo to the window, and then around the room. "It's winter, and since you're freaking out it can't be the same winter as before. I'm going to guess a year. Unless it's been two years?" She shook her head. "Can't be longer than that. You look different, but not that different. How long *has* it been?"

"It's been a year," Milo confirmed sullenly. "Where've you been?"

"Where've I been?" Meddy repeated. "You really want to talk about what my existence is like when I'm not here?" She hesitated, thinking. "I don't even know how I'd start to —"

"Never mind." Relief warred with frustration. Milo buried his face in his hands in an effort to keep himself under control. He wasn't sure if he wanted to laugh or scream or cry again.

Meddy looked from him to the school mess he'd dumped out of his bag. "What's wrong, Milo? You'd never leave your desk looking like that normally. Or maybe you've changed more than I thought."

"Never mind my desk," Milo said, exasperated. "I'll clean it up later, and yes, it would be driving me crazy if I had enough brainpower to think about it right now. Listen. Last time, you told me you came because you sensed something was off in the house. Don't you feel it now? Can't you tell?"

"I'm not a barometer, Milo." She watched him thoughtfully for a minute. "Though now that you mention it, yeah, I think I can tell something's off. But, Milo, I think . . . I think it's *you*."

"*Me?* What are you talking about?"

Meddy sank to a seat at the edge of his bed, staring at him. "Are you kidding? Milo . . . you look miserable. You're wound tighter than a spring. What's going on?"

"*I'm* not the problem, for the love of — It's everyone else!"

She put up her hands in a *Calm down* gesture. "Tell me, then. Tell me what I need to know."

Relief flooded through him, unimpeded at last. Milo yanked his chair away from his desk and sat. He felt weak, as if all the tension had been the only thing holding him up. He opened his mouth to start explaining the whole insane situation, but what came out was "I'm so glad you're here."

Meddy smiled. "Me too. Now talk."

When Milo finished filling her in on Clem and Georgie's heist, the arrival of the Waits, and the two maybe-accidents, Meddy sat back with a whistle. "Are you kidding? This all happened *tonight?*"

"All except the heist itself. That was day before yesterday." Milo hesitated. "And there's another thing. I . . . I can't find Negret."

"You . . . you can't *find* him? Like you lost him down a drain or something?" Meddy frowned. "Milo — he's *you*. Just like Sirin is me." Meddy picked up the little owl figurine from his bedside table and wiggled it at him.

"Yeah, okay, I know that, but I can't get to the *parts* of me that make Negret who he is. It's like, I need Negret to find those things, but I can't find them without getting to Negret first." He threw up his hands in frustration. "I can remember them. *Blend in. Control in Unexpected Situations. Athletic.* But the more I try to do those things, or have them, or be them, the less like Negret I feel. And then I get angry, and that makes it worse, and —"

"And you feel angry a lot lately," Meddy said quietly.

"Yeah. And I tried the Irresistible Blandishment exploit—I wanted to get them all telling stories again like last year, but it didn't work. It was chaos!" Milo kicked his desk. "It worked before. Why isn't it working now? Any of it! The stories, my exploits . . . They're out of control, Meddy! They're spoiling everything before I can even get started!"

"And by 'they,' you mean the people who are here."

"Obviously!"

"Okay, okay. Calm down."

"That is literally the worst thing you can possibly say to me right now."

"Fine, but it's what you need to do, so if you don't like me saying it, maybe try saying it to yourself. I need to think." She folded her arms and paced a few steps. "You said you've been having trouble getting to Negret, but maybe the problem is that you need something *other than* Negret. I mean, last year all you needed was to be able to out-sneak a bunch of people who were trying to out-sneak you. But this group—this group is more chaotic. You need a character better suited to dealing with a group as unpredictable as this one." She cleared her throat delicately. "Not to offend you, but you're a total bundle of emotional stuff yourself, Milo. I mean, you look like you're barely keeping it together. Any more chaos and you might straight-up self-destruct."

"It's been a crummy couple weeks," Milo admitted. "I thought . . ." This was surprisingly difficult to admit. "I thought maybe I only needed you to remind me. How to be Negret, I mean."

She looked at him for a long moment, then shook her head.

"No. Even if that worked in the short term . . . but no. You need something different. For this campaign, anyway, I'm certain you need something other than Negret."

That wasn't the answer he'd been hoping for, but it was so good to have her back, it almost didn't matter. The weight in his chest and on his shoulders began to feel just perceptibly lighter. "What do you suggest?"

"I have a thought. Where are your Odd Trails manuals?"

"You mean *your* Odd Trails manuals?" Milo pointed at his bookshelf. "I only have a few. The rest are still in the attic."

Meddy squatted in front of the bookshelf. "*Creature Compendium, Player's Guidebook, Game Master's Manual* . . . I see *Blackjacks of the Roads,* but nothing else on specific player classes. I think the one we want is called *Ostiaries and Summoners* or something." She stood up. "You know what this means. It's time for a trip to the Emporium."

"All right!" He bounced to his feet and opened the door. Then, abruptly, he yanked it shut again and turned to Meddy in shock. "Holy cow, I can't believe I didn't tell you this first thing — Meddy, I met your dad!"

Meddy took a faltering step backward. "You . . . you *what?*" Her eyes were like saucers. "My dad?" Milo nodded. Meddy put a hand out and felt for the foot of the bed. "I have to sit down." She sat. "No, I have to lie down." She sprawled onto the quilt and stared at the ceiling. "I think I'm ready. Tell me."

"It was just tonight." Milo pointed out his window. "Right out there. Well, not exactly right out there, but —"

"I know the place," Meddy said, turning her head to follow his pointing finger.

Milo winced. "Yeah." *Because you probably wouldn't forget the place where you last saw your father before he fell to his death,* he thought. *Even if only a minute later you fell to your own death.* Awkward. "Anyway, he said this Gilawfer guy—the fence who maybe double-crossed Georgie and Clem, who might still be after them? He was a rat for the customs department. He worked with Mr. Vinge!"

"Whoa. So then I guess it's not just Gilawfer and Cantlebone we have to worry about." She sat up. "What else did he say?"

"Exactly what you just did. Oh, and that it's possible that Violet Cross's derrotero might not be an actual book of maps. It might be something else."

"Right, right. What else?"

"What else?" Milo scratched his head. "I mean, that was kind of it."

"Can't be," Meddy insisted. "What *else?*"

"Oh." Milo smiled apologetically. "I'm so sorry. He said if you finally turned up, to come and wave."

Meddy's face broke into a smile like sunshine. "Thanks." She slid off the bed, went to the window, and walked effortlessly through it. Milo stayed by the desk in case she wanted privacy, but through the panes he could just see her yellow robe fluttering in the wind as she waved at the woods.

When she reappeared in the room, she looked a little glum. "Everything okay?" Milo asked. "Did he wave back?"

"I didn't see him." She squared her shoulders, but her disappointment was plain. "No big deal. He couldn't have known to look right at that precise minute. I'll try again later. In the meantime, we have things to do."

thirteen

THE EMPORIUM

THEY LEFT HIS ROOM and crept up one flight and then another until they reached the landing with the green and sepia Gate Window. Beyond that there was one more short staircase, leading to the place Negret and Sirin had dubbed the Emporium: the attic of Greenglass House.

Meddy went to the window ledge and lifted the pot that sat there, which held a pink flower made of wire and paper and glass. Underneath was a single key. She handed it to Milo. "Do the honors, will you?"

"Are we just here for the book?" Milo asked.

"Mainly. But we can take a quick look around for other useful things too."

He twisted the key, turned the milky green glass knob, and pulled the heavy carved door open. A soft whisper of frigid air puffed across their faces and slid down the staircase to rattle random doors on lower levels. Milo and Meddy stood on the threshold, each casting their eyes around the murk beyond. *Always check for traps,* Meddy had warned him last year.

"Look good to you?" she asked.

"All clear, as far as I can see. I'm going in." Milo ventured forward, waving his arms ahead of him until he found a knob dangling from a cord. He gave it a tug, and with a spark and a pop, a bare bulb overhead came to life, spilling bluish-gray light down in a little pool that spread just far enough to show him where the next pull-cord was. There were four bulbs total, and when he had them all alight, he looked around for Meddy.

"Over here." She was across the room already, tugging the cardboard box labeled *ROLE-PLAYING GAME STUFF —AW* from a pile. "I know I had the one we want," she said as he joined her. "It has scholiasts in it too. It's where I first saw them mentioned."

Milo held out his arms just in time to receive the pile of books and papers she chucked his way without so much as a glance. "You want me to look through these?"

"No. They were in the way." Her top third plunged headlong into the box. "Oh, here we go." She reappeared, brandishing an oversized hardcover. A pair of tough-looking fighter types, one with a glowing gem in the middle of her forehead and one with a radiant orb in one pawlike hand, mean-mugged on the garishly illustrated cover. Big golden letters announced this volume to be

Transmundane Warriors of the Realms: Harbingers, Summoners, and Ecstatics.

"Well, *there's* a lot of words I don't know," Milo observed, dumping his armful so he could take the book.

"Yeah, no kidding." Meddy perched on the edge of the box and reached over his shoulder to flip to the introduction. "*Transmundane* means something like . . . like beyond the physical, everyday world. The basic deal with this category of player is that, to varying degrees, in various ways and for various purposes, these guys all manipulate some combination of mental, emotional, and psychic power. The title says 'warriors,' but characters in these classes can still be captains, warders, or blackjacks instead, if you want."

"Okay." He turned back to the table of contents and skimmed the chapter headings. *Augur, Ecstatic, Harbinger, Ostiary, Solitaire, Summoner, Phrenic, Theurge.* In the margins were illustrations of different fighters. One of them caught Milo's eye. It was a girl whose garments and pose reminded him irresistibly of a Shaolin monk caught mid-move. "What's she?" he asked, pointing.

"Solitaire," Meddy said immediately. "They're like monks, except they're, well, solitary. Loners. Hermits. Usually they start out in some kind of monastic community and then go rogue for one reason or another."

"I like the idea of a monk," Milo said. "Are they all about controlling emotions and inner calm and things like that? But also martial arts and stuff?" Because whatever the illustrated solitaire was doing, it was clearly some kind of martial art. And although she wasn't drawn as Asian, now that the idea of a Shaolin monk had occurred to Milo, he couldn't get it out of his head. It reminded him of something he'd done while playing Negret: he'd created a Chinese blackjack father for his character, and it had been the first time he'd allowed himself to think about his own unknown Chinese parentage without feeling guilty.

Now the guilt was gone, but Milo felt a different twinge of unease. *You don't know anything about Shaolin monks.* The silent voice that said this in his mind bore a surprising similarity to Mr. Chancelor's. He forced the unease down. If he decided to play a solitaire, he wouldn't be building an *actual* Shaolin monk anyway. It would be something different, and surely he could still imagine a Chinese past for his new character.

"Yes, control is part of it," Meddy said. "All the monk types have some element of a mind-body fusion thing, and often they're martial arts fighters. Solitaires make good blackjacks, too." She flipped ahead to the solitaire chapter and pointed to a sidebar that listed recommended abilities. "Look how they suggest you rate yourself if you're building a solitaire. Dexterity, wisdom, charisma, athleticism."

"Those are a lot like what we gave Negret," Milo recalled.

"Exactly. But like you figured, less chaotic and more disciplined. In theory."

"And that's exactly what I need," Milo said. "Perfect."

Meddy made an uncertain noise. "Can I make an alternate suggestion?"

"Okay," Milo said reluctantly.

"I get why you're drawn toward a character class that depends on control. You feel out of control now. But if you play a solitaire, I guarantee you're going to try to tamp your emotions down and control them that way. And then you'll get frustrated, because you can't just decide to not feel something and then, you know, not feel it." She flipped back toward the front and landed on a chapter titled *Ecstatic*. "Consider the possibilities of a character that actually takes emotions and *uses* them. Ecstatic characters *focus* emotions. They channel them and make them work for the fighter."

The big illustration of the ecstatic on the first page of the chapter had weird energy lines radiating from his head. "Is an ecstatic like a psychic or something?" Milo asked dubiously.

"No, ecstatics pour their emotions and thoughts outward to influence the world around them. To boost the will of their allies and crush the morale of their enemies. To uncover secrets. And look." She turned the page and pointed to a subsection. "Fervent ecstatics get their power from emotions they themselves can barely contain. Often they're natural talents rather than heavily trained." She tapped the page triumphantly. "That, my friend, sounds like you right about now. Plus, you'd need to score high in some of the same abilities again: charisma, constitution, wisdom."

Milo hesitated, torn. What Meddy was describing did sound a lot like how he had been feeling, if only he could bring himself to believe that the very things that seemed to be the roots of all his problems right now could be turned into powers. But the solitaire *felt* right. A solitaire would be in control, and also, if he wanted, Chinese without having to explain it to anyone or answer for what he knew and didn't know.

Meddy watched him as if she somehow knew exactly what he was thinking. "Or there's a third option," she said after a moment. "You can combine character classes. Mix them together."

Now, *that* was interesting. "I can?"

"Sure. People do it all the time. Heck, Sirin isn't even technically a playable character, if you go strictly according to the manuals." Meddy found a page in the book that showed evidence of having been dog-eared long, long ago, a page belonging to the chapter describing *harbingers*. She pointed to the description for an exploit called *Summon Scholiast: You conjure a scholiast, a shape-shifting spirit familiar who can take the form of a bird as well as a human. Your scholiast can travel and operate semi-independently from you, taking its own turns. It typically remains within one hundred feet of you in order to maintain telepathic communications, but it can operate at greater distances and/or travel with another player character for short periods of time by means of a reliquary.* "Usually this is the only way scholiasts turn up in the game," Meddy explained.

"So if I wanted to combine a solitaire and an ecstatic, how would I do it?"

Meddy sat on the floor and leaned against the box. "Well, let's imagine how this could happen. Solitaires mostly start out in monasteries, so maybe that's where you were, studying one of the monastic fighter traditions, when you discovered — probably by accident, maybe during a stressful episode where all your training couldn't help you hold your emotions in check — that you could do miraculous things with your feelings if you opened the floodgates and let them loose. But maybe your order wasn't cool with your wanting to pursue both lines of training. Maybe they wanted you to complete your training with them before investigating your ecstatic nature."

Milo nodded. "If they were contradictory paths, then trying to study both could theoretically mess me up and keep me from learning either."

"Exactly. So for whatever reason — you should probably work out the backstory — you decided not to obey, but instead to leave the order and become a solitaire so you could study both paths, even if they sometimes got in each other's way. What do you think?"

"I like it. It's perfect. So I'm . . . what? A fervent ecstatic solitaire?"

"Yeah." She wrapped her arms around her knees and rocked back and forth. "I think you should imagine your solitaire as a captain-blackjack combination, like Negret was. You're a leader, and your presence affects everybody on the battlefield, whether they're friends or enemies. But your blackjack elements will let you be sneaky when you need to be. And the combination of inward focus from your monkish side and outward focus from your ecstatic side will help you figure out how best to use your feelings at any given time." She made a face. "At least in theory."

"Awesome. I love it." Milo tucked the manual into his rucksack. Later he could take a closer look at the exploits this character ought to be able to pull off. "What else?"

"Well, you're going to need a name." She got to her feet. "Oh, and do you still want to look for useful stuff while we're up here? You should probably have a locus, if we can find something likely."

"What's a locus?"

"Monks use them to focus their power. It's usually an object you can center your thoughts and energy on. Something with deep meaning for you."

"And we're just supposed to stumble on something with deep meaning searching the Emporium? Seems like a lot to hope for."

Meddy shrugged. "If I'm not misremembering, you found a sort of locus up here last year, didn't you?"

"Oh, I see." She meant the keys and hammered fob that he had discovered in the attic and that he later gave to Owen, Clem's now-fiancé, who had turned out to be related to the original owners of Greenglass House. Before Milo had given them away, though, he had decided they'd been a gift from Negret's blackjack father to his son. "Something of deep meaning to my solitaire, but not necessarily to *me*."

"Right." Meddy stretched. "So let's take a look before we head back downstairs. A quick one, though. It's got to be getting close to midnight, and there's still another thing we should do before we call it a day."

"All right. Oh, hey — what about you?"

Meddy frowned. "What do you mean, what about me?"

"Are you going to play a different character or stick with Sirin?"

She considered, then reached into her pocket and pulled out the owl figurine she'd picked up in Milo's room. "I'll stick with Sirin. I spent so long thinking about playing her, after all. I don't want to give her up quite yet. But I'll just be Meddy until you come up with a name."

Although the Emporium was technically one big open space, in practice, it was a warren of small chambers that had been carved out by garment racks and boxes and piles of lumber and broken chandeliers and a seemingly endless assortment of cast-off junk. Some of the piles were known quantities to the adventurers, like the boxes of broken glass (the Gems of Ultimate Puissance, in Sirin-speak) that were stacked near the long-dormant mechanism that had once run the house's dumbwaiter. Others were all mystery. Milo headed for one of the unexplored corners, a nook in a gable overlooking the rear of the house, mulling over possible names as he went. He'd taken Negret's name from *The Raconteur's Commonplace Book.* Maybe he could find his solitaire's name there too.

The gable was packed with stuff. The boxes in front, the most accessible ones, were all labeled and, if those labels were to be believed, were full of entirely uninteresting cargo. CLOTHES, 18–24 MONTHS; LEFTOVER YARN/FABRIC SCRAPS; YARD SALE STUFF (VASES AND MUGS). He muscled those aside. The next layer of boxes was unlabeled, but, when opened, these boxes were even more boring. Papers someone had probably put up here until they got around to shredding them, which apparently was never; a box of nothing but empty envelopes, possibly corresponding to the papers in the previous box; a flat wooden case with a pair of yellow metal clasps along one edge that opened to reveal a collapsible easel, half-empty tubes of paint, and the beginnings of a ship on a thin canvas. Whoever had painted the thing was, frankly, not good at painting. About all Milo could make out was that the figurehead had horns, which probably meant the vessel was supposed to be the smuggling clipper *Ganzander,* the ship Milo's grandfather had served on under Captain Ed Pickering.

He climbed over a few more cartons and a stack of garment bags until he was within arm's reach of the window. Sitting on the lower ledge of the casement was a red box about the size of a large pencil case. Milo reached for it and then clambered awkwardly backward over the piles. He sat on the box of leftover yarn and brushed off his find.

Under the layer of dust, the red case had a glazed surface that made it look like the scarlet color was emerging from under layers of transparent varnish. *Lacquer,* that was the word. On the top, just barely visible in the blue-gray light, was the sinuous shape of a long-necked, long-beaked bird. A crane, maybe?

Milo undid the clasp and lifted the hinged lid. Inside were a few slips of yellow paper, an improbably sharp red pencil, a long white feather, and a small vial made of some dull, goldish metal. Milo uncorked it and turned it upside down over his palm. It was empty, but it made a soft, almost bell-like ding when he tapped on it with one finger. Milo recorked it, stowed it back in the box, and tucked the box into his rucksack. He rooted around for *The Raconteur's Commonplace Book,* but his fingers encountered a different book first. Milo took it out, recognizing the cover by feel even before he saw it. It was the English-Mandarin dictionary, which had been in the stack on his desk before he'd dumped his school stuff out. He must've grabbed it by accident when he'd repacked his bag.

Accident or not, it was perfect. Milo found his spiral pad, flipped to a clean page, and started listing words in English. Then he started looking up those words. His dictionary showed the words in Chinese characters as well as in pinyin, a system that rendered characters into words spelled with the Latin alphabet. Milo jotted the pinyin translations down next to his column of English words. In some cases there were a number of options that Milo had a hard time differentiating between, but he made his best guesses. After a few minutes, he sat back and looked at what he'd written.

Monk: sēngrén
Hermit: yǐnshì
Ecstatic: kuángxǐ
Red: hóng
Gold: jīn
Flying: téngfēi
Crane: guàn

He liked the looks of all of them, and the sounds of them too. He spoke them quietly to himself, using the tone marks to figure out where to let his voice rise and drop and slide. But in the end, it was *téngfēi* that he kept coming back to. "Téngfēi," he said quietly. *Tung-fay,* with each part getting its own stress and the first syllable rising a bit, as if the name itself were leaping into flight. "The solitaire, Téngfēi."

"Did you say something, Milo?" Meddy called.

"Oh." Milo shoved everything hastily back in his bag and got to his feet. "Yeah. Did you find anything?"

"Are you kidding?" It sounded as if she was rooting around near the door. He glanced that way, and a small hand waving a book appeared over the top of a garment rack. "Tome of Unutterable Algorithms." The hand disappeared, then reappeared. It looked empty at first, but then, as Meddy moved her wrist, Milo caught a slight flash from one knuckle. "Ring of Wildest Abandon." Then Meddy's head and shoulders appeared as she climbed up and leaned over the top of the rack. With her other arm, she brandished a carved walking stick. "Eglantine's Patent Blackthorn Wishing Stick, guaranteed to offer considered advice before granting requests. What about you?"

Milo laughed. He held up the red case. "Slywhisker's Crimson Casket of Relics, including the Ocher Pages of Invisible Wards, the Ever-Sharp Inscriber of Rose-Colored Destinies, and the Flask of Winds and Voids."

Meddy whistled. "You don't mess around."

"I learned from the best." Milo put it away again. "I think I'm done here for now. What's the other thing you wanted to do tonight?" He made his circuitous way back to the door, turning lights off as he went, and found Meddy rigging a belt across her chest, the better to secure Eglantine's Patent Blackthorn Wishing Stick to her back. The leather edges of the Tome of Unutterable Algorithms poked out of one of her robe pockets, and the Ring of Wildest Abandon glinted on her finger. "Hey, didn't you tell me once that it's better to wear your magic rings on your toes?"

"Yeah, but this isn't for me, so it isn't my toe it's going on. It's yours." She popped it off her hand and passed it to him. "An ecstatic can use things like rings to boost his magic, the way a solitaire uses a locus."

Up close, it wasn't a ring at all. It was hardware, not jewelry, and it had plainly come out of a toolbox. "And I'm supposed to wear this on my toe?"

"It doesn't matter where you wear it," Meddy told him. "No one here is going to cut your finger off with an edged weapon, and since it looks like a washer or whatever, probably nobody's going to try to steal it."

Milo tried it on his ring finger, then his middle, then his index finger, where it finally fit well enough to stay put. Then he took it off again and bounced it lightly in his palm. "And what are we saying it does?"

"The lore is unclear," Meddy declared. "There are conflicting tales from varying sources."

"Great. I guess I'll figure it out. Oh, and I picked a name."

"Cool. Which is?"

"Téngfēi," Milo intoned. "It means 'flying' in Mandarin."

"Téngfēi," Meddy repeated, careful to mimic his pronunciation. "Am I getting that right?"

"Yeah, I think so."

She nodded approvingly. "I like it." She reached into the pocket that didn't have the Tome in it and produced her blue-lensed spectacles. She opened them with a single flick of her wrist, perched them on her nose, and held out her palm. "Pleased to meet you, Téngfēi. I'm Sirin."

Milo slipped the ring back onto his index finger. The solitaire shook the scholiast's hand solemnly. Then he turned off the last light, and together they left the attic.

"Where to now?" Téngfēi asked when the door was locked again and the key was back under its flowerpot.

"Let's start with this heist of Georgie and Clem's," Sirin suggested. "Do you think they're still awake?"

"If they're not, they're about to be."

In addition to his specialized transmundane skills (which he still had to figure out), Téngfēi was, like Negret before him, a black-jack. Therefore, getting down to the fourth floor without making noise was well within his capabilities, and his feet instinctively found the quietest paths down the stairs.

On four, the lights were off in Clem's room, but a glow spilled out from under Georgie's quarters next door. "We're in luck," Téngfēi said.

"Okay. Let's go." Sirin started down the hall, but Téngfēi grabbed her sleeve.

"Wait. Your dad said not to mention him to anyone if I could help it, but what about you? Do we tell Georgie and Clem you're back?"

She considered. "I think let's do what we did last time and keep me invisible to everyone else. The fewer people who know I'm here, the better, unless there's a good reason to tell them."

"Okay." He led the way down the hall, and the door of 4S swung open before he could knock. Georgie's face went from blank to relieved. "Hey, you. Come on in." She stood aside to reveal Clem sitting cross-legged on the bed. "Look who came to tuck us in, Clem."

"Hi, Milo." The red-haired thief stared past him into the hallway. "And is that *Meddy?*"

Georgie, who had been about to swing the door shut, yanked it open again. Sirin blinked in the doorway. "Well," the scholiast said coolly, "looks like that whole staying invisible thing is a nonstarter."

"I'm so sorry, Meddy! Here I was, about to slam the door in your face." Georgie waved her in and closed the door after her. "It's great to see you again. We were hoping you might turn up."

"Thanks." Sirin followed Téngfēi inside and sat in the chair by the desk. "So I hear we have some excitement going on. You guys have been busy."

Georgie snorted. "You could say that. And it just keeps on getting more exciting."

"I told Si—Meddy everything I know so far," Téngfēi said, sitting awkwardly on the unused luggage rack by the door. "But she had some information I don't think you have." He glanced at Sirin and sent out a silent prayer that she'd follow what he was about to say and pick up her cue. Maybe this fell under the category of ways in which his skills as an ecstatic could influence his allies. A guy could hope. "Tell them what you told me about Gilawfer, the fence."

Sirin looked at him blankly for a second, then snapped to. "Oh, yeah, of course. Back in my dad's day, he was a known informant. He passed information to the customs department by way of our old friend Mr. Vinge."

"Are you *kidding?*" Georgie swore. She banged the back of her head against the wall. "*Vinge?* I cannot believe my research didn't bring that to light. Just one more thing I screwed up. We'll add it to the list."

"Knock it off, Georgie." Clem sighed. "I'll keep saying it until you believe me — this is *not* your fault. But we could stand to waste less time on me trying to make you feel better."

"Got it," Georgie said through gritted teeth.

Clem stroked her chin thoughtfully. "I suppose this also means picking locks in front of Emmett might have been somewhat poor judgment on my part after all."

Téngfēi cleared his throat. "So the big question. Do we think the stuff that happened tonight is connected to Gilawfer or Cantlebone and your heist?"

"Yes," Georgie and Clem said sourly, and in unison.

"Oh," Téngfēi said, taken aback. "I didn't realize you'd be so . . . so confident about it. I guess then we have to assume someone in the house is either Gilawfer or Cantlebone or one of his people in disguise."

"Or a customs agent in disguise," Sirin added.

Georgie nodded grimly. "My money's still on Syebuck, but we can't rule out the possibility that it's one of the Waits, either."

"So how do you know?" Téngfēi asked. "I was pretty sure it had to all be connected because it's the simplest solution, but you seem totally certain."

"Oh, wait," Sirin interrupted, sending a sharp glance Téngfēi's way. "Before I forget, there's another thing I can tell you. Based on, you know, stuff I know from back in Dad's day. Milo said you thought the derrotero wasn't in the cache you found, but considering this is Violet Cross we're talking about, you can't count on her derrotero having been anything as obvious as a book. It might look like something entirely unrelated. She would've found a way to hide it in plain view, even if you were staring right at it."

"So maybe we should take a look at what you *did* find with fresh eyes," Téngfēi suggested. "It might turn out you already have it."

"That is such a good idea," Georgie said.

"Really, a truly great idea." Clem held up her index finger. "Just one problem."

Georgie held up two fingers, very close together. "Tiny problem."

"Okay." Téngfēi and Sirin exchanged a glance. "Well, what's the problem? Where's the stuff?" Téngfēi prompted.

Georgie folded her arms on the dresser and dropped her head onto them. Clem leaned back against the headboard and massaged her temples. "This brings us back to the question of what makes us so sure all the things tonight are connected," she said tiredly.

"It's all gone." Georgie spoke in a muffled voice without raising her head. "Somebody stole it all. So we clearly aren't the only thieves on the premises."

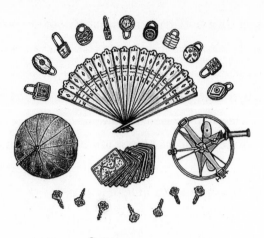

fourteen

PLUMS

I T'S ALL *GONE?*" Téngfēi repeated in disbelief.

Clem nodded. "Indeed. Part of the cache was in this room and part was in mine, and none of it's here anymore. Everything's gone but the lock I gave you to practice with. Assuming you still have it."

Téngfēi unearthed the lock from his rucksack. "I've got it."

"Well, that's all that's left."

"This was part of Violet Cross's hidden stash?" Téngfēi asked. Sirin appeared at his side and he passed it to her for a better look. "So cool. What else was there?"

Georgie answered. "A whalebone fan, a deck of cards, a small spherical chalkboard—it looks like a black globe with a chalkboard surface, only it's made of paper, and frankly seems too delicate to write on — and about ten other weirdo locks and a handful of even weirder keys. Interestingly, though, they're not the keys to those particular locks; they appear to be mechanical bump keys you can adjust to open random locks that might otherwise give you trouble. There's also a reflecting circle, which is a type of navigational instrument. It looks like a small, spoked wheel with a little telescope mounted on top and a knob handle attached to the bottom. Oh, and a pack of playing cards. All totally suspicious if you're looking for something that's possibly been disguised as something else, but nothing that obviously looked like it might be the derrotero."

"My money's on the fan," Clem said. "It was carved all over, in relief in some places and clear through in others, and the pattern changed depending on whether the fan was unfolded all the way or only partially, or if you unfolded it in the reverse direction." She shook her head in disgust. "I can't believe we didn't hide it all better."

"You had no way of knowing so many people were going to turn up and wreak havoc tonight," Téngfēi said as soothingly as he could. But he knew he'd be kicking himself too. "What else can you tell us?"

The thieves considered. "There's only about a two-hour window when the theft could've taken place," Georgie said at last. "I checked on the items that were in my room when I came up to get my sweater, so they had to have been taken between approximately nine fifteen and the time when Clem and I turned in for the night, half an hour ago or thereabouts."

"I was out of the house for at least part of that time." Téngfēi frowned and looked at the clock: just after midnight. "But wait. You had already gone up to bed when I came back in, and that was only at ten. Where have you been since then?"

Clem and Georgie exchanged a guilty glance. "We, ah . . . we searched Emmett Syebuck's room," Georgie said, wincing. "And then he almost caught us in there and we had to go out his window and come back up by way of the fire escape, and it was a whole thing getting inside again —"

Téngfēi groaned. "You didn't."

Georgie threw up her hands. "The guy won't leave me alone. We had to."

"Did you find anything?" Sirin asked, apparently unconcerned with how irate Milo's parents would be if they found out about this.

"Nothing," Clem told her. "Nothing but a bunch of sketches and art stuff, a bagful of film canisters, and a couple cameras. He's old-school for such a young guy."

"And his drawings are decent," Georgie admitted grudgingly. "If he's a poser, he's at least a semi-talented one. But if he's our thief, he didn't hide the stuff in his room. Which, honestly, only an amateur would've done in the first place. We should've known better than to do it ourselves."

"All right, all right," Téngfēi said before Georgie could get down on herself again. As an ecstatic, he figured he was the morale guy. He glanced at Sirin. "Anything else?"

"Was anyone missing while Milo was out on his walk?" Sirin asked.

"Five that we know of," Clem said. "Marzana and Barbara Kirkegrim, of course, plus Mr. Pine and Lucky had taken Mr. Larven upstairs. After that, we were the next ones to go up."

"All right." Sirin clapped her hands on her knees and got to her feet. "We have work to do."

"Keep us posted." Georgie said. "Wake either of us up if you need to. Any hour. I doubt we'll be sleeping much anyway." She frowned at the single-cup coffeemaker on the desk. "Though I should probably let you know my coffeemaker's broken, and we've already gone through the packets in Clem's room."

"That's weird. They're all pretty new. I'll let Mom and Dad know. And I'll bring you more coffee. You need the other stuff, creamer and sugar and whatever?"

"No thanks. We both drink it black."

After saying hushed good nights, Téngfēi and Sirin crept back through the darkened stairwell to the third floor. They had just started down to the second when Téngfēi stopped abruptly. "Someone's coming up." More than one someone. There were at least three sets of footsteps on the stairs below. Maybe more.

Mrs. Pine turned the corner first. "Oh, Milo." Then her eyes popped as they fell on Meddy. "And . . . hi," she said in a lower tone. She glanced over her shoulder. "Looks like we're going to have guests for the night," she added, putting a cheerful expression back in place and tossing her head meaningfully over her shoulder.

"You can see me?" Sirin asked warily. "And hear me?"

Mrs. Pine nodded rapidly. But before she could say anything else, Lucky turned the corner too. "Hey, Milo. Looks like we're going to have to impose on you after all." Sirin held her breath, but Lucky didn't give even the slightest indication that she saw a blue-bespectacled girl in a yellow robe and fur-lined hat lurking on the stairs ahead.

"I'm going to put Lucky and Mr. Hakelbarend in the empty rooms on four," Mrs. Pine said. "Rob and Sylvester drew the short straws, so they're stuck up on five."

"Right. Okay, we—well, I'm going to bed now. See you all in the morning," Téngfēi added as he edged around the three Waits clogging the stairwell.

"Good night," Lucky called back. Mr. Hakelbarend nodded as Téngfēi passed him, and Sylvester Alforn gave a tired salute. Neither of them appeared to notice Sirin, either.

The two adventurers hurried back to Milo's room in the gable. Sirin kicked the door shut and exploded, "What the heck is going on? Why can some people see me and others can't? And how am I going to be any good at this if I'm walking around in plain view all the time? A scholiast is supposed to be invisible. I need to be out of sight!"

This much, at least, made perfect sense to Téngfēi—both her discomfort with being visible when she'd rather be unseen and unnoticed, and the reason she was probably visible to some people and not others. "I totally understand why you're upset, but I bet the only people who can see you are the ones you showed yourself to last year. Remember? Maybe once you intentionally show yourself to someone, it sort of sticks. And it hardly matters if those folks see you. You don't have to hide from them."

"I guess." She paced a few irritable steps, then exhaled and shook out her shoulders. "All right, I'll get over it. What about you?"

"What do you mean, what about me?"

"Do you feel like Téngfēi?"

He considered. "Maybe. I think he'll take some getting used to, but I didn't *not* feel like him. I think I stopped thinking about it about it once we found out Georgie and Clem got robbed."

"All right, well, then don't think about it now, either, because we have more work to do before you turn in for the night." She plopped onto the bed. "Let's work out what we know." Téngfēi got his spiral pad and pen and sat cross-legged at the other end. "Before we forget, write down where your mom said everyone's sleeping," Sirin suggested. "Who's on three?"

Téngfēi wrote GUEST ROOM ASSIGNMENTS at the top of the page, then made a little grid underneath.

3N	Barbara Kirkegrim	4N	Lucky Julnissen or Peter Hakelbarend?	5N	Rob Gandreider or Sylvester Alforn?
3S	Marzana	4S	Georgie	5S	Rob or Sylvester?
3E	Emmett Syebuck	4E	Lucky or Mr. H.	5E	Rob or Sylvester?
3W		4W	Clem	5W	Rob or Sylvester?

"Mr. Larven must be in three W," Téngfēi said, penciling Nicholas Larven into the corresponding space. "There's no way they dragged him all the way up to five."

"What's Marzana's last name?" Sirin asked.

Téngfēi frowned. "I don't know. Mr. Hakelbarend just introduced her as Marzana. And I'm only fifty percent sure I've got everybody else's last names right."

Sirin shook her head. "You're going to have to tell me what we know about everyone. Make a page for each of them, then we'll come back to it. I want to make a list of what was in Violet Cross's stolen cache before we forget that, too."

Téngfēi duly labeled pages for each of the Waits plus Emmett, then wrote VC'S TREASURE CACHE at the top of the next one and began to list the items Clem and Georgie had mentioned.

1. Whalebone fan
2. Spherical chalkboard
3. Locks (11)
4. Keys ("a handful")
5. Reflecting circle
6. Deck of cards

"Excellent," Sirin said, rubbing her palms together as she looked over what Téngfēi had written. "Plums. I love a good bunch of plums."

Plums were little prizes or rewards you could find in Odd Trails over the course of the bigger quest. And this list would make for an interesting assortment of plums, if they could track them all down. "It's the chalkboard that's messing with me," he said. "Everything else I can imagine hiding fairly easily, but a globe?"

"So maybe we look for that first and hope we get lucky and find all the rest of the stuff with it."

"We're not that lucky," Téngfēi observed. "All right, what else?"

"Go back to the Waits," Sirin suggested, taking the notepad and pen. "I'll write, you talk."

"Okay. Who's first?"

"Barbara Kirkegrim."

"Hmm." Téngfēi leaned back against his pillows. "Well, she's the one who caught fire out on the lawn and didn't remember about Rob having to go in first. Lucky called her a noob, so I think this is her first time out with the Waits. She's older, though. Not *old*-old, just oldish. Married, I think. Mr. Larven called her Mrs. Kirkegrim, so that's what we've been calling her too. Oh, and she said she'd accidentally upset Marzana twice tonight. The second was when she called her by a dumb nickname. I wonder what the first time was."

"Got it." Sirin finished writing and looked up. "Marzana."

"She's the youngest, the one who was dressed as the hobby horse. I think she might be fifteen or sixteen."

Sirin gave an involuntary shudder. "I remember the hobby horse."

"The Waits have been coming here forever, huh?"

"Since before I was born, at least."

"Well, Marzana's definitely uncomfortable around strangers, or maybe around people in general. She said part of the reason she came this year was for a better look at Greenglass House. And I think she and Lucky are friends. Lucky said she was the one who convinced Marzana to come caroling, even though Marzana didn't necessarily want to. Also, Rob called her Spookypants. She's a little odd. Even ... well, even considering she's from the Liberty. Because not all of them come across as odd, you know?"

"I know what you mean." Sirin paused in her writing. "Wait, Marzana wanted a better look at Greenglass House?"

"Yeah, that's what she said. Or a better look at the windows, maybe. She said something like that on our way up to the second floor, before she got conked."

"Huh." Sirin scratched her head with the pen. "But you can't see Greenglass House from the Liberty of Gammerbund, can you?"

Téngfēi shrugged. "I have no idea."

"I mean, it's not like you can see any part of the Liberty from here, right?"

"Well, no, but I'm pretty sure if you hike up the hill through the woods and kept going, you'd reach the grounds eventually, wouldn't you? Maybe she takes walks. Long ones."

"I don't think people from the Liberty leave the grounds much," Sirin argued.

"Okay, maybe not, but it's not like they *can't* leave the grounds."

"No, I guess not. Nonetheless." Sirin put a star next to the line where she'd written *Prior interest in Greenglass House, or at least its windows.* "Maybe you should still try to find out more about this item."

"Okay, fair enough."

Sirin flipped the page. "Lucky Julnissen."

"She's about Clem and Georgie's age. Her real name is Lucia. She seems much more outgoing than most of them. Sylvester tried to kiss her and she smacked him in the face." Téngfēi grinned and Sirin snickered. "And I got the feeling it wasn't the first time that happened. Anyway, she says she's been caroling with the Waits since she was my age. I think maybe she feels responsible for all the stuff that went wrong tonight." He thought for a minute. "I suspect she's the one who knows the most about the traditions and stuff, but Mr. Hakelbarend is the leader somehow. Not like he's exactly in charge, though. I don't know how to describe it. Like he's the grownup among them or the chaperone or something."

"Come back to him. Nicholas Larven's next, if you're done with Lucky."

"He's the oldest. Tall, with a fussy little mustache, fancy green suit. He's the one who drank all that punch and passed out, although I think Clem suspects somebody put knockout drops or something in it. Mr. Hakelbarend said he was a doctor, but he didn't say what kind."

"Who made the punch?" Sirin asked as she wrote.

"Mr. Larven did. He said it was some kind of super-secret recipe. But of course anybody could've added something afterward."

"Okay. Sylvester Alforn. That's the one who tried to kiss Lucky?"

"Yeah. He's about the same age as she and Lizzie and Clem and Georgie. Wild reddish hair, blue face paint, lots of bells that he said drive him crazy but are tradition."

Sirin waited. "That's all?"

"That's all I can think of," Téngfēi said with a shrug.

"Peter Hakelbarend, then."

He scratched his head. "Just what I told you before — he seems to be the one who's got an eye on everyone and who's trying to keep them in line. But he's pretty reserved. He came dressed like a hunts-man. He was sort of the handler for Marzana's hobby horse, I guess, since you probably can't see much from inside the costume."

"All right. Last is Rob Gandreider."

"He's youngish, too. He has dark hair and a goatee. His real name is Rupert, and he's the sweep, but I don't think he's done this before."

"Done what, caroling or chimney sweeping?"

"Either. He was supposed to come in right-foot first and kept forgetting. Plus, he's terrible at cleaning chimneys. Wait till you see the mess downstairs. It sounded like Lucky only picked him for the sweep because he looked right for the part. Because he's tall, dark, and handsome, he said."

"I'll be the judge of that," Sirin said archly. "Anything else?"

Téngfēi shook his head. "He spent all night fighting with the fireplace. I barely saw him. But we can probably rule him out as a suspect, because he definitely never left the living room, and I think my dad was with him the whole time."

"Well, that's something, I guess." Sirin made a final note — *Unlikely Suspect*— and flipped back to the page where Téngfēi had written out everyone's room assignments. "So we have five people who've been targeted by our mystery maniac," Sirin observed. "We know why Clem and Georgie were marks for this guy, but why these others?" She tapped the boxes corresponding to Marzana, Mrs. Kirkegrim, and Mr. Larven. "You'd have to be an out-of-control psycho to attack three strangers for no reason."

"Plus, how the heck did anyone manage to pull off clobbering Marzana and Mrs. Kirkegrim without being seen?" Téngfēi asked. "It's like some kind of locked-room mystery. There seems like no way it could've happened, but it *did* happen."

"Never mind the *how* yet, let's focus on why."

Téngfēi shrugged and reached for the notebook. He glanced over their entries for each of the injured Waits. "Obviously there was a reason, so what do these three people have to do with anything?"

"I don't know. You tell me."

"Well, whoever attacked them didn't seem to be out for blood or anything. Marzana and Mrs. Kirkegrim weren't even knocked unconscious, and if it was poison that dropped Mr. Larven, it wasn't anything fatal. He passed out for a bit, threw up, and fell asleep. It was just enough to—" Téngfēi stopped speaking for a minute as the very simple reason for all of it occurred to him, clear and crisp and undeniable. "Just enough to keep him from being able to leave. Same with the other two. *Someone wanted to make sure the Waits couldn't leave tonight.*"

Sirin made a noise of frustration. "So either Emmett is Cantlebone or a customs agent, and a bunch of innocent carolers stumbled in just in time to give him the chance to arrange for some extra suspects to cover his movements, or Cantlebone or a customs agent somehow infiltrated a bunch of innocent carolers and conked a few to buy himself time to work."

"And there's still the Gilawfer guy," Téngfēi reminded her.

"But we can assume Clem and Georgie would recognize him, right? Or do you think he somehow snuck into the house and managed to stay hidden?"

"No, not without our knowing it. You're right. Cantlebone is the unknown quantity—the master of disguise." He tossed the notebook onto the bedspread between them. "Now what? I don't know how long they're likely to stay tomorrow."

Sirin made a thoughtful face. "I don't know, Téngfēi. How tired are you?"

Téngfēi waved a hand. "Not in the slightest," he fibbed.

"Okay, because I need a favor." She took off her blue-lensed glasses. "Will you go and see if you can find my dad? I can't wait any longer. I'll go out of my mind."

Milo slipped the Ring of Wildest Abandon off his finger and glanced at his clock. It was past one in the morning. "You want me to go out there *now?*"

Meddy's face took on a very uncustomary imploring look. "Please. I'll cover you. Would you try?"

He hesitated, but only for a minute. He'd gone nearly out of his mind waiting for Meddy to come back after only a year. She'd lost her father ... what was it? thirty-four or thirty-five years ago? ...

and had only seen him once since then, just long enough to wave to him from the fire escape. Naturally she was desperate, knowing that he was so close but hadn't shown himself.

"Sure," Milo said. "Of course I'll go."

Meddy left the room first, to scout ahead and make certain they weren't going to run into Milo's mom and dad. There was no good explanation for why Milo needed to go for a walk alone in the middle of the night. He'd have to tell the truth, and one of his parents would insist on going along, because obviously they would. And since Doc Holystone had made it clear that he didn't want anyone but Milo and Meddy to know he was out there, if an adult tagged along, the smuggler's ghost might not show himself. And then Meddy would probably lose it completely, which Milo couldn't have happening in the middle of everything else. If anyone was going to lose it completely, Milo was reserving the right to be that person.

He waited in his room until Meddy peeked around the door frame and gave him an *All's clear* wave. They tiptoed down the hall, passing his parents' closed door, then Mrs. Caraway's, then Lizzie's. Thin slicks of light slid out from under all three, but there were no sounds coming from any of them.

Milo willed his feet to be quiet as a blackjack's as they made their way down the stairs. The first floor was dark and deserted, of course, but he kept tiptoeing all the way to the foyer and slipped his boots and coat on as quietly as possible, just in case.

Meddy shifted from foot to foot as she waited for him to finish bundling up. Finally he unlocked the door and eased it open. Mercifully it was about as soundless as Milo figured it was possible for a door to be. They stepped out onto the porch.

"Where was he when you saw him before?" Meddy asked.

He pointed in the direction of the railcar landing. "There, on the platform." Then he realized something and frowned. The gap in the trees, the place where deeper shadows marked the landing, wasn't visible from where they stood. "Actually, I can't see the exact place from here. I was halfway across the lawn before I saw him last time. Do you see those three little pines, the ones in front of the giant one?"

"Yeah."

"He was on the other side of those. Where did you see him the time you waved to each other?"

Meddy pointed to a spot a short distance away. "There."

Milo frowned. "Are you sure?"

"I think so." She hesitated. "I guess I could be wrong," she said thoughtfully. "I think the woods are thicker there now than they were then."

"That's possible. Those pines grow fast. Dad cuts saplings down every year at the edge of the tree line. He says the woods are coming for the house eventually." Milo looked at his friend. "But if you can't leave the house and he can't leave the woods, do you think that means you won't be able to see him even if I go and tell him you're here?"

"That's what I'm—" She stopped, shook her head. "Never mind. Let's not assume anything until we try."

Milo nodded. "Okay."

"Okay. Then . . ."

"Then what?"

She threw up her hands. "Then *go*, Milo! Jeez! The suspense is killing me here!"

"Okay, okay!" Milo trotted down the stairs.

"And, Milo?" He turned back. "Stay away from the edge," Meddy said grimly.

"Yeah. I will." Milo shoved his gloved hands into his pockets and hurried across the lawn until the dark opening in the pines became visible.

"Doc!" he called in a loud whisper as he neared the edge of the woods. "Doc, are you there?"

Something moved in the shadows, and then the shape of Doc Holystone emerged, peering at Milo from beneath the brim of his hat. "Milo?"

It was going to work! Milo glanced over his shoulder and waved eagerly at Meddy back on the porch. For some reason he'd been certain Doc wouldn't appear to him again. But here he was, and all he had to do was come about two more yards closer to the house for him to be visible to his daughter.

But when Milo turned back to the woods, Doc's ghost had stopped moving and was standing at the edge of the wooden platform of the railcar landing. "Doc, Addie's here," Milo called as he reached the clearing. "She's on the porch!"

Doc immediately craned his neck, rising up on his toes and twisting his body this way and that to try to see past the little pines that were, just as Milo had feared, blocking them from a direct view of the house. "Where is she?"

Milo's heart sank. "You can't see the porch from here, can you?"

"No," Doc said miserably. "She's there? She's that close?"

"Can't you come just a little farther this way? If you can just get around these little trees, you'll be able to see her."

Doc wilted. "I can't believe this. So close, after all this time!"

"How far can you go? Maybe if you just try . . ."

The ghost shook his head. "I'll show you." He strode to the edge of the platform and came to a sudden, jarring halt, as if he'd run straight into an invisible wall. "Same thing if I try to leave this way." He crossed to the other side and came to another abrupt stop.

"We were afraid of that," Milo said sadly. "We were afraid you'd be stuck here the way she's stuck in the house."

The smuggler paced the length of the platform, arms crossed over his chest. "We have got to figure out a way around this."

"We will," Milo insisted. "We just have to work out the rules governing the two of you."

"All right. Tell her I love her, and I'm so sorry I can't say it to her myself, and that I promise we'll find a way." He fixed Milo with a sharp stare. "In the meantime, what about you? Did you find anything out?"

"Nothing specific. But all the items my friends found in Violet Cross's cache were stolen tonight."

"Stolen?" Doc repeated. "Do you have any idea who the thief is?"

Milo shook his head. "Everyone's suspicious. But at least no-body left tonight. Whoever took the stuff, they're still in the house, so the stuff has to be there too."

Doc paced a few steps again. "I suppose I can keep an eye out for anyone who leaves the house overnight — not that I can do any-thing to stop him if he tries to sneak away by another route."

"But unless he's got a car stashed on the hill road somewhere, this is the easiest way," Milo pointed out. "He could light a lantern down on the dock and call for a ferry. We'd never see it from up here, so even if he had to wait, he could still escape."

"Let's hope you're right. What will you and Addie do?"

"Well, I wanted to try and get them all telling stories. Some-times you can learn interesting things that way. But my attempt was a total failure," Milo said grouchily.

Doc made a sympathetic noise. "That's a shame. It's a good idea."

"I know." Then a thought occurred to Milo. "If I can't get them to tell stories, I wonder if maybe there's another way to accomplish the same thing."

"What are you thinking?"

Milo looked at the smuggler's ghost. "You knew Violet Cross, right?"

"I did. Why?"

"She got up to some pretty epic stuff, huh?"

Doc nodded. "She certainly did."

"Do you think maybe before I go back, you could quickly tell me about one of those ventures? Something most people might not know about?"

Doc's smile stretched wide. "I imagine I could, Milo. Yes. Let me think."

fifteen

MISTLETOE AND HOLLY

TEN MINUTES LATER, Milo darted out of the woods. Meddy was stalking back and forth on the porch — the short, girl version of Doc pacing in the woods. She managed to restrain herself until Milo was only a couple yards away, but then her impatience got the better of her. She flung herself off the porch, but before her foot hit the lawn, she vanished.

Milo stopped short. He'd seen Meddy do this before, of course, but only when she'd meant to. Even then it was jarring — she could hold things, touch things, and carry things, and she appeared to be perfectly solid, yet she could dematerialize at will and pass through walls. But this was different somehow. "Meddy?" He turned in a circle at the foot of the stairs. "Meddy, where are you?"

She reappeared in the act of stepping back onto the porch. She looked angry and frustrated. "Right here. What an idiot."

"Who, me?"

"No, me. I got carried away. I knew that wasn't going to work." She made a frustrated noise. "It didn't work for Dad, either, huh?"

"Nope." Milo looked back in the direction from which he'd come. Sure enough, those stupid pines were as good as a black-out curtain, hiding everything deeper in from view. Turning on the strings of lights that illuminated the railcar platform might have done some good, but at this hour of night, that would look very, very odd to anyone inside who happened to notice. "Listen, I had an idea."

"Oh, good. I was wondering what took you so long. But what did he say?"

"I'll tell you about it inside. I'm freezing."

Meddy grabbed his arm and pulled him around to face her. "What did he *say?*"

Milo shook his head, feeling foolish. "I'm sorry. He said he loves you, and he's sorry he can't tell you himself. He said he promises we'll find a way for you to see each other."

Her eyes lit up so brightly, they seemed to faintly glow. "Thanks."

Milo grinned back. "Come on. I'm seriously freezing my nose off."

Just then, a sudden blossom of light spilled out of the living-room-side window behind them. They turned, and although the glare would certainly render him invisible to anyone inside, Milo instinctively edged away from the window, pulling Meddy with him.

"It can't be this easy," she whispered. "We've never caught anybody in the act before, have we?"

Milo shook his head. "Or at least when we have, it hasn't meant what we thought it did."

"Good point."

"I'll take a look." Meddy went up to peer against the glass. "Young guy, wild hair. That's Sylvester, right?"

"Yeah. What's he doing?"

"Not sure yet." She watched silently for a minute. Milo, meanwhile, was beginning to feel his teeth actually chattering in his head. "Now he's going into the kitchen." Meddy tilted her face, following his progress. "He's going into that closet by the bathroom. Come on. Now. Fast."

They slipped inside, quiet as church mice. Milo wiggled out of his coat and boots as quickly as possible, keeping an eye on the open door to the laundry room in the kitchen. Was Sylvester hiding the items from Georgie and Clem's stolen cache in there right now?

Milo took the Ring of Wildest Abandon from his pocket and slipped it onto his finger. "Be ready," he said softly.

Meddy nodded, took the Eyes of True and Aching Clarity from her pocket, and popped them on her nose. "Ready to do what, exactly?"

"I don't know," Téngfēi whispered. "Be scary or whatever."

Then Sylvester emerged at last, arms full of . . . cleaning supplies.

Téngfēi pressed back into the shadows by the front door, but Sylvester didn't so much as glance his way as he carried his contraband into the living room. He'd ditched his bell garters and the ragpicker's jacket and had done his level best to get rid of the blue-green face paint, although there were still traces of it stuck in the roots of the hair around his face. Téngfēi could just make out a pair of headphones half-buried in his wild hair before he passed out of view. Aside from his still-out-of-control mane of hair, he looked almost normal as he bopped along to whatever he was listening to.

Téngfēi tiptoed over to the dividing wall between the kitchen and the living room and peeked cautiously around it. In the middle of the oilcloth that still covered most of the floor, Sylvester arranged a plastic garbage bag, a roll of paper towels, a few bottles of cleaner, and the Pines' broom and dustpan. Then he stepped up onto the hearth, carefully removed everything over the fireplace, and began to wipe off the mantelpiece, nodding and singing quietly to himself all the while.

As Téngfēi watched, Sylvester carefully brushed a little pile of ash off the mantel and into a paper towel in his other hand. He stepped down, deposited it in the garbage bag, picked up a bottle of wood polish . . . and realized he wasn't alone.

He fumbled in one pocket to turn off the music, then took off his headphones and hung them around his neck. "Oh, hey there, Milo." He sounded tiredly sheepish, but not particularly surprised or upset to be caught.

"Hey, Sylvester." Téngfēi eyed the assortment on the oilcloth. Was he *cleaning?* "What are you doing?" Sylvester's T-shirt had a picture of a bird-beaked, masked superhero and the words UP IN THE AIR, JUNIOR BIRDMEN! on it. It was borderline cool, which was disorienting after the general looniness of the past few hours.

"Trying to make up a little for what we put you and your folks through," Sylvester said, tearing a fresh towel from the roll. "Rob swept up most of the ash and whatnot, but it's still all over everything. I raided your kitchen for supplies," he added, stepping back up on the hearth and spritzing polish on the mantelpiece. "I hope you don't mind."

"I want that T-shirt," Sirin muttered. "I should have that T-shirt."

"I'm pretty sure Mom and Dad would say you don't have to do this," Téngfēi said to Sylvester.

"Yeah, I know. That's why I didn't ask." He tossed the paper towel into the bag, hopped down, and started moving the decorations from the floor back up. "Also, if you want the truth, I have a hard time walking away from stuff like this until it gets done. And I knew Rob wasn't going to do it. The idea of trying to relax while there was a bunch of grime all over was just excruciating. I'd never have been able to sleep." He looked critically at the assortment on the mantel. "Do I have these back in their right places?"

Téngfēi stepped to the middle of the room for a better look. "The clock should be a little to the left. Scoot the candlesticks a little closer to it. You can stick the holly wherever, just so it looks pretty."

Sylvester adjusted everything accordingly. "Thanks."

"You didn't have to wipe off all the holly, too, did you?"

"I dusted it a little bit, but that's all. The real problem's going to be the Christmas tree." He rubbed his eyes tiredly. "I don't suppose you know if your folks have a proper duster, do you? Otherwise I'm going to have to wipe down every bulb by hand, and that'll get annoying pretty fast."

"I'll check."

"Thanks."

Téngfēi and Sirin went to the kitchen. "It looks like he's actually cleaning," Sirin said in disbelief. "And where did he get that T-shirt?"

"Forget the T-shirt," Téngfēi hissed. "There should be a feather duster in the pantry, but it falls off its hook all the time. Check the floor by the bucket of potatoes." He glanced around the kitchen. The punch bowl and cups were in the drying rack, but there was no sign of the tea ball Lizzie had gotten for Mr. Larven. Téngfēi checked the cabinet where his parents kept tea and coffee, but it wasn't there, either.

It was a little thing, but sometimes the smallest details were far more important than they seemed. So while Sirin slipped into the pantry, Téngfēi opened the lid of the trash can by the sink and peered in. Nothing visible but a bunch of orange and lemon rinds that had probably garnished drinks, a few bits of pie crust, and a mound of crumpled napkins. Téngfēi took a fork from the drying rack and reached in to shift the rubbish aside to see what was farther down. Fortunately there didn't seem to be anything too disgusting in there.

Sirin appeared at his side with the duster in one hand. "What are you doing?"

"Shh." The fork struck something that gave a sympathetic metallic *clink*.

Aha. Téngfēi steeled himself, reached in with his free hand to hold the assorted trash out of the way, and dug a little more with the fork. The curved, perforated shell of the silver tea ball surfaced. He snatched it up and set it in the sink. Then he took the duster into the living room, where Sylvester was now methodically removing the contents of the bookshelves on the wall over the sofa and stacking them on a clean bit of floor. "Oh, thank God," he said with a sigh.

"Don't mention it." Téngfēi handed over the duster. "I'm going to make myself a snack. Do you want anything? I can make coffee if you'd like."

Sylvester shook his head. Then he hesitated and smiled. "Yeah, you know, that would be really nice. I promise I'll turn the machine off before I go up."

"Okay."

Sirin was staring down at the tea ball when he got back. "Shall I open it?"

"Hang on," Téngfēi whispered. "The coffeemaker's loud. It'll let us talk easier." Once the machine was sputtering its way toward a full pot of coffee, Téngfēi spread a paper napkin on the counter and unscrewed the tea ball. "This is what went into the punch, along with the liquor. Somehow it wound up in the trash." He dumped the contents out onto the napkin. Most of what was in there looked as if it had come right out of the jar of mulling spices the Pines used to make hot cider: bits of dried orange peel, cardamom pods, some curls of cinnamon, and one of those star-shaped things he could never remember the name of. But that wasn't all.

Sirin saw it too. "What are these?" she asked, prodding a crushed red berry with one finger. There were four crimson and four white ones, all squashed, probably the better to let the juices out into the punch.

"Holly, I think," Téngfēi said. "And I'm not sure, but I bet the white ones are mistletoe."

"I didn't think you could eat those," Sirin said slowly. "Or drink them, or whatever."

"You can't. Didn't you ever get the speech about not eating the Christmas plants? They're basically all poisonous to some degree." He glanced around. "There's holly all over this house. And as for the mistletoe ..." His eyes fell on Lucky's candle-and-greenery crown, which was still sitting on the bar between the kitchen and the dining room. *Evidently some people can't handle being around a girl wearing mistletoe.* "That was part of Lucky's costume, but she took it off as soon as she came in, and it sat there all night. So anyone could've poisoned the punch. All this stuff was literally just lying around."

He swept the napkin and the contents of the tea ball into the trash, then gave his hands and the ball itself a good scrub. "I better make the snack I said I wanted."

"You do that, and I'll have a look around for myself," Sirin said. "Not that it seems likely the thief would've brought what he took down here, where it was so busy all night. I wonder how much time passed between when the last folks went up and when Sylvester came back d—"

She stopped speaking abruptly and looked sharply at Téngfēi. They both must've had the same thought at the same time: that cleaning a room down to the surfaces would be a great cover for hiding things in that room. He nodded.

"I'll check," Sirin said grimly, and headed out of the kitchen.

Téngfēi got out the ingredients for PB & J Specials. Over the sounds of the coffeemaker, he thought he could hear Sylvester replacing the books.

There was no knowing how long the Waits would stick around in the morning. Surely if one of them was the thief who'd taken Violet Cross's stuff, the carolers — or at least that one — would get moving early. Which meant he and Sirin (and Clem and Georgie, who had probably reached the same conclusion) only had tonight and part of the morning to find the missing things — or find some way of keeping the Waits from leaving until they did.

As he started assembling the peanut butter and jelly sandwiches, he thought back to the year before, and the ways Negret and Sirin had managed to acquire the information they'd needed to get to the bottom of the thefts and secrets that had filled Greenglass

House for the four days before Christmas. They'd gathered some of that information from sneaking around and working out clues. But a lot of it had come from the guests themselves, by way of their stories. Milo's attempt to prompt some storytelling that evening had been a total failure. But maybe Téngfēi would have better luck, especially now that he had insider information from Doc Holystone himself to start the ball rolling.

On the other hand, last year they'd had plenty of time to convince the guests to play along. Even assuming he could orchestrate things so that they didn't waste time on stories from his own family, the Caraways, Clem, or Georgie, that still left eight people of interest, which would almost certainly take way more time than they were going to have.

He finished putting the sandwich fixings away just as the coffeemaker gurgled and sputtered and fell silent. "Coffee's done," Téngfēi called.

"Magnificent." Sylvester came around the corner, brushing dust from his palms. "Cups are where?"

"There." Téngfēi pointed. "Sugar's in the red jar, milk's in the fridge. And one of these is for you. You're not allergic to peanut butter, are you?"

"No, thank all that's good in this world. Peanut butter and coffee is . . ." He kissed the tips of his fingers. "Thanks, Milo."

"Anytime." Sirin appeared behind Sylvester. She made a bemused face and shook her head: nothing suspicious. "Well, thanks for dusting everything," Téngfēi said. "It'll be a nice surprise for Mom and Dad."

"Do me a favor and don't tell them I did it," Sylvester said as he spooned sugar into his cup. "I mean, if you don't have to mention it and it doesn't come up, we can just leave it alone."

"Okay. See you in the morning."

"See you." Sylvester opened the fridge door, and while he was out of sight behind it, Sirin produced a book and shoved it into Téngfēi's hands.

"Spotted this and thought it might be useful," she said quietly as they headed for the stairs. "I'm going to stay down here to make sure he doesn't do anything weird once you're gone. I'll meet you in your room later." She paused on the second step and took a close look at his face. "On second thought, you look like you need sleep."

Téngfēi, who'd been just about to stifle a yawn, decided to be honest. "Yeah, probably."

She nodded. "See you in the morning, then."

Téngfēi smiled weakly and continued up. On the second-floor landing, he paused and held the book Sirin had given him up in a shaft of celery-colored moonlight that drifted in through the stained-glass window: *The Skidwrack: A Visual History*. Téngfēi didn't know whether to laugh or gulp. This book didn't belong to the Pines. It had been abandoned at Greenglass House last year, when De Cary Vinge had fled the howling ghost of Addie Whitcher.

He opened it and flipped through the pages. Here and there were illustrations of the Skidwrack and its inlets — illustrations Téngfēi now understood were nothing more than someone's best guesses. Sure enough, the caption under the elegantly tinted picture on the frontispiece offered a warning: *Engraving by James Minor, c. 1870. Not to be used for navigational purposes.* Every image he could find had a similar disclaimer underneath.

And then, without warning, a sharp noise came from above.

Creak.

sixteen

THE IMPORTANCE OF GOOD PLUMBING

OOD GRIEF," TÉNGFĒI muttered. He leaned around the turn in the staircase, looking for a telltale shape in the darkness. Who else could possibly be up at this hour? He stashed the book just inside the second-floor hallway leading to his family's private rooms, then climbed the stairs as silently as only a solitaire with some blackjack skills could. On the third-floor landing, he came face to face with Georgie. "What are you doing?" he demanded in a whisper.

"What do you think I'm doing?" she retorted, whispering too.

A light clicked on and the door to 3E swung open. Emmett peered out, blinking sleepily. "What's going on out here?"

"Georgie's toilet overflowed," Téngfēi said quickly. "I'm going for a plunger."

Emmett frowned, confused, then faded back into his room and shut his door.

"Were we talking that loudly?" Téngfēi asked.

Georgie shook her head, still looking suspiciously at Emmett's doorway. Then she motioned toward the stairwell. "Take me to the plungers, I guess. You couldn't have come up with a story where I didn't clog the toilet?" she asked in an undertone.

"I didn't say *that*," Téngfēi protested as he led the way back down to the second floor. "It's an old house, the plumbing's ancient." Then he grinned. "Are you worried about being *embarrassed* in front of *Emmett?*"

"Good grief, no," she said, affronted. "Never mind. It was quick thinking. Thank you."

"So you were up to what, exactly?"

"Just having a look around. We figured everyone on this floor was more likely to be sound asleep than the folks on the upper floors, who came up later, so I got three and Clem took four and five."

"You're *both* out prowling?" Téngfēi said as they reached the second floor. He opened the utility closet and took out a plunger. "Great."

"We're not going to break into anyone's rooms," Georgie assured him. "We'd never do anything to get your folks in trouble." Téngfēi bit his tongue to keep from pointing out that she and Clem had already done that very thing only a little earlier in the evening. "Is someone still downstairs?"

"Sylvester. He's cleaning."

Georgie gave him a dubious look. "Cleaning? It's almost two in the morning. Are you sure?"

"I was just down there for like twenty minutes. And Meddy's down there now. If he's doing anything dodgy, she'll see." Georgie didn't seem convinced. "I made him a pot of coffee before I came up. If you want to see for yourself, go ahead. Tell him the plunger story and say I sent you down for a cup while I fixed your toilet. You can emphasize the old, old plumbing if you want."

Georgie rolled her eyes. "I just might do that. I could use some coffee."

"In that case, I'll go up to your room and pretend to fix it," Téngfēi said. "Just for show. And I'll leave you and Clem more coffee packets for later."

"Here." Georgie took her key from her pocket. "Come get me when you're 'done.' And then for crying out loud, go to sleep."

A few minutes later, Téngfēi climbed the stairs with the plunger clutched in one hand like a sword and his pockets stuffed with single-cup coffee packets. On the third floor, the door that had been open before, the one behind which logic said Nicholas Larven had to be sleeping off the combined effects of alcohol and Christmas-plant poisoning, was closed now. The light under Emmett Sye-buck's door was still on.

Back on the fourth floor, all the lights were off. Téngfēi paused to listen for an indication that anyone else was awake, but there was none. He went to Georgie's door — no point in trying to be solitaire-quiet when he was only doing this in support of the plunger story — unlocked it, stepped inside, and turned on the light.

The room looked exactly as it had when he and Sirin had been there earlier, down to the depression in the bedcovers where Clem had been sitting. Clearly neither of the thieves had so much as considered calling it a night. Téngfēi rolled his eyes. With guests asleep in all the rooms, how thorough a search did they think they could make?

He sat on the luggage rack, passing the plunger from hand to hand and thinking. If the thief wasn't one of the Waits but had manipulated events to make sure they stayed overnight, then the thief was Emmett. In that case, there was no way he'd have stashed his stolen haul in any of the empty rooms, because seven of those rooms would have occupants by the end of the night, and he'd have no way of predicting which ones.

If the thief was masquerading as one of the Waits, then maybe he could take a chance on finding some way to wind up in the room in which the things had been hidden. Rob had been the last one to go up, and he could be fairly certain that he'd have little or no company on the fifth floor, because nobody who didn't have to hike up there would choose to. But Rob was the only one who hadn't been out of sight for the entire window during which the thefts had to have taken place. And unless there was a good reason to hide things on the top floor of a creaky old house, it made far more sense to hide them on one of the lower levels, if only because it would take less effort to recover them when the time came to make an escape.

Still, anyone who knew Georgie and Clem for the highly skilled professionals they were and was still willing to tangle with them was taking a tremendous risk no matter where he hid the goods. He had to know they would discover the loss quickly and would immediately focus their considerable talents on combing every inch of the house they could get to. Which, considering Clem was a cat burglar, was literally almost every inch of the house. So under the circumstances, what the heck could possibly constitute even a halfway decent hiding place?

And then Téngfēi put a fist to his face and nearly stabbed himself in the eye with the end of the plunger he'd totally forgotten he was holding. There *was* a logical hiding place—a place that wouldn't be subject to the combing-over the rest of the inn was likely to undergo. There were *two* such perfect hiding places, as a matter of fact, and Téngfēi was already inside one of them.

He stood up and turned in a circle. "They're here," he murmured. "Some of them, at least. They have to be."

It would've been nice at that moment to know which items Georgie had had and which ones had been in Clem's room, and where they'd originally been hidden—but whatever. There were limited places you could hide anything in a guest room without the resident guest knowing.

Téngfēi looked around, remembering to examine his surroundings with the eyes of an ecstatic solitaire blackjack who didn't already know these rooms like the back of his hand. Bed, dresser, luggage rack, desk and chair. Wastebasket. Georgie's broken coffeemaker and its tray of plastic-wrapped packets holding stirrers, sugar, creamer, and napkins. The main light was a bump of glass attached to the ceiling; the one on the desk next to the coffee stuff was the hollow, clear kind you could fill with decorative stuff like shells or corks. This one was about half full of bits of sea glass. There was a single window with long sand-colored curtains, which he tugged aside to reveal Emmett's favorite window, the one with the four round medallions decorated by gilded portraits. Except for the light fixture, the ceiling was an unbroken sheet of painted pressed tin.

If he was right about this, the thief had to have chosen a hiding place that Georgie wasn't likely to interact with, so stashing stuff in the linings of the curtains or the soaps and shampoos and towels in the bathroom probably wouldn't work. He examined the coffeemaker, but of course the thief had no way of knowing it didn't work and would've had to assume it would get used first thing in the morning. All that was in the coffeemaker now were the grounds Georgie had dumped into the brew basket and the water she'd poured into the reservoir before she'd discovered it was broken.

He unplugged the lamp, unscrewed the little finial on top, took off the shade, and set it aside. The harp-shaped part that held the light bulb unscrewed too, and there was just enough play in the electrical wires that ran through the base for it to be moved out of the way. Téngfēi took his lockpicks from his bag, selected one, and reached in to stir the glass pieces until he was satisfied that there was nothing hidden among them. It was far too obvious, but still, it would've been nice to have found something so quickly.

The desk had no drawers, just a pullout panel on each side for extra workspace. The chair had a woven seat, but the weave was too thin for anything to be hidden inside. Finally Téngfēi went into the bathroom and looked through the medicine cabinet. Reluctantly, he glanced at the toilet. It had a tank on the back, the kind with a big ceramic lid. You could hide a lot of stuff in there. Just as he reached for it, someone spoke from the other room.

"I don't know who you are, but you are so busted." Clem appeared in the doorway. "Oh. It's just you. What are you doing, Milo? Where's Georgie?"

"Downstairs." He explained his run-in with Georgie and the story they'd fed Emmett. "But then I had this idea. Did you and Georgie search your own rooms after the thief took your stuff?"

"Did we search . . ." Clem's eyes widened. She leaned back against the wall and put a hand over her mouth. Téngfēi figured that meant no. "Oh, boy. So that's what you're doing?"

He nodded. "I should have gone to get Georgie first, but the idea just occurred to me and I thought maybe I could . . . I don't know . . . just solve things myself now."

Clem looked angry, but Téngfēi was pretty sure she wasn't mad at him. "I'm going to go check my room. Let me know if you find anything."

"Okay. What did Georgie have in here and what did you have next door?"

"I had the locks and keys and the reflecting circle. Georgie had the fan, the spherical chalkboard, and the pack of cards. Knock on the wall if you need me." And with that, she stalked out, muttering irritably under her breath.

Téngfēi turned back to the toilet tank and lifted off the lid. He looked at the tangle of plumbing inside: no plastic baggies full of whalebone fans or playing cards. Of course not. If the stolen things had been rehidden in Georgie's space, they had to be hidden really well. Too well for a kid to —

Something in there didn't look right.

Téngfēi turned on the light over the medicine cabinet and leaned down for a closer look. He had no idea what did and didn't belong in the tank of a toilet, but he was pretty sure none of it needed to be made of engraved metal. And there was a piece in there that was: an arc of silver that had initially appeared to be part of the plumbing, until he spotted the lines and numbers cut into its sides that made it look a bit like a curved length of ruler.

Téngfēi rolled up his sleeve, reminded himself that the water in the tank wasn't in any way gross except by basic toilet association, and reached in.

"What on earth are you doing?"

His heart lurched for the second time, but it was only Sirin, standing beside him as if she'd been there all along. "You couldn't have come two minutes earlier, when Clem was in here, so I'd only have to explain it once?" he demanded. "And who's watching Sylvester?"

"Georgie's down there now, so I came looking for you. Only to find you up to your elbows in potty water. Explain, please."

Once again, Téngfēi recapped his suspicions about the missing things and where they might be. "So I checked the tank, and I think I just found something." He turned back to the task at hand, and the curved bit of metal came loose without the slightest resistance.

He shook it off, ran both it and his wet arm under the faucet, and dried them on a towel. Then he took a long look at the thing he now held. It didn't look like anything on its own except a curve on a base. "I was right," he whispered in delight.

Sirin took it gingerly from him and examined it closely. "What is this?"

"It's got to be part of the spherical chalkboard — the base that holds the globe. So the rest has to be around here somewhere." But where on earth did you hide a sphere that, judging from the engraved curving part of the base, had to be at least the size of a big cantaloupe?

"Georgie said it was made of paper," Sirin reminded him. "The thief could've flattened it, like those maps that show the earth like a flattened orange peel? Hiding a sphere would be tough, but flat pieces of paper would be easy."

"But if any of the items in the cache could be the derrotero in disguise, then could the thief really afford to take any of them apart?"

"Sure, as long as he could put them back together again," Sirin reasoned.

"I guess. And you're right about paper — it can be flattened. Or folded." Téngfēi looked around the bathroom, not entirely sure what he was searching for except that it had to be something Georgie wasn't likely to interact with. "Not the medicine cabinet, the shower curtain, or the towels . . . Georgie might notice."

"What about there?" Sirin pointed to the little curtained window next to the shower. "Who opens the window in a hotel bathroom, especially in winter?" She reached up, tugged the curtain aside, and frowned at the empty ledge behind it. "No luck."

But Téngfēi had noticed something else. The curtain had moved when she'd tugged at it, but the rings from which it hung had stayed stuck, refusing to glide along the rod. "Hang on." He moved the pile of towels off the little stool that held them, pushed the stool over to the window, and climbed up.

There was something threaded horizontally through the curtain rings, right alongside the rod, that definitely didn't belong there.

Téngfēi reached up, found one end of whatever it was, and pushed it carefully through the rings. "Can you catch this when it comes out?"

Sirin obligingly drifted up off the floor and tugged at the opposite end of what turned out to be a thin, cylindrical rod made of metal. "Slowly, now," she said after a minute. Téngfēi glanced over and saw that what was emerging from the rings was thicker and had the deep, dark gray color of a blackboard.

They worked carefully, easing the thing loose bit by bit, until Sirin announced, "Got it," and sank back down to the floor. Téngfēi hopped off the stool, and together they looked at the object in the scholiast's hands.

It was narrow and about a foot and a half long, and at first glance it looked something like a collapsed umbrella. Except *this* umbrella seemed to have far more ribs than any Téngfēi had ever seen, and instead of being unattached at one end so that the umbrella could open wide and provide shelter, it was closed at both ends and capped by wooden rings. "Clem had a short tube with her when she and Georgie arrived," Téngfēi said. "I bet this is what was in it."

"Hold this," Sirin said, and Téngfēi took one end in each hand. The scholiast gave one of the wooden rings an experimental push. It glided easily up the rod, and as it did, the dozens of flexible ribs inside the blackboard-gray paper bowed into arcs. Instead of opening into an umbrella, it puffed out into an almost-perfect sphere. Here and there, the dark surface was marred by the decades-old ghosts of imperfectly erased chalk marks.

When it reached its final shape, it gave a soft click. Téngfēi retrieved the base he had found in the tank. The central rod fitted neatly between the ends of the arc, and there it was. "That's our chalkboard," he said.

seventeen

THE RELIQUARY

ⒹNE DOWN," Sirin said, giving the sphere a gentle turn on its axis. "Now, what else are we looking for?"

"A whalebone fan and a deck of cards. I'm going to let Clem know we found this first, though. I think maybe we should get Georgie."

"I'll go get her," Sirin offered, and dematerialized again. Téngfēi gave the wall that adjoined Clem's bathroom a quick series of raps, then took the reassembled spherical chalkboard out into the bedroom. He set it on the desk just as Clem returned. She made a little sound of delight and reached for the globe. "Milo Pine, you are a wonder. Where on earth was it?"

"The base was in the toilet tank and the round part was

collapsed like an umbrella and threaded through the bathroom-window curtain rings. Did you find anything?"

Clem shook her head. "I was beginning to think you were mistaken, but maybe I'm just overtired and overthinking things."

"Or you could be right, and they're not there. He could've hidden Georgie's stuff first, then gotten interrupted before he could do the same with yours."

"All right, for the moment let's focus on this room and hope the fan and the cards are still here." Clem touched the engraved silver arc that held the globe. "And now we know our thief's willing to take things apart to hide them."

Together, Téngfēi and Clem began to comb the room a second time. They had just stripped all the linens from the bed when Georgie and Sirin arrived.

"You two better not be short-sheeting my bed," Georgie said drily. She picked up the spherical chalkboard and shook her head. "I can't believe this was here all along. It's embarrassing. Hurts my professional pride."

"Not gonna lie, it is a bit of a slap in the face," Clem agreed as she unzipped one of the pillows and reached in to hunt through the batting. "Meddy, come give me a hand over here. Check the other pillows."

"Did somebody check this already?" Georgie asked, reaching for the lamp.

"I did," Téngfēi said, "but I only looked in the base. Can't hurt to look again."

Georgie unplugged it a second time and handed the shade to

Téngfēi. Then she took a roll of tools from her satchel, flicked it open, and confidently disassembled the lamp. Téngfēi turned the shade over and over in his hands as he watched. True, the hollow base full of glass *seemed* obvious, but maybe exactly for that reason, the thief could assume that anyone searching it would look no farther than that. Téngfēi certainly hadn't. Georgie, of course, wasn't going to make that mistake. She was going to examine every part of the thing, just in case, and she'd surely taken apart far more complicated wiring than this before.

Every part... Téngfēi looked down at the shade. It had stiff, ridged fabric on the outside, ruffled like the surface of a crinkle-cut potato chip, that was attached to a cone of smooth plastic on the inside. A sea-green ribbon capped the top edge, and a matching fringe of tassels ringed the bottom. He took his lockpicks out again, sat cross-legged in the middle of the floor with the shade on his lap, and poked the hooked end of one pick under the ribbon. It had probably been glued on at one point, but it wasn't now. One side lifted easily away, revealing a slender crack of space between the ridged potato-chip outside and the plastic cone. The space wasn't empty.

"Um... Georgie?" he said slowly. "Clem?" Then, holding the space open with the pick, he turned the shade upside down. Four thick paper rectangles fluttered to the floor. A queen of clubs looked up at him from one. She was not a traditional queen; she'd clearly been painted to resemble someone specific, though Téngfēi had no idea who. The other three had fallen face-down and showed only printed images of twisting rivers, each subtly different from the others.

The two thieves descended upon him. "Unbelievable," Georgie said. She took the shade and the pick and worked the instrument gently around the top edge, shaking loose handful after handful of cards, which Clem collected into a pack.

At last the shade held no more. "Fifty-four," Clem announced, setting the deck on the desk next to the globe. "Including two jokers."

"All right," Sirin said briskly. "One more stroke of genius and we're halfway there. What else you got?"

"The last thing that was in this room is the whalebone fan, right?" Téngfēi leaned back against the wall and thought hard.

"It's off-white, carved into lacy patterns, and stitched together with blue thread," Clem said. She held up two fingers about eight inches apart. "The sections are about this long."

"So it would come apart into sections pretty easily."

"Absolutely," Georgie confirmed. "You'd barely have to try. The thread was very thin, very old."

Téngfēi cast his eyes around, searching for inspiration, and found himself looking longingly at the coffee stuff. He was, it was time to acknowledge, fairly exhausted. He didn't drink coffee, but the idea of a potion that could zap him awake seemed magical. Of course, the busted coffeemaker wasn't zapping anyone awake ever again.

Which really was strange, because the Pines had only put

coffeemakers in the rooms a couple months ago. Appliances were supposed to last longer than that.

Oh. Téngfēi put a hand to his mouth. He'd assumed the thief had bypassed hiding anything in the water reservoir because the coffeepot fell into the column of things that were likely to get used by the room's occupant, and the thief couldn't have known it was broken. But what if the thief *did* know it was broken? What if the thief was *responsible* for the machine being broken? It wouldn't be for the sake of hiding anything in the coffeemaker itself, because Georgie would probably find out it didn't work by dumping coffee and water into it and turning the thing on. But if no coffee actually got brewed, then there would be no reason for her to mess with the *other* packets — the long, thin ones that held napkins, stirrers, sugar, and powdered creamer.

He went to the tray and picked one up. It was heavier than it should've been, and it was already open at one end. Téngfēi reached in, and between the folds of the thin napkins, he found two carved, off-white, tapered slats of a flexible material that logic — and the sharp inhalations he heard from the others — told him must be whalebone.

He passed them to Georgie and examined the other four packets. Each one yielded two or three fan segments. "This is the whole thing," Georgie said in disbelief. "He broke my coffeemaker. This person is not just tricky, he's *evil*. Who messes with someone's coffeepot? That's hitting below the belt."

Téngfēi had no good answer for that. He felt suddenly, completely done in. "I think I have to sleep now."

"Please go to bed," Clem said. "You've gone above and beyond the call of duty. And your parents are going to kill us when they find out we kept you up this late."

"But then we'll tell them you found all this stuff and they'll be too impressed with you to care about that," Georgie added, squeezing his shoulder. "Thank you."

"What about the other things?" Sirin asked.

"We'll comb Clem's room again. If there's anything there, we'll find it."

"I have a thought," Sirin said. "A safer place to hide what we just found than anyplace else, probably."

"Where?" Clem asked.

The scholiast held out her arms. "Me. Before I showed myself to you guys, before you could see and hear me, anything I wore or carried was invisible to you too. I don't know how it works, but I don't see any way the other thief can possibly get at your stuff if I have it."

"That," Téngfēi said, "is brilliant. It'll be like the stuff is in another dimension. Or what's the thing you use with the Summon Scholiast exploit in Odd Trails? The thing you can use to carry one over distances? Some kind of magical container . . . A reliquary! You'll be like one of those."

"This sounds great in theory," Clem said. "But will it really work?"

"I'll make sure it's secure, I promise," Sirin said, holding a hand to her heart.

"And you won't . . . I don't know, vanish and not come back?"

Georgie asked hesitantly. "You were gone for so long—is there a way to reach you if that happens?"

The scholiast's face got very serious. "When I left last Christmas —when I went back—I did that by choice. And I came back by choice, not by chance." She looked apologetically at Téngfēi. "It is true that I don't fully understand how time moves for you when I'm not here, but as long as I don't leave your . . . your plane of reality or whatever, that shouldn't cause us any problems."

Georgie and Clem glanced at each other. "I hate to let go of it," Georgie said, "but I hate the idea of trying to hide it all again even more."

"I'll keep it safe. You have my word." Sirin held out her cupped hands.

"All right." Georgie handed over the cards and the fan, then disassembled the chalkboard. Sirin tucked the smaller items in the pockets of her robe. The collapsed chalkboard globe went down the back of her shirt, and she hung the brass stand from her belt like a clunky, curved weapon.

They said their good-nights, with Clem promising to leave a note if she and Georgie found the missing pieces of the cache, and the two adventurers headed back downstairs. The clock in the Pines' living room chimed three in the morning as Téngfēi stopped briefly to pick up the Skidwrack book he'd left in the hallway.

"Not a bad night's work," Sirin said. "Feel better?"

"A little," he admitted. "Mainly I'm so tired I could sleep standing up."

Sirin pushed him gently down the hall. "I'll see you in the morning."

As he stumbled toward his bedroom, Téngfēi entertained very briefly the idea of giving *The Skidwrack: A Visual History* a closer look before he turned in, or calling Sirin back so they could examine the found items, but he could barely stay awake long enough to put the book in his rucksack and get into his pajamas.

A knock sounded on his door as his eyes drifted shut, and his mom stuck her head inside. Her face stretched into a weary smile as she came in to smooth the patchwork blanket up over his shoulders and kiss his forehead, which was the last thing Milo registered before he fell asleep.

eighteen

THE SOLITAIRE AND THE CRANE

DESPITE HIS LATE NIGHT, Milo woke up relatively early to a bleak sky out his window that somehow managed to look both drab and gray and yet not at all like the kind of sky that meant snow. He glanced blearily at his clock: nine in the morning. His eyes darted immediately to the floor by his bedroom door, but there was no note from Clem and Georgie, so the reflecting circle, keys, and locks still had to be missing.

Milo smoothed out his covers, then retrieved his rucksack from the floor by his desk, where he'd dropped it before climbing into bed. He took out his notebook and pen and the big *Transmundane Warriors* manual. He'd had to leap right into Téngfēi the night before; now maybe he could take a few minutes to get a deeper feel for who this new character was.

To most of the inhabitants of the known worlds, the introduction began, *the word* realms *conjures up maps of countries laid edge to edge, stitched together by the very borders that mark their limits. But the transmundane adventurer knows that there are more realms than any map can show, and that not all of them are places of the body. There are realms of the mind and the spirit in addition to the physical, and the transmundane is proficient at traveling all three. In the course of his studies, the transmundane has learned to convert the energy created by passage between these planes into power. At least, this is one way in which these adepts explain the mysterious, even miraculous ways they manipulate thought and emotion to make changes to the visible worlds around them.*

"Cool," Milo murmured. He flipped to the descriptions of solitaires and ecstatics and read through those, but Meddy's explanations had been pretty clear, and the manual's summaries didn't add much. He skipped ahead to the exploits chapter, which was divided into different sections that listed the special feats each type of character could perform.

Most of the solitaire exploits were all about combat, which Milo didn't need. But some did look useful. There was *Clear-Sighted Perspicacity: The weaknesses of your enemies become as clear to you as the bluest sky, as do the most elegant ways to exploit them.* And *Pensive Elutriation,* which Milo wished he'd been able to perform after the embarrassments in social studies: *Through the power of silence and mind, you purify yourself of pain and damage, emerging from your reverie at full strength.* And the *Spinner of Lore: At will, you tap into a reservoir of obscure information that can be used to manipulate your audience to your chosen purpose.*

He jotted down a few words in his spiral pad about a few different exploits, then riffled the pages until he got to the section about what ecstatics were capable of. Logically, Milo figured, these skills would be about channeling emotion into some kind of big whomp of a strike, like an invisible projectile of energy or something. But as he skimmed the descriptions, he started to get a picture of something subtler. Oh, the big power whomps were there, for sure. But there were also exploits where the ecstatic's released emotions could affect specific enemies or allies. A lot of them depended on the ecstatic's anger, or on his having already been wounded and feeling pain. *Ecstatic Fervor: As you absorb a blow, your outpouring of energy spurs your allies to greater feats.* Also *Ecstatic Wrath: As you absorb a blow, your anger destabilizes your enemies.* So the ecstatic didn't just channel emotion to empower him- or herself; his emotion affected those around him. That was something to chew on.

There were other sorts of exploits available to ecstatics too. *The Unfurling Eye: Your consciousness reaches tendrils into the minds of your confederates, allowing your perception to expand into multiple viewpoints.* And apparently ecstatics could bend time now and then too. That would be useful in his current situation. *Darn you, real-world game setting.*

The manual also had more information about the solitaire's power locus and the ecstatic's rings. It seemed that some of an ecstatic's abilities got even fancier if you had a magical implement like a ring. He slipped the circle off his index finger with his thumb and examined it. The Ring of Wildest Abandon, Meddy had called it.

The solitaire's locus got its own special sidebar on one page. *A power locus is an object or device, often devotional in nature, that channels and focuses the solitaire's energy to enhance a particular strength.* There was a whole list of different loci — the plural of *locus* — that solitaires could use.

"'Cataract Locus,'" Milo read softly. "'This delicate scrap of cloth is embroidered with a fragment of a holy poem in a dead language. As you let it flow from hand to hand, your inner energy channels the power of a pounding waterfall.'"

He thought for a moment. Negret's blackjack father had gifted him with a set of keys. Téngfēi would have something similar, Milo decided. Something that carried deep meaning because it anchored him, a roaming solitaire with fathomless reserves of powerful emotion, to the family he had left behind somewhere.

He reached into the rucksack and took out the red lacquer box with the crane decoration. Inside were the yellow paper, red pencil, white feather, and empty metal vial. He took the vial out and turned it over and over in his fingers as he let his imagination roam. If Téngfēi possessed this box, where would it have come from? What would these items have meant to him? What energies could they channel?

You should probably work out the backstory, Meddy had said. Milo looked down at the vial. "So what's my backstory, then?"

First: Téngfēi's monastery. Milo thought immediately of an Odd Trails campaign he and his father and some friends had played over the summer called *The Worlds over the Ways*. One of the places the adventurers had visited was a monastery in a range of high, wooded mountains where the monks made wings from paper and hammered copper.

For the head of the order, Milo imagined a tall, wizened abbot who was both a fighter and a redsmith, his hands scarred from long years of working with copper and decades of training as a warrior. When he'd learned of Téngfēi's unexpected discovery of ecstatic capability, he'd declared that it was impossible for Téngfēi to explore his newfound power while also studying the monastery's specialized fighting forms, which took their inspiration from flight and therefore required consummate control to master. *Remember Icarus, who flew too close to the sun,* Milo imagined the abbot saying. *If he had not flown so near, he would have survived. But there is no safe place to fly if you carry a sun within you. This is the power of an ecstatic: your emotions are the stuff of a burning star. You must choose one path or the other, for you cannot strap wings to the sun and expect them to survive the heat.*

Where would the despondent young monk of the air have gone then? To his family, of course. And for whatever reason—perhaps because the first picture of a solitaire that Milo had seen had been the female fighter in the manual—the image that arose in his mind was of a lady: Téngfēi's mother. But unlike the illustration in the book, this woman was human, and despite the decidedly non-Asian monastery he'd just conjured in his mind, she was also Chinese.

Here Milo felt a quick pang that, a year ago, would've deepened into the guilt that he'd always felt when he'd imagined alternate family situations involving his unknown birth parents rather than his mom and dad. It had taken some time and some emotional conversations with his folks, but he'd come to realize that they completely understood his need to wonder and speculate about the birth parents he'd never known. His father, in particular, had been helpful with this. Whenever they started role-playing games now, he encouraged Milo to create elaborate backstories and lineages for his characters. So today, when the pang came, it was a gentle thing — a flash of emotion that glowed for a moment like a tiny, warm candle flare.

Milo imagined Téngfēi's mother listening patiently and even sadly as her son explained the conundrum he faced. *Our winged fighting traditions and my ecstatic powers are both part of me, Mother. How can I possibly choose only one? Is there really no way to be both an ecstatic and a monk of the air?*

Téngfēi, his mother replied, *the abbot speaks the truth: these two paths are fundamentally at odds with each other. It is impossible to foretell the ways in which they will come into conflict. But I can see that you, too, are right: they are both part of who you are. You did not choose to be both things, and to deny either one would be to deny part of what makes you Téngfēi.*

However — and here her voice took on a warning tone — *I also know that life would be easier for you if you could be simply one or the other. In situations when you need the parts of you that trace their lineage to the monks of the air, the ecstatic in you will still be present, keeping you from flying as effortlessly as a monk who does not carry a sun. And at times when you need that sun to burn its brightest, the part of you that is a monk will shiver its wings. Perhaps your greatest challenge will be finding a way to be at peace with yourself. As your mother, I could wish you did not have to face that trial. But I would not have you face the agony of denying who you are, either.*

Then the only thing to do, the young monk said with a sinking heart, *is to leave this place and try to reconcile my paths for myself.*

Yes. But you need not go alone. Téngfēi's mother presented him with a red lacquer box he had never known her to be without. *Remember that you are ever and always a monk of the air, and you are always my child. Each of these things will be a locus for you, and a reminder that I am always with you, my solitaire son, however far you roam.*

Milo felt a press of emotion swirling up from his gut to curl into a knot in his throat, and it made him certain he'd found the right history for his solitaire. There was plenty of time to work out what kinds of power Téngfēi's loci would channel for him. For now, it was enough to know where they — and Téngfēi himself — had come from.

Milo stowed the box in his rucksack along with his spiral pad and *Transmundane Warriors*. As he did, his hand bumped the eye-engraved lock that was all that remained of the missing set. It would probably be safest if he gave it to Meddy to keep along with everything else, he thought reluctantly. On the other hand, it occurred to him that even if the mystery thief could identify this one lock as part of the cache, the only guest other than Georgie and Clem who knew he had it was Emmett. Therefore, if it went missing from his bag, at least they'd know the identity of the thief. Pleased with his logic, Milo zipped it into a pocket inside the rucksack, slid off his bed, got dressed, and opened his door.

Meddy was waiting in the hallway. "Morning, sunshine." She had added buttons to the pockets of her robe that held the fan and the cards, and she had rigged a strap to the collapsed chalkboard to hang it across her back next to Eglantine's Patent Blackthorn Wishing Stick. The stand still bumped her hip. "Ready to get cracking?"

"I am." Milo slung the rucksack over his shoulder and followed Meddy into the hall. "What's our situation? Have you been downstairs?"

"Yeah." Meddy hesitated. She stopped in the doorway to the living room and turned to face him. "Except actually, no. I watched Sylvester downstairs until he fell asleep, but since then . . . well, I've been on the roof."

Milo blinked. "You've been on the *roof*?"

She winced. "I know I should've been . . . I don't know, patrolling or something, keeping an eye out . . . but I went up there thinking maybe I'd just check. Just for a couple minutes."

"Check for what?" Milo asked. Then he got it. "For your dad."

"Yeah. You can be mad at me if you want," she added with a flicker of defiance. "But I had to look. I thought maybe from higher up, the view would be different, and maybe those pines wouldn't get in the way. Or that maybe he'd keep trying and find a different place to wave from. So first I went to the balcony, where you can see the stretch of woods where . . . where we waved to each other that one time before, the time Fenster saw us."

Which also happened to be the same stretch of woods where Doc Holystone had fallen to his death. "Right," Milo said casually, hoping it wouldn't look as if that macabre thought had just occurred to him.

"The fire escape outside your window would've been better, or outside any of the guest rooms above yours, but I didn't want to freak you out if you woke up. Or risk one of the others seeing me for whatever reason, like Fenster did that time he saw me wave to Dad. But Dad didn't show up." She sounded as if she was trying not to seem hurt. "So I went to three W, which has the best view of the lawn out of all the empty rooms. I opened the window and waited there for about an hour, but he didn't come. Then I worried that maybe he'd turned up at the back of the house as soon as I came to the front, and I realized that from the roof I could see the whole tree line along the cliff, so I went up there. I only meant to wait for a little bit, but then I just couldn't bring myself to leave, because what if, you know? Once I saw a flash of something pale and I thought—" She shook her head. "But it was just an animal. A deer, I guess. And then all of a sudden, the sun was coming up."

He patted her arm awkwardly. "I get it. I'm sorry."

She stood there with her arms folded for a moment. Milo couldn't picture Meddy crying, but it definitely looked as if she was working on mastering some strong emotion. "I just don't understand. I mean, it makes sense—our theory about those newer trees blocking our views of each other — but I'm sure I remember where he was before. If I'm right, he should be able to go there and we should still be able to see each other. Or maybe it's just that I want it so badly I'm getting details wrong."

Milo had no idea what to say to comfort her. The idea that she and her father could be so close and something as simple as a bunch of trees could keep them from seeing each other just seemed so . . . so *unfair*. But then, they were talking about ghosts, and it wasn't as if Milo understood the rules and physics governing them.

"Whatever's holding him back," he said carefully, "we know it isn't that he doesn't want to see you. You know how much he loves you, and how much he wants to be with you."

Meddy looked up at Milo reluctantly. "Yeah, I do."

"And he promised he'd figure it out. *We'll* figure it out. There has to be a way, and we'll find it."

"Let's talk about something else." She swiped her sleeve across her eyes. "The entire time I watched Sylvester, all he did was clean. And if you can believe it, he *did* dust off the tree ornaments and wipe down the holly, Milo. I mean, maybe that was just to cover a search, but if he was pretending, there was no need to be quite so thorough about it. There was nobody around to fool."

"Except you," Milo pointed out. "Is it possible somehow he knew you were there?"

"That thought did occur to me," Meddy admitted. "I'm still a little freaked that Clem and Georgie and your mom saw me last night. But it was also perfectly clear that none of the new guests could see me. So I think Sylvester was telling the truth: he was just trying to undo some of Rob's mess." An uncomfortable expression flitted across her face. "One thing, though. When he was done, after he put all the cleaning stuff back in the kitchen, he just lay on the couch and fell asleep. He's still sleeping there now, but I can't swear he didn't get up in the night."

Milo shrugged. "It's okay. I understand. At least we can be pretty certain nobody snuck out with the rest of Violet Cross's stuff. You would've seen anybody who left as they crossed the lawn."

Meddy brightened. "Oh, that's true!"

"Right. So don't beat yourself up about it, okay? Let's get moving. We have a lot to do and maybe not much time."

nineteen

THE FEATHER LOCUS

O N THE FIRST FLOOR, they were greeted by the smell of coffee and the quiet noises of Mrs. Caraway puttering about in the kitchen. She turned at the sound of Milo's footfalls in the dining room. Then her good-morning smile froze for a moment on her lips as her eyes flicked sideways. Next to Milo, Meddy stiffened. "This is so awkward," she muttered.

But Mrs. Caraway quickly worked out who the oddly dressed stranger was, and her expression brightened into a welcome. "Good morning," she said warmly. "How lovely to see you!"

"Thanks," Meddy said a little self-consciously. "Nice to see you, too."

Mrs. Caraway hadn't called Meddy by name, Milo noticed.

Somebody else must be downstairs. "Anybody else up?" he asked casually.

Mrs. Caraway put a finger to the side of her nose. "Not that I'm aware of. We'll likely be serving brunch rather than breakfast today. But one of the young men — Sylvester, I think? — seems to have camped out down here."

Milo and Meddy headed into the living room, and they surveyed the sleeping caroler. "That's how he was when I checked on him last," Meddy said. "It doesn't look like he's moved at all."

Mrs. Caraway spoke from behind them. "I'll start some hot chocolate if you'd like, Milo." She looked uncertainly at Meddy. "Can I get you anything, sweetie?"

Meddy looked at Mrs. Caraway with an expression that made Milo think of a cornered animal. She glanced at the sofa, but Sylvester still looked dead to the world. "Um. No. Thanks."

Mrs. Caraway patted her shoulder awkwardly, as if she thought maybe her hand would go straight through Meddy's body. It didn't, of course, but Meddy flinched anyway. As soon as Mrs. Caraway returned to the kitchen, Meddy grabbed Milo's arm and dragged him to the loveseat by the living room's bow window.

"They're going to give me away if they're not careful," she complained in a low voice.

"I'll talk to them," Milo promised in a whisper as he put his rucksack on the floor. "Listen, I had an idea last night that I never got to tell you about. Remember I tried to get a storytelling thing going, but the Waits ruined it?"

"Yeah."

"Well, I figured maybe if I can't get the Waits to tell stories, then I'll try telling one myself. I asked your dad to tell me something about Violet Cross, a story I can tell the guests to see how they react. Then this morning I found this exploit solitaires can do, and I'm thinking that as Téngfēi, I might actually be able to pull it off."

"Which exploit?"

"It's called the Spinner of Lore."

Meddy's face screwed up in thought. "Which one is that?"

"The one where you can just spout stories or information or whatever and it has some specific effect on your audience. Think it has a chance of working?"

She considered, then shrugged. "Can't hurt, that's for sure. And we've got to do something."

"All right. Then I'll try at breakfast, assuming everyone turns up around the same time." Milo stopped whispering and smiled up at Mrs. Caraway, who had appeared beside the loveseat with a mug of hot chocolate. "Thank you." She ruffled his hair and bustled back to the kitchen. Outside, the gray clouds were brightening and breaking up to reveal scraps of a disappointingly blue sky. No snow today.

Milo's dad came yawning into the dining room a few minutes later. He wandered over to kiss Milo good morning, took bleary, confused notice of the newly clean living room, then shook his head and headed for the kitchen. Lizzie came down next, followed closely by Mrs. Pine. To Meddy's very great annoyance, all of them came over to say cheerful good mornings to Milo and to whisper awkward, cryptic greetings to her.

Fortunately, Sylvester Alforn slept on. Mrs. Pine gestured at the sleeper on the couch with her coffee cup. "He didn't sleep in his room?"

Milo shook his head. "He's the one who cleaned the living room. I came down last night and saw him doing it."

"Really? I assumed it was Mrs. Caraway and your dad. I was just about to go and say thank you."

"It was Sylvester. But don't tell him I told you. He asked me not to. I think he didn't want a big deal made out of it."

"Huh." She gave Sylvester a long, curious glance, then wandered back to the kitchen.

Emmett Syebuck was the first guest to surface. He came trotting down the stairs, looking fresh as a daisy and cheerful as whatever kind of flower is even more cheerful than a daisy. "Morning, all!" He whisked into the kitchen and returned with a cup of coffee. "Morning, Milo," he called as he breezed past the loveseat and out the door to the screened porch, presumably to get some painting in before breakfast. He barely glanced at Sylvester on the couch.

"Okay, I think we can confidently say *he* doesn't know I'm here," Meddy observed, relieved. "Now if we can just keep friends and family from spilling the beans, maybe we'll be okay."

"I'll go talk to them now," Milo said. But just as he got up, a herd of footsteps sounded on the creaky old stairs. Into the dining room came Lucky, Rob, Marzana, and Mr. Hakelbarend.

It was interesting, seeing them in daylight. Despite the varying degrees to which they were still dressed as Waits, they all seemed much more like . . . well, like ordinary folks. Except maybe Marzana, Milo noted. She still looked haunted. Or maybe she was just that uncomfortable being around people.

"Morning, all," Lucky called. She looked slightly embarrassed, which wasn't particularly mysterious. Lucky seemed to be the most invested in the tradition she and her cohorts had been attempting to carry out the night before. And that tradition had most definitely gone right off the rails. Milo felt a little sorry for her. None of it had been her fault, as far as he could tell.

Rob, on the other hand, looked like a guy who didn't have a care in the world as he sauntered toward the kitchen right in time to be the nearest person to Mrs. Pine when she asked, "Who can I get coffee for?"

"Oh, me, me, me," Rob said, holding out his hands for the cup she'd just poured. "Thanks, Mrs. Pine." He took a long sip and headed into the living room, where he stopped short at the sight of Sylvester snoring lightly on the couch. Then he glanced around. A tiny cascade of soot drifted out of his goatee as he scratched his chin in thought, taking in the absence of the ash-covered oilcloth and the gleaming surfaces that had sprouted in its place.

Lucky joined them and gave the room the same once-over. She glanced at Rob. "Did you do this?"

He shook his head. Both turned to the couch and the snoozing shape sprawled across it. "I'm guessing Sylvester did," Rob said over the rim of his cup.

Lucky's face softened. She went into the kitchen. When she

returned a moment later, she set a second mug on the coffee table, where it would probably be the first thing Sylvester saw when he woke. Then she went back to the dining room.

Rob glanced at Milo, who, along with Meddy, had watched this entire exchange over the back of the loveseat. The sweep took no notice of Meddy, but he waggled his eyebrows goofily at Milo. Then he went over to the couch and gave Sylvester's shoulder a gentle shove. "Wake up, Sy."

Two slightly less gentle shoves later, Sylvester finally yawned and stretched. "What's the big idea, jerk?" he asked sleepily.

"Oh, nothing," Rob replied breezily. "Only Lucky just brought you coffee and I figured you wouldn't want it to get cold."

That got Sylvester upright fast. "She what?" He stared in disbelief at the mug. "*Lucky* brought coffee for *me? What for?*"

"Because you didn't clean up that mess for my sake, and I'm pretty sure Lucky knows it just as well as I do." Rob winked, then left.

"What's he mean by that?" Meddy asked quietly.

Milo ducked down behind the back of the loveseat. "Maybe he wasn't just cleaning after all," he whispered. "Maybe those two know something we haven't figured out yet."

"Lucky," Sylvester called.

Milo peered over the back again. At the dining table, Lucky glanced up with an arch *Yes, can I help you?* look. She'd picked just about the only seat on that side of the house where she had a clear sightline to the couch.

Sylvester raised the cup. "Thanks."

"No, no," Lucky replied, raising her mug too. "Thank *you*."

"Oh." Meddy chuckled. "I get it."

Milo turned back to her. "Explain. What are they up to?"

"Isn't it obvious?" Meddy looked at him incredulously. "You said Lucky took this whole thing pretty seriously, right? And that it seemed like she felt responsible for all the craziness last night?"

"Yeah, so?"

"So, the biggest thing that went wrong was the chimney cleaning, wasn't it?" Meddy prompted. Milo nodded. "Well," she said with exaggerated patience, "I bet cleaning everything up was Sylvester's way of trying to make Lucky feel better. He stayed up all night to give her one less thing to worry about this morning." She smiled. "Better than flowers."

Milo rolled his eyes. "So what you're saying is that it has nothing to do with what we're trying to figure out."

"I'm *saying* I think it's kind of charming," Meddy repeated sourly. "But that doesn't mean he wasn't also up to something. Or that Lucky isn't up to something. So when are you going to do your lore-spinning thing?"

Milo craned his neck to look over the back of the seat. "We're still missing Mr. Larven and Mrs. Kirkegrim, plus Georgie and Clem. Might as well wait until everyone comes down. More of the Waits to watch, and more of our friends to keep an eye on them while I talk."

"Makes sense," she replied, which was a relief because he wasn't exactly feeling confident about his ability to work the Spinner of Lore, and although his excuse for not wanting to try it yet was legitimate, mainly he just wanted to put off being the center of attention for as long as possible.

Of course, he thought, *I don't have to pull off the Spinner of Lore. Téngfēi will do it. Might as well start getting into character.* "Let's get campaigning," Milo said quietly, slipping the locus ring onto his finger as Meddy pulled Sirin's blue-lensed spectacles from her pocket.

Téngfēi took his notebook from the rucksack and flipped to his notes on exploits. Only one looked useful just now — Clear-Sighted Perspicacity: *The weaknesses of your enemies become as clear to you as the bluest sky, as do the most elegant ways to exploit them.*

The problem was that he still wasn't sure he felt like Téngfēi. The solitaire took a few deep breaths, figuring if you were going for focus and calm, deep breaths had to be a good place to start. But he felt anything *but* focused and calm. *I couldn't get to Negret,* he thought nervously. *What makes me think I'll be able to just hop into this entirely new character I don't even know?*

"Use a locus," Sirin suggested softly. "Remember, you have tools to help you channel your energy."

"Right." He took the lacquered box from the rucksack. Sirin watched with interest as he lifted the lid and considered the contents, turning his mind to the backstory he'd created only a little while ago.

Remember that you are ever and always a monk of the air, and you are always my child. Each of these things will be a locus for you, and a reminder that I am always with you.

After a moment he took out the white feather. He ran it through his fingers once, twice. It had to be old, but it felt soft and fresh. He closed his eyes and slid the feather between thumb and forefinger again. *Remember flight,* he imagined Téngfēi's mother saying. *Remember wings brushing the clouds from the sky, just as this feather brushes the clouds from your mind.*

And Téngfēi opened his eyes to survey his surroundings.

twenty

TOO NORMAL

$\mathfrak{T}$HE GROUP IN THE DINING ROOM had the look of a mixed bunch of oddballs meeting in a tavern. It felt almost familiar to Téngfēi; oddballs often met up in taverns in Odd Trails games.

Marzana had commandeered one of the little breakfast tables, and no one had dared try to take that table's other chair. Mr. Hakelbarend sat at the opposite end of the dining table from Lucky, silhouetted against the green-tinted window. He had not, apparently, worn street clothes under his woodsman outfit, or presumably he would've come down to breakfast in something other than the leathers he'd worn the night before. Rob sat near him, talking away and occasionally pausing for Mr. Hakelbarend to reply, although those replies tended to be brief and disinterested. Now and then, Mr. Hakelbarend glanced at Marzana. But he never spoke to her, and she kept her eyes turned in the direction of the cold landscape outside. Sylvester seemed content to sit alone on the sofa, drinking his coffee and gazing into the freshly cleaned fireplace — when he wasn't glancing surreptitiously at Lucky.

Yes, Téngfēi realized, they all knew each other, but — and this came as something of a revelation — they weren't any more comfortable with each other than with the regular denizens of Greenglass House. They had undertaken the traditional caroling together, but they weren't old friends. Why hadn't it occurred to him earlier that this might be important?

"I'm going to talk to Lucky," Téngfēi whispered. He took his cup into the kitchen for a refill, then went to the table. "Hi," he said, sliding onto the bench next to her.

Lucky glanced at him, surprised. "Hey, there."

Téngfēi gave her a guileless smile. "Can I ask you something?"

She smiled back. "Sure thing."

"Were you here the last time the Waits came to our house?"

Lucky raised an eyebrow. "You mean the time we came and got turned away?"

The calm, focused solitaire blushed. "Um."

Her smile deepened into a grin. "No, no, it's okay. I'm just messing with you. Yes, I was here that time, but listen: that back-and-forth where you bid us in or don't isn't based on any expectation. We don't assume we're going to be invited into every house we visit. The idea is that when we *are* invited in, it's a true welcome. It's a gift. But it's not an insult when we're not." She tilted her head. "You understand?"

"I think so," Téngfēi said. "So our not inviting you in last time isn't the reason you didn't come back?"

"Well, last year no band of Waits made it out of the Liberty," Lucky said. "You remember that storm. But before that . . . well, yes, it was why we didn't come back for a while. We figured — and I hope you aren't offended by this, Milo — we figured we'd freaked you out, and we thought we'd give you some time before we tried again. You were much littler then. A couple years makes a big difference."

"I was freaked out," he admitted. "But I'm glad you came back."

"No hard feelings, then?" Lucky held out one hand.

"None." They shook. "So," Téngfēi said. "Who else was here last time?"

"That would've been what, three years ago?" Lucky thought for a moment. "Peter might've been the only one. Sylvester's gone caroling before —"

"Four times," Sylvester interjected from the couch. "Don't let her act like she and Pete are the only ones with history here."

"But he wasn't in our band that particular time," Lucky finished loudly. "Hey, Peter?"

Mr. Hakelbarend looked up. "Lucky?"

"You were with us last time we came to Greenglass House, right?"

The big man nodded. "It was you and I, the Wilkens brothers, and someone else. Who played the hobby horse that year?"

"Ada Cosset," Lucky supplied.

"Only five?" Téngfēi asked. "But there are seven of you now."

Lucky shrugged. "The number varies. It depends on how many people show up each year."

Lizzie stepped out from the other side of the island between the kitchen and the dining room and sat on one of the barstools. "How does that work, by the way? I was wondering." Téngfēi sent a silent *Thank you* in her direction. That was going to be his next question.

"You remember how we were explaining about the Raw Nights?" Lucky asked. "Well, that stretch of days makes up the caroling period. Each morning during that time, anybody who wants to take part comes to a particular meeting place. The people who show up get divided up into bands. We practice for most of the day, then head out and hit as many houses as we can. You guys are pretty isolated, but there's the other side of the hill, there's the monastery up at the top, plus some bands go into the Harbors and some go even farther down the hill, toward the city proper. Carolers can decide which band they want to go with, in case they're not comfortable venturing that far from home." She shrugged. "That's it. Some people only volunteer for one day. Some people volunteer for more."

"That's it?" Téngfēi asked. "People volunteer and there's a practice?" He thought back to the night before, when the bells and voices had seemed so otherworldly as they'd come in their ghostly procession through the trees. How outlandish and unknowable the group had appeared as they'd stood there singing with their glowing candles and gleaming bells. And the hobby horse! The idea that all that atmosphere, all that unfamiliar emotion and creepy beauty could come from just a bunch of volunteers with one day's practice just seemed too . . . too . . .

"Seems too normal?" Marzana asked quietly, as if Téngfēi had spoken out loud.

He hesitated. Because yes, that was it exactly—it did seem too normal. But then, so did all the members of the band, even haunted-looking Marzana, now that they were just lounging around his house. And he didn't want to admit that he'd expected them to be unusual, because they might think he'd assumed that because they'd come from the Liberty of Gammerbund. And that wasn't true. Or was it?

Téngfēi felt himself getting confused and embarrassed. Next to him, Lucky had stiffened too. She definitely thought he'd meant *too normal for folks who live in a madhouse.*

This was bad. He *hadn't* meant that, Téngfēi decided. But how could he explain it now? He could feel his face reddening.

I have an exploit for this, the solitaire thought desperately. For getting rid of pain and damage. *Pensive* something. *Pensive* he knew—it meant something like *thoughtful.* But the other word he couldn't remember. Téngfēi wiggled in his chair, trying to force the embarrassment and confusion away and get back some of his poise. But before he could manage the Pensive . . . *Pensive Elutriation,* that was it! He still didn't know what *elutriation* meant, but—

"We probably all seem a bit too normal to you today."

Téngfēi blinked and turned his head. It was Peter Hakelbarend who'd spoken into the awkward pause. He didn't look angry.

And Marzana, whose *too normal?* had thrown him for such a loop, was watching him with something like curiosity, and he realized that she genuinely wanted him to answer. Lucky might've decided she already knew what he thought, but Marzana hadn't made up her mind. She was waiting for him to explain himself. Their eyes met, and the strangest thing happened. Her strained expression softened for a minute. It wasn't exactly a smile, but the meaning behind it was clear. *I know what you're feeling. It's okay.* And as they looked at each other, Téngfēi also immediately understood something else about the strange girl. She hadn't merely *guessed* what he was feeling. She knew firsthand what that felt like.

The embarrassment. The conviction that he'd just said the completely wrong thing without having a clue that it would be the wrong thing. The sense that it had turned out to be the wrong thing in a way that he wasn't sure he could possibly have foreseen. The certainty that everyone else could see his discomfort. The not knowing how to fix any of it.

She feels this way all the time, Téngfēi realized abruptly. And his own expression must've shown his discovery, because Marzana's face bent briefly into something sympathetic, maybe even regretful. *Yes, we understand each other,* it said.

Something clicked, and the solitaire Téngfēi—or no, Téngfēi the ecstatic—made a mental note to think more deeply about this later.

For now, he decided to tell Marzana the truth. "Yes, I think *too normal* is what I meant, but I didn't want to say it. It's just that there *was* something about all of you coming through the night like that — the candles and bells, and . . . well, *you*," he admitted, feeling embarrassed again. "But I don't mean *you*, you," he added quickly. For some reason, Marzana actually grinned. She leaned her chin on one palm and waited for him to elaborate. So he tried to explain, even though he desperately wanted to climb under the table and hide. "You as the hobby horse, I mean — not the actual you." Flustered, he decided to quit talking and hope he hadn't just dug himself into a deeper hole than he'd already been in.

Marzana was still grinning, not that Téngfēi was particularly comforted by it. "That's why we didn't bring the hobby horse inside, you know," she said. "You can't just hang it up on the coat rack like a scarf."

"I'll tell you something about the hobby horse that'll put some of the mystery back into the Waits for you," Lucky offered. She was smiling now too. Téngfēi tried to decide whether he was relieved to know she wasn't mad or mortified at the possibility that he had gone from saying something *offensive-because-insensitive* to saying something *cute-because-funny*.

"Okay," he said helplessly.

Lucky's face went very serious. "There are five skulls used for hobby horses that we know of. So we can never have more than five bands — nobody would travel with a band that doesn't have a hobby horse, because the lore goes that during the Raw Nights all kinds of uncanny things rise up and walk the earth, but not even the worst of them will bother carolers in the company of a hobby horse. And all of the skulls are old. Maybe even ancient. There's one that's weirdly heavy, and the wrong color. Looks like petrified wood, not bone." She glanced at Peter. "The one with the blackbuck horns, isn't it? Big ridged corkscrews."

Mr. Hakelbarend nodded again. "The one our band used this year was gilded once upon a time, though most of the gold leaf is gone. Another one we think isn't an actual skull at all but a chunk of whalebone shaped to look like a horse's skull. Except it almost doesn't even look like it belonged to a horse. It looks like . . . like I don't know what. Some mythological creature that resembles a horse. Like what you'd get if you described a horse to someone who'd never seen one and asked him to carve its bones. It has an oryx horn, but just one — it's about four feet long and it curves backward, away from the skull's face. The whole assemblage is carved all over with scrimshaw. And it was red at one point."

"In between uses," Lucky continued, "for the entire year, except for the Raw Nights, they're all kept buried, mostly underground, in different places around the Liberty. One under the threshold of the oldest house; one under the altar of Saint Whit's Chapel; one in the middle of a garden, where nobody can get anything to survive but nettles that always grow taller than they should . . . . I think the tradition of burying them comes from England or Wales, because as I understand it, that's where the hobby horse originated — but there are plenty of oldsters in the Liberty who disagree. The truth is, nobody knows where the skulls came from. Nobody knows who made them, nobody knows why they're buried between uses, and nobody even knows how many there are. We have the five, but there could be others." She sat back with an expectant look. "Mysterious enough for you, sir?"

"Yeah," Téngfēi admitted. "That's pretty mysterious."

"What about the rest of the costumes?" Lizzie inquired.

"There are a bunch of traditions governing those, too," Sylvester put in from the living room. "But pretty much the only things that are consistent are that every band needs a sweep and a hobby horse. And the bells. There are always a metric ton of bells," he said sourly. "I pack aspirin."

"So Lucky and Sylvester and Mr. Hakelbarend are old hands at this," Téngfēi looked at Rob. "What about you?"

The sweep snorted. "First-timer. Couldn't you tell?"

Téngfēi thought back to the night before, and Lucky's dismissive *Noobs*. The comment hadn't been directed only at Rob. "You and Mrs. Kirkegrim, right?"

Marzana spoke up again. "And me."

Lucky cast an apologetic smile in her direction. "I know Marzana from work," she said. "She mentioned being curious about it all, and I convinced her to come along. Are you still going to speak to me when this is all over, by the way, Marzana? Or am I totally dead to you now?"

"Only mostly dead," Marzana replied. "Supposedly you can come back from that."

Téngfēi made another mental note to follow up on: he'd thought Marzana wasn't much older than him, but if she had a job and worked with Lucky, maybe he was wrong. "And you?" he asked Rob. "What made you join up?"

Rob shrugged. "I don't know. I kind of did it on a whim. I'm not usually a big 'holiday traditions' kind of guy."

"What about the other two?" Téngfēi asked. "Mrs. Kirkegrim and Mr. Larven?"

Lucky spoke up almost before he'd finished the question. "You should ask them." Something about her tone made Téngfēi shrink a little again. It wasn't brusque, exactly, but there was just the faintest hint of reproach in it.

Not long after that, Lizzie returned to the kitchen, and Mr. Pine went outside and brought back an armful of firewood, declaring, "Seems a shame not to use the fireplace when it's been freshened up so nicely." The enticing brunch smells beginning to drift out of the kitchen finally brought Emmett in from the porch. He glanced around, looking a little disappointed, then mumbled his good mornings and slid onto one of the barstools. Mrs. Kirkegrim appeared a few minutes later, looking exactly like someone who'd suffered head trauma and a migraine. Her eyes were almost as dark-rimmed as Marzana's.

"Morning, Mrs. Kirkegrim," Mr. Hakelbarend said, half rising from his seat. "I don't suppose you saw any evidence of Nick, did you?"

"Nope," Mrs. Kirkegrim said shortly. "But if the bender he went on was as serious as I heard, I bet he sleeps until noon." The poinsettia by the dining table, which was looking rather sad this morning, dropped two petals as she squeezed between it and Mr. Hakelbarend's chair on her way to the vacant breakfast table by the bow window.

A vaguely embarrassed silence followed. "We were just talking about what brought everyone to the band this year," Lucky said at last in an obvious effort to change the subject.

Mrs. Kirkegrim made an interested face. "Oh." Another silence followed. Either she hadn't picked up on the prompt or she'd just chosen to ignore it.

Téngfēi decided not to let her off the hook so easily. "What about you, Mrs. Kirkegrim?"

She regarded him curiously. "What about me?"

There was something in her expression that made Téngfēi absolutely certain her response was not so much a question as a challenge. Milo might have withered a little under the weight of that challenge, but Téngfēi merely thought, *Well, that's curious.*

He was just about to clarify his query when Rob spoke up. "Should we try to wake him? Nick, I mean."

Lucky made an exasperated noise. "I guess. We should be going. Asking for hospitality is part of the tradition, but this is ridiculous."

"No one's leaving until after brunch," Mrs. Caraway said decisively, setting a basket of biscuits and a rack of butter and jams in little jars on the table. "It'll be ready in a half an hour. So let's not hear any more about it until then. These should tide you over."

"Exactly what I was going to say," Mrs. Pine added, coming over with a stack of plates and a huge handful of cutlery.

Sirin had been lurking in the vicinity of the loveseat, probably to avoid giving any of the regulars the temptation to talk to her. Now she hurried to Téngfēi's side. "If they get moving after breakfast, we have about an hour and a half to find the rest of what's been stolen before it has like an eighty-seven percent chance of walking out the door."

She spoke quietly, but of course she still was perfectly audible to Mrs. Pine, who nearly dropped her collection of cutlery in surprise. "Stolen?" she repeated in a shocked tone.

Sirin and Téngfēi turned to stare at her in horror. *Of course*, Téngfēi realized. They hadn't told his parents about Violet Cross's cache having gone missing the night before.

Unfortunately, everyone else turned to stare at Mrs. Pine too.

"I'm sorry, did you say, 'stolen'?" Rob asked.

"Stollen," Mrs. Caraway said smoothly, giving the word a slightly different pronunciation. "It's a family specialty. Lizzie's stollen is legendary. It would be a shame to miss it."

Lizzie blanched, then picked up her cue. "Mom, you were supposed to remind me to start the stollen this morning. I completely forgot about it."

"What's stollen?" Marzana inquired.

"It's a kind of sugar-dusted fruit pastry," Lizzie said over her shoulder as she hurried into the kitchen. "Halfway between bread and cake. It's traditional at this time of year in Germany. I don't know if it ever came up last night, but I'm a baker."

Téngfēi slid off the bench and headed for the stairs, relying on the discussion of international baked goods to cover his exit. Sirin fled up the stairs after him, fuming. "We have got to do something about them, Téngfēi. They're going to ruin everything if they can't play it cool."

"I know, I know," Téngfēi muttered. "But how was I supposed to remind them once all the Waits started turning up?"

"I'll tell them," Sirin said irritably. "That's what we should've done in the first place. I can tell them without any of the others overhearing. But right now we have work to do. We have to find this stuff before it's too late. Where do we start?"

"Let's check in with Clem and Georgie first." Then Téngfēi stopped halfway between the second and third floors. "Sirin, what if the thief has it all on him right now? The only things left are the reflecting circle, which according to Clem isn't that big, and a bunch of locks and keys."

Sirin chewed her lip. Then she shook her head decisively. "None of them look like they're ready to walk out the door."

"Oh. Good point. But," Téngfēi reasoned, "whoever our thief is, he's got to be ready to go quickly, right?"

"Presumably. Or she," Sirin reminded him as they started up again. "We can't rule out the girls. But yeah, whoever it is probably can't be planning to run all over the house collecting a whole bunch of stuff."

"And remember what Georgie said — that she and Clem figured it was unlikely the thief would stow stuff in his or her own room because —" Téngfēi stopped on the third-floor landing just in time to hear a very soft click. Only because he'd lived in the inn his entire life did he know immediately what that click was. 3N had a weird defect in the door. If you wanted to close it quietly, you had to push up on the doorknob to lift the entire door up and over the jamb, but doing that made the slightly misaligned top hinge that was the root of the problem click.

"Because," Téngfēi continued through gritted teeth, "Georgie and Clem were guaranteed to search everyone's rooms first."

Sirin followed his glare. "That's Barbara Kirkegrim's room, right?"

"Yup." Téngfēi walked down the hall and knocked on the door of 3N. "Room service." He opened the door and swung it wide.

The room appeared to be empty, but come on. Sirin closed the door, and Téngfēi glanced around. The bathroom door was ajar. He leaned in, yanked the shower curtain aside, and glared at Georgie, who was standing in the tub trying to look as if she belonged there. "Morning! Did we miss breakfast?" she asked innocently.

"It's almost eleven, and no, because we're having brunch today, and did you or did you not tell me only an amateur would've hidden the stuff in their own room?" Téngfēi demanded.

"No stone unturned," Georgie said with an attempt at a charming smile.

"Did you or did you not tell me you and Clem weren't planning to break into anyone else's rooms?"

"Any port in a storm?" Georgie hazarded.

"Out," Téngfēi ordered, pointing. Sirin put on a matching severe face and pointed too.

"We figured once they left their rooms, they were probably done with them," Georgie explained as she stepped out of the tub.

"And yet, while you were—I believe the term is *tossing*?—while you were *tossing* the room, you could not have failed to notice that." Téngfēi pointed to Mrs. Kirkegrim's red cloak, which was folded neatly across the luggage rack.

"Yes," she said, eyeing the cloak. "*Tossing* is the word you want."

"Out," Téngfēi said again.

Sirin left first to make sure the coast was clear; Téngfēi and Georgie followed. Georgie closed the door after herself and scowled up at the clicking hinge. "I guess that's how you knew, huh?"

"You should leave the searching to us," Téngfēi hissed back. "We know how to avoid that kind of stuff."

"To be fair," Georgie protested, "so do Clem and I. We just don't have the luxury of putting every little trick into practice. Time's short. Who knows when these guys'll cut out?"

Sirin had paused next to the door of 3W. "I can tell you it's not going to be anytime soon. Not the way that guy's snoring."

"In any case, we're going to take over the hunt now," Téngfēi said firmly. "No more searching other guests' rooms. Mom and Dad would be so mad."

Georgie sighed, walked back down the hall to 3S, and rapped a gentle pattern on the door. A moment later Clem slipped out. She stopped short on seeing Téngfēi and Sirin. "Ah." She gave them a guilty wave.

"These were the last two rooms anyway," Georgie admitted. "We did Sylvester's last night while he was cleaning—that dude never even used his room—and everybody else's as they came downstairs. No luck." She glanced at Clem. "Unless you found something."

"I did not."

"You're cut off," Téngfēi said. "Both of you."

Clem opened her mouth, but whatever she was about to say was silenced in an instant as the big old bell on the front porch gave one and then another deep but brittle bong. "Wow," Clem said when she found her voice again.

Sirin laughed. "Because of course someone else was going to show up."

Georgie just dropped her face into her palms.

Téngfēi shook his head. "Somehow I still didn't see that coming."

After a brief, hushed conference, the four of them decided that another person showing up might prompt the others, or at least some of them, to get themselves in gear to leave. So with one last admonishment from Téngfēi to stay out of occupied guest rooms, they split up to make a thorough search of the halls and staircases before that happened. Sirin took the third floor, since it was most likely to be visited first if the Waits decided to get a move on. Georgie took the fourth and Clem the fifth.

"I'll take the second floor," Téngfēi suggested. "We know people were in and out of our living room already. And it's a logical spot to hide something, especially since my family was too preoccupied to spend any time there."

As it happened, though, he barely had time to begin before he heard someone coming up. Two people, and he didn't have long to wonder who they were. "Hey, Milo?" Mr. Pine called.

Téngfēi came out of the living room. "Yeah?"

Mr. Pine emerged from the stairwell. "Seen Clem anywhere this morning? Is she awake yet?"

"Um. Yeah," Téngfēi answered, hoping he sounded less cagey than he felt, since he didn't especially want to say *where* he'd seen her. But then he spotted the newcomer on the stairs behind his father. It was a young man, smiling and waving. Owen, Clem's fiancé.

twenty-one

TALKING TO GIRLS

ILO TOOK THE SOLITAIRE'S RING from his finger and shoved it in his pocket. He couldn't decide whether to be delighted for his own sake — Owen was the only other Chinese adoptee he knew — or apprehensive for Clem's.

"Want to show Owen up?" Mr. Pine asked.

"Sure thing," Milo said, trying to sound as if he was in no way involved in Clem's lies, which Owen had apparently not been remotely fooled by. "Let's go."

Mr. Pine stood aside and Owen trotted up the stairs. He had a backpack over one shoulder, and he put his other arm around Milo in a hurried hug. "Can't wait to chat," he said. "Gotta check in with the ladies first, though."

His tone was light and friendly, but since the one thing Milo understood about the idea of a "bachelorette weekend" was that the groom wasn't supposed to be there, he figured Owen couldn't possibly be feeling as lighthearted as he sounded.

"I totally get it," Milo said as the two of them continued on together.

Owen shot him a dark look. "Do you?" he asked.

"Um." Milo put on some speed, taking the stairs two at a time so he reached the fourth floor a few steps ahead of Owen and with just enough time to wave frantically at Georgie, who had stopped searching and was standing in her own doorway, waiting to see what this new arrival signified. She took the hint and slipped into her room.

Clem was technically staying on four, of course, but she was more likely still searching on five. Milo hesitated, then decided the problem was best solved by shouting. "Hey, Clem!" he yelled, trying and failing to make it sound casual. "I think she's in four W," he added to Owen as the young man arrived on the landing behind him.

"Let's not pretend we don't know what's going on here," Owen said drily as he headed for the door Milo indicated.

Buddy, Milo thought sympathetically, *you don't know the half of it.*

As Owen raised his fist to knock, Milo felt a hand on his shoulder. Clem moved him gently aside. "I'm right here."

Owen turned to look at her, and Milo was surprised by his expression. He'd expected that Owen would be angry. And he was, or at least frustrated. You could tell from the set of his mouth, some-how. But the rest of his face was relieved.

"Clem," he said. His voice matched his face.

Before anybody could reply, the door of 4W flew open. Georgie burst out, already protesting. "Don't be mad at her! It was my fault. It was *all* my fault."

Owen held up one finger in warning, but Clem put a hand on his wrist. "Georgie," she said tiredly, "please, not this time." She opened the door to her room and pushed Owen inside. "I'm tell-ing him everything," she said to Milo and Georgie. "If you could keep watch and warn me if any of the others come up, but . . . you know. Give us what privacy you can." Translated: *You're going to hear everything we say, and we all know it. But please pretend not to.*

Side by side in the hallway, Milo and Georgie nodded. Clem cracked her neck, then went into her room and shut the door. Milo slid down the opposite wall. Georgie ducked briefly back into her room and returned with a small handful of fabric and glass, then sat next to him. They looked at each other, then away without saying a word. Georgie set the fabric in her lap and began carefully sorting through small pieces of mirror.

"What are you doing?" Milo whispered. "Where'd you get all that?"

"New project," she whispered back. "This was the glass in my satchel. Mirrors can be useful during"—she glanced at Clem's closed door—"during adventures, so I usually keep a few pieces with me."

Across the hall, hushed voices began speaking. "Two weeks, Ottilie."

Oh, that's right, Milo remembered. Ottilie was Clem's middle name. "He's the only one who calls her that," Georgie mumbled, staring at the glass in her lap.

"It was supposed to be my last hurrah," Clem said. "That was the whole idea."

"Did you really need a last hurrah when you were only quitting for two weeks?"

Her voice spiked in volume. "No, I needed a last hurrah because I was *quitting* quitting!"

Both Milo and Georgie winced. "Too loud," Milo said under his breath. At that volume, Clem would be audible in the stairwell.

A short silence followed. "What do you mean, *quitting* quitting?" Owen asked quietly.

"You know what I mean." Clem sounded cranky. "Just because you hadn't asked yet—"

"Wait a minute, Clemence. It's not that I hadn't asked *yet*. I *never* asked, except for this one time because I wanted to have a wedding and honeymoon without worrying. And yes"—here Owen lowered his voice even further—"I know how good you are, but that's probably never going to stop me from worrying when you're on a gig. This wasn't, like, a way to get you used to the idea of getting a straight job." Another silence. "For crying out loud, is that what you thought?"

Silence.

"It is, isn't it?"

Silence.

A very small noise.

Owen's next words were muffled, just barely audible: "Ottilie, how could you even stand to look at me if that's what you thought?"

Georgie gave a quiet hiss. Milo glanced over and saw that she had cut her thumb on a piece of mirror. She stuck the finger in her mouth and whacked the back of her head against the wall.

A moment later, Meddy appeared in the stairwell. She looked at Milo and Georgie in disbelief. "What are you doing?" she demanded.

"Sentry duty," Georgie said dully.

"Well, wrap it up," Meddy said. "Mrs. Pine says it's time for brunch. And that had better be the last time anyone talks to me in view of anyone who can't see me." She jabbed a finger at Georgie. "Including you." She jabbed the same finger at Clem's door. "And you can pass the word that it includes them, too."

"You go," Georgie said to Milo. "I'll wait for them."

"Okay." Milo got to his feet. "But you guys should come down as soon as you can. I have a plan, but I need all the eyes and ears I can trust."

"What plan?" Georgie asked.

"Stories. I'm going to make it work this time."

Georgie tapped two fingers to her forehead in a halfhearted salute. "Copy that."

"I guess you didn't find anything on the third floor," Milo said as he and Meddy started down the stairs.

She shook her head. "Not before your mom came looking for

us. I think it was less about brunch, actually, and more about finding out what I was talking about when I mentioned stolen stuff. I had to tell her. I told her you'd meant to, but then I showed up last night and you forgot." Meddy gestured back toward the floor they'd just left. "That's Owen, right? How's all that working out?"

"I don't know. I think Clem's crying, but I can't tell if it's a good thing or not."

"We're not getting anywhere," Meddy grumbled. "This is just going to be another distraction."

"I don't know," Milo said thoughtfully. He stopped on the second-floor landing, under the red and green window. "I think we did learn some stuff this morning. I wasn't sure how it would've been possible for the thief to be one of the Waits. I mean, for any of them to be involved in Georgie and Clem's thing, it would've had to mean that either that unknown master thief, Cantlebone, or someone working for the other guy, Gilawfer, had managed to get himself or herself into the Liberty of Gammerbund and into the band. Now that we know the Waits are all volunteers and the bands only came together yesterday morning, that seems a lot more possible."

"But some of them did know each other beforehand," Meddy reminded him.

"Yeah. I think I need to work this out on paper."

"And then you'll tell your story?"

He couldn't put it off much longer if he was ever going to try it. "Yes. But first, maybe I can figure out who we should be watching, at least. Narrow things down a little."

As she often did when there were large groups, Mrs. Caraway

had set the meal out buffet-style on the big dining table. The guests, with the exception of Clem, Owen, Georgie, and Mr. Larven, were already in various stages of getting food and finding places to sit and eat. "Meet me at the loveseat," Milo said quietly to Meddy, when he was certain no one was looking their way.

"Right." Then she stopped short. "Or not." Milo followed her pointing finger. Barbara Kirkegrim was already there with her plate.

"Well, that's inconvenient," he said under his breath. His other usual spot, the corner behind the Christmas tree, was almost certainly guaranteed not to have an adult in it, but it had some problematic sightlines if you wanted to be able to observe anyone while having your quiet time.

"Inconvenient, but not the end of the world." Now Meddy was looking toward the dining room window. "How are you at talking to girls?"

"What?" He picked up a plate from the pile at the end of the table. Although they had a certain amount of cover due to the hubbub of a bunch of people filling dishes and looking for places to sit, he couldn't stand in the middle of the room apparently talking to nobody.

"Girls, Milo. How are you at talking to girls? Live ones, I mean. Or at least, I assume she's alive." Meddy pointed to where Marzana was still sitting by herself at one of the little breakfast tables. "If you sit with Marzana, you'll have a view of all three rooms. Not perfect, but decent. And maybe there's more she can tell you."

Milo couldn't answer aloud, but he hoped a truly incredulous look would convey to Meddy what he needed it to. Sit at one of those little tables with a girl who was, he was pretty sure, not that much older than he was? Inconceivable. What would she think? What would he say?

Yes, Meddy got the message. The look she gave him in response seemed as if it should be physiologically impossible: she managed to lower her eyelids and lift one eyebrow at the same time, all while molding the rest of her face into an expression of complete disdain and amusement. The expression informed Milo with perfect clarity that, while a lesser person would've had to choose between ridiculing him for a general lack of pluck or a more specific lack of courage related to the most basic, level-one boy-girl relations, Meddy was *not* a lesser person. *Meddy* could comment witheringly on the full spectrum of cowardice and generally ridiculous boy behavior Milo was currently displaying, all without wasting a single word.

"How are you doing that?" Milo whispered, awed.

Lucky, who had found a spot at the end of the table where she'd been sitting earlier, looked up from her plate. "Doing what?"

"Saving the bacon for last," Milo improvised. "I always try, but I end up eating it first."

"Easy," Lucky replied. "I sit by the bacon plate so I can just get more."

"Smart," Milo said. "Maybe I'll join—"

"Get over there," Meddy ordered. "Immediately."

"Never mind," Milo mumbled. There was nothing to do in the face of such authority and scorn but obey and hope he could prove himself worthy of Meddy's approval again. Even if it meant talking to a real, live girl.

Meekly, he finished filling his plate. As he did, first Clem and Owen and then Georgie descended the stairs, which bought him another minute or two of time while Owen introduced himself to the group at large. But in the end, there was no putting it off any longer. Milo edged around Lucky to Marzana's table. "Um." He cleared his throat. Marzana looked up from her french toast. "Can I sit with you? Here," he corrected himself. "Can I sit here, I mean?"

Her eyes shot sideways to Lucky, who was definitely within earshot but who — thank heavens — pretended not to have heard and kept her eyes on her own plate. Marzana glanced around, probably checking to see if there was somewhere else Milo could've chosen to sit instead. Fortunately the place was looking pretty crowded.

Feeling Meddy's eyes on his back, Milo forced himself to wait out these indignities. Her contempt would be titanic if he backed down now.

"Sure," Marzana finally said. "If you want." She moved her mug and orange juice closer to her plate to make room for Milo's stuff. Her drinks had been a bit too far away from her to have been placed there naturally. Probably she'd arranged them that way so that nobody would try to sit with her.

"Great," Milo said weakly. He set down his plate and pulled out the chair. This was awkward. "So I guess . . . are you feeling better?"

Her face, which had started looking a little too amused for his comfort, twitched into a frown for a moment. "Feeling better?"

"Yeah, you know, since last night. When you and Mrs. Kirkegrim got knocked in the head."

"Oh, that." She cut a piece of french toast. "Yes. Much better, thanks."

Milo ate a bite, then two. He tried to think of something else to say. Plenty came to mind, all questions Meddy was probably expecting him to ask — what did she do for a job with Lucky, what was her last name, how had she wound up playing the hobby horse and where had they left the costume, why did she live in the Liberty (a question he longed to ask every member of the Waits) — but somehow every question seemed as if it would add to the awkwardness.

Before he could choose one and forge ahead, Marzana herself spoke up. "Can I ask you a question, Milo?"

That was unexpected. "Sure."

She suddenly looked shy, and Milo remembered that talking to people made her nervous too. "Which do you think is the best window in the house?"

Oh, right. Marzana, like Lucky, had been curious about the windows even before coming here. Milo thought for a moment. "If you mean which one do I *like* best, the one in our upstairs living room. The huge one. You saw it, but I don't know if you remember it." *Since you got conked right after that. Sorry.* "But there's a cool enameled glass window on the fifth floor — it's painted, not stained — and there's the chandelier here in the dining room, which is pretty neat even if it's not a window. It's a ship, though you have to look at it just right to see that."

Marzana looked thoughtfully at the chandelier for a long moment, then brightened. "Oh! I do see it!"

"I forgot that you said you'd been curious about Greenglass

House. How do you know about it?" Milo asked. She'd seemed uncomfortable when he'd asked before, but maybe since she'd opened the door to conversation this time, she wouldn't mind answering.

"Well, it isn't like the Liberty doesn't get news from outside," she answered a little defensively. "It's a big place. Bigger than you probably realize. We have about as many citizens as any of the regular Nagspeake districts, just concentrated into a smaller space, and plenty of Liberty dwellers come and go all the time. We're not required to stay there. It is, technically, still Nagspeake, and we're free citizens."

"Most of us," Mrs. Kirkegrim put in as she crossed from the loveseat to the table to get seconds. "Most of us are free citizens." Interesting.

Being honest with Marzana had been a good choice last time. "I don't really understand how the Liberty works," Milo admitted. "Do you think you could tell me a little bit about it? It's okay if not," he added hastily, remembering that while he truly hated when people made assumptions about him as an adopted kid, he didn't much like strangers asking even well-intentioned questions about it either. And still no one from the Liberty had done either of those things, which continued to be remarkable to him.

"Maybe I shouldn't have asked," he said. "I'm sorry."

"I like that you did." Marzana hesitated. Something shifted in her posture. Before, it had been as if she was held together with rubber bands that all pulled her inward, closing her up. Now she straightened and some of the nervous tension seemed to dissipate. "You know, the person you should ask is Peter. He knows a lot about the Liberty, and he could tell you how it came to be the way it is — sort of a whole second city within the city of Nagspeake. But I was born in the Liberty and I've lived there my whole life. It's all I know, so I'm not sure I can tell you how it's different from your part of Nagspeake." The surprise Milo felt must have shown on his face, because some of the defensiveness in her posture returned. "It's not that I've never left the Liberty," she clarified quickly. "I have. I've seen some of the rest of the city, and I've traveled a little, so I've seen other cities too. But I've never seen your house before. I only heard about it."

"You heard about it? From who?"

She hesitated again. "From my mom."

Milo brightened. "Then I bet I know her! What's her name?"

Marzana smiled, but she shook her head. "No, you wouldn't have met her. I think she visited the house once, and it would've been before you were born." She paused, then admitted, "I was going to say, I guess I do have some idea of how the Liberty is different. But all the things I was thinking of, the things that set us apart . . . well, those exist in other cities too. Like the citizens being sort of insular and not wanting a ton of visitors — that happens all over the world. And the wall. Maybe we've held on to ours a little longer than most, but there have been walled cities for thousands of years."

She was calling it a *walled city,* but that didn't quite jibe with what Milo thought he knew about the Liberty of Gammerbund. "But wasn't the wall around the Liberty meant to keep people in, not out?" he asked cautiously. "At some point?" After all, the Liberty was, or had been, an asylum. That was why less sensitive people than the Pines often called it the madhouse.

Marzana shrugged. "Ask Peter. People say different things about that, but Peter's a good source. I trust what he says."

Mr. Hakelbarend spoke up from the far end of the big dining table. "You do?" He snorted, but there was humor in the sound. "That's news to me."

"I don't always *like* what he says," Marzana amended loftily, "but I almost always trust it." She gave Milo a curious look. "You said something about stories last night, didn't you? Lucky was telling me so this morning."

"I thought it would be fun," Milo replied. Had she just handed him the perfect opening? Why, yes, she had. "I'm a fan of *The Raconteur's Commonplace Book*. Do you know it?"

"Yeah, I like that one too." Thoughtfully, Marzana took a sip of orange juice. "Okay, well, I gather it didn't go so well last night, but I bet if you asked Peter to tell a story about the Liberty, he'd do it. And you should ask Lucky about the—which is it, Lucky?" she asked, swiveling in her seat. "The hobby horse skull with that very cool story behind it?"

"They all have very cool stories," Lucky said. "But I think you mean the one I told when I invited you."

"Would you guys really do that?" Milo asked, pivoting to address the Waits at either end of the big table.

"Tell stories?" Mr. Hakelbarend pushed back his sleeve and

consulted a watch that was a bit too modern and nice to go with his huntsman outfit. Then he glanced at Mrs. Pine, who was filling her plate. "I don't know."

Rob spoke up from the bar between the kitchen and the dining room. "Come on, what's the rush?" He gestured toward the stairs. "Nick isn't even up yet, for crying out loud."

"We should do it," Mrs. Kirkegrim said brusquely. She'd been standing near the table, eating on her feet, apparently employing Lucky's post-up-by-the-bacon strategy. "If I hadn't been unconscious last night when Milo suggested it, I would've told one then."

Georgie spoke up from the sofa. "I think it's a perfect idea. A story from a guest is a gift to the host. There are all kinds of folk traditions where that's true."

In the dining room, Lucky nodded. "That's the whole thing behind caroling. That's what a song is, after all. It's a story."

"I think it would be fun," Emmett's voice said. Milo couldn't see him but figured he must've been sitting on the hearth.

"Anyway," Mrs. Kirkegrim said drily, "unless Miss Caraway has some magical capabilities with bread that makes the dough not have to rise for hours, we still have a good wait ahead of us if we're sticking around for stollen."

From where she stood kneading dough at one of the counters in the kitchen, Lizzie couldn't see Mrs. Kirkegrim, but she could hear her. "I'm modifying the recipe," she grumbled loudly, giving the mass a sharp punch with one fist. "It won't have to rise nearly that long."

Mrs. Kirkegrim carried her plate into the kitchen. She leaned over Lizzie's shoulder and examined the clump beneath her hands. "If you say so." She refilled her coffee cup and positioned herself just outside the kitchen to address both the living and dining rooms. "We've imposed upon the residents of Greenglass House to a ridiculous degree. This is a small way to give something back." She turned to the dining table. "Lucky, Peter, I know Marzana sort of volunteered you, but are you willing? If, of course," she added, almost as an afterthought, "it's okay with the Pines."

Milo's father, who was sitting at the dining table to one side of Mr. Hakelbarend, nodded easily. "We love a good story around here. Nora?"

Mrs. Pine had taken the second stool at the bar. "Absolutely. We'd be honored."

"Then sure, I'll do it," Lucky said immediately. Mr. Hakelbarend took a moment longer, but he, too, agreed.

"Good. Three would be a good number." Mrs. Kirkegrim looked expectantly at the rest of the group. Her eyes settled on Georgie. "Maybe one from you, too, for variety . . . ?"

Emmett clapped his hands. "I second that."

Georgie gave him a low-lidded glare. "You know, I just bet you do."

Somehow, though Milo could not remotely fathom the science behind it, Emmett managed not to wilt under the weight of that glare. Was it a skill that came from years of weathering girls' disdain? Whatever it was, it was impressive. *I need to know how to do that,* he thought wistfully.

Meanwhile, Meddy appeared at Milo's shoulder. "This is so very definitely Téngfēi's cue, Milo."

He straightened and raised a hand. "I have one, Mrs. Kirkegrim."

Mrs. Kirkegrim looked at him appraisingly. "That's great, Milo. Thank you. Maybe you want to start things off?"

"No, I'll go last," he said. Meddy's hand clamped on his shoulder and squeezed, which he interpreted to mean she thought he should get on with it. But he wasn't just putting off the act of getting up and speaking in front of everyone. He didn't want to risk the others changing the stories they might have told as a result of their reactions to his tale about Violet Cross. "And if anybody else wants to tell one, that's fine too," he added quickly.

"All right, then, it's settled," Clem said, getting to her feet. "I vote non-storytelling guests volunteer for kitchen patrol first, and then we have the stories afterward so no one misses anything. Stories are awesome, but someone else doing the dishes is a truly epic gift too. What do you say, Mrs. K?"

Mrs. Kirkegrim sighed. "I would be a horrible person to refuse, wouldn't I?"

"Yes," Clem agreed, linking her arm through the older woman's. "You would. Also you, Smoky," she added, pointing at Rob. "Get in here. And, Sylvester, you can clear the table."

Marzana spoke up, though she waited until Sylvester had come as far as the dining table. "I'll do it." She rose, edged around Lucky, and gave Sylvester a little push toward the table. "Sylvester, you sit."

Sylvester smiled an embarrassed little smile, but he allowed himself to be maneuvered to the seat next to Lucky. "Thanks, Spooky."

"Not my name," Marzana said as she started piling up dishes.

twenty-two

FORTRESSES AND FIREWORKS

CLEM KICKED MRS. CARAWAY out of the kitchen. Lizzie was allowed to remain until she had worked the stollen dough into two loaves and set it aside to rise by the stove. Then she, too, was ejected. Marzana cleared away the remnants of brunch while Clem, Mrs. Kirkegrim, and Rob tackled the dishes: one washing, one wiping, and one putting away.

Meddy slid into the seat across from Milo. "Can I see you in private, please?"

He stood and headed for the living room and the space behind the tree, pausing along the way to pick up his rucksack from where he'd left it by the loveseat earlier that morning. A quick check told him the engraved lock was still inside where he'd left it. Owen had joined Marzana in clearing the table, and now the only people left in the living room were Georgie, who was drinking her coffee on the sofa and seemingly intent on not being disturbed as she sketched something on a paper napkin between sips, and Emmett, who was drinking his coffee on the hearth and plainly waiting for Georgie to quit looking so forbidding so he could try to strike up a conversation with her. "What are you working on now?" he asked finally.

"A stereoscope," she said without looking up.

"Cool. You're going to need some—" Emmett stopped speaking as, without so much as glancing his way, Georgie reached into the pocket of her sweater, produced two mirrors, and held them up, fanned like a pair of playing cards. "Oh."

He was way too close to the tree cave. Milo thought about going back to the loveseat, but if he and Meddy were going to have a real conversation about everything they'd learned and not get caught at it, they needed more cover than that spot could provide. He coughed, caught Georgie's eye, and gave a quick, significant jerk of his head in Emmett's direction. Georgie's eyes narrowed. Then she sighed.

"Hey, Emmett," she said halfheartedly, setting down her pencil.

The art student brightened. "Yes?"

"Come tell me about the painting you're working on."

"Really?" He glanced at Milo in disbelief. The guy might have had a crush, but he was no idiot.

Milo returned what he hoped was an encouraging nod. *What are you waiting for, nerd?*

"Unless you don't feel like talking about it," Georgie said, retreating back into her coffee cup, as cool as anything. "No prob-lem."

"No, no." He was on his feet in a flash. "Shall I show you?"

Georgie managed a reasonably convincing smile and followed him to the screened porch, leaving Milo and Meddy alone in the living room.

Once they were safely hidden away behind the tree, Meddy all but exploded. "Talk!"

Milo put on Téngfēi's ring, then dug his spiral pad out of his bag and opened to a clean page. "Hang on," he said quietly. "We have to write down what we learned just before Owen showed up. Because I think it's clear that whoever we're looking for, Cantle-bone or Gilawfer, we have to focus on the Waits."

Meddy put on the blue glasses. "You're eliminating Emmett?"

"For the moment. Because *the Waits aren't leaving*. Granted, Mom started it this morning, saying nobody was leaving until after brunch, and at first I thought *we* were the ones buying time to look for the missing stuff. But now they're the ones stringing out their stay, probably so the thief has time to find a way to recover what was left in Georgie's room."

He wrote down the names of six of the Waits in two columns: Lucky, Mr. Hakelbarend, and Sylvester on one side; Marzana, Rob, and Mrs. Kirkegrim on the other. "These three are regular carol-ers," Téngfēi said, tapping the first column. "And these three are first-timers this year. Mr. Larven I'm not sure about. We'll put him over here." He wrote the mustachioed man's name in a separate spot with a question mark.

"You think the person we're looking for has to be a first-timer, right?"

"I think it's most likely. Either Cantlebone or Gilawfer's henchman passed himself or herself off as a Liberty resident in order to volunteer for the band of Waits coming to Greenglass House. From what Marzana told me, the Liberty certainly has enough people, and they come and go often enough for an outsider to claim to be from there without anybody knowing. And since the bands only come together the day of the caroling, there was definitely time for Cantlebone or Gilawfer to settle on this plan and put it into action."

"Okay, so theoretically these are our suspects." Sirin pointed to the second column: Marzana, Rob, Mrs. Kirkegrim.

"Right. And we're looking for a person who could do three things: poison Mr. Larven's punch, conk Marzana and Mrs. Kirkegrim, and steal Georgie and Clem's stuff."

"I suppose Mr. Larven's passing out is all the delay the thief needed," Sirin pointed out, "but let's not forget that there was also the botched chimney cleaning — which was all Rob — and this storytelling session, which was Mrs. Kirkegrim."

"Well, Marzana kind of suggested the storytelling first," Téngfēi said slowly. For some reason he didn't like the idea of considering Marzana a suspect, but just because she was a kid wasn't a good enough reason to eliminate her.

Sirin shook her head. "But Marzana joined the Waits this year because Lucky invited her. Plus, she was one of the conking victims. I think that rules her out."

"So that leaves Mrs. Kirkegrim and Rob," Téngfēi said. "But

Mrs. Kirkegrim was one of the conking victims too, so that eliminates her, as well. And even though Rob was directly responsible for the chimney-cleaning debacle, he's the only one in the house who has an ironclad alibi for everything else. *Because* of the chimney-cleaning debacle. He's the only one whose whereabouts we definitely know for the entire evening."

"Well, there's also Mr. Larven," Sirin said, tapping the lonely name in the corner of the page. "But he gets a pass due to poisoned punch."

Téngfēi sat back and frowned at the lists. "So there's actually nobody among the first-timers who could've done everything."

Sirin nodded silently, then yanked the pad from Milo's hands and started turning pages. "Maybe we're confusing things by worrying about who could do it all. Let's start from first principles. We know there was a theft, and that's the main thing, right? So who could've done the theft?"

She found the page she wanted and held it up. Téngfēi read the notes he'd made after they'd learned about the theft from Clem's and Georgie's rooms. "During the time you figure the theft had to have taken place, the only people we know left the first floor were the three who were out of commission — Marzana, Mrs. Kirkegrim, and Mr. Larven — and the two people who carried Mr. Larven upstairs — your dad and *Lucky*."

"Lucky?" Téngfēi repeated in a whisper.

"Yeah, Lucky. What if we made a false assumption when we decided it had to be a newbie caroler? If it's true that a stranger could sneak into the Liberty and pass himself off as a resident, then the opposite is also true." She paused for extra dramatic effect. "A resident could have a double life outside the Liberty! And look at all the things it would explain." Sirin held up a hand to tick off items on her fingers. "Lucky convinced Marzana to come. Lucky insisted on Rob, a newcomer who doesn't know how to clean a chimney, to play the sweep. Lucky wore the mistletoe crown—she carried the poison in with her, in plain sight! And who would question her? Lucky's the group's expert on the Waits—even the others who've done this before defer to her. She could have any detail of the caroling trip exactly the way she wanted, probably."

Sirin sat back, shaking her head in wonder at her own deduction. And Téngfēi had to admit, if you put it that way, the pieces did seem to fall right into place. He scratched his head. "Let me think about this."

"You said Mr. Larven is tall, right?" Sirin persisted. "Unconscious, he would've been totally dead weight. Lucky doesn't look like a weakling, but seriously, how much sense does it make that it wasn't, say, Mr. Hakelbarend or Sylvester who helped your dad carry an unconscious man up two flights of stairs? I bet if you ask, we'll find out that Lucky insisted on going. I bet she made that happen."

"Maybe," Téngfēi said slowly.

"But you're still not convinced?"

He hesitated. Lucky as the thief they were looking for didn't have the sudden, satisfying sense of completion he wanted. Pieces had fallen into place, yes, but there were some left over. "Maybe it's because we still have unsolved bits," he suggested. "If we could just find the missing things. Do we think Lucky is Cantlebone or some-body connected to Gilawfer?"

"That I don't know," Sirin admitted. "Let's hope we learn something from her story. Or yours."

Just then, Owen returned from the kitchen with a mug in each hand. He sat on the hearth. "Hi," he said, nodding to Sirin in order to include her in his greeting.

"Hi," she said a little sullenly, pulling off the glasses. It didn't seem to be getting any easier for her to handle being visible.

"So I know a little of what's going on," he said quietly, "and I'm sure you've got a ton on your minds, but do you think I could talk to Milo for a few minutes in private?"

Téngfēi stuck his hand in his pocket and worked the Ring of Wildest Abandon off his finger. "Okay," said Milo.

"Sure. I'll go." Meddy flickered once, managing a slightly re-proachful look at both of them between vanishes, and then disap-peared altogether.

"That's so weird," Owen said.

"She's completely freaked out that some people can see her," Milo told him. "Make sure you don't talk to her in front of any of the new guests."

"Got it." Owen passed him one of the mugs.

Although Mrs. Caraway and both of his parents had been ex-iled from the kitchen, it was hot chocolate done up just the way Milo liked it. Maybe Owen had asked his mom what he preferred. "Thanks."

"You're welcome." Owen set his own drink aside. "Milo, I've

been thinking about you. It's really good to see you again. How's it going?"

Milo opened his mouth to say what he would've said to anyone —*Fine,* accompanied by a not-quite-glower to let him/her know what they should already have surmised: a kid who climbs into the corner behind the Christmas tree doesn't go there so you'll follow and annoy them with your presence and/or conversation. But "Fine" and a glower weren't what came out. Instead, to his own surprise, Milo said, "School is awful and I don't know what to do about it."

"Huh. That sounds crummy." He didn't say, *Do you want to talk about it?,* but he didn't change the subject or go back to his coffee, either.

"Yeah." Milo wasn't sure how much he wanted to talk about this with anyone, but . . . Owen was a Chinese adoptee. Telling him might be different from telling anyone else. And if he didn't tell him now, who knew when — or if — he'd ever have the chance again.

"It's my teacher," Milo said experimentally.

Owen nodded, waited. Milo took a deep breath, and the story of his difficulties with Mr. Chancelor came pouring out. Clem and Georgie, and Sirin's Lucky theory, and all the rest of that mess melted right out of his head. Milo swiped angrily at his eyes as he talked and tried to ignore the burning in his cheeks. He couldn't look at Owen while he spoke, or even for a few minutes after he finished. He just sat there in his Christmas-tree cave, taking deep breaths and willing himself not to lose his composure.

Owen blew out a breath as if he'd been holding it for a while.

"Man. I had a couple things like that happen to me back when I was in school. I can remember one time in particular . . . It wasn't a Chinese thing; it was a more general adoption thing, but if you want to hear, I'll tell you."

"If you don't mind."

"I don't. It was a long time ago." Owen scratched his head. "Have any of your teachers had your class do family trees?"

Milo thought, then shook his head. "I don't think so."

Owen gave him a crooked smile. "It's probably going to happen at some point, so maybe it's good we're talking about this. I got assigned the family-tree project in fourth grade. I had a little bit of a struggle at first, because as you probably remember, I didn't know anything about my birth family except my middle name until just last year. But my parents are my parents, even if they didn't give birth to me, so I settled on doing what you'd probably do too: drawing my family. The one I grew up with, beginning with my mom and dad. And I felt fine about that, until the teacher gave us a handout with information about ways of showing relationships in genealogy."

He hesitated, then continued. "There are a few ways to show adoption on a family tree. One is with brackets around the adoptee, or a dotted line between the kid and the parents, or sometimes both. Or with a slash in that line, which is what my teacher suggested I do. I probably don't have to tell you why that upset me at age ten or however old I was."

He didn't. Every one of those three options made Milo think immediately of separation. Of a weak connection, or a severed connection. A relationship without the comforting integrity of a solid line to describe it. "I think I get it," he said quietly.

Owen nodded. "*You* get it, but my teacher had no clue. And I didn't know how to tell him. Heck, I couldn't bring myself to tell my *parents* why I was so upset, because I didn't want to upset *them* with the idea that maybe there was this . . . this *slash* in our relationship. This broken line. So I didn't tell them about the family tree at all. I just . . . didn't do it. And then I had to explain why I failed the project."

Milo sat in numb silence while Owen paused for a sip from his mug. He could feel the pain of it as plainly as if it had happened to him.

"The thing is, in retrospect, I'm sure the teacher would've been fine with my drawing the same line everyone else got to draw if I'd just explained why that was important to me. And my parents would've explained that pencil marks on paper don't define a family. *If* I'd told them. But I didn't tell anyone." He shook his head. "Still happens now and then. Different stuff, same old feelings."

"Still?" Milo protested.

"Sure. At my job, sometimes when I'm out with people I don't know well . . . It's what people do, isn't it? They make assumptions about others—who they are, what they're like. Sometimes they don't even realize they're doing it. But it's harder for people like you and me, because *who we are* and *what we're like* is . . . complicated."

Complicated was right. "But it never stops?" Milo swallowed back a lump. "Do you . . . Does that mean I'm always going to feel like this?"

Owen looked at him thoughtfully for a long minute. Milo's heart sank. The answer he'd wanted shouldn't have taken that much consideration.

Owen must've known what Milo was thinking. He smiled, but his thoughtful expression was tinged with sadness. "I wish I could say it goes away, Milo, just like that." He snapped his fingers. "That one day you'll wake up and just . . . feel . . . I don't know. *Confident* isn't quite the right word, I don't think . . . It's not quite enough." He scratched his head. "I wish I could say that one day you'll wake up and you'll know who you are and feel good about it — but more than *good:* you'll feel *exactly right* about it, and you'll know that for the rest of your life, nothing anyone can say or do will be able to shake that certainty. Or if not that, then you'll wake up one day and feel like a . . . a fortress. Strong enough that nothing anyone can throw at you gets through to what's inside, so that even if the doubts don't go away, no one else can reach them."

The lump hovered somewhere between Milo's collar and his tongue. "But you can't say that."

Owen shook his head slowly. "No. In the first place, because that certainty, the feeling exactly right about who you are forever and ever, amen? That's not real. Everybody doubts themselves now and then. Ask anyone here. If they're honest, they'll tell you they question themselves all the time. And nobody's a fortress."

Milo shook his head. "That's not the same."

"I know, I know. And I agree; I think you and I and lots of other folks have it even harder than most."

"Then it never stops," Milo said miserably.

"Well, there's two answers, I suppose." Owen sat back and scratched his chin. "I think the first one is, every day that you're aware of yourself and who you are, you'll be aware of the fact that you're not exactly like the people around you. How you feel about that . . . well, that'll probably be different every day. Will it always make you feel like it did in school this week?" He shook his head decisively. "No, absolutely not. Will it always be uncomfortable?" He made a hesitant face, as if he wanted to say no again but wasn't quite as sure about it. "Often it will, and for a hundred different reasons, but not always."

"Well," Milo said with effort, "I guess it could be worse than 'not always.'"

Owen nodded apologetically. "I wish I could tell you differently, I really do. The good news, I suppose, is the second answer, which is that, over time, you can come to feel like you *do* know who you are. All the parts of who you are come together, and even if they don't quite come together perfectly, you make peace with them. They make sense to *you*. But you never get to a point where you're a fortress and nobody can get through, unfortunately."

"People say stupid things," Milo said quietly.

Owen sighed. "People have an endless capacity for being thoughtless, heartless, and yes, racist. Even good people. The problem is, even when the person who says or does the hurtful thing is essentially a good person who you know means well —"

"It doesn't make it hurt any less," Milo finished.

Owen nodded again, sadly this time. "And then there's that hard decision of whether you say something or not. If it's someone you like or care about at all, you want them to know they hurt you so they don't do it again. And you've got to figure they'd want you to tell them so they can avoid making you feel bad in the future. But knowing all that doesn't make it any easier to speak up." He leaned back against the brick of the fireplace. "For one thing, it's embarrassing to have to do it. And if you do, you have to relive all those feelings again. Not to mention—I wish this didn't matter to me, but it does—you run the risk of hurting the feelings of people you care about when you tell them they hurt yours." He leaned away from Milo and raised his voice. "Hey, Clem, can I tell Milo about that time at Leo's dinner party?"

"No," she shouted back immediately and indignantly. Then her face appeared around the wall dividing the living room from the kitchen, looking penitent. "Yes, of course you can."

"You don't have to tell me," Milo said as Clem faded back into the kitchen.

"Well, suffice to say, Clem had a thoughtless moment and I decided the one person I'd better be honest with was the person I loved most, if for no other reason than because she'd never forgive me if I didn't tell her. And, listen, I like your parents a ton and I get the feeling that in some ways they're a lot like mine: they love you wholly, and they truly want to respect both your Chinese heritage and your place in this family and this city. Is that pretty accurate, do you think?"

Milo found he couldn't speak over the lump at that moment, so he just nodded.

"Okay, good. But that doesn't mean that even *they* aren't ever going to make thoughtless mistakes, Milo. And when they do, you absolutely have to find a way to tell them, even if it's difficult." His smile faded. "But you've got a different situation with your teacher, don't you?"

"Dad wants to talk to him. I told him no, and he said that he wouldn't if I would."

Owen took a sip from his mug. "That's a tough one. Teachers can be unpredictable. A great teacher would listen and think about it with an open mind, but I think we both know not all teachers are great, and the handful that aren't can make your life harder if they take being told they did something dumb the wrong way or just can't handle it."

"Exactly!" Milo exploded. "What if he gets mad at me? What if I make it worse?"

"It's a tough one," Owen said again. "I'm not going to lie, Milo. If you asked me what I'd do if I were you, I'd say let your mom and dad talk to him, because I'm an adult and that's my instinct looking at this situation now. But Kid Owen would've insisted that if anyone was going to have that conversation with my teacher, it would be me. The thing is, then I wouldn't have done it. And looking back now, even if I had, I'm not sure I could have put it all into words without falling apart in the moment." Owen gave him a sharp look. "Which is not a reason not to do it, by the way."

Milo slumped.

"So I guess," Owen continued, "what I suggest to you, Milo, is that you figure out what you'd say to him yourself, because you have to find a way to put those words together, whether you talk to this teacher specifically or not. You have to find a way to talk about it when people say or do hurtful things — to you or to anyone else. It's important to be able to speak up."

"But I don't know where to start," Milo said. "I get hung up on everything and it's just this big jumble of awful feelings."

"Feelings are a good place to start," Owen told him. "For this particular conversation, I'd also think about your teacher's, if only because you've got to figure out how best to get him to listen and understand how *you* feel. Mind you," he said quickly, "I'm not saying this because it's about your teacher's feelings. It's not; it's about yours. But with someone who has the potential to make your life miserable, like a teacher — or, in my case sometimes, someone I work for — if you want him to hear you, you have to frame the conversation so he's inclined to listen. So let me ask you this: why do you think he said what he did?"

"I think he was excited because he thought he was doing something good," Milo admitted grudgingly.

"Okay, then that's how I'd start out. 'Mr. Whoever —'"

"Chancelor."

"'Mr. Chancelor, I understand that you meant to be appreciative of my heritage last week when you asked if I could translate the name of that ship. But since I'm only just learning the language, and since there's more than one system of written Chinese and thousands of characters to learn, jerk —'" Owen broke off with a chuckle as Milo threw his hands up in frustrated agreement. "Yeah, only probably don't call your teacher a jerk to his face because of that whole getting-him-to-hear-you problem, and also because it'll land you in detention. Anyway, 'Because I'm in the process of learning, the chances that I'd know a group of random written characters are pretty slim. And because I'm Chinese in a white family, things that point out gaps in my knowledge of Chinese culture, especially in front of other people, make me feel bad. I feel the same way when you suggest that I'm wrong about things that I do know, like about the Bluecrowne family having a Chinese boy in it and being here during the War of 1812. So it would be great if you wouldn't call attention to me that way in front of everyone.'" Owen paused and watched Milo for a minute. "Make sense?"

"It does," Milo admitted, "but I can't imagine saying that to Mr. Chancelor. I feel like I'll forget what I'm supposed to say as soon as I start talking."

"That's why you should practice what you'd say, regardless of what you finally decide to do. If you know you have the words to describe how you're feeling and what you'd like to go differently the next time there's a potentially awkward situation, then you won't feel quite as helpless next time it happens. Because unfortunately, it will happen again, Milo." He sighed. "And by the way, sometimes the right words to have ready are 'Quit being a flipping jerk.' But, again, probably not with your teacher."

Milo laughed despite himself. "He's not going to believe me about the Bluecrowne family and this house, though."

"Aha." Owen straightened. "There, at least, I can give you some good news. Remember I said I'd been thinking about you?"

"Yeah."

"Well, after I learned the origin of my middle name last year from you and Mrs. Hereward, I placed a couple ads seeking information about the Bluecrowne family in Nagspeake." He reached into the breast pocket of his shirt and took out a small envelope. "There wasn't a lot, as you can imagine—the Bluecrownes were privateers, for one thing, and not inclined to leave a massive paper trail. For another, we all know that records in this city are ridiculous. But I did get a few interesting replies. When I followed up on one of them, I wound up in a fireworks shop, of all places." Owen passed the envelope to Milo. "Take care. The paper inside is very old."

Milo carefully drew the yellowed page out of the envelope and flattened it on the hearth. It was a letter, in handwriting that was at once elegant and childlike—swirly and fancy in that way that old script always seems to be, and yet uncertain, as if the writer had still been acclimating to cursive.

Owen spoke as Milo read the date at the top: *March 1813*. "The shop's files included a bunch of correspondence from the days of one of the owner's predecessors. And he had a long-standing relationship with a customer named Liao Bluecrowne."

"That's your ancestor?"

"Yes. I could be descended from either him or his sister. I may never know. But read it."

Esteemed Mr. Fulgor,
Greetings from Java! I hope this finds you well and doing splendid business. I

have just learned that we shall be passing through Nagspeake waters again in October or thereabouts, and I should very much like to pick up some of the items you introduced me to on my visit to the city last year. I have included a list below. If you will not be in Nagspeake in October, will you please suggest another seller who might provide them, or can do business on your behalf? (Anyone but Ignis Blister, please, as we have discussed.) I will check the post exchange at the Bazaar if you would leave a reply there.

Yours sincerely,

Liao Bluecrowne

And after the English signature but before the shopping list were five Chinese characters.

Owen tapped the page there. "That's his name. And, as you probably remember, Liao Bluecrowne translated his English surname to Mandarin when he was just a little kid, much younger than you. These four symbols at the end mean 'the crown that is blue,' or *lán sè dè guān,* from which we get the Englishified *Lansdegown,* the first name of this house and my middle name."

"Lán sè dè guān," Milo said, trying to replicate Owen's pronunciation. Owen repeated the phrase, and so did Milo. "But you're probably going to have to come in and show this to him," he added as he folded up the letter and slid it into its envelope. "I bet I could tell him about it and he still wouldn't believe me."

Owen's smile returned. "How about if *you* show it to him? I brought it for you, anyway. It's yours. I have about a dozen letters from after that. Liao was apparently a lifelong customer of this Mr. Fulgor."

"It's for me?" Milo clutched the envelope in both hands. "But how did you know?"

"That you needed it just now?" Owen laughed. "I didn't have a clue. But once I figured out that this was where Clem and Georgie probably . . . ahem . . . decamped to, it occurred to me to grab one of the letters on my way out the door. I guess I wanted to show you what I'd managed to find out with the information you and Mrs. Hereward gave me. That I'd put it to good use."

"Thank you," Milo managed. "Thank you so much."

Owen squeezed his shoulder. "I'll leave your folks my phone number. Call and tell me how it goes with Mr. Chancelor. Or just call me anytime. Okay?"

Milo nodded, blinking hard. "Okay."

"Great." Owen held out his cup. "To Liao."

Milo clinked his mug against Owen's. "To Liao." Then Owen winked, stood up, and left the room.

twenty-three

A PERSON OF INTEREST

FOR LONG MINUTES, Milo held the precious envelope in both hands and watched the little flashes of color the twinkling tree lights splashed across the old, old paper. He was on the verge of losing his battle with the tears that wanted to overflow his eyes when the telephone rang.

It was just the distraction he needed. He tucked the envelope into his rucksack, then sprang out from behind the tree and rushed to the phone that hung on the wall by the bar. "I'll get it," he called as his mother, who'd been lying on the loveseat, straightened up and his father rose from the dining table where he'd been speaking to Mr. Hakelbarend. Milo picked up the receiver and winced at the crackle. "Hello, Greenglass House."

"Well, hello, is that Milo?"

The voice was vaguely familiar, but Milo couldn't place it. "Yes, this is Milo speaking."

"It's Dr. Wilbur Gowervine, Milo!" the voice announced cheerfully. *That's why I didn't recognize the voice,* Milo thought. *I don't know if I've ever heard Dr. Gowervine sound cheerful before.*

"Oh, hi, Professor," Milo said. "Merry Christmas."

Mrs. Pine got up from the loveseat and drifted closer. Clem stacked plates quietly on the bar.

"Merry Christmas," Dr. Gowervine replied. "Say, I happened to stop by my office and found I had several messages from Miss Candler, asking me to call her there at the inn. Is she about?"

"Yes, she's here." Milo glanced meaningfully at Clem and mouthed, *It's for you.*

"Take it upstairs," Mrs. Pine whispered.

Clem nodded. "Get Georgie. She can listen down here."

"I think she wanted to ask you about a student," Milo said to Dr. Gowervine as Mrs. Pine went out onto the screened porch and Clem darted up the steps.

"Yes, I got that part." The cheer dropped out of the professor's voice. "I think I'd better talk to her directly. It's complicated."

"She's going to get the phone upstairs. Did you recognize the name?"

"I recognized the name, all right," Dr. Gowervine said. "But—"

Silence, then a dial tone.

"Dr. Gowervine?" No answer. Milo shook the receiver, even

though he knew it wasn't going to accomplish anything. Then he listened again. Nothing but the tone.

Georgie came over, trying to look as nonchalant as possible. "For me?"

"Hello?" That was Clem's voice, sounding far away on the upstairs extension.

"I think he's gone," Milo said.

"What do you mean, gone?" both thieves asked at the same time.

"I mean he's not on the line anymore. There's nothing but a dial tone."

Georgie rubbed her forehead irritably. Upstairs, Clem sighed. "I'll try calling him again. Thanks, Milo."

"You're welcome, I guess." He hung up the phone. "Gone," he said in answer to his parents' questioning looks.

Mrs. Kirkegrim wandered over, polishing a dish with a towel. "You look stricken," she said to Georgie. "Is everything okay?"

Georgie reassembled her face into something less freaked out. "Everything's fine, Mrs. Kirkegrim. Thanks for asking. Just someone we wanted to say Merry Christmas to, but we lost him."

"Sorry to hear that." The older lady stacked the plate and went back to the sink for another.

Milo thought for a minute. Then he slid Téngfēi's ring onto his finger and went out onto the screened porch.

The solitaire found Emmett pacing at the far end of the room. There was something different about him. Something about how he was standing, maybe — there was less of the squirrelly student about him now. He looked . . . older. Definitely more in control of himself than he had ever seemed before.

What had Mrs. Pine said when she'd gone out to the porch? *Georgie, you have a phone call?* Surely not anything as obvious as *Georgie, Dr. Gowervine's on the phone.* But it definitely seemed as if Emmett had known that whatever the call was about, it had something to do with him. And he looked as if he'd resigned himself to it.

Téngfēi decided not to mince words. "You aren't who you say you are."

Emmett's face did the strangest thing. His eyes and mouth opened wide, as if for a heartbeat the young man had considered a show of shock, surprise, and disavowal. But only for a second, before snapping immediately back to a neutral, almost blank state. He blinked a single, slow blink. "How do you figure?" There was no denial in his voice. Just curiosity. "The phone call?" He laughed. "Gowervine finally picked up his messages, I imagine."

"Yes."

"If you talked to Gowervine, you already know the answer," he said easily. "What's left that you feel requires explanation?"

He's calling my bluff, Téngfēi realized. *And since I don't actually know what Dr. Gowervine was going to say, I'm stuck.*

Emmett nodded. "That's what I thought."

Téngfēi touched the locus ring on his index finger. What did he have in his arsenal that would be useful just now? Perhaps the Clear-Sighted Perspicacity: *The weaknesses of your enemies become as clear to you as the bluest sky, as do the most elegant ways to exploit those weaknesses.*

There'd been another reason, beyond the one he'd given Sirin, to eliminate Emmett as a suspect: Emmett had come to Greenglass House first. Yes, he had been unaccounted for during the time frame when Clem and Georgie's heist had gone off the rails. Yes, he'd extended his visit just before they'd arrived. And yes, Téngfēi could understand why his friends needed to be suspicious of everyone until they worked out where the dangers really lay. But he just didn't believe that either Cantlebone or Gilawfer could have anticipated that the two young thieves would come here to hide out. He could fully believe that they had been followed here, despite the relative secrecy of the Belowground Transit System, and he could believe that with a whole day to work on it, either Cantlebone or Gilawfer might be able to infiltrate the Waits and use them as cover to sneak in. But to guess they would come to Greenglass House before they'd even decided to do it themselves? No. That was stretching it. Emmett hadn't come to Greenglass House because of the Violet Cross heist.

Still, Dr. Gowervine's tone on the phone made it clear that the professor knew who Emmett was, and that there was more to him than he'd revealed. And even without the professor's information, Téngfēi was going to work out what that was.

He kept coming back to the change in Emmett's bearing just now. Emmett had clearly been anticipating that Georgie would return to confront him with new information. But if he'd planned to stick to his cover story of being a student here for a working vacation, he still would have been in Emmett-the-art-student mode. *This* Emmett Syebuck, the one waiting for Téngfēi to make a move, was a different creature. No, he'd planned to confront head-on whatever he thought Georgie now knew.

Emmett folded his arms. "Is there something else you wanted to say?"

"You're not who you say you are," Téngfēi repeated. "But you're not who Georgie thinks you are, either." He took a deep breath and took a big chance. "Dr. Gowervine got cut off before he could tell her whatever he knows about you, so she still thinks what she thought before: that you're the thief who robbed her and Clem last night." *There.* Emmett's confident expression flickered and his eyes sharpened. "I'm betting you know there was a theft," Téngfēi continued, "but you aren't the one who did it. So maybe you'd better just tell me the truth now. If you can convince me, maybe I can convince Georgie and Clem."

The art-student-who-probably-wasn't considered Téngfēi for a moment. "All right, Milo. I think I'd rather have you on my side than not. I'll make a deal with you. You tell me what was stolen and where it came from, and I'll tell you what I know."

Oh, snap.

Emmett waited, one eyebrow hitched up. "This much I'll give you to help make your decision: yes, I know there was a theft in the house; no, I am not the one who did it. I know Georgie and Clem have been snooping in every room in the inn, including mine, although I will say I'm impressed with how thorough they were able to be without leaving any real trace. I also strongly suspect that even if they were the victims this time, your friends are both highly capable thieves themselves." He eyed Téngfēi closely, and the solitaire forced his face not to shift a muscle. "What I want to know is, if whatever went missing is recovered and returned to Georgie and Clem, is it being returned to its rightful owners or not?"

Of course Téngfēi was automatically going to be on Georgie and Clem's side. They were his friends. But they also made their livings from stealing, and from the direction this conversation was taking, it was looking more and more as though Emmett was involved in some way with law enforcement. Dr. Gowervine knew him, so maybe he also was, or had been, an art student interested in glass. But if Téngfēi was right and Emmett Syebuck had come to Greenglass House because of his involvement with the law and not because of a passion for stained-glass windows, then he was probably with customs. In any case, there was no way Téngfēi was confirming to this guy that Georgie and Clem were thieves.

But . . . but that wasn't exactly what Emmett was asking, was it? He was asking if *these particular items* had been stolen. And that, now that Téngfēi stopped to think about it, was a good question.

They all kept referring to the operation by which Clem and Georgie had acquired Violet Cross's cache as a heist. But how accurate was that? They'd gone in to retrieve the stash through the floor of Gilawfer's warehouse, but they'd had Gilawfer's permission. And the structure beneath the warehouse hadn't belonged to Gilawfer —he hadn't even known it was there. Most importantly of all, the rightful owner, if it was anyone other than Clem and Georgie, was Violet Cross, and she had been presumed dead for thirty or forty years.

"Georgie and Clem are the rightful owners," Téngfēi said decisively. "The stuff in question was lost years ago, and they worked out where it was. The previous owner is long gone, and they didn't take it from anyone else's property."

Emmett was silent for a moment. "That's what they told you and your parents."

"Yes."

"And you believe it?"

Téngfēi nodded. "They would have no reason to lie to us," he said simply.

Emmett shook his head and held up a hand. "Don't explain that to me. What was it, the stuff that was taken from them?"

Téngfēi had no intention of mentioning the derrotero or Violet Cross by name, not if this guy was law enforcement. Fortunately, he could be specific enough to satisfy Emmett without giving away either of those details. "A spherical chalkboard, a bunch of locks and keys, a fan, a deck of cards, and a reflecting circle." He considered and decided against telling him they'd recovered half of the cache.

"Seriously?" Emmett asked dubiously. "That's . . . well, it sounds like a truly random assortment of junk."

"You're telling me," Téngfēi agreed. "I'm pretty sure it's not exactly what Georgie and Clem expected when they first found it either. So when you asked me if Georgie was single, that was supposed to explain why you were watching her and Clem so closely?"

Emmett winced. "For the sake of my own dignity, I should probably say yes and leave it at that. It seemed like the kind of clumsy thing the character I was playing would say. I've been watching everybody in this place, same as you have. I wasn't expecting other guests to show up at all. But as to your friends . . . all right, yes, I suppose I was watching them in particular."

"Why?"

"Because Clem knows how to pick locks." Emmett gave him a long look through narrowed eyes. "And," he said at last in a slightly different tone, "because I find Georgie and her oddball projects interesting."

"Interesting, as in, a person of interest?" Milo asked.

"No, the other kind," Emmett said coldly. "That much was true. But then all the other insanity happened, and when she and Clem started lurking around, I figured they were either attempting to steal something or attempting to get something back."

Téngfēi grinned. "I'll pretend to forget the first half of that answer. Now you talk. Why did you have to play a character at all? Who are you?"

Emmett unfolded his arms and reached for the partially completed watercolor on the little tabletop easel. He'd taped the painting, which was just on a piece of paper, to a slightly larger piece of thin brown board that Téngfēi had assumed was meant to keep the paper from warping. Now Emmett peeled back the top piece of tape, reached between the board and the painting, and extracted another bit of paper. This one was smaller, rectangular, and covered with print. He handed it to Téngfēi.

What the solitaire saw made his stomach drop down to somewhere around his knees. He—or rather, Milo—had once seen something very similar. He'd seen it a year ago, and it had belonged to a customs agent who had come to Greenglass House in search of the last cargo belonging to Meddy's father, Doc Holystone.

```
Be it hereby known and confirmed throughout the
City and Beyond that Emmett Ryan Syebuck is an
agent in good standing of the Customs Department
of the Sovereign City of Nagspeake...
```

There was no way this wasn't terrible news. The language was slightly different from the previous document like this Milo had seen—the bearer of that one, De Cary Vinge, had been *deputized* by the customs department but had only been an employee of the Deacon and Morvengarde catalog company empire. Emmett was an *actual* customs agent. Did that make it better or worse? Everyone knew that Deacon and Morvengarde was out to destroy the smugglers who undermined their chokehold on the flow of goods in and out of Nagspeake. The customs department was generally assumed to be in the pocket of D&M, but even if it wasn't, cracking down on smuggling was still part of its job.

It wasn't widely known that the clientele of Greenglass House was mostly made up of smugglers, but one person who probably did know was Mr. Vinge. In the end, he hadn't turned up any evidence last year that could've proved illegal activity went on at the inn, but he'd been angry and humiliated, and he definitely held grudges. Had he convinced customs to take a closer look at Greenglass House? Or was Emmett here for another reason?

Gilawfer, now — him *I know,* Doc Holystone's ghost had said. *He was also known to many of us runners to be an informant for the customs department.*

"Do you know anyone named Gilawfer?" Téngfēi asked. "Toby Gilawfer?"

Emmett shook his head. "Doesn't ring a bell." He took the identification paper gently from Téngfēi's fingers, folded it, and put it in his back pocket. "No point in hiding that again, I guess. Yes, I came here to investigate the house and your folks, Milo. There were stories circulating — but the source of those stories was, shall we say, not entirely trustworthy. A little nutty, and a guy with ties to organizations that might've made him biased." He was definitely talking about Mr. Vinge. "But I haven't seen evidence of anything untoward here," Emmett continued in what was probably meant to be a comforting tone.

"Then why did you extend your stay?" Téngfēi demanded.

"Because, believe it or not, before joining customs, I actually *was* an art student. Dr. Gowervine was my adviser. I wrote my dissertation on Skellansen, and I did original research on Ellamae Wellshowe." Emmett smiled. "I figured my other work was done, so I asked to stay an extra day because I like it here. Nothing more elaborate than that. Actually, I had started to have a theory about that window up on the fourth floor . . ." His voice trailed off thoughtfully. "If it *does* contain recycled grave markers, and if they *did* come from that church in Shantytown . . . well, there are some crazy theories about some unidentified remains in those catacombs . . ."

It looked like a genuine enough bit of nerding-out, but Téngfēi wasn't quite ready to let his guard down. "So we're supposed to believe you came for the smugglers and stayed for the windows?"

Emmett's smile faded into seriousness again. "Milo, a smuggler's having owned the house in the past isn't a crime, and neither is letting smugglers stay here as guests, as long as they don't commit crimes on the premises. You and your parents have nothing to fear from me."

"I don't have anything to say," Téngfēi said defiantly.

Emmett held up his hand again. "I don't want you to say anything more."

"Can I tell my parents?" He was going to tell them no matter what Emmett said; he just needed to know how sneaky he had to be about it.

"Sure, but I should probably tell them myself. I'll do it now, unless you have any other questions."

"No. Or yes. What will you do next?"

"Well, if you can convince Georgie and Clem to believe what I've just told you — that I have no interest in them from a legal standpoint — I'd like to help recover what they lost. Then I'll go back to my department and tell them they can consider Greenglass House a non-issue."

Téngfēi looked at him thoughtfully. Could he be trusted?

Yes, the solitaire realized. Because even if Emmett had come to

Greenglass House as part of an undercover assignment looking for evidence of illegal activity, *he had never intended to find any.*

Emmett had said, *A smuggler's having owned the house in the past isn't a crime, and neither is letting smugglers stay here as guests, as long as they don't commit crimes on the premises.* By that logic, he would've had to have seen evidence of a smuggling crime being committed at Greenglass House to report that the Pines posed a customs threat by operating a haven for runners. But he'd also said, *I wasn't expecting other guests to show up at all.* So he'd come looking for evidence of a smuggling crime at a time when he already knew there probably would be no smugglers staying at the inn. The only reason he'd have done that was if he'd already made up his mind about the house and how he'd report on it.

Emmett smiled, as if he'd been following Téngfēi's train of thought. "Not everybody in customs is in somebody else's pocket. I'm not Vinge."

Téngfēi returned the smile. "I can tell. You know, you should probably tell Georgie and Clem the truth too."

"I will. Let me talk to your parents first, though. I don't want you worrying about that."

"Okay. Shall I send them in?"

"I think so."

twenty-four

BLAME TRADITION!

I T SOUNDED AS THOUGH the brunch cleanup was winding down when Téngfēi returned to the living room. He could hear the creaking of cabinet doors and the gentle clatter of dishes being put away. Lizzie and Mrs. Caraway were lounging on the couch. Lizzie appeared to be snoozing. Mrs. Caraway had her feet up on the coffee table, and she was sipping from her mug and looking, as she always did, as if it took an effort to relax when someone else was messing around in the kitchen.

He didn't see Sirin anywhere, or his mother, but Mr. Pine was adding wood to the fire. "Where's Mom?" Téngfēi asked.

"She and Georgie went upstairs. You were gone for a while,"

Mr. Pine noted, nodding toward the screened porch. "Is Emmett still out there?"

"Yes. He wants to talk to you," Téngfēi told him. "You better go now, and I'll get Mom."

"Am I going to hear something that freaks me out?" Mr. Pine asked, standing and brushing his hands off on his jeans. "Is it serious?"

"You'll think so at first, but I'm pretty sure it's not as bad as it's going to sound."

Mr. Pine took a deep breath. "Milo, is it ever comforting to you when I tell you something isn't going to be as bad as it sounds?"

"Nope." Téngfēi shrugged. "Sorry."

He took his rucksack from behind the tree and hurried to the stairs. On the way, he checked on the group in the kitchen. The last few dishes were moving from sink (Marzana) to drying towels (Mrs. Kirkegrim). Rob was putting leftovers in the fridge, and Owen was busy making a fresh pot of coffee. In the dining room, Lucky and Sylvester were deep in conversation.

Téngfēi gave them a long look as he passed. Could Sirin possibly be right about Lucky? He definitely didn't *want* her to be right, but that didn't count for much. They knew she'd been upstairs during at least part of the time period when the thefts had taken place, and Mrs. Pine had said the soot and chaos had been too thick downstairs during the conking of Mrs. Kirkegrim and Marzana to rule out anyone but Rob. And Sirin was right—Lucky had carried one of the two poisons that had been in the tea ball in Mr. Larven's punch into the house herself. Finding holly hanging around in a big old house during the holidays was a pretty safe bet, but if there hadn't been holly, mistletoe probably would've been enough. He glanced at the poinsettia by the window at the end of the dining table, which now looked as if it might be dying. There were other things around during the holidays she could've used if she'd had to improvise.

He ran upstairs and into his family's living room. Mrs. Pine was pacing by the big window. Georgie was leaning against the wall, running a piece of sandpaper against the edge of one of her mirrors. Clem had the phone cradled against her ear, but a moment later she put it back on the receiver. "Still nothing."

"No luck?" Téngfēi asked.

Clem shook her head. "The problem seems to be at his end. I don't get it. What are the chances of Dr. Gowervine having phone troubles right at this minute?"

Actually, considering Emmett had the considerable resources of the customs department at his disposal, Téngfēi didn't have a particularly difficult time believing there could be some kind of fix in on Dr. Gowervine's phone that would go into effect if a connection was made between his office and Greenglass House. But to explain that, Téngfēi would have to explain what he'd just learned, and since the customs agent was ready to come clean, there was no need to waste time on that. "You guys all have to talk to Emmett," he said. "But Mom first. Dad's with him already. He's on the porch."

Mrs. Pine dropped her head into her hands. "When does it end?" she moaned.

"It's not that bad," Téngfēi said, patting her shoulder.

"Unless it's *good,* I don't care," she growled as she stalked out of the room.

Georgie looked at Téngfēi. "Spill."

Téngfēi sighed. "He's customs."

Clem groaned and Georgie dropped onto the couch with a muttered curse. "Well, there's our answer."

"No, I don't think so, Georgie. He's not here because of Gilawfer. He's here because of Mr. Vinge. Remember Mr. Vinge, from last year?"

"How could I forget?" Georgie's eyes narrowed. "Emmett told you this?"

"Yes, and he wants to tell you, too."

Her eyelids dropped even farther. "Why?"

Téngfēi decided not to go into the person-of-interest angle. "He guessed about the thefts. He wants to help." Georgie snorted. Clem laughed outright. "I believe him," Téngfēi insisted. "But I didn't tell him about Violet Cross or the derrotero."

"Well, I guess I'll listen if there's something he wants to say, as long as it's not 'You're under arrest.'" Georgie chewed on her lip for a minute. "So if he's not our guy, it's one of the Waits."

Téngfēi hesitated. "Si — Meddy thinks it's Lucky."

"Lucky?" Clem frowned, thinking. "Well, she could've been in all the right places at the right times, I guess. But you don't agree?"

"I don't know." Téngfēi dropped onto the couch next to her. "My money was on one of the others, one of the first-time carolers. But there's no other person who could've done everything."

"Good morning, my dears!" Nicholas Larven burst into the room, looking dapper and exactly as if he hadn't ingested an entire bowlful of poisoned punch the night before. Maybe that was what sleeping until noon got you. "Where on earth is everyone?"

"Downstairs," Clem said. "This is the second floor."

"Morning," Téngfēi added with a wave. "How are you feeling?"

"Like a new man," Mr. Larven replied. "What a lovely rest. And do I smell coffee?" He wandered blithely out.

"I wish I could sleep off a hangover like that," Georgie muttered, sanding with a vengeance.

"Hey." Sirin appeared without fanfare in the middle of the room. Georgie leaped up onto the couch in shock and Clem stifled a scream. Sirin ignored them. "Get a move on," she said to Téngfēi. "The kitchen's done. They're ready for storytelling."

"And you should probably go talk to Emmett," Téngfēi reminded the thieves.

"I'll go," Georgie said to Clem. "It'll look weird if it's both of us."

"Try to keep your voice down," Clem suggested.

"Yeah, okay." Georgie pocketed her stuff, steeled herself, and left the room.

Téngfēi filled in Sirin on his conversation with Emmett; then they and Clem headed down. Another petal dropped off the sad poinsettia by the window at the bottom of the stairs as they arrived on the first floor. Clem joined Owen on the loveseat. Mr. Larven,

Mrs. Kirkegrim, and Rob were in the kitchen refilling their coffee cups. Georgie, too—his parents must still be out there with Emmett. From the aroma curling through the air, it seemed that Lizzie had managed to get her loaves of stollen into the oven at last. Téngfēi thought he could smell cider, as well.

"Here," Georgie said, putting a cup into Téngfēi's hand. Yup, definitely cider. He followed her into the living room, where the others were already getting comfortable. Marzana had settled on the side of the hearth near the tree. Mr. Hakelbarend had taken the chair in the opposite corner. Lucky was on the couch, and Sylvester was sitting on the floor with his back to the other end of it—not sitting with her, precisely, but not far away from her, either. If Lucky was the thief, Téngfēi wondered, was Sylvester in on it?

Georgie sat on the couch next to Lucky. Téngfēi took the other end of the hearth, and Sirin sat next to him as the remaining three trickled in from the kitchen. Rob turned the chair next to the loveseat around to face into the room and dropped into it with a huge sigh. "And here we all are."

"Are you recovered, Nick?" Lucky asked.

Mr. Larven beamed from the chair near the sofa where he'd settled. "My dear, I feel like a new man. Though it does seem that I might have made the punch a bit stronger than I'd intended."

Sirin elbowed Téngfēi hard and gave him a big, serious glare accompanied by a significant waggling of eyebrows.

What the heck. "Actually," Téngfēi said, "this is kind of weird, but I think some mistletoe might've fallen into it somehow. And some holly berries. You might've gotten a little . . . um . . . food poisoning."

Mr. Larven's jolly expression flickered. "I beg your pardon?"

"That seems unlikely," Lizzie said slowly.

Mrs. Caraway was indignant. "Impossible. There's no mistletoe or holly anywhere in that kitchen."

Téngfēi nodded, still looking at the mustachioed man. "There were mistletoe and holly berries in the punch you drank."

"I made that punch myself," Mr. Larven said stiffly.

Téngfēi shrugged. "I don't know what to say, Mr. Larven. Although I could've been more accurate when I said the berries fell in. I found them in the tea ball with all the spices."

"Uh-oh." By the window, Rob guffawed. "Milo discovered the secret ingredient to the mysterious Shutter Club Punch." Against all logic, even Mr. Hakelbarend grinned at that, his teeth a flash of white against his dark face.

"In the *tea ball?*" Mrs. Caraway repeated, aghast.

"Then someone put them there on purpose," Georgie said.

"What the devil?" Mr. Larven crossed his legs and folded his arms angrily. "Well, it wasn't me! I certainly wouldn't have drunk it if I had! You can't think—"

"Whoa, whoa." Sylvester spoke up. "Pretty sure nobody's suggesting you did, Nick. You're the only one who drank it. I don't see any motive you could've had for poisoning yourself."

"I do," Rob said. "If you needed a nap that badly, old man, you could've just said so."

Mr. Larven leaned around the side of his chair and pointed

furiously at Rob. "You are a damned nuisance, Rupert. If you hadn't been so all-fired impossible at chimney cleaning—"

"Oh, good grief. I did my best. Anyway, Lucky made me do it. Blame her."

"That's right," Lucky retorted. "Blame it on me. Blame the whole thing on me. This whole wretched experience is all my fault."

"Hey, hey," Sylvester protested. "Nobody's saying that."

"I suppose we can't blame her that I'm the only one who's tall, dark, and handsome who's not also a fire hazard," Rob said. "Or too big to fit up a chimney," he added with a nod to Mr. Hakelbarend. "So maybe it's not totally Lucky's fault." He held up a triumphant, accusatory finger. "Blame tradition!"

"Enough," Mr. Hakelbarend snapped from the chair in the corner. He leaned forward. "Milo, are you saying you actually found poisonous berries in the punch?"

"I found the tea ball in the trash," Téngfēi told him. "Someone threw it away, but all the spices and stuff were still in it."

"And you definitely put spices in a tea ball in the punch?" Mr. Hakelbarend asked Mr. Larven.

"Not mistletoe and holly!" Mr. Larven exploded.

"Yes, we get that." Mr. Hakelbarend scratched his head. "Then —But you're all right now, Nick?"

"I feel fine," Mr. Larven said defensively. "I'm not even sure I believe this ridiculous assertion."

Milo would've interpreted that as a suggestion that he was mistaken or, worse, lying, and reacted appropriately. But Téngfēi merely shrugged. "Believe it or don't. The poisonous berries were there."

"You did sleep until noon, Nick," Sylvester said. "And you passed out cold last night. Passed out *hard*."

Just then, Mr. and Mrs. Pine emerged from the screened porch. Emmett leaned out the door. He located Georgie on the couch. "Hey, can I have a word?"

Georgie gave him a deceptively charming smile. "Why, Emmett, I thought you'd never ask." She got up and swept past him.

For a moment, Emmett looked terrified. Then the door shut behind them. "I'd give a lot of money to hear that conversation," Sirin said with a chuckle. "Oh, wait. Back in a minute." And she vanished from Téngfēi's side.

Téngfēi studied Mr. and Mrs. Pine, but it was impossible to tell anything from their carefully guarded faces. "Is it time for stories?" Mrs. Pine asked with forced cheer as she took Georgie's spot on the sofa.

Everyone else shifted uneasily. Mrs. Kirkegrim spoke up from the chair nearest the hearth. "I think it is. We can come back to the other conversation later."

"Oh, I didn't mean to derail anything," Mrs. Pine said.

"You didn't," Mrs. Kirkegrim said firmly. "And it's high time we—"

From the screened porch came a shattering noise—a small one, or maybe two small ones in rapid succession. The kind of noise you'd get if you threw a pair of little mirrors on the floor in a fury. Georgie's voice shouted, "Don't *overreact?* Are you *kidding me?*"

Uh-oh. So much for Georgie's stereoscope.

"Told her to keep her voice down," Clem muttered.

"Should we . . . ?" Lucky asked hesitantly.

Clem and Mr. and Mrs. Pine all answered at the same time. "Nope."

"O-kay." Mrs. Kirkegrim glanced from Lucky to Mr. Hakelbarend. "Milo said he wanted to go last. Who's going first?"

Mr. Hakelbarend stretched in his chair. "I suppose I will."

twenty-five

THE SAINT IN THE HALLWAYS

"So I believe," Mr. Hakelbarend began, "that I was nominated as a storyteller because Milo was asking to hear a little bit about the Liberty of Gammerbund." He glanced at Marzana, who had clearly picked her spot on the hearth for the same reason Milo crawled behind the tree, although she hadn't gone quite that far in her efforts to become invisible. Probably because she was (a) a guest, and (b) too old to crawl behind trees in unfamiliar company. "True?"

She nodded, and again Téngfēi was struck by her abrupt transformation from a withdrawn creature made of too-tight rubber bands to an open, ordinary girl as she answered, "True."

"All right." Mr. Hakelbarend stretched his legs out and crossed them at the ankles. "Well, the history of the Liberty goes back further than I have time to tell you about today. It's been up on the hill, in one form or another, at least as long as the rest of the city has been here. Maybe longer, if you believe some of the old-timers."

Sirin reappeared at Téngfēi's side. "What did I miss?" she asked. Téngfēi gave the tiniest twitch of his head to shush her.

"The term *liberty* comes from a tradition in England that goes back to feudal times and the idea of *tenure*. Certain areas were exempt from certain rules of governance because they were held, for one reason or another, by someone other than the Crown. It gets quite complicated. Suffice it to say, something similar cropped up here, where a parcel of land within the boundaries of Nagspeake was — and is — governed by someone other than the city itself. The oldest tenure holder we know of was Whittacre Gammerbund, hence the Chapel of St. Whit and the name of the Liberty itself. But the story goes that even he was a mere citizen at first, just another person who came to the Liberty for asylum."

The non-Waits in the room fidgeted a bit at that word, *asylum*.

Mr. Hakelbarend glanced at Milo. "I don't know if you know this, but *asylum* has more than one meaning. Around Nagspeake, when people say, as they often do, 'The Liberty of Gammerbund is one big asylum,' usually what they really mean is 'The Liberty of Gammerbund is one big *insane* asylum.' A madhouse. A place for crazy people to be hidden away."

Now the Waits in the room reacted. There was a soft snort from Lucky, a low chuckle from Sylvester, a yawn from Rob.

"But in actuality, the Liberty started out as the *other* kind of asylum. In older times, when people said 'The Liberty of Gammerbund is one big asylum,' what they meant was 'The Liberty of Gammerbund is a place where you can *seek* asylum.' A place to go and be safe if one is being pursued."

"Like claiming sanctuary in churches," Mr. Pine guessed.

"Exactly," Mr. Hakelbarend confirmed. "*An asylum* can mean *a refuge*. A haven. And that's what the Liberty was when Whit Gammerbund threw himself at the gates. It had no other name than the Liberty then, but already it was known far and wide as a place where safety could sometimes be found.

"Back then, just like now, the Liberty was entered through the office of a gatekeeper called the warder. It's the warder's job to decide who may enter the Liberty and who may not. And it is true that the warder often turns people away, but rarely those who seek asylum. So he welcomed Whit Gammerbund, who was a mere boy. Not much older than you," he added, looking to the hearth, where Téngfēi and Marzana sat, along with Sirin.

"I always imagine him arriving out of breath, scratched and scarred from running through the woods to get to the gates. There was a road straight to the entrance to the Liberty — a good road too; but he had come over rock and river, through forest and God knows what else, instead of using it."

"It's still there, that road," Lucky put in. "Supposedly it's one of the *really* old ways, the ones the roamers use."

Téngfēi and Sirin sat up straighter. They had heard tales of the mysterious itinerants called roamers before — roamer folklore was a big part of Odd Trails; plus, one of the tales that had given Negret and Sirin a clue to unravel the goings-on last year had been the story of Julian Roamer, the first of all of them. But Peter Hakelbar-end waved off Lucky's interruption with one hand.

"Whit stayed as far off the roads as he could. Even so, he'd been chased the whole way." A sad, faraway look crept over Mr. Hakel-barend's face. "I imagine the sounds of pursuing dogs and horses being silenced as the door of the warder's office shut behind him. Because Whit was a wanted man. He was wanted in Nagspeake because he was a smuggler, part of a famous crew at the time, and he was wanted in the United States because he was a fugitive slave. Now, in those days, Nagspeake was a lawless sort of place —"

"'In those days'?" Mrs. Kirkegrim asked, deadpan. "'Was'?"

Mr. Hakelbarend gave a single nod. "Was, and still is, in many ways. Fair enough. But back then, there were certain folks who made careers out of flouting even the good laws we had on the books. And although it wasn't *technically* legal to hunt down the es-caped slaves who reached the city, it wasn't unheard-of. There was a particular man who, among other business ventures, would, for a fee, assist bounty hunters in working under the radar in Nagspeake. His name was Morvengarde, and he'd been consulted on the matter of finding Whit Gammerbund."

Now everyone shifted in their seats, the non-Waits in surprise, and the Waits as they looked around the room and savored the as-tonishment on the others' faces.

"Morvengarde, as in Deacon and Morvengarde?" Lizzie asked.

"The very same, though this was before the partnership with Octavian Deacon that resulted in the empire we know today. Now, in addition to acting as a fixer for visiting bounty hunters,

Morvengarde had hunters of his own, and they were fierce and nearly impossible to shake once they were on your trail. They were expensive, too — somebody wanted you back badly, if he or she was willing to hire one of Morvengarde's hounds to find you. It was one of these who was on Whit's tail, and he arrived at the gates only minutes after Whit had been admitted.

"The sound of the hunter's fist battering on the door when Whit had barely settled himself in the warder's guest chair must have brought the boy's heart to his mouth. 'Don't open it,' he begged.

"But the warder was unconcerned. 'My job is to greet those who come to this place, no matter who they are. Whether they're allowed any farther into the Liberty than this room is another matter. But you have been granted asylum,' he reminded Whit. 'You have nothing to fear from outsiders any longer.'

"Well, Whit couldn't quite believe that yet. 'He's come for me, dead or alive,' he argued. 'And he doesn't care a fig for your sanctuary.'

"The warder gave him an unreadable look. 'Then why did you come all this way to ask for it?' he inquired. 'Trust in the Liberty. But there's no need for you to stay and watch what happens next.' He handed Whit a small piece of thick, folded paper upon which he'd been writing. Then he pointed to a second door opposite the one that was currently being hammered upon by the Morvengarde bounty hunter. 'Go home.'

"*Go home* was clearly an order to proceed into the walled city itself, and to consider it his new abode. But the warder's previous words—*There's no need for you to stay and watch what happens next*—well, Whit understood they meant *get on out of here so you don't complicate things,* but it was a strange way to put it.

"A creeping unease worked its way through his bones. But the warder was right: he'd come all this way for asylum. Even if he couldn't quite believe it would be enough to protect him from the hunter, it was the only chance he had. So Whit obeyed the warder's instructions and departed the office through the inner door."

Mr. Hakelbarend paused to take a sip from his mug. Téngfēi glanced toward the door to the screened porch; there hadn't been anything audible since Georgie's eruption earlier.

"There was a world on the other side of the warder's office," Mr. Hakelbarend continued, "and if Whit had walked into it under any other circumstances, he would've stood in awe of what he found. But even the miraculous can fade into the background and become invisible when you can't look past something that seems closer and more menacing. Whit's fear made him nearly blind to everything but the specter of the hunter. Nor could he bring himself to put his trust in the asylum he'd been granted and simply flee into the depths of the Liberty. Instead, he turned and watched with a pounding heart through a small, many-paned window next to the door he'd just come through as the warder let the hunter in.

"The hunter spoke, and the warder nodded. The hunter spoke again, and the warder shook his head. The hunter took a step closer and spoke once more. The warder stood his ground, and this time he held out his arms: *You shall not pass.* The hunter took a knife from his belt and flipped it over in his fingers as easily as a magician cascades a coin over his knuckles: *I can and will pass, even if I have to cut my way through you first.*

"And then," Mr. Hakelbarend said slowly, "without waiting for the warder's next move, the hunter flashed out with his knife hand. For a moment, the room was still. The only thing that changed was the color of the hunter's face. Then the warder fell. The hunter stepped over his body, wiping blood from his cheeks, and at last Whit turned and ran. He plunged into the first passageway that opened up before him. The hunter followed, and the Liberty swallowed both of them whole."

Mr. Hakelbarend lifted his cup again and took a long, placid sip.

"Is that the end?" Sirin asked.

Téngfēi glanced down the hearth at Marzana. Her face was painted with anticipation. She'd heard this story before, and she knew it wasn't over. From the looks of it, the good parts were still to come.

Sure enough, as soon as he'd fortified himself, Mr. Hakelbarend spoke again. "At first Whit didn't see anyone else. Remember that he was little more than a child, and he ran as an animal does, aware only of the predator on his heels. He allowed the turning ways and alleys to lead him deeper into the Liberty, giving no thought to the walls around him, to the windows that glinted briefly as he passed, to the balconies whose creeping vines brushed the top of his head or the doorways that appeared in the walls and then fell behind as he ran on.

"And then one of the doors opened, and a face peered out. Something about that face stopped the boy in his tracks. It belonged to a woman wearing glasses, but he could make out nothing more of her appearance.

"She looked over Whit's shoulder, and suddenly he could hear the pounding footsteps of the hunter, though they seemed to be coming from a good distance away. There were unnatural acoustics in those alleys.

"The stranger in the doorway turned her gaze on Whit. 'Have you a passport?' she asked.

"Whit took the warder's paper from his waistcoat and handed it to her. She unfolded it and read the words written inside. Then, from her pocket, she took a little copper-colored ink stamp, which she used to mark the passport. She returned the document and drew Whit inside the shadowy room. 'I grant you asylum, Whit. Follow the hallway with the lights.'

"Just then, the hunter turned the corner, spotted her, and threw himself at the closing door. It flew open, pushing the woman back, but she didn't fall. Instead, she faced the hunter and asked, 'Have you a passport?'

"The hunter took out his knife. 'Here is my passport,' he snarled, and he lunged at her.

"Whit cried out and reached for the woman, sure that she would fall just as the Warder had, with silence and a spray of blood. But his hands were knocked aside by the four huge, dry-rattling beetle wings that unfolded from the woman's back: two chitinous red wing covers and two translucent gray-brown flight wings.

"Beetle wings?" Téngfēi repeated dubiously.

"Shh," Marzana hissed.

"It's all right, Marzana," Mr. Hakelbarend said with a smile. "I think Milo is just confused by the sudden genre switch."

"I thought we were hearing a historical thing, is all," Téngfēi apologized. "Something real. I like fantasy, I just wasn't expecting it."

"No problem. Shall I continue?"

Sirin gave Téngfēi a little push. "Yes, please," he said to Mr. Hakelbarend.

"All right. Well, the beetle wings unfolded, and the woman screamed right in the hunter's face. *'No asylum for you!'* Her voice was as unexpected as the wings: high and otherworldly and full of fury. There was no challenging that voice, or cutting past it with a knife. The hunter stumbled backwards, and he was so cowed, the woman didn't even bother to slam the door in his face. She glanced back at Whit and said again, 'Follow the hallway with the lights, Whit.'

"At the back of the shadowy room was the entrance to another passageway. Sconces flickered here and there on the walls until the hallway meandered out of view. Whit managed a thank-you and hurried down it.

"The sconces cast a patchy light, and Whit found himself passing in and out of pools of illumination as he went. One wall was broken up at uneven intervals by uncurtained windows, through which Whit could see the hunter rushing along a course parallel to his own. Sometimes the hallway turned a corner, but even when it did, the hunter outside seemed able to turn a matching corner. Sometimes it went up a flight of stairs, but there were always windows at the next level that showed the boy that his pursuer had followed him. *There may be asylum in the Liberty,* the boy thought helplessly, *but perhaps there's no escape here.* In all this time, Whit saw no other person but the hunter.

"At last, the hallway came to an end at a door. Peering out, Whit saw a small courtyard ringed with brick and overhung with more eaves and balconies. The passage had been leading him upward for some time now, but even so, there were levels higher than this one. Across the courtyard was another door.

"There seemed to be nowhere to go but to that door across the yard, and there was certainly no time to waste in doing it. He darted into the courtyard, and the moment he did, the door opened. A figure stood on the threshold. It was a man, and he, too, wore spectacles, only his reflected too much light to show his eyes at all.

"Whit rushed to him. 'Do you have a passport?' the man asked. Then he adjusted his spectacles with the air of someone who had all the time in the world and studied the paper Whit handed over. As he read, the hunter vaulted over the courtyard wall.

"Before Whit could do more than flinch, the man in the doorway lowered his spectacles and looked over them at the hunter. 'Wait your turn,' he said mildly.

"The hunter stopped in his tracks. He didn't appear to be frozen, or anything as dramatic as that. He just looked as though he'd decided to pause in his crossing of the space, and he looked a bit confused about why he'd made that particular choice. The stranger pushed his glasses back up his nose, and Whit found himself wishing he'd gotten a look before the fellow had hidden his eyes again.

"'This all seems in order.' From his pocket the stranger produced a silver seal and a stick of wax. He took a candle from a table beside the door, melted the wax, dripped some onto the passport, and stamped it alongside the beetle-winged woman's stamp. Then he handed back the document. 'Come in, Whit. I grant you asylum. Follow the hallway with the vined carpet.'

"Whit entered the bright room. A carpet woven through with branching, twisting creepers covered the floor of the chamber, then narrowed and ran out along another passage.

"In the doorway behind him, the man spoke again, this time to the hunter. 'I can see you now. Thank you for waiting.'

"The hunter crossed the courtyard in a blur, knife already in his hand. The man lowered his glasses again, and a heartbeat later the hunter was standing still once more, caught mid-lunge with his knife mere inches from the man's nose. 'Do you have a passport?' the man inquired.

"The hunter managed to summon a surprising amount of vitriol, considering he was as helpless just then as a bug in amber. 'To hell with your passports!' he spat.

"The spectacled man laughed, and from his back sprouted a massive pair of goose wings: ash-colored, with nearly black pinion feathers edged in white. His laugh was terrible — there was no anger to it, only the amusement of a being so much more powerful than the thing facing it that anything that lesser creature did could only be entertaining. Until it became annoying, at which point the lesser creature was likely to be squashed underfoot like an insect.

"He took off his glasses and wiped his eyes as he laughed on. 'No asylum for you,' he said through his terrifying hilarity. Then he beat his wings once, and the hunter flew backward off his feet and straight over the courtyard wall.

"Then the man faced Whit. Without the glasses, his eyes were swirls of mist in sockets like deep caves. 'The hallway with the vined carpet,' he repeated."

"I like this story," Sirin said with relish. "Any story with empty eye sockets in it is okay by me."

The door to the porch opened and Georgie stalked out. She peered around the room with a mutinous expression on her face until she located Clem and Owen, looking into the living room over the back of the loveseat. Arms folded, Georgie went and leaned against the loveseat next to Clem. She put a hand on Georgie's back, but neither spoke. Georgie must've believed at least some of what Emmett had said or she'd be upstairs packing by now, but she certainly wasn't happy about it.

The customs agent followed a moment later, red in the face but a looking bit defiant at the same time. "Sorry to interrupt," Emmett said, closing the door. "Is there still coffee? Never mind, I'll just go check for myself."

Mrs. Kirkegrim got up. "I'll make another pot."

"I can do that," Mrs. Caraway offered, getting to her feet too.

"No, you sit," Mrs. Kirkegrim said. "I've heard this story before. It doesn't matter if I miss a little of it. Go ahead, Peter."

Mr. Hakelbarend nodded. "When we left Whit Gammerbund,"

he continued, picking up the thread of his tale, "the boy was in the bright room, about to start down the hallway with the vined carpet. This passage was illuminated by thick candles that stood on piles of books lining the walls. And like the last hallway, it was broken up by windows on one side. As Whit hurried past the first of these, the hunter appeared on the other side of the glass, pressing himself against a pane with his hands cupped around his face. He spotted Whit immediately.

"The hunter curled one hand into a fist around the handle of his knife and punched the glass. His fist bounced off without causing so much as a scratch. Whit didn't wait to see what his pursuer would do next. He took off down the hallway as fast as his feet would carry him and as fast as he could navigate its turns. And this hallway was nothing *but* turns.

"They started out as gentle curves, but before long, they became shorter and tighter. And this would've been troubling — a hallway can't spiral in on itself endlessly after all — except that the curving passage was also angling *downward*. And somehow, just as improbably, as the hallway made its descent, coiling itself ever tighter, Morvengarde's hunter kept pace on the outside. He appeared now and then in the windows like the monster Whit had been sure lurked in the forest beyond the fields when he was a child, back in the days before he learned that monsters lived in houses just like everyone else.

"The hallway went on pitching downward, yawing inward. Was he still aboveground? When he dared glance at the windows, behind the shape of the hunter, Whit saw fleeting glimpses of details that suggested there was still a town out there: flashes from other windows, a slick of sunlight painting the corner of a rooftop, even the occasional human figure standing on a balcony. These sightings became more and more frequent, until it began to look like the denizens of the Liberty were coming out to watch the hunter chase after his quarry.

"Inward. Downward. The candles were becoming more abundant, and the piles of books they stood on had begun to spill out into the middle of the passage.

"And then, when the hallway had curled in to about the width of a spiral staircase and Whit had to pick his way through mounds of books that didn't quite leave enough space down the middle for even a boy to pass, the corridor came to an abrupt stop at an iron door. Flickering light in shades of blue and violet spilled out from under it. Although logically there was no room for anything on the other side of that door, Whit took a deep breath, pushed it open, and looked out into a courtyard that could not possibly have been there at all.

"This courtyard was paved in red stone and surrounded by an ordinary-looking wall of the same material, and the blue and violet flicker came from a motley collection of ironwork lanterns and lampposts that hung here and leaned there at improbable angles around the space. In and among these, dangling bare from twisted cords, were dusty glass bulbs with curls of sparking, glowing blue-gray wire inside."

"Sounds pretty," Lucky said.

"Sounds like a light bulb," Téngfēi put in. "But how could

there be light bulbs?" When had the United States finally done away with slavery? "This would've been more than a hundred years ago, right?" He wasn't totally clear when electric lights had been invented, but it had to be too recently for an escaped slave to have encountered them. Not only that, but Téngfēi had seen something matching the description of these bulbs recently, right down to the unlikely color of the light. Four of them, five floors up, in the Emporium.

"After winged creatures, you're worried about light bulbs?" Sirin asked.

"I'm just trying to keep everything straight," Téngfēi muttered defensively.

Mr. Hakelbarend shrugged. "The stranger thing for Whit was where they were. Above the top of the red stone wall, the rest of the Liberty towered overhead, as if he were seeing it from the bottom of a well. There was daylight up there, but it was far too distant to cast any illumination this far down. And, as he'd realized before, the final tight curves of the hallway could not have concealed a space bigger than a closet — certainly nothing as big as this courtyard. It was an impossible space. And set into the opposite wall, between two bent lampposts that curved over it like an archway, was another door.

"As Whit tried to make sense of what he was seeing, the hunter climbed over the wall. And — Whit gave a little start — the hunter looked *terrible*. He looked battered, for one thing, as if he'd had to fight his way here, or cut his way through unforgiving and overgrown territory. He looked gaunter than Whit remembered. And —

this surely wasn't possible, but he looked *older*. His hair was shot through with white that definitely hadn't been there before.

"The hunter gave a start when he got a good look at Whit, too. 'Impossible!' he hissed in a voice that crackled as if it hadn't been used in years. And then Whit discovered something else that was different about the hunter: he was, for the first time, *hesitating*. But before the boy could make sense of that, the door under the arching lampposts swung wide.

"The woman who stepped out was dressed in trousers and a vest of patterned tweed topped by a short cloak that reached only to her elbows. To Whit, who'd never seen tweeds before, the pattern in the wool made it look as if she were dressed in some sort of animal hide made of soft scales. She wore a gold-rimmed monocle, leaving one eye visible. That eye glanced from Whit to the hunter and back.

"'Who among you has a passport?' she inquired in a voice like the buzzing of bees. Whit came forward and presented his document. The woman took the passport with one hand and adjusted her monocle with the other. As she moved, Whit saw that her cloak had been hiding a pair of thin but leathery flaps of translucent green and gold flesh that connected her upper arms, from the shoulder to the elbow, to her torso, like the wings of a gliding lizard.

"'This seems in order.' She licked her thumb and pressed it onto the paper, then took a golden tube from her pocket, uncorked it, and tipped a stream of gleaming dust onto her thumbprint. She shook off the excess, opened the door of the nearest lantern, and melted the glittering powder carefully over the flame. When she handed the passport back, a seal with the look of molten metal lay alongside the other two marks.

"Then she turned to the hunter and held out her hand. He shook his head angrily. 'My directive was to return this child even if the hunt took me to the ends of the earth,' he said. 'I think not even my employer can say I didn't follow those orders. But if someone's willing to move heaven and hell to protect him . . .' And he spat on the red stone floor. He turned to Whit, and hate blazed from his face. 'I wish you joy of your freedom, if there's any joy to be had in this place.'

" 'Then you do not have a passport?' the woman inquired.

" 'To hell with your passports,' the hunter snarled. 'To hell with your doors. I'm going home.'

" 'Oh, I see. You misunderstand me.' Her lips peeled back, and her teeth were so white and perfect that Whit almost didn't notice how sharp they were. 'In my courtyard, the passport isn't for entry into the next passage. It's what lets you leave.'

"The hunter recoiled in terror as the woman held out her hands as if reaching for a dance partner. She waltzed across the red stones and took the hunter in her arms, wrapping him in her green and gold wings. The hunter began to howl—first protests, then threats. The woman, unfazed, waltzed back to the door, carrying him along with her as if they were dancers at a cotillion.

"The woman paused on the threshold to look back at Whit. 'Follow the sunlit passage,' she said, her buzzing voice somehow perfectly audible over the hunter's shouts.

"Whit turned, but the door he had come through was no longer there. 'Where?' he asked. She pointed her chin upward at the tiny spot of sunlight far above. 'How?' Whit protested. There seemed no way to ascend. One would have to fly.

"The woman spoke as if she had heard his thoughts. 'Of course you have to fly. What do you think *those* are for?' Whit turned to look over his shoulder again, and this time he saw something he hadn't noticed before: the top joint of a wing, like a bat's, but fashioned from copper and silver and gold.

"'You have your asylum,' she said. 'Enjoy it.' Then the door shut, leaving Whit alone in the iron-and-red-stone courtyard. And Whit stretched out his new wings and he rose up out of the depths, free at last of the hunter, and free of gravity, too."

Mr. Hakelbarend raised his cup. "The end."

twenty-six

SANCTUARY

ARZANA APPLAUDED. So did Sirin. Then the others joined in. Mr. Hakelbarend glanced over at Milo. "Not what you expected, I know, but did you enjoy it?"

"It wasn't what I expected at all," Téngfēi admitted. "But yeah, I liked it a lot." He thought for a minute. "So it was never . . . the other kind of asylum? Why do people think it was?"

"Because of the Liberty's other name," Sylvester said. "The one people who don't live there use. Saint Whit Gammerbund's Home for the Mentally Chaotic."

"There's always been confusion about that word, *asylum*," Mr. Hakelbarend said. "And there have been plenty of times when the denizens of the Liberty were content to let that confusion stand. It kept people away, you see."

"Whit became a saint?" Téngfēi asked.

Mr. Hakelbarend nodded. "The patron saint of the Liberty. And also the namesake of the chapel where one of the hobby horse skulls was found."

"He's a fascinating figure," Lucky put in. "He certainly existed, but there's as much myth surrounding him as there is actual, verifiable history. There's another story where —"

Mrs. Kirkegrim cleared her throat. "I think I need to stretch my legs before we dive into another tale, Lucky."

"Me too," Clem said. "Let's take a break." She grabbed Georgie's hand and the two of them hurried onto the screened porch while everyone else stretched and went for more coffee. Emmett watched the door shut behind them and sighed.

"So Whit Gammerbund was definitely a real person," Téngfēi asked, speaking half to Sirin and half to Mr. Hakelbarend. "But we're not supposed to believe that story was literally true, are we?"

Mr. Hakelbarend stretched comfortably in his chair. "Well, look. Plenty of people who were probably real have some fairly unbelievable stories told about them. And saints — to become a saint in the first place, you have to have performed a number of verified miracles, which are, by definition, phenomena that can't be explained by the laws of reality." Mrs. Kirkegrim appeared and handed a fresh cup of milky coffee to Mr. Hakelbarend, then she settled onto the sofa at the end near the porch. "I think," Mr. Hakelbarend said, taking a sip, "that the point of a story of the miraculous is to *convey* a truth, not necessarily to *be* true."

Which left the question: what truth was a story about a hunted boy and winged gatekeepers supposed to convey?

"Hey." Sirin gave Téngfēi a gentle shove. "Want to compare notes before Lucky starts?"

"Where?" Téngfēi muttered out of the corner of his mouth, then covered the syllable (he hoped) with a throat-clearing noise. Marzana was still sitting at the end of the hearth by the tree. He couldn't get into the cave without asking her to move, which would just be weird.

"The loveseat's empty right now," Sirin pointed out.

"Guess I better figure out what story I'm going to tell," Téngfēi said casually, picking up his bag. Then he and Sirin slid off the hearth and hurried over to the room's other halfway-private spot.

"All right, so what have we got?" Sirin asked as Téngfēi got out his spiral pad and pen. "Did that story give us anything useful? What did we learn, apart from the fact that apparently anyone can disappear into the Liberty?"

"I think we learned the opposite, actually," Téngfēi whispered, twisting the pen between his fingers. "I think we learned that *not* everyone can disappear into the Liberty — or at least, not safely — but whoever does is pretty much untouchable. I don't know what that has to do with anything, though. Unless . . ." He leaned over the back of the loveseat. Lucky was talking to Emmett near the dining table. "You watched Lucky during the story, right? Did she do anything?"

Sirin scowled and shook her head. "Nothing. She just listened and looked interested. Masterful performance."

"If it *is* a performance," Téngfēi said, wanting to be fair.

"Let's just hope her story tells us something," Sirin grumbled.

Téngfēi started to speak, then stopped as Marzana approached the loveseat and peeked over the back. "Mrs. Caraway said there's more hot chocolate coming," she said a little shyly. "Do you want a cup?"

"Say yes," Sirin ordered immediately.

"All right," Téngfēi said awkwardly. "Yes. Thank you." Marzana headed kitchenward. "What was that about?" he hissed.

"We still need more information from her," Sirin said. "Like how she and Lucky know each other, for one thing."

But Téngfēi was thinking back to Mr. Hakelbarend's story, and how Marzana had looked as if she'd heard it before. Of course, if it was a well-known tale about a local saint, a hero of the Liberty, maybe that was all the explanation they needed. Still, another idea was starting to take shape.

He recalled the earlier exchange between Marzana and Mr. Hakelbarend. Marzana: *Peter's a good source. I trust what he says.* Then, Mr. Hakelbarend, in a voice with a touch of amusement in it: *You do? That's news to me.* And Marzana again: *I don't always like what he says, but I almost always trust it.*

There was too much familiarity, too much humor, and too

much history implied there for it to be a conversation between two people who'd only met the day before. Then he remembered how Mr. Hakelbarend had introduced them both. *My name is Peter Hakelbarend. This is Marzana.*

Whenever the Pines met someone new, his parents did the same thing. "I'm Nora Pine. This is Milo." Or, more often, "This is my son, Milo." But never did they bother to say his full name, first and last.

"I know what Marzana's last name is," Téngfēi whispered. "It's *Hakelbarend*. She's Peter's daughter."

"What?" Sirin turned to stare over the seat, first at Mr. Hakelbarend, who was still sipping his coffee quietly in the chair in the corner, then at the entrance to the kitchen, where presumably Marzana was waiting for two hot chocolates. "But why on earth — they're definitely pretending otherwise, right?"

"Definitely. I don't think any of the other Waits know. Not even Lucky, and she appears to have been acquainted with both of them before the caroling began. But I'm right. I'm sure of it."

As he explained the details that made him so certain, Sirin's disbelief turned to a thoughtful expression. "All right, that all makes a certain amount of sense. But they don't look anything like each other," she observed. Téngfēi raised an eyebrow and treated her to every ounce of disgust he could put into a single glance. "Oh. Right. I guess they don't have to look alike, do they?"

"No," he said stiffly. "They don't. That doesn't mean anything at all. Maybe she was adopted. Or maybe she just looks more like her mom than her dad."

"Then why are they pretending?" Sirin persisted. Abruptly, she shut her mouth and made a zipping motion across her lips as Marzana came around the loveseat with two mugs. Téngfēi hastily took off his ring. Sirin tucked her blue glasses into the pocket of her robe.

"Here," Marzana said, handing one of the mugs to Milo. "Mrs. Caraway said this is how you like yours."

"It's—" And then Milo lost his entire train of thought as something derailed him completely. It wasn't a realization so much as the sudden awareness that there was something he *should* realize, but wasn't getting to. What was it?

"Is something wrong?" Marzana asked.

"Oh. No, thank you. This is perfect," Milo said, confused.

"Ask her if she wants to sit," Meddy prompted, sounding annoyed at his lack of chivalry. "I'll move."

"Er." Milo shrank a little. "Do you want to sit?"

"No," Marzana said immediately. "You look like you want some alone time."

"Oh. Thanks," he said, surprised.

She shrugged. "I know what it looks like when someone wants alone time. And you said before that you need to work on your story."

"That was the idea," he fibbed. Marzana started to leave. "Wait a second. I have a question for you, if it's okay to ask one."

She turned back slowly. "Okay, shoot."

Milo cleared his throat and, feeling a little self-conscious, waved her closer. He lowered his voice. "Why are you and Mr. Hakelbarend pretending not to be related?"

Marzana's dark-rimmed eyes narrowed. She didn't say anything for a minute. Then she sat down, forcing Meddy to scoot hurriedly out from under her. "How did you know?"

"You were too familiar before, when you told me he was a good source of information. You wouldn't have said all that if you'd just met." Milo hesitated. "Is he your dad?"

"Yes." She gave a little chuckle. "You're probably the only one who would've guessed that, you know?" Then she shook her head, annoyed at herself. "Do you think everyone knows?"

"I . . . I don't know. I haven't told anyone. The other Waits don't know, either?"

Now Marzana hesitated, then shook her head. "No."

There was something off about that response, but he couldn't quite work out how to follow up on it, so he circled back to the first question he'd asked. "I won't say anything. But why the charade?"

She clutched her cup in both hands and stared out the window over the rim. "It's cold out there, huh?"

Milo followed her gaze to the white-crusted lawn with its dead grass and meager layer of frost. "Probably."

"It's what we do whenever we leave the Liberty," Marzana said slowly, and it took Milo a moment to realize she was now, finally, answering his question. "Not that we leave the Liberty all that often. I can't explain the reason. It isn't that I don't trust you, but I still can't tell you."

"So it isn't something to do with this particular caroling trip, then?" Milo asked.

"We do it whenever we come down the hill," she repeated. "That's all I can say. I'm sorry."

"I'm sorry to have pried," Milo responded, not sure what else he could say in response.

"It's all right."

"Can I ask you something else, then?"

She shrugged. "Go ahead."

"I know Lucky invited you, and she said you work together. But if she doesn't know the truth about you, how well would you say you know her?"

Now Marzana looked confused. "Lucky? Why do you ask?"

"I can't tell you." Turnabout was perfectly fair play, under the circumstances. "But it's important."

Marzana clearly didn't like his refusal to share, but she accepted it. "Lucky doesn't know the truth about me. Not unless she guessed, like you did. I suppose that's possible. And Lucky owns a bookstore where I like to shop."

Ah. So when Lucky had said she knew Marzana from work, she hadn't meant they worked together. That made more sense.

Marzana gave him a long look. When she spoke again, her voice was skeptical. "You don't think Lucky's . . ."

"Lucky's what?"

"Nothing." She stood with a strained smile. "I can't wait to hear whatever story you're going to tell."

Meddy, who'd been leaning against the window with folded arms, watched her go. "I'll bet you a hundred invisible pancakes this has to do with the asylum thing. Sanctuary."

Milo watched over the back of the loveseat as a brief but meaningful glance passed between Marzana, as she settled back onto the hearth, and Mr. Hakelbarend in the corner chair. Mr. Hakelbarend looked at Milo and raised his coffee cup.

Mrs. Kirkegrim, still curled on the sofa by the screened porch, followed the man's gaze and lifted her mug too. "Are we toasting Milo?"

"Um. Cheers," Milo said, then ducked back down again. "What were you saying about sanctuary?" he whispered to Meddy.

"*That's* why they live in the Liberty, I bet," Meddy said. "Mr. Hakelbarend and Marzana." She turned and pointed out the window and across the grounds to a place where the skeletal winter remains of a garden encircled a little stone bench, one leg of which was Meddy's own headstone, marking the place where her mortal remains lay. She took the glasses from her pocket and polished the blue lenses on a yellow silk hem before perching them on her nose. "When someone in your family isn't safe everywhere, it requires you to take extraordinary precautions sometimes."

"You're saying Mr. Hakelbarend is some kind of wanted man?" Milo whispered as he put on Téngfēi's ring.

She nodded. "That's exactly what I think. Pretending they're not related when they're outside the Liberty is his way of making sure if he gets picked up for any reason, she won't automatically become a target too. I wonder who he really is."

Now his telling of the story of Whit Gammerbund began to make a bit more sense. A hunted person finding some kind of miraculous amnesty inside the walls of the city-within-the-city would naturally appeal to someone who had found asylum there himself. Minus, presumably, the wings.

Then Sirin gave a start. "That's it! *He's Cantlebone.* A world-famous thief in hiding would definitely have to protect his family. It explains everything!"

"Nope," Téngfēi whispered, shaking his head. "In the first place, I'm pretty sure Mr. Hakelbarend was down here the whole time last night. And in the second place, isn't the thing about Cantlebone that nobody knows who he is? He's practically a myth. Maybe there are people who'd like to figure out his identity, but that's not the same kind of 'wanted' as, say, Doc Holystone was, or somebody who's on the run like Whit Gammerbund in the story." Sirin didn't look convinced, but Téngfēi was positive. "I think probably there are a lot of wanted people who've gone to the Liberty for asylum. Maybe he's one of them. But I don't think he's who we're looking for."

A bell-like *ding ding ding* sounded from the dining room. "Attention," Lucky sang out, plinking a fork against the rim of her cup. "Storytelling Part Two begins as soon as I'm back from the bathroom."

Sirin nudged Téngfēi's shoulder. "This is it, Téngfēi. This is where we get our answers, I can just feel it."

"Great," Téngfēi replied. Maybe it was true that Lucky could've pulled off all the incidents that had plagued Greenglass House in the last two days, but he still couldn't completely believe she was

Cantlebone or working for Gilawfer, any more than he could cast Mr. Hakelbarend in those roles. Still, Sirin was right. At this point, Lucky was the simplest answer.

It would be nice, he thought, *if for once somebody turned out to be who they said they were. Just once.*

twenty-seven

LUCIA AND THE SKULL

LUCKY BEGAN HER TALE the way a folklore nerd ought to. She began with *Listen*.

Everyone had reassembled in the living room. Even Clem and Georgie had finally emerged from their lengthy conference. Whatever they'd decided, Georgie had made the grand gesture of sitting next to Emmett on the sofa. He'd given her a questioning look. "Don't read anything into it," Georgie had muttered, folding her arms. "We'll talk afterward." Then, a moment later, she'd added, "But I will say I like your painting so far."

Now Lucky held the room. If she felt any reluctance or nerves, she didn't show them. Sirin was watching her like a hawk from the middle of the hearth. Téngfēi sat at the end farthest from the tree—

Marzana was still at the other end — and he watched the others. If his gut feeling was right and Lucky wasn't the person they were after, then he needed another suspect. But who? He looked from one face to another.

Sylvester, standing against the wall by the porch door, had eyes only for Lucky. Rob was leaning with his arms folded on the back of the chair next to Téngfēi's end of the hearth, looking bored. He seemed to have been ready to leave since that morning. But Mr. Larven, who was sitting in that chair, appeared to be staring right past Lucky at *Georgie*. And Mrs. Kirkegrim, who had shifted to the other end of the sofa, had her eyes pinned on Clem, sitting cross-legged in the chair next to the loveseat.

Interesting.

"Listen," Lucky said, taking the center of the room. "Once a little girl was playing hide-and-seek, and although she was supposed to be hiding, she found something instead.

"The little girl was part of a clique that ran through their part of the Liberty as wild and fearless as cats. When they played hide-and-seek, it was an all-day affair. Inevitably there were two winners: whoever *appeared* to win, and the last kid left hiding, which is to say the one who was forgotten about and trudged home long after the game had ended. On one particular day, the big winner was a girl named Lucia."

As she spoke, she pivoted little by little, so that although her back was always to someone, she was never facing away from the same part of the room for long. *Lucky has told stories like this before,* Téngfēi thought.

"Lucia. That's Lucky's real name, isn't it?" Sirin asked in a whisper. Téngfēi nodded.

"Lucia had half expected to be forgotten. She had found a truly epic hiding place. There was a loose board among the handful that had been used to secure the door of a long-closed shop, and when she'd pried that board away, it left a hole just big enough to crawl through. Although she'd left the board slightly ajar in an effort to make her hiding place just a little less awesome, she'd been pretty sure nobody would find her, so she'd taken the opportunity to explore the empty space.

"The shop had once been a bookstore, she thought. She half remembered when it had been open, years before. Whoever had last owned it had left the insides mostly intact when he or she had closed up for the final time. The books were gone, but plenty remained: dusty brocade furniture, shelves that still bore the uneven grime showing where the missing volumes had been, and dozens of mounds of wax, the only remnants of long-ago expended candles that probably had never quite provided enough light to read by. And on one wall there was a single very wide brick step that led to a pair of small wrought-iron doors just Lucia's size.

"They were irresistible. They looked like they absolutely had to lead to someplace fantastic, Narnia or the Hollow Wood or an outpost of Fiddler's Green. And surely, she thought, it could be no accident that she had found these doors while playing hide-and-seek, just like Lucy Pevensie when she found her path to Narnia! And in a bookshop! Sal Mayfly had found the Old Route to Fiddlersport in a bookshop! Lucia climbed tremulously onto the brick stair and grasped the handle on the right. Did it feel *warm?* She turned it and hauled open the door, which was heavy and reluctant . . . and found nothing but cold ash and half-burned kindling. Because of course, it wasn't a door to Narnia." Lucky pivoted a quarter-turn and gestured to the wall behind Téngfēi and Sirin. "The brick stair was a hearth, and the doors hid nothing but a fireplace.

"Lucia was so disappointed, she hauled off and kicked the nearest branch in it. And then, just as she was about to close the door again, something glinted and caught her eye: a stray drift of sunlight had found a patch of something reflective on the branch. She looked again and realized that the thing she'd kicked wasn't a piece of kindling at all. It was an antler, and it was covered patchily with something that glittered like gold.

"Lucia dug into the debris and unearthed the thing that was buried there. Then she sat back and considered it for a few minutes, trying to determine whether she wanted to take it from its place or not. It was the skull of a horned animal with gilded antlers, and Lucia couldn't decide whether it seemed eerie and magical or simply terrifying. But Lucia was a fanciful girl, and in the end she couldn't leave it in the fireplace. It was too bizarre and too beautiful. So she pulled it from the ashes, carried it to the counter where the register had probably once been, and found a rag to try to clean it off as well as she could.

"'Thank you,' the skull said.

"'You're welcome,' Lucia replied, wiping its jaw with the cloth. 'Had you been in there long?'

"'Years and years,' the skull replied. 'Who knows how much

longer I would've had to stay if you hadn't come by. I think I've been forgotten about.'

"'I'm Lucia,' she said as she scrubbed at the stained bone.

"'I'm the hobby horse,' said the skull.

"'You don't look like a horse. You look like a pair of antlers on the wrong head.'

"'That's because I'm not a horse,' the skull explained patiently. 'I'm a *hobby* horse.'

"'Well, whatever you are, you're cleaner,' Lucia told it. 'Where would you like to be put now?'

"'That depends very much upon what time of year it is.' The hobby horse glanced at the nearest window, but of course it was boarded up, like all the rest.

"'It's summer,' Lucia reported. 'August.'

"'Hmm. Then I suppose I must stay here until at least the start of December,' the hobby horse said sadly. 'Winter is my time of year. It used to be that I would be taken out of my fireplace in December to go caroling with the Waits, but it's been a long time since that happened. Do you know the Waits?' he asked Lucia hopefully. 'They're who I need to find.'

"Lucia thought and thought, but she didn't know anyone named Wait. 'If I find them, can you come out into the Liberty?'

"'Yes,' the hobby horse said. 'But not until December.'

"'Then I'll find them by then,' Lucia promised.

"'You could come and visit me in the meantime,' the hobby horse suggested. 'If you wanted to.'

"Lucia went to visit the hobby horse every weekend after that.

Each time she crept through the hole in the boards, she found the skull half buried in ashes in the fireplace again. She would take it out and wipe it clean with a fresh cloth from home, and they would discuss her week at school — usually terrible — and whatever progress she had made in searching for the mysterious Waits — usually not much. The hobby horse, not having been out in the world for years and years, had very little to add to the conversations, but it liked listening to Lucia, and occasionally it made useful points and asked important questions. The little girl always felt better after a visit to the hobby horse, no matter how tough a week she'd had. Then she would leave the skull polished and gleaming darkly on the dusty, dim bookstore counter, because she figured it was nicer there than in the ashy fireplace. But that's where she would find it when she came back — buried in soot behind the iron doors.

"The weeks passed, and summer trailed away into autumn. October came and went, and then it was the cold end of November. In the shuttered bookstore, Lucia came and went, visiting her friend and bringing it updates, but still she had no leads in her search for the Waits. December was looming, and Lucia was afraid. If she didn't find the people her friend needed, winter would pass into spring without the hobby horse being able to leave the bookstore, and then it would be stuck there for another year.

" 'I have an idea,' she said one crisp afternoon right on the doorstep of December. 'Suppose you and I go out into the Liberty and look for the Waits together?'

" 'I don't know,' the hobby horse fretted. 'Just go out there? Is it safe?'

"'Of course,' Lucia assured it. 'I'll be with you.' And that began a new time in their friendship. In the afternoons, after school and before dinner, Lucia went to the shop, retrieved the hobby horse, and took it on long walks through the Liberty. It was unwieldy at first; the hobby horse wasn't precisely heavy, but its antlers were almost as wide as Lucia's outstretched arms, which made it difficult to carry. And the night came on earlier and earlier, too — even earlier in the Liberty than in other parts of the city because there were so many tall buildings overhanging the passages and courtyards of Lucia's neighborhood. She needed light to see by, but carrying a lantern or a flashlight was out of the question since she needed both hands to carry the hobby horse.

"In the end, they settled on an arrangement that made perfect sense to the two of them but that looked completely bizarre to anyone who saw them on their perambulations: Lucia tied the hobby horse on top of her own head like a bony hat, with a candle fixed in the open mouth of the skull to light their way."

"Creepy," Téngfēi said.

"Probably," Lucky agreed. "But they hadn't meant it to be — it was just what they came up with. And it worked.

"As they walked along, Lucia sang to help her friend relax in the unfamiliar alleyways. And because it was December and the hobby horse had once mentioned caroling with its mysterious friends the Waits, she sang her favorite Christmas songs.

"December slipped by. The days grew shorter, the nights grew colder, and, unbeknownst to Lucia, word started to spread through the Liberty of the strange girl who wandered the streets at dusk, singing Christmas carols with a gleaming and glittering antlered skull on her head. And this was how it came to be that, on the first evening of the Raw Nights, the Waits found her.

"The candle in the skull's mouth was burning with an aroma of bayberry and oranges, and she was singing 'The Holly and the Ivy.'" Lucky pivoted to face Mr. Hakelbarend in his chair opposite the tree and Mrs. Pine and Lizzie, who were sitting cross-legged on the floor at that end of the room, and began to sing. *"The holly and the ivy, when they are both full grown, of all the trees that are in the wood, the holly bears the crown.*

"And suddenly the two friends heard voices singing the same song somewhere up ahead." She made another quarter-turn to face Téngfēi, Sirin, and Marzana on the hearth and began to sing again. *"The rising of the sun and the running of the deer, the playing of the merry organ, sweet singing of the choir.* A moment later a figure turned the corner before them. It was a woman wearing a crown of candles on her head. Then came a man carrying the tools of a chimney sweep. Then came a woman carrying a branch lit with tapers and hung with glass bees, and then came others, all singing 'The Holly and the Ivy.'

"Last of all came a creature that gave Lucia a terrible fright at first. Then she realized that she was looking at something very much like how she herself must have appeared just then. It was a horse's skull, except with two curving horns like a ram's protruding from its temples. Delicate silvery webs had been woven in the circular spaces formed by the horns. There were candles in its eye sockets, and its body was covered in layers of white shrouds. It was different from her friend, but it was unquestionably another hobby horse."

"Heck, yeah," Sirin whispered. "*Two* stories with eye sockets."

"Lucia stopped walking and stopped singing as the group of strangers came to stand before her. But *they* didn't stop singing, and after a moment Lucia joined back in. When the song ended, they began the first verse of 'Greensleeves.'

" 'Are these the friends you were looking for?' Lucia whispered to her companion. The hobby horse had a lit candle in its mouth, so all it could do was whinny, but the sound was so happy the answer was clear. They had found the Waits.

"Lucia joined in again on the next verse, and when the carolers resumed walking, Lucia followed. She and her antlered friend sang with the Waits every evening of the season, caroling throughout the Liberty of Gammerbund. And when the Raw Nights came to an end, Lucia returned the joyful hobby horse to its resting place in the shuttered bookshop. 'Will you come back again?' it asked.

" 'I promise,' Lucia said. And she did. Every year at the start of the Raw Nights, she retrieved the gold-antlered skull from its hiding place and went to join the Waits. She returned at other times too, and although the hobby horse never did have all that much to say, it continued to be a good listener." Lucky smiled a little sheepishly and turned her palms up. "And that's how the fifth of the hobby horses, the one Marzana played this year, was found."

"By you?" Téngfēi asked.

"By me. When I was about ten. The end, I guess." The room applauded. "And before you ask," she said to him as the clapping died away, "yes, I really did walk around with it tied to my head."

That was what she thought he'd be struggling with after that story? "But . . . the parts about the skull talking?"

Lucky hesitated, then shrugged. "I was a lonely kid. It seems crazy now, but that's how I remember it." She scratched her head. "You know what, though? Even if it was true, rather than a mistaken memory, it still wouldn't be the strangest thing about these skulls. Not to mention, there's some really out-there lore about them. That they've been seen on Raw Nights long after the caroling's done, drifting through the streets on their own, or that carolers have put on a certain hobby horse costume and gone out with a particular band, only to take off the getup and discover they're wearing a different skull and accompanied by a completely different group of Waits. That sort of thing."

"And the bookstore?" Marzana asked. "Is that the one you own now?"

"Sure is."

"So you've been caroling since you were ten?" Mrs. Caraway asked.

Lucky nodded. "And I've been the . . . steward, I guess, of that skull ever since. It's my job to dig it up and bring it every year, and I get to pick the person to play the hobby horse in our band." She winked at Marzana. "Usually only a few people know where any particular hobby horse skull is. It's not that it's exactly a secret, but somehow it sort of works out that way. I think that's how ours got lost for so long—the only person who knew where it was must've been the former owner of the bookshop, and he or she probably died without passing the information along." She turned to where Milo's parents sat and gave a shy curtsy. "Thank you."

Despite all her evidence, Sirin had to be wrong about Lucky. Téngfēi was more certain than ever. If anybody in the room was exactly who and what they said they were, he thought, it had to be this woman. She was there because caroling as one of the Waits was something she loved doing, something that had been part of her since she was a little girl. And she would never have sullied this most beloved thing by using it to sneak into someone else's house.

"No, thank *you*," Mrs. Pine said. "I'm so honored that you shared such a personal tale with us."

Lucky beamed, then turned that high-wattage smile on Téngfēi. "Your turn, Milo."

Before he could even start feeling nervous, Mrs. Kirkegrim sniffed the air. "What's that smell?"

Now everybody sniffed. Lizzie lurched to her feet and darted to the kitchen. Téngfēi heard muffled cursing from the other side of the wall. He followed the swearing and the smell of burning and found Lizzie furiously waving a dishtowel at smoke billowing from the open oven. "What happened?"

"Heck if I know. These loaves should've had another few minutes to go, but—" She folded the towel around her hand, reached into the oven, and pulled out the baking sheet. On it sat two oblong objects, lumpy and shrunken and thoroughly blackened. "Unbelievable."

Téngfēi glanced at the temperature dial. "Is the oven supposed to be set to five hundred degrees?"

Lizzie followed his pointing finger and swore again. "No, it is not. Somebody must've bumped it or something." She sighed and set the baking sheet on the stove to cool off. "I'll throw something easy in. Cookies are fast."

Téngfēi knew better than to hang around in the kitchen when anybody needed to do anything in there fast. He went back to the living room. "I guess there was a mishap with the oven," he announced to the room. "Lizzie's making cookies instead. And in the meantime, I need to practice for a little bit before I tell my story. Upstairs." With a quick, sharp glance at Sirin, he grabbed his rucksack. "I'll be back."

"Okay, okay," Sirin conceded as she followed him out of the living room. "After that story, I think you might be right. Maybe Lucky's not our guy. You have a better idea, though?"

The last petal fell off the poinsettia by the dining room window as the two of them breezed past. Téngfēi stopped in his tracks and gave the plant a long look. "I kind of think I do."

"What?" Sirin asked.

Téngfēi glanced over his shoulder, but nobody seemed to be paying them any attention. Then he leaned close to the damp soil in the pot and took a deep sniff.

"This feels familiar," Sirin said. "You think something's hidden in a plant again? That seems like a stretch, Téngfēi."

"Oh, I think something got hidden in there, all right." He grabbed the sleeve of the Cloak of Golden Indiscernibility and pulled Sirin up the stairs. "Come on."

twenty-eight

FALSE ASSUMPTIONS

TÉNGFĒI SHUT THE DOOR and tossed his bag on the bed. "Okay, so Lucky's not the thief." He leaned against his desk, thinking. "Mrs. Kirkegrim and Mr. Larven were watching Clem and Georgie really, really closely during her story."

"They're ruled out," Sirin said mechanically. "Tell me about the poinsettia."

Téngfēi shook his head. "According to the assumptions we've made so far, *everybody's* ruled out. We have to look at it all differently somehow."

"But even if we allow that the victims aren't necessarily innocent, there's still no one of them who could've done everything!"

"Yeah, I know," Téngfēi said wearily. "But I think we made

another false assumption. We assumed, whether we're looking for Cantlebone or a henchman of Gilawfer's, that we're *only looking for one person.*"

Sirin had begun to pace, but now she stopped cold. "What?"

This was starting to feel right. "We know that, other than Lucky, there's no one person who could've done everything. But what if it was *two* people working together?"

"Mrs. Kirkegrim and Mr. Larven?" Sirin frowned. "You're going to have to explain to me how they could've done any of it when they were both unconscious."

"They could have done plenty if they *weren't* unconscious," Téngfēi argued. "And I think the poinsettia just convinced me that I'm right. That flower was fine yesterday, and today it's practically dead. What if Mr. Larven *poisoned the punch himself;* then, each time he poured himself a cup of it, instead of drinking it, he dumped it in the flowerpot? He was over by that window a lot. Plus, at one point he spilled practically a whole cup on himself. Maybe he didn't drink *any* of it."

Sirin thought for a minute. "Wouldn't it have been simpler to just pretend to have passed out from drinking too much? It would've accomplished the same things — preventing the group from leaving and getting him upstairs alone, theoretically tucked in to sleep it off, but really with the run of the place. Why complicate it with a fake poisoning? What if somebody had found the tea ball with the stuff in it earlier and called Emergency Medical Assistance?"

"I thought about that, and I think it's the same reason Mrs. Kirkegrim didn't just pretend to fall down the stairs or something instead of faking an actual attacker. The point wasn't just to keep the group from leaving. They also wanted to stir up a bunch of chaos and confusion in the house. That's why he poisoned the punch, and that's why he left the berries in the tea ball to be found. If somebody else drank some and got a little sick . . ." Téngfēi shrugged. "Well, that's just more confusion in the mix. Or maybe there wasn't even enough poison in the punch to actually affect anyone, since Mr. Larven only needed to *look* like he got sick. But even if someone *had* called EMA, do you have any idea how long it takes an ambulance to get up here from town?"

"Yes, I remember that much," Sirin grumbled.

"Well, then you know he'd have plenty of time to poke around up here in the meantime, while he was supposed to be tucked in. Or maybe if anyone had suggested it, he'd miraculously have recovered just enough to tell them not to bother."

She turned pale. "Let me see your notebook." Téngfēi passed it to her and she flipped pages until she came to the one where they'd written down which rooms everyone was in. "Oh, I am such an idiot," she groaned. "Téngfēi, he was in three W!"

He looked at the page, then up at her. "Yeah, so?"

"*So,* that's the room with the good view of the front lawn!" She fell onto the bed and buried her face in the pillow. "The room I was in last night for like an hour, looking for my dad," her muffled voice explained. "It was empty the whole time I was there. I am *such* an idiot."

Téngfēi sat at the edge of the bed and patted her shoulder. "Don't beat yourself up. I didn't realize it either. But in that case, now that we know he wasn't sleeping off the effects of the punch, we have to assume he certainly could have stolen Georgie's and Clem's stuff earlier that night, as long as Mom and Lucky didn't stick around after taking him up. And why would they? Mom had too much to deal with, and we know Lucky felt terrible about how the caroling was turning out. I bet she went back downstairs to try to get things under control as soon as she could."

Sirin rolled over and stared at the ceiling. "We still have the question of who hit Mrs. Kirkegrim and Marzana, and Mr. Larven was definitely downstairs at that point, right? So he couldn't have been the impossible third person in the room." She turned her head to look at Téngfēi. "But under our new theory that there was more than one person behind all these events, there doesn't have to have been a third person in the room at all, huh? Not if Mrs. Kirkegrim conked Marzana, then pretended to have been hit herself to deflect suspicion. The impossibility of it could only add to the confusion."

Téngfēi nodded. "And to give herself an excuse to be upstairs. Two people searching a house this big makes way more sense than one."

Sirin got up and paced a few steps. "So now what? We know who our culprits are, but how do we get them to talk?" She brightened. "Do you think we can get Emmett to question them? He's sort of a law enforcement officer, isn't he?"

"Possibly." Téngfēi hesitated and reached for the spiral pad Sirin had left on the pillow. "But there are still pieces of the cache missing—the keys, the locks, and the reflecting circle. What if we ask Emmett to question those two and they don't crack? Unless he can hold everyone here until those things are found, once they know we're onto them, won't they just leave?"

"They could, but in order to leave with the stolen things, they've got to retrieve them first. They could lead us right to the stuff we didn't find."

"Maybe."

"You don't think it would work?"

Téngfēi scratched his head. "It might, but that's not what's bothering me. Sirin, why would they have hidden the things the way they did in the first place? It doesn't make sense. Why put them anywhere you'd have to go back and get them? Especially Georgie's room. It was risky enough sneaking in there the first time. Why make it so you'd have to do it twice?"

"Now that you mention it," Sirin added, "why bother putting them anywhere? Why didn't the two of them just keep the stuff, make miraculous recoveries once they had what they were looking for, and get out of here as fast as possible?"

"Because Marzana presumably really was hurt," Téngfēi pointed out, "and Rob really was making a mess of the living room, and the rest of the Waits wouldn't have left before those two things were resolved."

"All right, but if Mrs. Kirkegrim is one of the thieves, why is she extending their stay now?"

"Mr. Larven was awfully late coming down," Téngfēi said thoughtfully. "Maybe he went to collect the stuff and discovered that it was gone. It could be now they're buying time to find it again.

Plus, Sirin, if there are two crooks among the Waits, how do we know there aren't more?"

"Let me completely blow your mind." She took a deep breath. "What if there *are* more crooks, and *what if they aren't all working together?* What if the reason some of this stuff doesn't make sense is that we've been assuming that either Gilawfer *or* Cantlebone snuck a couple Waits in here, when in fact there's at least one Wait present who's working for Gilawfer, and at least one other who's working for Cantlebone?"

Téngfēi buried his face in his hands. "And one of them stole the stuff and the other one's trying to steal it from *that* person?" he said through his fingers.

"Could be they've just been stealing things back and forth from each other all night. It would be funny if it weren't so frustrating."

"So what do we do?"

They looked at each other for a long moment. "I think it's time for you to go tell your story, Téngfēi," Sirin said. "It's the plan we have." She looked wistfully out his window. "I wish we could talk to Dad about it."

"I could go back out there," Téngfēi offered. "After the story."

Sirin sighed. "That isn't what I meant."

Of course it wasn't. She'd meant *I wish I could talk to Dad, about this or anything.* "I know. I'm sorry."

"It's not your fault." She straightened and adjusted her hat. "Come on. You have a story to tell."

"Right." Téngfēi glanced at the corner of the red box, which was just visible inside his rucksack. "I think this is going to call for a locus."

Sirin nodded. "I'll leave you to it and go check in downstairs."

"Okay. See you there." Téngfēi waited until she had dematerialized, then took Slywhisker's Crimson Casket of Relics from his bag and opened it. Inside were the feather, the Ocher Pages of Invisible Wards, the Ever-Sharp Inscriber of Rose-Colored Destinies, and the Flask of Winds and Voids. The feather already had a purpose. Which of the others should he use to focus the Spinner of Lore exploit?

He pulled the big *Transmundane Warriors* from his bag, too, and double-checked the exploits he'd marked as particularly interesting. There was the Spinner of Lore, of course, but he took a moment to read through the ecstatic's skills as well. After all, he didn't only need to be able to tell the story and bend it to his purpose. He needed to get an emotional reaction from his audience. That seemed more like an ecstatic's strength than a solitaire's. The ecstatic's exploits all required vulnerability and uncertainty; to make this work, Téngfēi would have to let go of his solitaire's tendency to be in control of everything, including his emotions. From somewhere under the surface of the character Téngfēi, the player Milo wanted to freak out a little at that idea. And what if he somehow managed to do it — to let himself be vulnerable, to let his emotions loose into the world — and his storytelling was just . . . bad? What if the listeners simply didn't like his tale? So much could go wrong.

He picked up the feather and ran it through his fingers. *Uncertainty is always frightening,* came the voice of Téngfēi's mother.

And you were raised a monk of the air, so it must be doubly troubling for you — uncertainty is anathema to flight. I am no ecstatic, so I can't offer much in the way of advice. But remember that no matter how well your wings are calibrated, no matter how precise your calculations or how ideal the wind, it always requires a leap of faith to leave the ground. If you cannot take that leap, you cannot fly. So perhaps you can think of unleashing your emotions as just another leap into flight. And as for vulnerability — well, what is more vulnerable than leaping off a cliff into the air?

"I can do this," Téngfēi said aloud. He looked down at his hand and saw the Ring of Wildest Abandon on his index finger — a gift from his adventuring partner. It occurred to him then that he had never learned Sirin's parentage and background. But he did know that behind the blue spectacles was someone who would be listening to his story and trying as hard as she could to hear her father's voice in the tale. Even if the ploy failed — even if they didn't learn what they needed to learn from it — he was going to do this right for her.

And then, just before he closed the book, he noticed something else that he had marked earlier. *The Unfurling Eye: Your consciousness reaches tendrils into the minds of your confederates, allowing your perception to expand into multiple viewpoints.* That was the final thing he needed for this to succeed. There were just too many variables here, too many people to watch. But maybe there was a way to work around that.

He repacked his rucksack and left his room. On his way down the stairs, he met his mom coming up. "Oh, hey, kiddo. I was just coming up to check on you. Do you honestly feel like telling a story? There's absolutely no reason you have to."

"I know," he said, surreptitiously sliding Téngfēi's ring off his finger. "But I think it might be helpful."

Mrs. Pine nodded thoughtfully, then sat down on one of the stairs and dropped her head into her hands. For a horrible moment, Milo thought maybe she was crying. "Mom, are you okay?"

"I have a tearing headache," she said, her words muted by her palms. "And this is just totally out of control. Poor Lizzie, with her stollen. And nobody's leaving. *Why is nobody leaving?*"

Milo patted her shoulder hesitantly. He had a pretty good idea why no one was leaving, but explaining his and Meddy's theories on the matter would probably not do much to comfort his mother. "I think because I'm supposed to tell a story."

Mrs. Pine snorted. "Milo, nobody was leaving long before that. I don't know what to do. If not for the"—she lowered her voice— "for the missing items, I think maybe I'd invent some story about our needing to be somewhere else in an hour, but I don't want to chase anyone out who might be carrying Georgie and Clem's stuff."

It was extremely weird to see his mom look so helpless and frustrated. "Can Emmett do anything, do you think?" Milo hadn't liked that idea when Meddy had floated it, but it seemed a logical question to ask.

"We thought about that. He did say he wanted to help, but he doesn't have the authority to detain anyone, and he doesn't seem to have any contacts in the Liberty that could provide information about these folks. I think the best he can do is help find what's gone missing before it leaves the house. If he can even manage that." She sighed and got back to her feet. "I don't know, Milo. But thanks for listening to me." Then she sat down again and looked up at him. "How are you, sweetheart? I'm so sorry about all this, and if it's driving me crazy, it's got to be driving you up the wall too. Can I do anything to make this less obnoxious for you?"

Milo started to say that he was fine — it wasn't totally true, but he definitely thought he was in better shape than she was. Then a wave of homesickness for the quiet family Christmas he hadn't had in two years swept over him and he changed his mind. He sat down at her side, put his arms around her, and hugged her tight. "I'm okay. It'll be okay, Mom."

Mrs. Pine made a choked little noise as she hugged him back. "I wish you didn't think you needed to make *me* feel better right now, Milo."

He shook his head and held tight for a minute more, not wanting to leave the quiet, uncomplicated love of that moment. But little by little, the voices from the first floor broke in and reminded him that he had work to do.

He fidgeted and let go at last. "The reason I offered to tell a story was that I thought maybe we'd learn something from how people reacted. So I'm going to go tell it." He got to his feet. "But I need help."

"What kind of help?"

"Can you get Clem and Georgie and Dad to come up to the second-floor living room? And Meddy, but try not to talk directly to her. I want to tell everyone what my plan is."

Mrs. Pine saluted and went back down. She looked amused, which was definitely better than how she'd looked a minute earlier. Even if it did make Milo suspect she wasn't taking him totally seriously.

He put Téngfēi's ring back on his finger and went slowly up to the Pines' floor, thinking through the story Doc had told him the night before and making sure he had all the key points clear in his mind. It truly was a perfect story for this crew, he reflected. *As long as I can get it right in the telling.*

Sirin appeared in the room just as he reached it. "They're coming," she told him. The other four trickled up over the next few minutes: first Georgie, then Mr. Pine, with Clem and Mrs. Pine following not long after.

"I'm going to tell a Violet Cross story," Téngfēi said without preamble. "One I think might get a reaction." He could see immediately that it was a good plan, because everyone in the room reacted. His parents merely made surprised faces, but Georgie and Clem recoiled. "I'm telling you this now for two reasons," he explained quickly. "For one thing, the whole point is to see who does what when I tell it, and you guys can't give anything away by reacting weirdly like you just did. And the second reason is that I need you to help Si — Meddy and me watch to see what the guests do."

"Are you sure that's a good idea?" Georgie asked. "To whoever our mystery person is, it'll look like you're involved. And last year, things went right off the rails when Mr. Vinge thought you were involved in things."

"They're already off the rails," Clem pointed out grimly.

"Where did you pick up a Violet Cross story to tell?" Mr. Pine asked. "That is, I'm guessing if you're sure it'll get a big response, it isn't one of the stories everybody already knows."

Sirin spoke up. "He got it from my dad. I mean," she explained hastily, "I told him a story I remember my dad telling me back in the day."

"The four of you plus Owen and the Caraways should be able to keep an eye on all seven of the Waits," Téngfēi continued. "Meddy can tell them the plan. And she'll make sure you're not all watching the same people, since she can talk to you and she won't be overheard. Just remember not to respond to her."

"Thank you," Sirin said primly.

"And when I'm done, hopefully we'll know who came here looking for Georgie and Clem, and who just wanted to sing Christmas songs."

The adults looked unconvinced, but none of them had a better idea. "Okay, Milo," Clem said at last. "You're the boss."

"Should we tell them who we suspect?" Sirin asked quietly.

Téngfēi shook his head. "No. Just make sure everybody's watching someone different."

"Can I offer one more observation?" Georgie interjected. "If this works, not only might one of the Waits give something away, but they might figure we're on to them and do something desperate. I realize I'm the only one who's concerned about things going horribly wrong, but remember how Vinge had a *gun?*" She said the last word in a furious whisper.

"We have a customs agent in the house," Clem argued. "We can ask Emmett to be ready in case of emergency. Maybe he'll turn out to be good for a little muscle."

Mr. and Mrs. Pine glanced at each other. "Do you think we have to worry about guns?" Mr. Pine asked.

Mrs. Pine rubbed her face. "If we do, at least this time we know the person likely to be carrying it is after Georgie and Clem, even if Milo does tell an interesting story." She winced. "I'm sorry, girls. You know what I meant."

"Of course." Clem patted her shoulder. "And we have the same priority if the unthinkable does happen."

Téngfēi clapped softly to get their attention back. "So everyone's clear?"

Everyone was. They began a staggered return to the main floor, which was just as Téngfēi had left it: full of the smell of burned fruitcake, thick with thieves and carolers and family and friends — and he was starting to realize just how much overlap there was between those categories.

Mrs. Pine went into the kitchen and started a fresh pot of coffee. Georgie followed her. "Do you have an old newspaper I can tear up? And maybe could I borrow a butter knife?"

"Absolutely," Milo's mom said, as if these were the most normal things she'd heard all day. They probably were.

Rob was sitting on one of the stools by the bar, likely stalking the cookies Lizzie had put in the oven earlier. He and Téngfēi watched Georgie tear the paper into squares and stack them neatly.

"Are you planning to paper-train a very small dog?" Rob inquired.

"New project," Georgie said as Mrs. Pine handed her the butter knife from breakfast. "Thank you. This will do nicely."

"Hey." Rob chucked Téngfēi on the shoulder as the solitaire passed him. "Ready for your story?"

"Ready," Téngfēi confirmed. "I think I have a good one, too."

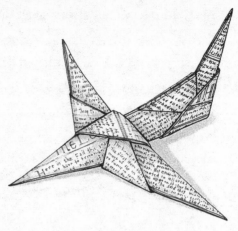

twenty-nine

THE FLIGHT OF MAPS

WHEN THEY WERE ALL SETTLED with an assortment of beverages, Sirin passed among the conspirators who would make up Téngfēi's extended network of unfurling eyes: Lizzie in the chair to the left of the hearth, his parents and Mrs. Caraway on the sofa, Clem and Owen in the loveseat, and Georgie on the floor by the coffee table. When she'd finished, the scholiast sat by the tree.

Téngfēi took center stage, sitting on the hearth and taking calming sips from his mug of hot cider as he rotated the Ring of Wildest Abandon on his index finger with his thumb. *I can do this. I can do this. I am a solitaire. I am an ecstatic. I am the Spinner of Lore, and I can make people feel things.* His parents and Mrs. Caraway smiled encouragingly from the sofa.

Well, if nothing else, he knew how to begin. "Listen." Out of the corner of his eye, he saw Georgie nod her approval as she folded a square of newspaper into quarters and flattened the creases with the butter knife. He took a deep breath and plunged in.

"There was once a girl who grew up to be a famous smuggler. She did things that even today no one can explain, and then she disappeared. Maybe she died, but I don't think anyone knows for sure. Her name was Violet Cross."

He paused, hoping it looked as if he was doing it for the sake of drama, and scanned the faces that surrounded him. Each of the Waits looked politely alert. Marzana, sitting on the floor near Mr. Hakelbarend, was smiling. In the chair by the loveseat, Lucky wore an encouraging expression. Nobody flinched or fidgeted.

Well, fine. The story was only beginning, anyway.

"I know about Violet Cross from school . . . and everywhere, I guess," Téngfēi said. "Everybody knows how good she was at what she did. But I heard a story once that I was told was a secret. It has to do with the problem of maps."

Somebody to his left shifted, causing a spring in one of the chairs to make a boinging noise.

"As I understand it, there are two problems with maps in Nagspeake." Téngfēi held up one finger. "The first is that the city is just plain hard to map. I don't really understand all the reasons why. Maybe nobody does. But since basically forever, people in Nagspeake just assume they kind of have to take anything they use to navigate by with a grain of salt." He turned to Mr. Pine. "That's right, isn't it?"

"That's what the tars in my family always used to say," Mr. Pine confirmed. "Still do."

"Right. And because of this problem, Deacon and Morvengarde got the licenses to be the exclusive makers and sellers of maps in Nagspeake. They claimed they could do it right and nobody else could, so they should be the only mapmakers for the city because all the errors and weird things that happened when anybody else tried to do it made travel unsafe."

"I remember when that happened," Mr. Larven said from where he leaned on the wall midway between Mr. Hakelbarend's chair and the Christmas tree. "Not to interrupt you, dear boy. But you're absolutely right. Of course, the licenses that Nagspeake granted to Deacon and Morvengarde didn't apply in the Liberty of Gammerbund, so several of the city's finest cartographers rented studio space there. There are still several very famous shops in the Liberty that earned their reputations back in the days when they were the only places where one could get Nagspeake maps actually made by Nagspeakers."

"I didn't know that," Téngfēi said politely.

"We are a locale of loopholes," Mr. Larven said with a bow. "Apologies. Carry on, young man."

"Okay. Well, like I said, there are two reasons that good Nagspeake maps are hard to come by, and the first is that Nagspeake is just hard to map. But the second is that, despite what Deacon and Morvengarde said about being able to do it right, the maps they sell in the city are—"

"Awful." Four voices said this at once: the Pines and Lizzie

Caraway for sure, and Téngfēi thought the other might have been Mrs. Kirkegrim. "You wouldn't believe some of the adventures I've been on trying to make deliveries when I've been stuck with a D and M map," Lizzie grumbled.

"Right," Téngfēi continued. "Even the supposedly good maps are inaccurate. But instead of admitting that they can't get it right either, Deacon and Morvengarde claim the problems people were finding were traps—things they'd mapped wrong on purpose so that if anyone tried to copy them, D and M would know. And maybe some of them are. But either way, their maps are lousy—maybe worse than the ones they were supposed to replace. And this is where Violet Cross comes into the story.

"There were a handful of cartographers in the city who knew they had done better work than Deacon and Morvengarde's mapmakers." Téngfēi glanced at Mr. Larven. "I didn't know the part about some of them going to the Liberty, but it makes sense, because what I heard was that Violet Cross got a few of them together, the ones who were willing to take a chance, along with some equally daring printers, and found them a secret place to work where they weren't technically breaking the law. But then the finished maps had to be smuggled back into Nagspeake, of course. And the folks at D and M weren't idiots. They knew there was a market for illegal local maps. They just couldn't figure out how those maps were getting in.

"D and M had customs investigating every paper shipment that came into the city, and every market where paper was traded. They kept an eye on bookstores and stalls on the street and all the places where people purchased maps, and they didn't see anything. But suddenly people had maps that hadn't been ordered from the Deacon and Morvengarde catalog, and they couldn't figure out where the contraband was coming from."

Emmett spoke up from a spot near the door to the screened porch. "In other words, business as usual on any given day in Nagspeake," he said drily. Everyone who knew who his real identity glanced at him in surprise. Georgie actually laughed. Mr. Hakelbarend snickered too. "Excuse me," Emmett said with a grin.

Téngfēi returned the smile. "No problem. Anyway, meanwhile, another thing was happening that year, something nobody at D and M or customs paid much attention to: throughout the city, everybody had gone crazy for kites."

"Kites?" Georgie asked, eyeing the geometric form that was beginning to take shape in her lap from interconnected pieces of folded newspaper.

"Kites," Téngfēi confirmed. "New shops opened up that sold nothing but kites. Each of the city's big museums had exhibits on kites through history, or photography done with kites, or something kite-related. Dance theaters put on kite ballets. Universities hosted lectures on new scientific techniques using kites for power and weather studies and all kinds of experiments."

"Interesting." Georgie began to methodically disassemble her unfinished sculpture and flatten the papers out again.

"Every weekend it seemed like somebody was having a kite contest, with prizes for the best decoration, the best design, the highest flight and the longest flight and all kinds of other categories. The fight houses in Shantytown had kite-fighting competitions, where the idea was to use your kite to mess up your opponent's kite. Everybody was flying kites. Kites were *in*. But if you were really serious about it, you made your kite with paper. If kites were cool, old-school paper kites were the coolest of all.

"And that, of course, was how Violet Cross got the locally made, more accurate city maps onto the market. They were sold at kite events, as part of the kit for a paper kite called the Orienteer. If you needed to get rid of one fast, it included special line markings that showed you how to fold it up into a structurally sound kite in less than ten seconds so you could toss it into the air and let the wind take it, leaving no evidence behind. And in order to prevent her kite kits from attracting attention, Violet Cross rallied the entire city to make kite-flying the most popular activity in town for an entire year, which was long enough to break Deacon and Morvengarde's monopoly. And I guess . . ." Téngfēi hesitated. He sort of knew how to start a tale, but not how to finish one. "The end?"

Everyone applauded. Everyone except Marzana, who was no longer smiling. "The Orienteer wasn't a kite kit," she said as the applause died down.

Téngfēi looked at her in surprise. "What?"

She folded her arms and propped them on the knees she had drawn into her chest. It almost looked like a defensive maneuver. "It was a paper airplane set," she said in a voice that was at once shy and defiant.

"Paper airplanes?" Téngfēi repeated. He shook his head. "I definitely heard it was kites, and I heard the story from somebody who knew her."

"Marzana," Mr. Hakelbarend said quietly.

Marzana almost looked angry. "It was a paper airplane set," she insisted. "There were instructions for six different planes and the map was cut into six sheets. But she could put maps on anything. It was just a means of figuring out how to orient them."

"Marzana." Mr. Hakelbarend was louder this time. Around the room, others shifted uncomfortably, but no one else spoke.

"There *was* a kite map — there were *two*, actually, but they were called the Windrose and the Portolan. You don't know what you're talking about."

"It doesn't matter," Mrs. Kirkegrim said from the chair at the other end of the sofa. "It's just a story, Marzie." Evidently Mrs. Kirkegrim had forgotten the cold reception she'd received last time she tried to give the girl that nickname.

"It's *not* just a story," Marzana snapped. Mr. Hakelbarend put a hand on her shoulder. She shrugged him off and shrank down into herself behind her folded arms. "Everybody tells those stories," she said, awkwardly wiping at her eyes with her shoulder. But evidently the tears were too persistent, and finally she just dropped her face into her arms. "Stories of smugglers they never saw or met or knew, turning them into folklore like they weren't real men and women doing real things," she went on in a muffled voice. "I'm so sick of people telling those stories and getting them wrong. Aren't you?"

Mr. Hakelbarend patted her shoulder again. Everybody tried

not to stare at the crying girl. For his part, Téngfēi was confused and embarrassed. This wasn't remotely what he'd wanted to happen. Yes, he'd hoped to get a reaction out of someone, but not this kind of reaction—and especially not from Marzana. What must it have taken to work up the courage to fight through her discomfort and speak up like that, even if it meant losing control?

And if she was right . . . how did she know all that?

Sirin's voice broke the awkward silence, though of course she was audible to only half the room. "Everyone remember who you're supposed to be watching," she snapped. "Don't get distracted."

Those who could hear her shuffled a bit and tried in various ways to be casual about looking around before their eyes settled on their assigned surveillance subjects. Téngfēi hadn't been given a specific person to watch, so he swallowed his own discomfort and went over to where Marzana was sitting with her face hidden and her father's hand on her shoulder. He crouched at her side. "Hey, I'm sorry." She shrugged and said nothing.

And then, out of nowhere, Téngfēi felt a twinge of recognition —not of this situation, precisely, but of what Marzana seemed to be feeling. "I'm sorry I got it wrong," he said quietly. "Thanks for setting me straight."

She turned her head so that one angry, wet eye appeared out of the shadows in the crook of her elbow. "But you don't believe me, do you? I thought you got everything from someone who knew her."

"I did, but . . ." And then it clicked. This whole thing was reminding him of the situation in social studies class with Mr. Chancelor. And—*Oh God*, he realized. *I'm Mr. Chancelor in this scenario.*

Maybe Marzana's family had a connection to one of the cartographers who'd worked out of the Liberty. Maybe Mr. Hakelbarend was even one of those mapmakers. It sounded as if Marzana had some knowledge of mapmaking, after all. *She could put maps on anything,* she had said. Maybe Mr. Hakelbarend had gone to the Liberty to work, and had just never left. Or maybe the answer was even simpler: Maybe Mr. Hakelbarend had been a runner. Maybe that was why he and Marzana had to live in the Liberty, and why they pretended not to be related when they left it. It could be he had even sailed with Violet Cross herself.

"I did get it from someone who knew her," Téngfēi said, "but that person could've gotten it wrong. Or maybe I misunderstood what he said." He sat next to her. "How do *you* know that story? It sounds like you feel strongly about it."

Mr. Hakelbarend cleared his throat. "The problem when a real person becomes a legend is that then people feel like his or her stories belong to everyone. And in some ways, when it's someone like a Violet Cross or a Doc Holystone or a Gentleman Maxwell and the whole city benefitted from their actions, those stories *do* belong to everyone. But they still belong to some people more than others."

"Are you a mapmaker?" Téngfēi asked him on impulse.

Mr. Hakelbarend shook his head with a slight smile. "No. Good guess, but wrong. An enthusiast, maybe, but not a cartographer myself."

A runner, then. Had to be.

"On the topic of Violet Cross and maps," Mr. Larven spoke up,

"I have to admit, young man, that I was hoping your story would have something to do with her famous Book of Ways."

"Book of Ways?" Téngfēi repeated. "What's that?"

"You don't know about the Book of Ways?" Mr. Larven laughed. "Why, my boy, that's the Grail. Violet, they say, did the impossible: mapped the Skidwrack. Found a way to compensate for the shifting of the banks and inlets and shoals."

All motion in the room lurched to a halt, and Téngfēi heard the collective sound — or maybe the absence of sound — that told him a bunch of people had stopped breathing. *Oh, please,* he thought, *please let everyone still be watching their targets.* "There's another name for it," Mr. Larven continued. "I can never remember. But surely our Marzana will, if she's such a fan." He looked down at the huddled girl. "What's that word, again, Marzana? I'm sure you know it. Starts with a *D.*"

Marzana looked up at the mustachioed man with a faintly insolent expression. "I don't know what you're talking about, Mr. Larven." Then she got to her feet, shoved past him, and stomped out onto the screened porch.

"Ahem." Lizzie Caraway tapped on her cup with a fork. "Anybody for cookies? And who needs a refill?"

Sylvester, who had been listening from where the living room met the dining room, followed Lizzie into the kitchen. "Can I help?"

Mr. Hakelbarend got to his feet and stared down at Mr. Larven, who looked small and old and unimpressive next to him. "I suppose I'll have some coffee."

"Let's get a breath of fresh air," Clem said to Owen. She shot a significant glance at Sirin, who trailed the two of them to the foyer. It was going to be a bit of a challenge, getting everyone's observations, but if anyone was up to the kind of logistics it would take to do it without being overheard by the Waits, the scholiast was that person. Téngfēi left her to it. He got up and went out onto the porch.

Marzana stood at the tabletop easel, looking at Emmett's unfinished painting. Her arms were still folded, and she gave Téngfēi a rebellious look as he came in. "Who do you know who knew her?" she demanded. "It can't be your parents. They're too young, aren't they?" She scratched her head. "But your dad has seafaring connections — or was it someone who's stayed here?"

Téngfēi shook his head. "I can't tell you. But the map thing isn't *that* big a secret, is it? I mean, if people were buying the kits and putting them together —"

"No, because the other thing you got wrong is that the actual customers didn't buy the kits, the people who distributed the maps bought them. Then they took the kits apart, put the maps together, and sold them that way." She snorted. "If everyone was aware of how the maps were coming in, how long do you think it would take before somebody from D and M managed to buy one and work the whole thing out? No, the story you told isn't well-known at all. Whoever told you was probably involved in the scheme. He or she was involved in the cartography, the printing, the smuggling, or the distribution. Had to be."

"Well, what about you?" Téngfēi countered. "She was gone

before either of us was born, so you know one of those same people too, right?"

Marzana's eyes narrowed. "I can't tell you."

"Can you tell me why you lied about knowing about the derrotero?"

She gave him a long, irritated glare. Then she dropped onto the wicker sofa. "All I want to do is get out of this place."

"Nobody's keeping you here," Téngfēi pointed out. Marzana just flopped back against the cushions. He sat at the other end of the sofa. "So you won't tell me what you know about the derrotero or how you know so much about Violet Cross?"

"Not if you won't tell me what *you* know, and how."

"Fine. Then I guess we're at a stalemate." Téngfēi flopped back too. They sat in silence for a minute. "I really am sorry I got the story wrong," he said at last. "I've had people not believe me about stuff *they* got wrong when they were being know-it-all-ish. I hate when people do that, and I'm sorry I did it to you."

"It's okay," she mumbled without looking over.

"You said she could put maps on anything, you just had to figure out how they were oriented. What's that mean?"

Marzana glanced thoughtfully at him. She seemed to be calculating how much she could tell him without answering the questions she'd already refused to answer.

"Orientation is one of the things that makes a map work," she said at last. "You have to know what you're looking at. And you probably think a map always looks like a map—north is always north, which is usually at the top of the page, that kind of thing. But that's not true. You and I could make a map of the same space and wind up with two totally different pictures if we were orienting them differently."

"Explain," Téngfēi said. "Please. I'm trying to picture what you mean."

"Well, the easiest way to try it is to just turn a map upside down so south is at the top of the page. You probably wouldn't recognize even a familiar part of town if you flipped it that way."

She got up and poked around among Emmett's art stuff until she found a sketchpad and pencil, then came back to sit next to Téngfēi. "Here's how Nagspeake looks on a regular map." She drew a little stretch of coastline with a big sheltered bay to the east and a river to the south, then marked the city's districts inside it. "But I could also draw it this way." This time she wrote the names of the districts in a single line, with the Liberty of Gammerbund at one end and the Quayside Harbors at the other. "This is what you'd get if you imagine snipping the city's border at its most westward point, stretching it out in a single line, and drawing the map as if Nagspeake were stretched out that way too."

"But it *isn't* stretched out that way," Téngfēi pointed out.

"And the world isn't flat, but that's what you'd think if you took any map literally. Maps don't show reality, they give you a way of visualizing it." She set the pencil down. "Every map focuses on some things and leaves other things out. Making a map means making choices about what's important to you. What the world is really, truly like in every single detail doesn't matter; what matters is what specifically about the world you want to show. Orientation's part of that — it can help emphasize what information is significant. And you can orient a map however you want, as long anyone else who needs to read it can figure out how to orient it too."

"Sounds like you're talking about breaking a code, almost," Téngfēi said. "And the orientation is like the code's key."

She nodded, pleased. "That's a good way of looking at it."

Téngfēi was just about to reply when, at the end of the room, Sirin poked her head literally through the middle of the door. Téngfēi stifled the urge to yelp in surprise. "Information exchange at your earliest leisure," Sirin said. "Meet you behind the tree." Her head withdrew again.

"Well, good talk." Téngfēi got awkwardly to his feet. "Thanks for letting me apologize. I'll leave you alone now." But Marzana sighed and shook her head and walked back to the door with him.

As they emerged, Georgie looked up from the coffee table. "Hey." She held up an elaborate paper airplane made of folded newspaper. "This is for you, Marzana." She tossed it into the air. It sailed over the back of the nearest chair and made a single loop before it landed in Marzana's hands.

"Thank you," Marzana said curiously, turning the plane over in her palms.

"You're welcome. There are six pieces of paper in that plane," Georgie added in a *no big deal* tone, spinning the butter knife between her fingers. "And check out those creases. Like razors."

Marzana's taut expression slowly loosened into the beginnings of a smile. "It's beautiful."

thirty

MORE PERSONS OF INTEREST

SIRIN WAS WAITING behind the tree. "Talk," she said as he settled in and got out his notebook. "What's Marzana's connection to Violet Cross? Did you find out?"

Téngfēi shook his head. "She wouldn't say," he whispered. "But my guess is that Mr. Hakelbarend is a smuggler, and I'm willing to bet he served with the Great One herself. I think Marzana's connection is that her father knows the truth firsthand."

"It holds together," Sirin agreed. "And you were totally right about Mr. Larven! That whole thing about Violet Cross's book? Between that and his being out of his room, I think for sure he's the guy we want. Or one of them. Georgie was watching him. I wouldn't have believed it was possible to do all that folding and still pay attention, but I guess that's just a thing she can do — she said he looked really interested during your story, and when Marzana interrupted, his face completely lit up for a minute. Then you know the rest."

"Yeah, and despite what she said about not knowing what Mr. Larven was talking about, I think Marzana gave me a clue about the derrotero, if we can only find those last three things and get a good look at the whole haul."

Just then, Marzana sat down on the hearth and held out a plate with a pair of cookies on it. "Here." Her voice was shy. "Thank you." And then, before he could respond, she was gone, off to sit with Lucky on the sofa.

Sirin peered through the tree branches at the other girl. "I agree with you that she's not our guy any more than Lucky is, but she definitely knows something."

Téngfēi nodded. "Yeah, but I'm not sure how to get her to talk to me. What about Mrs. Kirkegrim? Who was watching her during the story?"

"Lizzie was. She said Mrs. Kirkegrim looked amused for most of it, like she thought it was funny or something. But when Marzana spoke up, she looked angry for a second, and then when Mr. Larven said what he did, she looked annoyed."

So their two primary suspects had had very different reactions to Téngfēi's tale and Marzana's contribution to it. Curious. "What time is it?"

Sirin checked the big watch she wore under the sleeve of the Cloak of Golden Indiscernability. "Past four."

"Good grief." The only thing forcing this situation to go on was that Mr. Larven and Mrs. Kirkegrim needed the pieces they thought Clem and Georgie had, and the Pines didn't want to kick anyone out until they'd gotten back the ones that were still missing. "We've got to find the last of the stuff, Sirin. Think."

She chewed on her thumbnail. "Locks, keys, reflecting circle. The reflecting circle is the biggest thing, so where could that be?" She sat up straight. "What about outside? Could either of them have snuck stuff out easily, and without drawing suspicion?"

Milo considered. "Maybe by lowering something out a window? Sylvester would have seen if anyone tried to go outside."

"Or there's always the fire escape."

"Yeah. Okay, I'll run outside and take a quick look to see if anything got thrown out a window to pick up later. You check the fire escape. Especially where the ladder lowers down, right outside the second-floor study window. Maybe the reflecting circle would blend in with the moving parts there."

"Done."

They left the tree together. Téngfēi headed for the foyer. It looked as if a number of the guests had gone upstairs: Clem and Georgie were nowhere to be seen, and Milo suspected that was because Mrs. Kirkegrim, Mr. Hakelbarend, Mr. Larven, and Rob had all apparently gone up to their rooms too. Sylvester, Emmett, and Owen were sitting at the dining table having what seemed like a friendly enough conversation. And Milo's parents and the Caraways were in the kitchen, looking stressed. Lizzie tipped the two blackened stollen loaves into the garbage, then yanked the trash bag out, tied it up, and tossed it angrily out the kitchen door into the outside rubbish bin, where it landed with an audible *thunk*.

"Hey, Mom, Dad," Téngfēi called. "I'm going for a walk." He stuffed his feet into his boots and grabbed his coat, and as he yanked it down from its peg, it jarred one of the bell-encrusted coats that had come in with the Waits. Téngfēi tried to catch it, but it slid heavily down with a jingling clatter onto the floor.

"That thing is such a menace," Sylvester said disgustedly from the dining table. He got up and took the coat from Téngfēi. "Sorry about that, Milo. These bells . . . Somebody remind me to take some aspirin before we head home."

"Speaking of that," Lucky said from the living room, "we really should get everybody under way pretty soon."

"Yeah," Sylvester agreed in a preoccupied tone. He was examining one sleeve of the patchwork coat with a frown.

"What is it?" Téngfēi asked.

Sylvester looked at him in confusion. "This is weird. Hey, Lucky? Come here, would you?"

The elbows of his coat were hung with bells that dangled from lengths of braided leather. Sylvester lifted one of those braids, and Téngfēi's heart sped up. Hooked through the spaces between the strands near the end was a small silver padlock with the number 22 engraved on it in old-fashioned type.

"I thought it felt heavy." Sylvester picked out another braid and stared at a second, larger padlock shaped like a heart. "Where did these come from?"

Milo leaned around the foyer wall and tapped Owen's shoulder to get his attention. "Get Clem," he whispered.

As Owen made for the stairs, Emmett strolled over. "Wow. Look at that. It's a bunch of locks." He glanced at Sylvester. "And you say you have no idea how they got there?"

There was a clatter as a chair fell over at one of the little breakfast tables, and Mr. Larven appeared in the foyer, pop-eyed with surprise. Apparently he hadn't gone upstairs after all. He wiped the shock off his face fast, but not before Téngfēi saw it. Whatever else Mr. Larven was up to, *he* clearly hadn't hidden the locks there.

Lucky touched one. "These aren't part of the costume."

"No kidding, they're not part of the costume." Sylvester turned to Emmett. "And no, I have no idea how they got there. They weren't there last night. Not when I wore the coat, not when I hung it up."

Lucky lifted the other sleeve and examined its bell braids. "There are more on this side. A bunch of them!"

By now, Milo's parents had joined the group by the door. "I believe we're going to find that those belong to one of the other guests," Mrs. Pine said tightly. "You're sure you don't know anything about this, Sylvester?"

"Anything about what?" Sylvester exploded. "You think I stole a bunch of old locks from somebody and hung them all over my own coat?"

Over Mrs. Pine's shoulder, Téngfēi saw a flash of yellow as Sirin returned. She gave a triumphant lift of her eyebrows, reached into her robe, and produced a round brass object: a small spoked wheel with a knob on the underside and a little telescope mounted on top. The reflecting circle.

Mr. Larven dashed up the stairs, completely oblivious of the ghost girl in his way. Sirin sidestepped him easily, then scrambled up in his wake. Téngfēi followed as quickly as he could shove his way through the adults.

He met Clem, Owen, and Georgie coming down the steps. "Did you see Meddy? All that's left is the keys." Both girls' faces broke into huge, beaming smiles, but neither they nor Téngfēi wasted any more time with talking.

He called up every ounce of silent solitaire speed he possessed and sprinted up to three, then paused at the top of the stairs and listened. Yes, there were angry voices coming down the hall. From 3N: Mrs. Kirkegrim's room.

Sirin waved from outside the door. Téngfēi crept down to join her. The voices within could be heard clearly. "— said absolutely that you couldn't find anything!" Those clipped tones belonged to Mr. Larven.

"And neither could you," Mrs. Kirkegrim retorted in a low, dangerous voice. "Or so you said. Until now, I was willing to believe the girls had hidden the stuff somewhere else — maybe before they got here, maybe somewhere on the grounds — but at this point, the only two possibilities are that one of us is lying or there's someone else fooling with things."

The stairs creaked behind them. Téngfēi froze. Sirin darted

down the hall in a flash, then returned. "Just Mr. Hakelbarend on his way down. He's gone."

Téngfēi relaxed and turned his attention back to the voices coming out of 3N. "Sylvester, maybe," Mrs. Kirkegrim was saying. "Maybe he was up cleaning all night, like he said, or maybe he was doing something else with that time."

"Sylvester's the one who showed everyone the damned things hanging from his coat," Mr. Larven seethed. "Don't be ridiculous."

"Knock it off, the two of you," interrupted a third voice. Its tone was so authoritative Téngfēi had to work through who was downstairs and who was not to identify it, and then it took an extra beat or two before he could believe his conclusion.

Sirin must have made the same calculations, and she couldn't believe it either. "Is that *Rob?*" she whispered.

On the other side of the door, Rob kept speaking. "Almost a full twenty-four hours, and we have nothing to show for all this ridiculousness. Exactly how long do you think we can hang around here? Come on. I need ideas, and fast." Evidently the hapless chimney sweep was actually in charge. Was he Cantlebone, or Gilawfer's henchman?

"The girl knows something," Mr. Larven said.

Mrs. Kirkegrim sighed. "The girl knows stories, Nick. Lay off. She wasn't part of the heist, and she's just a kid. What do you want to do, stick her toes in the fire?"

"Just a kid." Mr. Larven snorted. "You're too tender for this kind of work. At some point, we're going to have to consider getting a little rough. This charade isn't going to play out much longer."

"We're outnumbered three to one," Mrs. Kirkegrim said. "How exactly do you propose we get rough without being completely overwhelmed?"

"People don't like to see kids get hurt," Mr. Larven pointed out. "We've got two kids here. That's pretty substantial leverage."

Téngfēi stiffened. "Try it," Sirin muttered, cracking her knuckles.

Rob spoke up again. "Let's save that for a last resort. Other ideas?"

"Why don't we just call in the cavalry?" Mr. Larven asked.

"I'm asking what options we have *before* we do that," Rob said irritably. "Once we call them in, those girls will recognize the boss, and then there's nothing to do but fight it out, and we're still outnumbered. Other ideas."

Téngfēi and Sirin exchanged a glance. If "the girls" were Georgie and Clem, and if they would recognize "the boss" if he showed up, then "the boss" had to be Gilawfer. Not only that, it sounded as if Gilawfer was nearby. And he wasn't alone.

"Well, if Nick isn't lying—"

"Barbara, why don't you just—"

"Keep your voices down," Rob snarled.

"If Nick isn't lying," Mrs. Kirkegrim repeated calmly, "then there's someone else making trouble in this house. We need to know who that is. But if we stay up here much longer, we're going to be pretty obvious suspects."

Sirin plucked Téngfēi's sleeve. "Let's go. They're going to come out any minute."

Together they crept back to the stairwell. "Where did you find the reflecting circle?" Téngfēi asked.

She had hung it from her belt opposite the brass base of the spherical chalkboard. "Right where you suggested: shoved in among the pulleys for the fire-escape ladder."

"So now it's just the keys." Téngfēi rubbed his palms together. "Game on."

"Game on. Listen, I'm going to keep an eye on these guys here. I'll check in with you in a few."

"Okay."

Back on the first floor, things were tense. Sylvester was pacing, looking as if he was pretty sure everyone thought he was guilty of something. Lucky stood nearby, chewing her fingernail. Mr. Hakel-barend sat at the bar by the kitchen, fuming. Marzana and Lizzie were at the dining table, watching Clem in fascination as she sat with Sylvester's coat before her, methodically picking the locks open one by one.

"Where's Georgie?" Téngfēi asked Mrs. Pine, who was leaning against the kitchen bar looking more frazzled than he'd ever seen her.

"Searching," Mrs. Pine muttered. "She and Emmett."

Téngfēi pulled her over to the stairwell and told her what he'd overheard on the third floor. Mrs. Pine rolled her eyes so far back in her head they were all whites for a split second. "Ben," she called to Milo's dad. "A word."

Clem looked up, spotted Téngfēi, and waved him over. "Hey, got your picks?"

He joined her at the table, and she passed him a section of hem with two locks worked in among the bells. "Give these a try. If you can't get them open, don't worry. I'll be done with these others in a minute or so."

"Okay." He took his picks from his bag and selected a torsion wrench and the curved pick Clem had started him off with. He positioned the padlock in his palm, tweaked the keyway to one side, and felt for the pins. *One, two, three.* He started pressing the pins up and out of the way, pretending there was nobody watching and that he was just practicing on his own.

"Keep pressure with the wrench," Clem said softly. The one in her own hand popped open, and she added it to the growing pile of those she'd already removed. Téngfēi adjusted his grip on his torsion wrench and started over. *Snick.* That was Clem's next lock popping open. He shook his head — *This isn't a race* — and . . .

Snick.

His padlock snapped open. Marzana and Lizzie applauded as he slipped it out of the braid and added it to the pile. He smiled sheepishly and went to work on the next one. Clem finished all the others, but just as she tossed her final one on the pile, the hasp of Téngfēi's second lock clicked open.

"Nice work." Clem counted them, snapping each one closed again as she did. "Ten. That plus the other one" — the one still in his rucksack, she meant — "makes the full complement." She turned with Sylvester's jangling coat hanging from two fingers and offered it to him. "I believe this is yours."

"I swear —" he began.

"I know," Clem interrupted. "You didn't hear me make any accusations."

"They're so beautiful." Marzana reached out to touch one of the locks. "What are they?"

"My collection," Clem said shortly. "They were stolen last night. Along with a few other things." Mrs. Caraway handed her a brown paper lunch bag and Clem began dropping them into it one by one.

Lucky made a miserable noise. "This just keeps getting worse and worse."

"You don't know the half of it, Lucky." Clem folded the bag shut.

Mrs. Kirkegrim emerged from the stairwell. Sirin followed close on her heels. "Why does everybody look so glum?" the older woman asked.

"Nothing more to report," Sirin said quietly. She nodded at the bag in Clem's hands. "You want me to take those?"

Clem hesitated, probably trying to work out how she could reply to Meddy while appearing to answer Mrs. Kirkegrim. Lucky spoke first. "Evidently someone among us is a thief, Mrs. Kirkegrim."

"A thief?" Mrs. Kirkegrim put on an admirable show of dismay. If Téngfēi hadn't known better, he might even have believed it. She glanced at the Pines, who were standing watchfully near the bar. "What's this about?"

More footsteps pattered on the stairs: Mr. Larven, followed by

Rob. Instinctively Téngfēi got up from the table to put some distance between himself and the man who had pointed out that kids might make for good leverage.

Clem stood, holding the bag in one hand, and folded her arms across her chest. "What it's about, Mrs. Kirkegrim, is that someone broke into both my room and Georgie's last night. A number of things were taken." She rattled the bag. "Some of them are in here."

"You mean there was *more?*" Lucky's misery was audible. Milo felt terrible for her.

"There was more," Clem said evenly. "And I think it's time somebody answered for it. There's still one thing that hasn't been recovered. Or *one set of things* is maybe more accurate. If those are returned, Georgie and I will overlook this little adventure. No questions asked. But if not, we'll get the law involved."

"Point of order, Miss Candler." Mr. Larven's voice was open, cheerful, and polite. "We're citizens of the Liberty. No officer of the law from outside would come into the Liberty of Gammerbund after anyone for mere theft."

Every pair of eyes in the room flicked back and forth between Clem and Mr. Larven. Every pair, Téngfēi noticed, except Mrs. Kirkegrim's. Hers darted into the kitchen.

"Nick," Sylvester protested. "Don't be a jerk. If one of us is responsible—"

"I'm merely observing that Miss Candler's threats aren't quite the thing. It's not polite to make threats, and it's even less polite to make pointless ones."

"It's not a pointless threat." Emmett pushed not entirely gently past Rob, who was blocking the stairwell. He reached into his pocket, took out his wallet, and flashed a badge at Mr. Larven. "Nagspeake Customs."

thirty-one

CANTLEBONE

EMMETT HELD UP the open wallet the way a teacher holds up a book to show a class the pictures and pivoted so the whole room could see. Clem took advantage of the moment to pass the paper bag to Sirin, who vanished it into her yellow robe.

"The thing about Liberty citizens being protected from Nagspeake laws," Emmett said, "is that it only counts if you're *in* the Liberty. You can't claim sanctuary without being *in* the sanctuary, especially if you committed a crime and there happens to be someone present with the legal authority to arrest you. So I suggest strongly that if anyone here knows where the final missing items are, he or she speak up immediately and take advantage of Clem's very generous offer. Since she said she won't press charges, I also won't make any arrests if the items in question are returned now."

"Are you going to keep us from leaving?" Mrs. Kirkegrim asked.

Mr. Hakelbarend glared at her. "I for one will volunteer to stay for as long as it's helpful." She glared back, and there was something dangerous in her expression, something that Milo hadn't seen so much as a hint of before now.

"Me too," said Sylvester. "I know how it looks, those locks turning up on my coat. Whatever I can do to convince you I'm innocent, I'll do."

Mr. Pine stalked over to join Owen, who, by accident or design, stood between everyone else and the front door. "We appreciate that, Sylvester," Mr. Pine said grimly, his arms folded.

"And so will I. Please," Lucky begged, looking around at her fellow carolers. "I can't believe this is true, but please, if anybody knows anything at all, speak up."

"Yeah," Rob said. "Seriously, this is embarrassing."

Sirin snorted.

Marzana said nothing.

Mr. Larven said nothing.

"You didn't answer my question," Mrs. Kirkegrim said at last. "You can arrest the thief, but do you have the authority to detain us to *find* that thief? On the evidence you have, I mean."

Téngfēi held his breath. What evidence did Emmett have, after all? Even if Téngfēi told him everything he and Sirin had overheard, what would that accomplish? None of the three conspirators had admitted to anything more than wanting to find the items and (unless one of them was lying) *failing* to find them.

"I'll make it easy on you," Mrs. Kirkegrim said, stepping right up to Emmett. "I'm going upstairs to get my cloak. Miss Candler can join me to make sure I don't stash anything on my way up or down—or better yet, someone can just go and get it, and meanwhile, you and she can search me to your satisfaction. You'll find nothing on me and nothing in the cloak. But after that, I'm leaving. I've had enough."

"She's one of them," Sirin said, speaking rapidly and loudly enough for all the Greenglass regulars to hear. "She and Rob and Mr. Larven, but each of them told the others they hadn't found anything. Someone's lying, and it's probably her, because she was the first one upstairs yesterday. She might be telling the truth about not having the keys on her right now, but I bet she knows where they are."

"I'm waiting," Mrs. Kirkegrim said.

"Under those circumstances, I'm happy to let you leave," Emmett answered.

"What?" Clem asked, aghast.

Téngfēi wilted. "He can't hear her."

"I heard the lady just fine," Emmett said. "I think if she's willing to be searched, I'm satisfied." He didn't *look* satisfied, though.

Georgie appeared in the stairwell, empty-handed. She took in the situation and sighed. "Let me guess. Cards on the table time?"

"For some," Clem said grimly. "Mrs. Kirkegrim is leaving. No luck?" Georgie shook her head.

Emmett put his badge back in his pocket. "Georgie, how about if you go and get Mrs. Kirkegrim's coat for her?" He held out his hand to Mrs. Kirkegrim. "Key?"

The older woman tossed it underhand directly to Georgie. "The cloak doesn't belong to me. Try not to rip the seams while you search it."

Georgie actually snarled as she headed back up the stairs. Emmett turned to Mrs. Pine. "While Georgie's getting the cloak, would you and Clem go with Mrs. Kirkegrim for a search of her person? Maybe use the porch."

"Privacy," Mrs. Kirkegrim said coolly. "How civil."

Mrs. Pine looked as if she was holding it together by the barest of margins, but she agreed. When the three of them had gone, Emmett surveyed the remaining Waits: Mr. Hakelbarend and Marzana, Rob, Sylvester, Lucky, and Mr. Larven. "Anyone else feel they need to leave right now?"

A heated look flitted across Mr. Larven's face and dissolved a second later. "Not if there's coffee, I suppose." He flashed a grin at Mrs. Caraway and Lizzie, who stood like sentries near the kitchen entrance.

Lizzie snorted. "You can get it yourself," Mrs. Caraway said evenly.

"We already said we'd stay," Lucky said, gesturing at herself, Sylvester, and Mr. Hakelbarend.

"I'll stay too," Marzana added. She glanced at Rob. "What about you?"

"Sure, why not?" he said easily, though Téngfēi thought he saw a flash of anger in his eyes for a moment too.

Sirin tugged Téngfēi's sleeve. "Why is only one of them leaving?" she whispered as she led him to the loveseat. "Why don't Rob and Mr. Larven care that she's going?"

"They do care," Téngfēi whispered back. "They just can't do anything about it. Or maybe if they let her go, she looks guilty and it buys them more time to try to get the other stuff back."

"But she's got to be the one who took the stuff. It's the only way the timing works out, right? So then why is *she* leaving? You saw their faces, the other two, when she started making noise about walking out on her own. They weren't expecting that from her, so it wasn't a preexisting plan or anything. Is she just giving up?"

Téngfēi pressed his hands to his face and thought as hard as he could. "She knows we have everything but the keys. And she knows where the keys are, but they aren't on her or she wouldn't offer to be searched. She also has to know that once she leaves, she's never getting back into the house, so yeah — either she's giving up or . . ." The answer hit him like a ton of bricks. He forced himself to keep his voice low. "Or she knows *she can still get them,* even if she doesn't have a chance at getting her hands on anything else. Sirin, *I know where they are.*" He got up from the loveseat and made for the kitchen. He couldn't risk going to the foyer for his coat, which he'd dropped when Sylvester discovered the missing padlocks, but at least he already had his boots on.

"What? Well, tell me, and I'll go get them and your folks can kick everybody out and be done with it!"

"Can't," he said under his breath as a very frustrated-looking Georgie returned with Mrs. Kirkegrim's red cloak just as the porch door opened and the lady herself emerged, followed by an equally aggravated Mrs. Pine and Clem.

"Why not?" Sirin asked as Mrs. Kirkegrim accepted her cloak from the blue-haired thief and swirled it regally around her shoulders.

"You can't get them because they're not in the house," Téngfēi hissed through gritted teeth. He edged past the Caraways, calling on every blackjack skill he possessed to pass unnoticed. It worked. Mrs. Caraway patted his shoulder distractedly, but her attention — like everyone's — was riveted by the dark-haired woman who was about to walk out the front door.

"I do hope your . . . whatever they are . . . turn up, Miss Candler," Mrs. Kirkegrim said with a smile. "I truly do."

Stony silence was the only reply she got. Milo's parents, the Caraways, and Owen were merely angry, but Clem and Georgie seemed as if they wanted to breathe fire, and Mr. Larven and Rob looked capable of murder. Marzana had folded her arms in a huff. Mr. Hakelbarend's expression was unreadable. Emmett was watching Rob and Mr. Larven; maybe Mr. Pine had filled him in. Téngfēi, all but invisible, edged toward the back door at the far side of the kitchen.

"It's been a lovely time," Mrs. Kirkegrim continued as the rest of the room seethed. "I do wish you all a happy Christmas." And with that, she opened the door and stepped out into the whipping cold. Téngfēi waited until the front door shut behind her, then yanked open the kitchen door and plunged into the frigid twilight. He shivered as a gust of wind hit him head-on. When had it gotten so late?

The trash cans that usually stood just outside the kitchen were gone. Téngfēi groaned. Of course: tomorrow was trash day. Despite all the insanity, Mr. Pine had found time to drag them out to the road for emptying.

Sirin appeared on the step next to him. "Watch for Mrs. Kirkegrim," he said. "She'll be coming this way in a minute. Try to delay her somehow if you can."

"All right, and you take this." She pulled Eglantine's Patent Blackthorn Wishing Stick from her back and handed it over. "Just in case."

"Thanks." Then he took off for the uphill timberline at a run. He could reach the road fastest if he cut through the trees, which saved him the trouble of trying to figure out which way Mrs. Kirkegrim was likely to come around the house. It also might just put him out of sight before she spotted him. His rucksack flapped against his back. It would've been a thousand times better to have Sirin there.

He heard a voice shout behind him, but he didn't dare turn. He plunged into the trees, darting around them as fast as he could and holding the stick close to his body to keep from catching it on any stray roots or branches. It was bitterly cold, and now that he was in the woods, it felt as if night was falling in earnest.

Abruptly, the red brick wall of the outbuilding they called the garage loomed out of the shadows. Téngfēi cut around it, shuddering, and sprinted on until he came to the dirt road. Just a few yards away, a pair of wide, uneven, not-quite-parallel lines showed where Mr. Pine had dragged the trash cans from the house and down the driveway to the side of the lane. Téngfēi trotted over, flung off the lid of the nearest one, and untied the bag on top. There they were: the two burned loaves of stollen.

Lizzie had made it by pounding the dough down and folding it in half lengthwise so that when it was sliced, the pieces would look a bit like flattened Cs. This meant there was a sort of seam along one long edge. Téngfēi tucked one of the loaves under his arm, wedged his frozen fingers into the seam on the other, and pried it open. It broke apart with a crunch, and there in the cavity lay five very odd-looking keys baked into the dough.

He emptied them into his rucksack and wrenched open the second loaf, where he found six more keys. He stuffed those in his bag too, then crept back into the woods and headed uphill. He needed a place to hide for a couple minutes while he figured out what to do next.

He made his way to an outbuilding he used for a fort in warmer weather. It was small, and it had once had a peaked roof. Téngfēi crept toward it from the back, crunching over flattened drifts of frost-crusted leaves and between the branches of an overgrown but mostly thornless rosebush that covered the hole in the wall. Then he stopped and crouched just outside the hole. Something was already in there.

It was big — so big that it took up easily a third of the space, and too big to have gotten in by any means but the actual door, which he could see from the hole and which was still shut. Also, the thing wasn't moving. Téngfēi crawled cautiously forward for a better look.

It was a curved framework, bone-colored and skeletal, but not a proper skeleton and not made of real bone, either. Places where one piece crossed another were lashed with dark cords. But it was definitely animal-shaped. *Horse*-shaped. There was a broad back and a graceful neck that ended in a pair of leather straps. The neck contained a mechanism that reminded him of the time he'd taken apart a plastic grabber claw to see how it worked. Inside the shoulders was a structure with padded pieces. There was also a backpack lying against the wall; a corner of white fabric poked out where the zipper hadn't quite been pulled all the way closed.

So *this* was where Marzana and Mr. Hakelbarend had stashed the hobby horse costume. It made sense — they'd come through the woods, not from the road; they'd probably passed his fort on the way to Greenglass House. But in that case, the skull had to be here somewhere too. Téngfēi scrambled in and glanced around. It didn't seem that a thing as large as the antlered skull could escape his notice, but if it was there, he couldn't see it. Maybe they'd buried it, since, judging from what Lucky had said about the skulls, burying them seemed to be a thing.

He dropped onto a tree stump that served as a chair, fumbled in his bag for Wildthorn's Crackerjack Gauntlets, and pulled them onto his hands, which felt as if they were going to freeze at any second. He caught himself humming "The Holly and the Ivy." *Wow, Lucky,* he thought. *Way to tell a story that sticks. Focus, Téngfēi.*

The good news: he had the final piece of Violet Cross's haul. And once he could focus on anything other than the cold in his hands, Téngfēi began to suspect he had more than the final piece. He began to suspect he had the only piece that mattered. Mrs. Kirkegrim hadn't bothered to put any of the other items she stole in places where she was likely to be able to recover them quickly, or even at all. Georgie's room, the fire escape, Sylvester's coat—all of these were tremendously inconvenient places to hide something if you wanted to retrieve them later. Only the keys had been hidden in a way that broke that pattern.

And Mrs. Kirkegrim had taken a huge risk to hide them the way she did. She must've done it during the post-breakfast cleanup, right after Lizzie had finished the loaves, when everyone but the cleanup crew had been kicked out of the kitchen. And she would still have had to make sure none of the other folks in the kitchen saw what she was up to. But by doing it that way, not only had Mrs. Kirkegrim guaranteed that she'd be able to pick up the keys later, but she'd fixed it so she could retrieve them outside the house, without having to carry them out herself. She could even submit to searches by a pair of fellow thieves and not have to worry. All she'd had to do was find a moment to sneak back into the kitchen at some point and turn the oven up to Maximum Crisp.

It was brilliant. *She* was brilliant.

She had to be Cantlebone.

It was the only way it made sense. Gilawfer must've recruited thieves for this endeavor from among the more lawless citizens of the Liberty. But Mrs. Kirkegrim — Cantlebone — had gotten wind of it and infiltrated Gilawfer's group, which then proceeded to infiltrate the Waits and manipulate its way into the band whose route included Greenglass House. She'd taken all the confusion-sowing delaying tactics Gilawfer's team had planned and used them for her own ends.

And somehow, unlike everyone else involved in this heist, Cantlebone had known which part of the haul mattered: the keys. Téngfēi was itching to get a closer look at them. How could a handful of keys also be a complete and accurate map of a river that was known to shift and change? But there wasn't time to try to work that out now. He had to get back to the house before he froze.

The wind had picked up, but the walls of the fort kept most of it out. Unfortunately, there was too much rustling and clicking and whisking and whooshing out there among the trees for Téngfēi to be certain he was alone. He crept up a ladder that leaned against one wall for a look through the collapsed roof. The shadows had darkened into pools of night, and although there was still some meager light glazing the tops of the trees far overhead, none of it was coming through to ground level. Still, Mrs. Kirkegrim's red cloak and bright blue dress ought to be visible if she was out there. Téngfēi scanned the woods for a long minute but saw nothing. He hauled himself up, dropped Sirin's stick over the side, and climbed easily down the outside of the wall. Then he retrieved his sort-of weapon and started through the woods again, cutting south with the idea that he'd come up behind the house and make a break for the kitchen door. Maybe Sirin would still be there keeping watch.

He made his way through the trees, not running this time because somewhere to his right, the slope got very steep, eventually becoming the cliff that descended sharply to the river. Also, he was too cold to run anymore. And every time he saw something move out of the corner of his eye, it freaked him out. He kept thinking he saw flashes of something pale that he was pretty sure was Mrs. Kirkegrim's face, but he could never find her when he turned to look. Or maybe the cold was just making him see things. He focused on the slight aroma of woodsmoke that he thought he could detect among the trees. It smelled like warmth. He pretended it felt warm, as well. Humming helped too. *The holly and the ivy, when they are both full grown, of all the trees that are in the wood, the holly bears the crown. The rising of the sun and the running of the deer . . .*

And then, suddenly, a figure stepped out of the dark directly ahead of him and raised a lantern so that the light revealed his face. Téngfēi felt the air rush out of him, and he slumped in relief. "Doc."

"Milo. What are you doing out here? And without your coat!" Doc Holystone reached for the buttons of his own jacket, then came to his senses. "Sorry. I'd give you mine, but I suppose a ghost's coat does no good for the living."

Téngfēi shoved the stick under his arms and reached his hands instinctively toward the lantern to warm them. Its warmth couldn't be real either, but it was comforting somehow. He must have come farther than he realized, almost all the way around the house, if he had stumbled into Doc's small haunt. Good thing the ghost had found him, or Téngfēi might've stumbled right off the cliff without realizing he was anywhere near it.

"We found it," he said through chattering teeth. "We found all of it, Meddy and I."

"You did?" The ghost frowned. "But what are you doing stumbling through the woods in this freezing cold?"

"G-Gilawfer's men — only one's not his man —" Téngfēi giggled at how difficult this was to explain. Or was he just loopy from the cold? "Cantlebone double-crossed them. One of Gilawfer's people turned out to be Cantlebone, only he's a sh-sh-she. She's after me because I found the final objects she'd hidden. I think they're the actual d-derrotero."

Doc Holystone's eyes glittered. "You're joking."

"N-no. I've got them here. Not sure how they work yet." Téngfēi patted his rucksack.

"That's wonderful, Milo," Doc said. He glanced at Téngfēi's bag. "Would you like me to take a look for you? Maybe I can provide a little insight into how Violet's mind worked."

Téngfēi nodded. He started to reach into the rucksack, but his fingers were too numb to make sense of the buckles. "I think I have to warm up first, Doc. Which way is the house?" They had to be near the railcar landing, since Doc couldn't venture much farther, but Téngfēi couldn't get his bearings. Where *was* the railcar platform?

"Here." Doc reached for the bag. "I'll do it for you."

A voice spoke up from nearby. "You'd really let the kid freeze, wouldn't you?"

Téngfēi turned and found Barbara Kirkegrim hiking through the trees toward them. Who was she talking to? He frowned and glanced at Doc. The ghost's face had hardened.

"You can see him?" Téngfēi asked the approaching woman.

"Yep," she said, reaching up to unbuckle her cloak and swirl it off her shoulders as she walked. "Put this on," she said, tossing it to Téngfēi. "Then go home."

He dropped his stick, fumbled to catch the cloak, and stared at her in confusion. *Go home?* She was just letting him go? He glanced around, trying to figure out how he'd follow her instructions even if he wanted to. Why couldn't he get his bearings?

"It's below freezing out here. Your brain's probably feeling fuzzy," she said, surprisingly gently. "It's normal, but you need to get inside." She pointed back the way she'd come. "That way."

"Stay where you are, Milo," Doc said. "She's just trying to confuse you."

"But how can she see you?" Téngfēi asked as he wrapped the cloak around himself and clutched it tight. *Warmth. Oh, warmth.*

"I can see him because he's not a ghost," Mrs. Kirkegrim said. "He's lying to you. He lied to you about everything. That's not Doc Holystone. It's Toby Gilawfer, a costume, and a bunch of makeup."

thirty-two

STRANGE THINGS IN THE WOODS

OH, NO. But the clothes, the bright eyes, the pin in his hat!

"I don't b-b-believe you," Téngfēi stuttered through numb lips. *But,* came a logical voice in his brain, *the clothes, the hat, the pin, even the expression on his face the first time he stepped out from under the trees — that's Doc from the stained-glass window, the one that's been on display down in the city. Thousands of people have seen it. Anyone could have put that outfit together.*

Then Téngfēi remembered how he'd thought that Doc — this Doc, the one Mrs. Kirkegrim could see too — had looked much older than he'd expected. And although Meddy had vanished outright when she'd tried to pass beyond the border of her haunting-space, this Doc had merely come up short, as if he'd hit an invisible wall. Or as if he'd been *pretending* to have hit an invisible wall. And then there was the woodsmoke, which, the first time Téngfēi had smelled it, had been wafting through the trees when his own fireplace had been dead and cold and was being cleaned (badly) by Rob Gandreider. Somebody had had a fire going out here, and ghosts didn't need to build fires to keep warm.

Téngfēi turned to the man with the lantern. "Is it true?" But now the illusion seemed obvious. This wasn't Doc. This wasn't a ghost at all.

Doc — the false Doc — *Gilawfer,* Téngfēi corrected himself angrily — rolled his eyes. "Yes, it's true. Obviously."

Suddenly Milo felt very foolish, and the persona of Téngfēi slipped away from him like water down a drain. None of the adults could have been the target of this fakery. Gilawfer had put that outfit together to fool *him.* The thought made his cheeks burn. *Meddy is going to be crushed.* That thought made his heart feel as if it were breaking, which was far worse than his own humiliation.

But how could anybody even have known there was a ghost angle to play here?

"Milo Pine, meet Toby Gilawfer." Mrs. Kirkegrim knotted her skirt up over her jeans, put the toes of one foot under Eglantine's Blackthorn Wishing Stick, which still lay at Milo's feet, and flipped it neatly up into his hands. He grabbed it, although it was more an act of self-defense than any kind of cool catch. "Now go home, Milo."

"Not until I have that bag, he won't, Babs." Gilawfer showed his teeth. "Except I hear your name isn't Barbara Kirkegrim at all. I hear I'm in the presence of the infamous master thief, Cantlebone. Be still, my heart."

"Well, that's flattering." Mrs. Kirkegrim grinned. "Wrong, but flattering."

He still felt humiliated, but at least now that he was warmer, Milo's brain was working a lot better. Yes, this was definitely a situation to get out of, and fast. He wasn't sure why Mrs. Kirkegrim suddenly seemed so unconcerned about the keys she'd worked so hard to smuggle out of the house, but he wasn't about to stick around to see if she changed her mind. He started moving slowly, quietly in the direction she'd pointed, which, now that he wasn't hung up on reconciling the woods around him with the belief that he had to be close to the railcar landing, he recognized just fine.

"Stay right there," Gilawfer snapped.

"Milo, *go!*" Mrs. Kirkegrim paired those two words with a glance over her shoulder that made Milo move, and move *fast*. Nobody should be able to do that with two words and a glance, he thought. That much authority in the wrong hands would be dangerous. She'd crush it in a classroom.

But before he could make it more than three rapid steps, somebody else appeared in his path. "Hold it, please."

The newcomer was an older man with oversized tortoiseshell glasses on his nondescript face. Milo hadn't heard his voice in a year, but it wasn't one he was ever going to forget. It belonged to De Cary Vinge, Deacon and Morvengarde operative and deputized agent of Nagspeake customs, he of the endless collection of oddball socks — and the man who had once actually tried to shoot Meddy (before he'd realized she was a ghost).

"Toby didn't lie about everything, you know," Mr. Vinge said. His hands were in his coat pockets, but Milo would've bet money that one of them held a pistol. "He didn't lie about having customs connections, for instance."

Well, that explained where Gilawfer had learned that there were ghosts at Greenglass House. *One mystery solved,* Milo thought sourly. *Yay.*

Mr. Vinge raised his voice. "Kirkegrim or Cantlebone, whoever you are, you *stay* where you are, by the authority of Nagspeake Department of Customs." He took his left hand from his pocket — no gun, thank goodness — and held it out. "You can hand over that bag now, Milo."

Milo thought about swinging the stick at Mr. Vinge — it was supposed to be a weapon, after all — but one look at the guy's face told him that would be a very bad idea. As he tried to figure out how to get out of this without having to give up the keys, Mrs. Kirkegrim spoke.

"Oh, saints preserve us, *customs showed up.*" Her voice dripped with sarcasm. "Color me shocked. You know, there's another customs agent inside already. Didn't get the sense that he was in on Toby's shenanigans, though."

"Excuse me?" Gilawfer said. He and Mrs. Kirkegrim were behind Milo, so he couldn't see either of them, but the fence sounded surprised. Mr. Vinge's eyes narrowed just a bit.

It felt like a cue. "Oh, yeah," Milo piped up. "His name's Emmett Syebuck. Do you know him?" he asked Mr. Vinge innocently. Mr. Vinge's expression shifted subtly: Emmett's name meant something to him. "Of course," Milo continued, "his papers said he was a *real* customs agent. Not just a *deputized* agent. So maybe you guys wouldn't have met."

"You're supposed to be giving me that bag," Mr. Vinge said coldly.

"Oh, I'm sure they'll have met," Mrs. Kirkegrim said. "Right, Toby? All those customs guys know each other. Weird that two operatives would show up at the same place at the same time, isn't it?"

That was *definitely* a cue. And, Milo remembered, neither Vinge nor Gilawfer knew anything about what had been going on in the house all this time. "It's not that weird," Milo said, turning a little so he could see the other two as well. "Mr. Syebuck said he was here because of Mr. Vinge. He said he was investigating all the stuff that happened last year." He looked up at Mr. Vinge and made his eyes extra wide and kidlike. "You guys are working together, aren't you?"

"Not to *my* knowledge," Gilawfer growled.

Milo ignored him. "Mr. Syebuck's here with you, isn't he, Mr. Vinge? He's part of this whole thing. Jeez, that makes so much sense."

"What's the kid talking about, Vinge?" Gilawfer demanded.

"He's just a kid! He doesn't know what he's talking about," Vinge snarled back. "All we need is the bag."

"I'll tell you what he's talking about, Toby," Mrs. Kirkegrim said with a laugh. "He set you up. I knew it the minute I figured out the other guy in the house was an agent. I'm sure Vinge told you he'd take the Book of Ways and you'd get the rest, plus probably a payoff, but this is a *sting*, Gilawfer. He and his bosses at Deacon and Morvengarde get the derrotero, and Syebuck and *his* bosses at customs get *you*." She snorted. "That's why I cut and ran. I'm no Cantlebone, but I'm not stupid, either."

There was a warning tone in her voice, and Milo was pretty sure it was meant for him. If this ploy worked, things were eventually going to go south in a big way, and both he and Mrs. Kirkegrim were going to have to get out of here fast when they did. *I hope I know when to run,* he thought. *I hope I can run with this cloak on.*

"Vinge," Gilawfer began.

"We'll sort this out later," Mr. Vinge snapped. "Give me the bag, Milo."

There was an ominous click from Gilawfer's direction. "To hell with that. I'll take that bag, kid." A tiny flash of moonlight caught on the barrel of the gun his hand.

"Put it away, Toby," Mrs. Kirkegrim said. "Armed robbery is a whole other ball of wax from anything else he's got on you. And if you pull that trigger, it gets a thousand percent worse, and it brings everyone running. I'm sure a handful of them are already out in the woods, searching for Milo."

Gilawfer ignored her and snapped the fingers of his free hand. "Bag."

Milo knew better than to try to hang on to the keys with a gun in play. He started to pull the bag off, discovered the cloak around his neck was in the way, and reached up to take that off first. But somehow now the strap of the bag had gotten caught on the end of the stick he had tucked under his arm before. As he tried to straighten out all the things now tangling him up, Mr. Vinge took his other hand from his pocket, and then it was all Milo could do not to faint. Suddenly there were *two guns* pointed *at him.*

"Guys," Mrs. Kirkegrim said. Her teachery warning voice was tinged with a note of panic now.

"Don't," Mr. Vinge said. "Gilawfer, I said we'll sort this out afterward. But the derrotero is mine."

Milo stood paralyzed with indecision. His hands, tangled in cloaks and straps and sticks, shook. The guns glinted in the moonlight.

Except it wasn't moonlight playing on the firearms. There was a bright gleam visible on the barrel of each gun, but it was the wrong color. It had a *shape,* and Milo thought he knew what that shape belonged to. Once again, he saw a flicker of something pale out of the corner of his eye. Instead of turning to look, he focused on the reflection in the gunmetal in Mr. Vinge's hand. There was something there. It would vanish if he turned to look, and it would probably vanish again in a moment anyway, but right now, it was there, and no one else had seen it. But *why* was it there? And *how?*

The only explanation he could come up with was something Lucky had said the day before. And although that explanation felt like pure fantasy, a year ago Georgie had told Milo not to overlook folklore if he wanted to really understand the place it came from. Sometimes there were surprising truths buried in stories. So he took a deep breath. He kept his eyes on the pale reflection, and he began to sing. *"The holly and the ivy, when they are both full grown —"*

"Kid," Gilawfer said warningly, "do not mess around with us."

The bright gleam moved closer. He'd gotten the thing's attention. Now he could see it better. Milo sang louder. *"Of all the trees that are in the wood, the holly bears the crown."*

There was an animal snort from the trees to the right. Everyone turned to see what had made the noise.

"What on earth?" Gilawfer said slowly, warily. Mr. Vinge frowned, trying to make sense of what he was seeing. Mrs. Kirkegrim gave an involuntary gasp of disbelief. She knew exactly what she was looking at, and so did Milo.

"The rising of the sun and the running of the deer," he sang as he started working his hands loose from the strap of the bag and getting ready to run. It took effort, because it meant splitting his attention, and everything in him wanted to stop and stare at the spectacle coming their way.

During the Raw Nights, Lucky had said, *all kinds of uncanny things rise up and walk the earth, but not even the worst of them will bother carolers in the company of a hobby horse.*

The approaching creature was a palomino horse whose massive golden antlers perfectly matched its bright golden fur. It advanced through the trees without bothering to make its way around them. Instead, it *cut right through them,* as if the trees were imaginary things, each one a figment of someone's very detailed arboreal imagination. The golden horse strolled up to the group as casually as if it were joining a picnic. A memory clicked into place: Was this the "pale deer" Meddy had seen from the roof when she'd been looking for her dad?

It stopped in front of Milo and lowered its face to sniff at his nose. "Hi," Milo said uncertainly. Gilawfer's gun hand dropped slowly. Mr. Vinge's didn't, but his eyes were wide and stunned.

"Wow."

It would've been hard to imagine anything shocking the group after the arrival of a glowing, antlered horse among them. But that single word made every one of them jump almost out of their shoes, Milo included. Another newcomer had appeared in their midst, right out of nowhere, and it was he who had spoken.

This man was younger, thirty or so at most. He wore his reddish-blond hair swept straight back from his forehead. He had glittering dark eyes that pinned each of the four of them in turn as he whistled the last few bars of the verse Milo had begun. He looked strong, and he looked solid. But this time there was no mistake. He even looked like Meddy. He stood right beside Mr. Vinge, so close he could've put an arm around him. And that's exactly what he did. Vinge flinched, but didn't dare move. He was visibly terrified.

"Just look at all the strange things wandering in my woods tonight," said Captain Michael Whitcher.

thirty-three

WHAT THE MOONLIGHT SHOWS

YOU'RE REALLY HERE?" Milo said uncertainly. "And you are who I think you are?"

Captain Whitcher — Doc Holystone, the *real* Doc Holystone — grinned, and it was Meddy's grin. "I'm that guy."

"Impossible," Mr. Vinge spat, finally getting his nerve back. He pivoted to aim his gun at the ghost. "You're dead!"

"That," the captain replied, looking down with disdain at the firearm pointed at his chest, "is both completely true and completely irrelevant." He laughed. "After all that trouble to put me out of the way all those years ago, I thought you had the sense to stay gone, Vinge. And drop that gun. I think you know it won't help you against me this time." He glanced at Gilawfer. "You too, Toby."

Mr. Vinge started to lower his weapon. Then his eyes landed on Milo, and it was as if Milo could see his thoughts. *Kids. They make good leverage.* Mr. Vinge grabbed for him with his free hand, but Milo was already moving. He struck out wildly with the stick and felt it connect; then he threw himself out of the way. Out of the way of both of the guns, and out of the way of the spectral horse, who had moved even before Milo had.

The horse sprang between them in a single fast, fluid motion. Then it raised its front legs and brought one hoof cracking down on Mr. Vinge's gun hand. The pistol hit the ground with a thump, and Vinge staggered backward, holding his wrist.

The horse lowered its antlered head to stare Mr. Vinge in the eyes as it stalked toward him. The golden hide that had covered its face flew away on the breeze and sailed off through the branches overhead as if it had been nothing but a butter-colored scrap of silk all along — revealing a gleaming skull hung with ribbons and bells that were soundless as they bounced at the ends of their tethers. Candle wax dripped from the creature's glowing eye sockets.

Mr. Vinge screamed.

He backed up to where Gilawfer stood quaking in his boots, probably hoping if he stood still enough, the horned beast would somehow fail to notice he was there. But no such luck. The hobby horse twisted its head, maneuvering Gilawfer closer to Mr. Vinge with one branching antler. Gilawfer yelped and grabbed Vinge in terror.

Then the beast proceeded to *herd* the two of them — there was no other way to describe it — through the woods. Every time one of the men tried to break away and run in another direction, somehow, impossibly, the hobby horse was there too, antlers reaching like wide, bony arms to bring him back. When they emerged from the trees and stepped out onto the lawn, the moonlight falling on the horse revealed the rest of its hide to be nothing more substantial than spider webs, or more moonlight. It melted away to transparency, unveiling a belled and beribboned skeleton. Candles burned in the curves of its ribs as it drove the two horrified men across the grounds toward the road.

The trees on the far side swallowed them up one by one. The glow of the hobby horse was visible for a few more minutes as it passed through the pines, and then it, too, was gone.

thirty-four

NOTHING STAYS BURIED

"WELL," SAID THE GHOST of Doc Holystone, "that's a spectacle you don't see every neap tide."

Milo shook his head, stunned. "I don't understand what just happened." He looked at the ghost. "And you ... It's really, truly you."

"I think I know who you are," Captain Whitcher said. "You're Milo." He turned to Mrs. Kirkegrim, who was looking as shaken as Milo felt—maybe more. Milo, at least, had already reconciled himself to the idea of ghosts, and to meeting the specter of Doc Holystone. Mrs. Kirkegrim had both that *and* the phantom hobby horse to wrap her head around.

"I think I know you, too," Captain Whitcher said thoughtfully, the hint of a smile lurking on his face. "Are you who I think you are?"

Mrs. Kirkegrim pulled herself together. It looked as if it took some effort. "Just a fan. A big one. You wouldn't have heard of me."

"Are you sure?"

"Sure as sailboats. And I'd better be going, because there's a houseful of confusion back there Milo and I should probably go and take care of."

Now that hint of a smile broadened, and the ghost gave a short laugh. "Fair winds to you, then, stranger." They shook hands, but it didn't look like a handshake between strangers. *She* is *Cantlebone*, Milo decided. Captain Whitcher wasn't sure he recognized her because she would've been thirty-four years younger the last time he'd seen her.

Now the ghost turned to Milo. "You too, Milo. Maybe we'll meet again."

Milo shook his hand. It felt like shaking a real person's hand, but of course that should've come as no surprise. Meddy seemed solid when they interacted too.

Meddy.

"Wait," Milo said. "How do I find you again? There's someone you should see."

The ghost tilted his head. Then his eyes flashed even brighter. "Addie."

Milo nodded. "She's my friend."

Captain Whitcher put a hand over the lower half of his face, but even so, Milo saw his expression as it flickered through hope to pain and back again. Then the smuggler lowered his palm and took a deep breath. "If you can find a way, I'll be here. And I would be forever grateful." He frowned and peered into the trees over Milo's shoulder. Someone was calling Milo's name. Several someones, it sounded like. "Friends of yours?"

"That's my dad!" He cupped his hands around his mouth. "Over here!"

"I think I hear Peter, too," Mrs. Kirkegrim said.

"Can you come any closer to the house?" Milo asked, turning back to Doc Holystone. But the captain's ghost was gone.

Mr. Pine and Owen stampeded through the trees. "We found them!" Owen bellowed as Milo's dad sprinted forward. Mr. Hakel-barend's voice called back from a different part of the woods. There must've been other people searching too.

Milo's father arrived first, and he reached out to wrap Milo in a tight hug. His face and Owen's were both drawn and pale. "You gents look like you've seen a ghost," Mrs. Kirkegrim said. Her tone was jaunty, but her voice shook just a little.

"I think we might have," Owen said.

"Well, we have you beat," she replied with forced cheer. "We saw *two*. But Milo's freezing, so we can discuss it inside. Let's go. It's time we called a halt to all this ridiculousness."

There it was again: the Most Serious Teacher in the World voice. Milo had about a dozen questions, and it seemed like a good idea to get most of them answered before they let Mrs. Kirkegrim back through the door. But it was impossible to say no to that voice, so the four of them trooped back to the house. Mr. Hakelbarend joined them a moment later, sprinting in from whatever part of the woods he'd been searching. He put one restraining hand on Mrs. Kirkegrim's shoulder, presumably in case she got any ideas about trying to make another break for it.

As they crossed the lawn, Milo glanced in the direction the hobby horse had herded Gilawfer and Mr. Vinge, but there was nothing to be seen except a trampled path in the grass where their footsteps had disturbed the frosty ground.

Meddy was waiting at the kitchen door. Milo took one look at her worried face, then tugged his father's sleeve. "Dad, make the others go in first," he whispered.

Mr. Pine looked as if he wanted to argue, but only for a second before he relented. "Be quick."

He maneuvered the other three adults neatly up the kitchen stairs, leaving Milo and Meddy alone. "Meddy," Milo said in a rush, "I saw your dad. For real, this time. Right there." He pointed back toward the woods, but Doc was still gone.

"What do you mean, for real? And you saw him *there?* I thought—"

"It was Gilawfer, before, pretending to be your dad's ghost." Milo swallowed his embarrassment. "But out there in the woods— Meddy, the real Doc Holystone showed up, I swear. He and the hobby horse—a ghost hobby horse—saved me."

Meddy's eyes widened. "The fake one *was* in the wrong part of the woods. Why didn't I trust my memory?" Her eyes flooded. "And Dad's really there? Really?"

"Really." Milo put an arm around her. "When this is over, we're going, you and me. We'll find a way, I promise." His friend nodded, eyes glued to the trees. Then they went inside.

Mrs. Pine descended on Milo the minute he stepped over the threshold, simultaneously hugging him and yelling at him as she dragged him to the fireplace to warm up. He saw Rob try to sidle up to Mrs. Kirkegrim, with Mr. Larven a pace or two behind him. She ignored them and let Mr. Hakelbarend guide her to a chair.

Georgie came to sit at Milo's side as he huddled under the cloak, arms wrapped around his rucksack with its precious contents. "That was utterly stupid, running out into the cold like that without telling anyone and without so much as a coat. I don't know what you were up to, but if I find out it was about—"

"It was." Milo grinned over his still-chattering teeth. "And I found them."

Georgie made an angry face, and by some will of effort stood without asking any questions. "We'll talk later." She walked away, paused to say something to Emmett, who was leaning on the back of the loveseat, then went into the kitchen as the others came into the room in groups of two and three.

Emmett folded his arms and spoke loudly to address everyone. "It seems the last missing items have been ... recovered. So it appears that there's no need for arrests. But I think it's best that everyone get their things together and head out so we can give the Pines some well-earned privacy and peace."

"But we hope everyone has enjoyed their stay." Milo's mom was coming in with a mug he badly wanted to be for him, and Clem was heading his way too. But before either of them could reach him, Rob dropped onto the hearth at Milo's side, between him and the tree.

Milo stiffened as Rob put an arm around his shoulders and poked something into his ribs with his other hand. Milo glanced down, but Rob had his sleeve pulled all the way over whatever he was holding. "Before we go," the sweep announced, "there's just one matter left to discuss."

"Rob —" Lucky began sharply.

Mrs. Pine dropped the mug. Steaming cocoa splashed all over her feet. "Milo!"

"You all stay back until it's settled," Rob said quickly, putting up a warning hand. "Otherwise Milo might get hurt, and I'd like to avoid that. Babs, you have a lot of explaining to do, but start with this: does the kid have what we need?"

Mrs. Kirkegrim hesitated, then nodded.

"Great. Nick?"

Mr. Larven trotted cheerfully up to the hearth, unhooked Mrs. Kirkegrim's cloak from around Milo's neck, and took the rucksack. He opened it, peered inside. "Oh, how very interesting."

Rob couldn't risk taking his eyes off the room, but Milo could. Instead of reaching into Milo's bag, Mr. Larven picked up one of the candlesticks from the mantel.

"You find it?" Rob asked.

Mr. Larven hefted the candlestick, testing the weight. "I believe so."

At last, Rob started to turn to see what Mr. Larven had found, but just then, Sirin leaned quickly out from behind the tree and tapped

Rob's shoulder. "Hey," she said brightly. He turned, his eyes popping at the sudden appearance of the strange girl peering out at him through blue-lensed glasses. And in that moment, Mr. Larven swung the candlestick swiftly down, whacking him solidly on the temple. Rob tumbled sideways, knocked out cold. The butter knife Georgie had been using earlier tumbled from his hand. Milo leapt away and flung himself into his mother's arms. *Thank you,* he mouthed to Sirin. She nodded, removed the glasses, and glanced around the room, probably to be sure she hadn't inadvertently shown herself to anyone other than Rob. Fortunately, none of the other Waits seemed to have any more inkling she was there than they had before.

"And Lucky said I was less than spry." Mr. Larven *tsk*ed as he examined the candlestick for damage. He returned it to the mantel and set Milo's rucksack down on the hearth. "You know, Mr. Syebuck," he said as he dusted off his hands, "you probably should make one arrest after all."

"Just one?" Emmett asked wearily.

Mrs. Kirkegrim rose from the sofa. "One ought to do it, don't you think?" She picked up the butter knife, tossed it up so that it spun end over end, and caught it neatly. "Attempted armed robbery, in front of a roomful of witnesses. Even if it is just the Pines' very nice heirloom silver, it's still a knife."

Emmett cracked a tired smile. "Can't argue that."

"And I think some explanations are in order," Mrs. Kirkegrim continued. She glanced at Emmett. "If, that is, what you said earlier about not pressing charges if the missing items were returned still holds."

Emmett, in turn, looked to Georgie, then Clem. "Does what I said still hold?"

"Sure," Georgie said warily. "I'd quite like to know what the heck has actually been going on."

"Seconded," Clem added, folding her arms.

Mrs. Kirkegrim nodded, satisfied. "Very good. Unless Milo wants to do the honors. I suspect he's worked it all out at this point."

"She's Cantlebone," Milo said from his mother's embrace. He looked at Georgie and Clem. "You were right — Gilawfer followed you here. I'm not totally sure, but I think he must have had a contact in the Liberty — him." He pointed with one shoe at the sprawled and unconscious Rob Gandreider, who Emmett was busy hand-cuffing. "Then I bet he and Rob recruited two other crooks from the Liberty to help steal your haul." *Crooks* sounded bad. "Excuse me," he said, glancing from Mrs. Kirkegrim to Mr. Larven.

"No apologies needed," Mr. Larven said breezily. "It's accurate."

"But Clem and Georgie were also right about Cantlebone having been after the cache, too," Milo said. "Only Gilawfer didn't know that, or he and Rob would have been more careful about their recruits. He unknowingly recruited Cantlebone and got her right into the house."

"Along with a trusted lieutenant," Mrs. Kirkegrim said, smiling at Mr. Larven. "Poor Rob. He never had an inkling, I don't think."

"So *you're Cantlebone?*" Georgie was in total awe. "I'm, like, your *biggest fan!*"

"It's a tie," an equally stunned Clem managed.

"Good grief." Emmett sighed. He sat down on Rob's back as if the sprawled body were a park bench. "Fangirl thieves."

Mrs. Kirkegrim tried to look modest. "I'm honored."

"Wait till you hear how she got the keys out of the house," Milo said. He explained briefly about the burned stollen, then told what had happened in the woods. There were hisses and mutterings from those who'd met Mr. Vinge before, including some choice epithets from Emmett. Then Milo got to the part about the hobby horse.

"I think I . . . called it," he said haltingly, looking at Lucky. "I found most of it, the parts that were hidden in my old fort where I guess Marzana and Mr. Hakelbarend stashed them, but the skull wasn't there. And I started thinking about your story, and that got 'The Holly and the Ivy' stuck in my head. I was humming it as I was going through the woods. I think . . . I think it came because of that. And it chased them away. It *herded* them away. I don't know where to, but it did, and then . . ." He swallowed and glanced at Meddy, who was leaning out of the tree-cave with her elbows on the hearth and her eyes wide. "And then I saw Doc Holystone. He's really out there, haunting the woods."

A momentary silence fell as the assembled group digested this information.

"So what happens now?" Clem asked at last.

"You mean with the keys and the rest of it?" Mrs. Kirkegrim asked. She glanced at Milo's rucksack, which still sat on the hearth. "Well, I don't have them, so I suppose it isn't up to me."

Clem glanced at Meddy. Meddy, in turn, caught Milo's eye. He got up a little awkwardly. "Can we not decide anything for a minute? I . . . I have to go to the bathroom."

He tried to look as casual as possible as he walked out of the living room, through the kitchen, and into the bathroom under the stairs. Meddy followed him and pulled the door shut behind her. "Well. This is weird."

"Yeah. Didn't totally think it through."

"So what do I do?" Meddy asked, touching the globe stand hanging off her belt. "I could disappear it all right now. I think I managed to only show myself to Rob, so none of the rest of the newcomer crowd know I'm here."

Milo hesitated. Something had been bothering him, and it was still bothering him, but he was beginning to think it wasn't bothering him for the reason he'd thought it was. He twisted Téngfēi's ring, which was still on his finger, and willed himself to get back into character. "Sirin, help me think through this. I think maybe we still haven't solved the whole thing."

"Ooooh, really?" She put on her blue glasses.

"Yeah. Remember what Marzana said after I told the Violet Cross story?"

"She said a lot of stuff. Mostly that you were wrong," the scholiast said drily, leaning against the sink.

Téngfēi rolled his eyes. "Yes. But what she *actually* said was something like 'I'm so sick of people telling those stories and getting them wrong. Aren't you?'"

Sirin waited for him to elaborate. Then she got it. "Who was she talking to with that 'Aren't you?'"

"Exactly! At the time, we'd just worked out that Mr. Hakelbarend is her father, so I assumed she was talking to him. That's why I figured he had to be a smuggler. And then right after that, he said . . ." Téngfēi tried to recall the exact words. " 'Those stories *do* belong to everyone. But they still belong to some people more than others.' Even if *he'd* sailed with Violet Cross, that wouldn't quite explain why *Marzana* would get so upset about a wrong detail, or why she would think those stories belonged to her."

"So who would Violet Cross's stories belong to more than anybody else?" Sirin prompted. "Other than Violet Cross herself, obviously. Why *would* they belong to Marzana like that?"

"I wonder," Téngfēi said slowly, "if it isn't Marzana's *father* who's a wanted person. I wonder if it's her *mother*. I think her mother was in the room, and that's who Marzana was talking to. I think Marzana is Violet Cross's daughter, and *I think Violet Cross is here at Greenglass House.*"

Sirin's jaw dropped. "The only person old enough to be Marzana's mother . . ."

"Is Mrs. Kirkegrim," he finished. "I think she's Marzana's mother, and Mr. Hakelbarend's wife." He snapped his fingers. "That was the other thing that was bugging me, back when Marzana brought me hot chocolate. Mrs. Kirkegrim took a cup of coffee to Mr. Hakelbarend. Something I'd seen was off, but I couldn't put my finger on what it was. That was it: they were supposed to be almost strangers, but she brought him his drink already doctored up. She knew how he likes his coffee, without having to ask."

"Wow." Sirin frowned, shook her head, then made a *maybe* sort of face. "Wow. This is interesting."

"Right?" Téngfēi whispered. "And it works out agewise for Violet Cross, too. Violet Cross's ship caught fire and went down with all hands about thirty years ago, didn't it? And she was presumed dead, but if she *didn't* die, if, say, she escaped and went into hiding, then she'd be about the same age as Mrs. Kirkegrim." She did seem a little old to have a young teenage daughter, but it could be that, if you had gone underground for a very good reason, you might wait a while to start a family. You'd probably want to be absolutely sure you were safe. Then another piece clicked: maybe she hadn't been trying out a nickname for a new acquaintance when she'd called Marzana *Marzie*. Maybe it had been a slip—a mother accidentally calling her daughter by a familiar childhood name. "And this could explain the fake knockouts in the upstairs living room. It wasn't just Mrs. Kirkegrim pretending to have gotten conked. It was *both* of them. And then of course, four eyes are even better than two for finding a bunch of hidden stuff."

Sirin held her hand over her mouth. "This makes so much sense. But—" She scratched her head under the Helm of Revelations. "But I met her, you know. Violet Cross, I mean. Once or twice, I'm sure of it. Wouldn't I have recognized her? And what about Gilawfer? Marzana said the only people who could have known that story you told were the cartographers, printers, smugglers, and distributors who were involved. Gilawfer's a fence. I bet he was one of the distributors. Shouldn't Gilawfer have recognized her?"

"I don't know, Sirin. Thirty years is a long time, right? I've seen pictures of my grandparents when they were young, and they look like totally different people." Then he remembered something. "I think your dad recognized her, though. He asked if he knew her. She said no, but something about it—I don't know, Sirin, I think she only said no because I was there. And I think he knew it too. They were like two old friends meeting again."

He hadn't been quite certain at first, but now that he'd talked it out, he was positive. He took the ring off his finger. "Let's find out for sure."

Milo returned to the living room with Meddy in tow and walked up to Emmett. "I have a question. Is there . . . I don't know the phrase, exactly, but is there a length of time where after that, you can't prosecute a crime anymore?"

Emmett nodded slowly. "It's called a statute of limitations. Different crimes have different ones. Things like murder have no time limit, but other crimes often do." He gave Milo a long, curious look. "I'm not an expert on them, but in Nagspeake the statute of limitations on smuggling cases, for instance, is ten years."

"Okay, good." Milo took the center of the room. "Clem, Georgie? About the things from the cache." Everyone looked his way. "I think you have to give them to her," Milo said, pointing to Mrs. Kirkegrim. "They're hers anyway." He looked at the older woman. "Right? You're Violet Cross."

Mrs. Kirkegrim sat very still for a long moment. Then she shook her head, chuckling. "Lesson learned," she said. "If I've heard it once, I've heard it a hundred times: nothing stays buried forever."

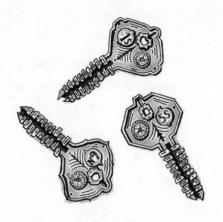

thirty-five

VIOLET CROSS'S SECRET CACHE

ILO'S PARENTS GASPED, Lucky put a hand to her mouth, and the others made assorted shocked mutterings ... but nobody paid any attention to these little reactions, because Georgie and Clem went *nuclear*. If they had fangirled out over Cantlebone, it was nothing compared to their responses to *this* revelation.

"Oh, my God!" Clem erupted, literally falling out of her seat as she tried to get up. "But ... but you're dead!"

"I'm actually not," Mrs. Kirkegrim said drily. "Although around here, I can see how there might be some confusion on the matter."

Georgie stayed seated, but she bounced in her chair like a kid. "You have *got* to tell us about the Gables job. That was you, wasn't it? Everybody says it was John Ferdinand, but I've never believed that."

"The whole story, though," Clem protested. "You falling in love with a customs agent, everything going to pieces, your ship going down—what about all that?"

Mrs. Kirkegrim smiled and shrugged. "Sometimes the only way to reconcile two people in an impossible situation is to change the situation. Isn't that right, Peter?"

Everyone turned to stare at Mr. Hakelbarend. "I *knew* it!" Emmett laughed out loud. "I thought you looked familiar, but I figured my mind was just playing tricks on me."

Peter Hakelbarend gave him a perplexed look. "How on earth could I look familiar to you? This all happened probably before you were born."

"Yeah, but your ID photo is still on file. I read up on a bunch of the old smuggling cases before I came here. Vinge's case—he was the guy who was here last year, the one whose crazy stories I came to investigate—went back to Doc Holystone, and there are plenty of jobs customs figures Miss Cross and Doc Holystone worked together on. So I read your file too." Emmett rubbed his forehead. "Although some of the crazier things Vinge said don't seem quite so crazy today, frankly." He glanced down at the unconscious thief he was still treating like a chair. "I'd better get this guy out of the room if we're going to talk about this any further. Nobody say anything interesting until I get back."

He stood and grabbed Rob under the arms. "Hang on," said

Owen. He took Rob's legs, and together he and Emmett hauled Rob out to the screened porch. Everybody waited silently until they returned.

"All right," Emmett reported. "He's still out cold and he's definitely not going anywhere. Carry on."

"So the story is that your ship was fired on by customs, the powder magazine was hit, and there were no survivors. But . . . that was all a lie?" Clem asked Mrs. Kirkegrim. "You just . . . just walked out?"

"As a matter of fact, we *swam* out, the whole crew, because that's the first thing you do when you've blown up a ship," the older woman said. "We wound up at the Liberty, and that's where we've been ever since. Except when I've ventured out on a few . . . let's call them *excursions* over the last few years." She winked at Mr. Larven, who gave a guffaw. "Since there's a customs officer in good standing present."

Owen spoke up from where he stood by the porch door. "Sounds like you found a way to be together." Even Milo didn't have any trouble interpreting the look he gave Clem. "Looks like people *can* find a way, huh?"

"That's encouraging," Emmett commented. Georgie rolled her eyes at him.

Milo went to sit by Marzana on the couch. She looked as if she couldn't quite figure out what to do with her face — whether to pretend to not know what was going on or to let her just-barely contained pride shine through.

She glanced at Milo. "How long have you known?"

"Only for about two minutes, but you gave me the clues," Milo admitted.

"I was worried about that." She shook her head. "But it's hard not to . . . to . . ."

Milo wanted to say *I know what you mean. I know how you feel.* But he didn't know if that was really true or if it only felt true. So he simply nodded and waited for her to finish talking.

"I always wanted to know what it was like," Marzana went on. "That's why I came on this trip. It wasn't hard to get Lucky to suggest it. I wanted to see Mom work, just once. To have one of those stories for my own."

It was hard to know how to respond. Then Milo had a thought. "You should meet my friend," he said. "Her dad was Doc Holystone."

Several pairs of eyes darted toward Meddy, who was once again leaning out from behind the tree with her folded arms on the hearth. She stiffened. "Milo—"

"But . . ." Marzana frowned and lowered her voice. "I thought she died too."

Milo nodded somberly. "She did. But she never left."

The former Violet Cross gasped. "*Addie?* Addie Whitcher is here?"

Abruptly, he realized he should've asked Meddy before he'd brought her up. He returned to the fireplace. "Can I introduce you?" he asked Meddy.

Meddy scowled at first. Then her face softened. "Yeah. Yeah, you can."

Milo returned to the couch, took Marzana's hand, and pulled her through the room of silent adults and over to the tree. Meddy climbed out and stood there, looking uncomfortable. "Should I introduce you as Meddy or Addie?"

Marzana frowned, confused. "What am I looking at? Was she reincarnated as a Christmas tree?"

Milo didn't actually see Meddy *do* anything. But it was clear that, to Marzana, one minute there was no one behind the tree, and the next minute there was a girl in a yellow robe and a fur-lined hat. Behind them, the adults in the room—the ones who couldn't already see Meddy—made noises of shock.

"Well, now," Mr. Larven said in a tone of wonder. Mr. Hakelbarend folded his arms and whistled. Sylvester gave a yelp, and Lucky, pop-eyed, swatted at him. Emmett looked from Meddy to Milo to Georgie and back again but said nothing.

Meddy studiously ignored them all. "Marzana, I presume," she said stiffly. "I'm Addie Whitcher. But you can call me Meddy."

"Wow," Marzana said, leaning close. "That's some trick. Totally looks like you pulled a Tarncap Reveal." She smiled shyly. "It's a—"

"A theurgist exploit from Odd Trails," Meddy supplied. She eyed Marzana for a minute, then nodded once. "Okay, she's cool." Then she took off her hat and faced Mrs. Kirkegrim uncertainly. "We met before, didn't we?"

Mrs. Kirkegrim stood. "Yes, sweetheart, we met on three occasions. I'm sure I look like a complete stranger to you now."

"I don't recognize you at all," Meddy admitted.

The older woman nodded sympathetically. "I was much

younger then. But I want you to know I've thought of you many times since you and your father passed."

I bet she has, Milo thought. Violet Cross had survived longer than Doc Holystone, but she lived the same kind of life. She had to worry about her own daughter's safety, and probably she thought of Addie Whitcher every time she did.

Mrs. Kirkegrim held out her arms, and Meddy buried her face in the older woman's shoulder. "Thank you."

It took the rest of the room a minute or two to get over the shock of having a ghost appear in their midst, but they all still had questions. "So at what point did you know we were looking for your stuff, ma'am?" Georgie asked.

Mrs. Kirkegrim smiled. "As a matter of fact, the two of you managed to fly under my radar for a bit longer than I'm comfortable with. I found out when you started hunting down all those old geologic surveys of the underground ironwork structures in the Quayside Harbors — the ones that led you to Gilawfer's warehouse. One of the booksellers who sold you those maps is a friend of mine."

"And obviously you know what, specifically, we were looking for," Clem said. "Mr. Larven all but slapped us in the face with it earlier."

"The derrotero. What Nick called the Book of Ways. He's very poetic, aren't you, Nicholas?" Mrs. Kirkegrim asked. Mr. Larven made a short bow. "Everyone looks for that. I hear the stories."

"It must have been there, or why else would you have come out of hiding to retrieve this cache?" Clem asked.

Mrs. Kirkegrim tilted her head curiously. "You think the

derrotero was the only thing I had that I might not want found again?"

The younger thieves frowned and glanced at each other. "Then what was it? What was in the cache that was so special?"

"Most of the tools I created would be . . . problematic in the wrong hands," Mrs. Kirkegrim said carefully. "And almost all of them I made sure to secure before I went off the grid. But this time it wasn't about what was in the cache. It was about Toby Gilawfer." Her face hardened. "He's the one who ratted on me. He's the reason things fell apart all those years ago. It was right after that map escapade, you know. He was a small operator in those days—in fact, he and I never actually met in person before this week—and he got arrested for something minor. Rather than face the consequences, he tried to bargain. Offered to turn over someone even bigger. *Me.* So you'd better believe I was never going to let him get his hands on any of my stuff if I could help it. And if I could humiliate him a little in the process . . ." She shrugged. "Well. Bonus. Plus, my daughter had been hassling me about wanting to see me work." She smiled over at Marzana. "This seemed like a nice, relatively safe caper to bring her on. Kind of a take-your-kid-to-work-day situation."

"Your daughter?" Lucky's mind was clearly blown. "And here I thought it was all my idea, your coming along."

Marzana blushed. "Surprise."

"Okay, but why did you hide the stuff under Gilawfer's warehouse in the first place?" Georgie asked. "He'd be the most likely person to find it."

"Oh, I didn't," Mrs. Kirkegrim told her. "The iron structure that came up through his floor was in an entirely different place when I stashed everything there. That's why I thought it was safe. I know more about those underground ironworks than almost anybody else in the city. I knew they shifted, but even I didn't think they were likely to work up to the surface. What were the chances?" She cleared her throat. "So. About the goods you recovered. I see the reflecting circle and part of the spherical chalkboard hanging from Addie's belt. I presume the rest are hidden somewhere very safe."

Clem and Georgie both started talking at the same time.

"They're yours, obviously."

"Please, don't say another word —"

"No, no." The woman who had been Violet Cross held up her hands. "Listen, I've heard of you two. I don't follow the scene in Nagspeake quite as closely as I used to, but I know what kind of operatives you are. And now I think I have some ideas about what kind of *people* you are. You're welcome to keep the stuff. And although the derrotero isn't among the items you're walking away with, I think you'll find that what you have is well worth the trouble you went to." She grinned. "Let's just say it'll provide many hours of study, and a lot of value if you put in the time. But I'd like to take a keepsake for Marzana."

"Of course," Georgie and Clem said at once.

"Lovely. Then it's a bargain." Mrs. Kirkegrim looked at her daughter. "Possibly this will be the only heist she ever pulls. I sort of hope it is. In that case, she should have something to remember it by. You did beautifully, my dear."

"I tipped off Milo in like five different ways," Marzana grumbled, but she was smiling.

"I have a feeling you should not judge yourself too harshly for being figured out by Milo Pine," Mr. Hakelbarend said from his chair. "Not just anyone could've put together that you and I were related. After that, it was only a matter of time."

"I can confirm that this is the truth, Marzana," Georgie said. "Definitely do not beat yourself up over it. Clem and I have learned not to even bother trying to keep secrets from Milo." Meddy chucked Milo on the arm. He blushed.

"So where is everything else, exactly?" Mr. Hakelbarend asked, glancing from Clem to Georgie. "We couldn't find anything after you recovered it."

"I have everything here." Meddy produced the pieces of the cache one by one and set them out on the coffee table. "And of course Milo has the keys."

"Oh, right." Milo grabbed the bag on the hearth and reached in. One by one he produced the eleven keys and set them out on the table.

"I thought these were so beautiful," Clem said, picking one up. "Adjustable bump keys, right?"

It was Milo's first good look at them, and they were even stranger than he'd realized. Where most keys had a straight channel cut down each flat side, these had slightly wiggly ones instead. There were teeth on both edges instead of just one, and some of the teeth had ledges and whorls cut into them. Furthermore, each tooth was a separate piece of metal that could be adjusted, moving in or out by means of tiny screws. On the big flat handles near the hole for the key ring, each had a dial that looked a bit like a clock with a couple too many hands. And each was engraved with a letter and a number: *1S, 2S, 3S, 4S, 5S.* The others were numbered *1–6N.*

He looked up from the line of keys glittering in the reflected lights from the tree. "You said it wasn't about the cache," Milo said to Mrs. Kirkegrim. "But these were the only things you bothered to smuggle out of the house. Why?"

"There really is no getting anything past you, is there?" Mrs. Kirkegrim winked at him. "Well, like I said, I wanted to make sure I left with a keepsake for Marzana, and the only way to do that was to make sure something made it out of the house. I couldn't assume I'd get everything out, so I made a choice. As to why I chose these, well." She lifted one up and turned it in the light. "That's easy. I'm terribly proud of them. They're one of a kind. I made them myself." She smiled at her daughter. "Although of course you can pick whatever you like, Marzie. It's not for me, after all. It's for you." This time Marzana didn't flinch at the nickname.

"You *made* these?" Clem breathed. "Unbelievable. They're works of art."

Clem was right. No wonder she looked so wistful — it was obvious what Marzana would pick for her keepsake. Everything else paled next to those keys.

"What would you like for your remembrance, Marzana?" Georgie asked, sounding just a little resigned. Yup. Everybody knew.

"I think I would like those, if that's okay," Marzana said, nodding to the glittering collection on the table.

To their credit, both Georgie's smile and Clem's looked totally genuine. "Of course," Georgie said.

"I can probably find a spare ring for them," Mrs. Pine said, getting to her feet.

While they waited, everyone crowded in to examine Violet Cross's secret stash. It was a little bit like getting to touch and hold pieces of a museum exhibit. Milo picked up the reflecting circle, the only part of the cache he hadn't had a look at. It needed a polish, but it was a beautiful device nevertheless.

"It's for determining longitude," Mr. Pine said, leaning over Milo's shoulder. "An antique method, but look at how lovely the thing is. Can you actually do lunar distance navigation?" he asked Mrs. Kirkegrim.

"Not well," she admitted. "I figured if I was going to fall in love with old-fashioned instruments, I'd better know how to use them, but I'll be the first to confess you wouldn't want me relying on one of those if we were lost at sea."

Then there were the cards, which Milo had gotten only glimpses of while shaking them from the lampshade in Georgie's room. Now that he had time to take a better look, he saw that the face cards were all images of famous smugglers. "I'll be damned," Emmett laughed, picking one up. "I've heard of these. They were issued to customs agents for a couple years back in the day. The courts were made up of the most wanted lawbreakers at the time."

"Close," Mrs. Kirkegrim said with a grin. "The customs agency made something similar, but they never knew the real identities of half the people their cards showed." She nodded to the deck. "*This* was the real Court of Runners in Nagspeake, once upon a time, and it's the only set there is. Hand-painted, every card."

"No way," Milo breathed as he, Meddy, and Marzana all dove at the cards and started hunting through them in search of relatives and acquaintances. "Here's Captain Pickering," Milo announced, holding up the king of clubs.

Marzana waved a queen. "I found Mom!"

Meddy sat back with a card cradled in her hand. She said nothing, just gazed down on it in silence. Milo had read about people having faraway looks in their eyes, but this was the first time he was certain he was seeing one.

Sylvester carefully opened the spherical chalkboard and fitted it into the stand. Lucky and Georgie bent over the pieces of the fan, discussing how to properly order them when they were put back together. Both seemed certain there had to be a right way to do it, but neither wanted to ask outright. Clem watched Owen try to open one of the locks with a pick and wrench he didn't look all that confident with. Probably she'd taught him just as she'd taught Milo.

Oh, but the keys. Milo kept coming back to the keys. He picked one up — 4N, as it happened — and turned it over in his fingers. *So cool.* He couldn't see how you could stick it in a lock, though, with teeth on both sides of it. Plus, it looked as if you'd need a toothpick or something to adjust the dial in the grip. "Hey, Clem, how do you use a bump key, anyway?"

She took it from his outstretched hand. "I've never seen one like this before," she admitted. "I'm guessing that each side allows for a different combination of bittings — those are the notches and teeth—so one of the adjustments you make while setting it is to withdraw the side you don't want to use—to pull that side all the way in. Then you'd be left with something that looks a bit more like a normal key, with bittings on just one side. Is that right, Mrs. Kirkegrim?"

"You can adjust them that way," the older thief confirmed. "There are other ways too."

"The wiggly grooves are confusing to me, though," Clem said, running her finger down the channel in the middle of the key. "I have seen keys with channels that didn't run straight before. But usually those are pretty specific to certain locks."

"Found one," Mrs. Pine said, holding up an empty key ring that dangled from a heavy, engraved brass fob as she returned to the living room. "I knew we had a box of these around somewhere."

Marzana took the ring and read the words carved on the brass piece. "'*Your Establishment's Name Here*'? Why didn't you get some that said *Greenglass House*?"

"Well you might ask. We didn't order those. A guest here once failed to let us know at the beginning of his stay that he lacked the ability to pay in actual currency. Instead, he left us a salesman's sample box of fancy key fobs. We eventually learned to start asking more questions when guests checked in."

Marzana collected the keys and threaded them one by one onto the ring. Then she tucked them into her pocket. "Thank you."

Lucky passed the pieces of fan she was holding to Georgie. "Listen, maybe we should think about getting under way. Or *I* should think about getting under way, and anybody who wants to can come with me. Now that things are sort of settled, we can finally get out of the Pines' hair." She glanced at Mrs. Kirkegrim. "Although maybe you want to stay and swap stories or something. I can get back by myself."

Sylvester had been arranging the playing cards in elaborate arrays on the rug. Now he swept them up and straightened them into a neat pack, which he handed to Clem. "I'll walk with you. If you don't mind, that is. I can carry the hobby horse stuff back."

Lucky shrugged. "Okay," she said coolly. Then she gave up on the cool and smiled. "Sure. I'd like that."

"We'll all go," Mr. Hakelbarend said. He stood with a stretch. "Lucky's right. It's time. We did what we came to do."

thirty-six

SNOW

T HE WAITS GOT their belongings together. It didn't take long — they hadn't brought anything besides their various coats and costume pieces. Lizzie packed a little bag of treats and a thermos of hot cider for their walk back up the hill to the Liberty.

There was a muffled shout from the screened porch. Rob was coming around.

"What do you want us to do about dear Rupert?" Mrs. Kirkegrim asked. "I hate to leave him cluttering up your porch."

"You can leave him with me," Emmett said from the sofa. "I called a friend of mine. He's coming with a car to pick us up. And then I promise both he and I will get out of your hair too, Mr. and Mrs. Pine."

Mrs. Kirkegrim shook hands with Georgie, then Clem. "Come up to the Liberty and visit sometime, if you like."

Georgie looked as if she might faint from delight. Clem tried to play it cooler and just wound up looking, in Milo's opinion, as if she was trying not to faint before Georgie did. Owen, who had been talking with Peter Hakelbarend at the dining table, gave Mrs. Kirkegrim a hug. "Thank you both. You have no idea how much this has meant to Clem and me, meeting you."

"I think maybe I have an inkling." Mr. Hakelbarend turned to the bar and the three friends sitting there. "You ready, Marzana?"

"Almost." Marzana sucked down the last of her hot chocolate and slid off the stool. She held out her hand to Meddy, and then to Milo. "Nice to meet you both."

"You guys should come down and visit again," Milo said. "We play Odd Trails sometimes, if you want in on a game."

Marzana's face lit up like a lantern. "Yeah, I'd like that. And maybe we can talk some more," she said to Meddy. "If that's okay."

Meddy grinned. "I can't make any promises. Milo can explain. But if I'm here, I'd like that a lot."

The Waits (minus the chimney sweep) made final adjustments to their cold-weather clothes. Mrs. Kirkegrim paused to light the candles on the branch she'd carried in on the first night, which still stood in a vase on the dining table. "For luck," she said, kissing Milo's mother on the cheek. "Keep it warm and watered, and it should flower before the new year—if I didn't kill it when I set myself on fire last night, that is."

Someone opened the door, and winter poured in on the back

of an icy gust. And then they were gone, filing out down the stairs. Milo and his parents watched from the porch as they crossed the lawn. They left the way they had come: through the woods rather than by the road, headed in a direction that would take them past his fort, where the frame and shrouds that made up the hobby horse's body were still waiting. Would the skull be there waiting for them too? Had it returned from wherever it had herded Gilawfer and Vinge?

Just before they disappeared into the trees, Milo heard Lucky's voice rise into the cold, cloudy sky. *"The holly and the ivy, when they are both full grown . . ."* The others picked up the song, harmonizing easily. *"Of all the trees that are in the wood, the holly bears the crown."*

And then they were gone.

When the Pines came back in, Emmett stood. "I think I'll get moving too. I'd like to be ready to go the minute my ride gets here."

"Are you sure you can handle that guy all on your own?" Georgie asked.

"Him? Sure." Emmett grinned. "You might not have picked up on it, but I only pretend to be a hapless artist."

"Oh, I picked up on the fact that you only pretend to be an artist," Georgie retorted. "Picked up on that when we searched your room yesterday. I just wasn't sure at the time that *you* knew you were only pretending."

"Ouch."

Clem coughed from the loveseat, where she was sprawled with her feet up on one armrest. "Actually, after we searched his room, your exact words were 'His drawings are decent. If he's a poser, he's at least a semi-talented one.' For the record."

"'Semi-talented'?" It didn't seem as if it should've been possible, but Emmett's grin got even wider. "Sounds like a compliment to me."

"It was not a *compliment*, it was an *observation*," Georgie said loftily.

Meddy made a gagging noise. "Jeez, get a room," she said under her breath. "I mean, there are like twelve of them right upstairs."

"Anyway." Emmett took a card out of his wallet and scrawled what looked like a phone number on it. "I'm leaving this here without comment." He took Georgie's hand and put the card in it. "Use it as a bookmark if you want."

Georgie raised an eyebrow, *Who are you kidding, mister?* style, but she tucked the card in her pocket as Emmett trotted upstairs to pack.

Clem stuck an elbow in Georgie's ribs the second the sound of Emmett's footsteps faded away. "You gonna call him?"

"Shut up, Red."

"'Cause you can totally bring a date to the wedding."

"Shut *up*, Red!"

Clem looked from Georgie to Owen. "We should probably figure out getting home, too, although I don't particularly want to leave until our captive out there on the porch is gone for good. Should we call a ferry, or see if Brandon can come out and pick us up?"

Mrs. Pine put an arm around her. "Why don't you three stay tonight and leave tomorrow? There's no reason to rush off. Lizzie and

Mrs. Caraway need to get out of here to meet Lizzie's little sister when she arrives tomorrow morning, but you're welcome to stay."

"You've got to be dying to have your house back," Georgie said. "Aren't you fed up with guests?"

"You aren't guests, Georgie," Mr. Pine said. "You're friends."

Georgie put a hand to her heart. "After all the trouble we caused you—all of you—"

"You needed help," Mrs. Pine said gently. "And I'm honored that you thought of us and trusted us enough to come here."

Georgie threw her arms around her. "Thank you. But no, I think I'll be on my way."

"I think," Clem said after a moment, "that Owen and I are going to head home too. But thank you so, so much for the invitation."

"In that case," said Mrs. Caraway, "I bet we can fit everyone in Lizzie's car. We'll get under way as soon as Emmett's ride arrives."

A companionable hush fell over Greenglass House. Mrs. Caraway passed out more hot chocolate; then she and Lizzie joined everyone in the living room. Everyone but Rob, who could still be heard making muffled threats out on the porch. Eventually he gave up and fell silent. Georgie and Clem played rock-paper-scissors every once in a while to determine who had to get up from messing with their Violet Cross souvenirs to make sure he was still securely tied to his chair. "Man, he's trussed like a turkey," Georgie said to Emmett, who returned to the first floor with his luggage right after one of these checks. "You weren't playing around."

Milo sat next to Meddy on the hearth, watching the two thieves with their haul. "Too bad about the derrotero," said Milo. "It was cool to think Violet Cross might have managed to do the impossible." Meddy turned to look at him as if he were crazy. "What?"

"Step into my office, would you, please?" Meddy dragged him back behind the tree. "You're kidding, right? She *did* make a derrotero. Maybe it wasn't in this particular cache, but she totally admitted it. Remember when she told Clem there was other stuff she might not have wanted found? Was I the only one who was paying attention to that?"

"I don't remember her exact words," Milo said defensively.

"Well, let me refresh your memory. Her exact words were 'You think the only thing I had that I might not want found again was the derrotero?' She never said there *wasn't* a Book of Ways. She didn't say 'I don't have a derrotero, but I had other things.' I'll bet you a million bucks it's still out there somewhere. Or maybe she never stashed it anywhere in the first place. She's probably had it all this time. Would you ever let go of anything that valuable?"

"Not unless I didn't have a choice about it." They hadn't gotten many details out of Mrs. Kirkegrim about Violet Cross's final, miraculous, presumed-dead escape. But if she'd had to pull it off fast, maybe she wouldn't have had time to gather up every single possession she'd stashed away for safekeeping. Also, there was the instability of the underground structure in which she'd hidden the cache Georgie and Clem had found. "She did say that buried building had shifted more than she'd expected it to. Maybe she hid the derrotero in a similar place and lost it herself."

Or . . .

Milo's rucksack was still by the fireplace where he'd left it after

taking the keys from it. He grabbed it and pulled out *The Skidwrack:
A Visual History,* then he opened the cover and examined the frontispiece illustration in the glow of the multicolored tree bulbs. "What
do you see here, Meddy?" She leaned over the book, pushing aside
a branch to get closer without losing the light. Milo pointed at the
inlets branching off the main curving body of the river. "One. Two.
Three. Four. Five. Five on the south side of the river. One. Two.
Three. Four. Five. Six. Six on the north side. Eleven inlets. And
each one has a channel, right? A deeper section running approximately down the middle, with shoals and banks that sort of shift?"

"Yeah, so . . . ?"

"You know what else has a channel sort of down the middle,
with edges that can be changed? *Those keys.* The so-called adjustable bump keys. The ones Marzana just happened to pick for her
memento of this weekend."

Meddy's eyes popped. "You think the *keys* are the derrotero?"

"Of *course* they are! Marzana said it herself—Violet Cross
could put a map on anything. You just had to figure out the orientation in order to read it. But the problem that makes the Skidwrack
so difficult to map is that everything changes. So the derrotero has
to be able to shift too. It has to be a movable map. Violet Cross must
have found a way to calculate the factors that make the banks and
channels so unpredictable. If you know what those factors are, I bet
it's just a matter of adjusting the keys so that the—what did Clem
call them?—the bittings reflect the shoals and banks." He tapped
the frontispiece of the book. "If you knew how to adjust the key
corresponding to a particular inlet, I bet it would look like one of

these illustrations." He sat back, shaking his head. "I knew, I *knew* there was something about those keys. And not once, but *twice* she arranged for somebody else to get them out of the house in a way that made it look like she wasn't even involved: first my dad, carrying out the trash, and then Marzana, carrying out the keepsake we all agreed she should have. We even knew she'd done it already, and she still got us a second time."

"That's crazy." Meddy shook her head, impressed. "Should we tell them? Clem and Georgie, I mean."

Milo considered. "I don't know what good it would do. It's over. Mrs. Kirkegrim has what she came for."

"I think we should tell them because it's just one more way that Violet Cross is a beast. I think they'll love it."

Yeah, they probably would. "Okay."

They climbed out from behind the tree and joined the thieves, Owen, and Emmett at the coffee table. Milo told them his suspicions. Owen sat back with a low whistle. Emmett closed his eyes as if trying to picture the keys, then opened them again with an expression of wonder. "Unbelievable."

Clem burst out laughing, and Georgie shook her head in disbelief. "I want to be her when I grow up," she said wistfully.

After that, Mrs. Caraway brought out sandwiches and a salad for a quick dinner while they waited for Emmett's friend to arrive. They were just finishing up when a pair of headlights flashed through the trees that hid the road.

The customs agent stood up with a yawn. "That'll be my ride. I'll see you all later, I guess."

"I'll get your luggage," Mr. Pine offered.

"Thanks." Emmett went out onto the screened porch and returned with a furious Rob Gandreider, untied but handcuffed. "Say goodbye and thank you, Rob."

"I have nothing to say to you or anyone but my lawyer," Rob retorted through clenched teeth.

"Yeah, I figured," Emmett said as he escorted his prisoner across the room. "Fair warning: it's a long drive back into town, and I tend to fill awkward silences by singing. I'm not good, but I'm loud." Rob muttered something about unethical torture of uncharged detainees as Emmett shoved him out the door.

They watched the red taillights of the car recede down the driveway until they faded into the woods. First Georgie, Clem, and Owen, then Mrs. Caraway and Lizzie headed upstairs and returned with their assorted luggage. While Mr. Pine and Owen loaded up Lizzie's station wagon, Milo realized he still had the lock engraved with all the eyes, the one Clem had lent him so he could practice with his lockpicks. He dug it out of the rucksack and carried it to where Clem and Georgie were sitting with Meddy at the dining room table. "I almost forgot this," he said. "Thanks for letting me borrow it."

"I'm glad you brought that up," Clem said with a smile.

Georgie patted a paper lunch bag that sat between them on the table. "We have something for you."

"What is it?" Milo asked, barely able to keep the excitement from his voice.

"I think you know," Georgie said, pushing the bag over to him.

He opened it, and there they were: ten more locks of assorted sizes, shapes, and designs. They glinted tantalizingly in the light of the candles burning on the branch in the vase, light that flickered as Mr. Pine and Owen came back inside along with a gust of cold air. "These are for me? All of them?"

"They are," Georgie said. "A little thank-you from both of us."

"From all three of us," Owen corrected, blowing into his hands to warm them up. "I want to be part of the thank-you present this time."

"Besides, you really need an assortment of pieces to practice on," Clem said reasonably. "Practice makes the picklock."

Milo clutched the bag tightly. "Thank you."

Georgie reached one closed fist out to Meddy. "And this is for you."

Meddy blinked, surprised. "For me?" She cupped her palms together, and Georgie dropped something small and silvery into them: a tiny, narrow-winged bird with a long, hooked beak.

"It used to be a quarter, but now it's an albatross," Georgie said. "Just in case you couldn't tell. I'm not a sculptor."

"Thank you." Meddy nodded, smiling. "I could tell."

More goodbyes and hugs all around, as well as congratulations to Clem and Owen. Clem promised to send the Pines a wedding invitation, even though it was last-minute. Hugs from Lizzie and Mrs. Caraway, too, who would be back in a couple of weeks. And then just four people were left in Greenglass House: Milo and his parents and Meddy.

"It gets quiet so suddenly sometimes," Mrs. Pine said. "I

thought I was going to have a panic attack at least five times this weekend."

Mr. Pine checked the clock. "Nearly eleven, you guys. How late are we staying up? Tomorrow's Christmas Eve."

"I have to enjoy the quiet for a bit before I turn in," Mrs. Pine said. "I need to sit and appreciate our nice clean fireplace. I think I'm just going to lie in front of it and maybe fall asleep there. Somebody make sure I wind up going to bed eventually."

Mr. Pine kissed her cheek. "Promise. You want a glass of wine?"

"Good grief, yes."

"Milo? Meddy? Hot chocolate?"

"Yes, please," said Milo.

"I'll pass," Meddy replied apologetically. "But thank you."

They went into the living room, and Milo started repacking all the stuff he'd taken out when he was hunting for the keys at the bottom of the bag.

He was reaching for the big hardcover *Transmundane Warriors* book when something occurred to him. "Meddy, I think I'm having an idea about a way to get you to your dad."

She looked up from where she was sprawled on the floor. "I'm listening."

"Remember how last year you tried carrying me through a door with you?"

"To be completely accurate, I smashed you face first *into* a door while trying to carry you through it," Meddy reminded him. "It didn't work."

"Right, I remember that part. You can't carry me, but I was thinking maybe I can carry *you*."

"How?"

"You showed me something in the book—an exploit called Summon Scholiast."

"A harbinger exploit," Meddy said automatically. "So?"

"Okay." Milo opened the book to the dog-eared page and read the description aloud. "'You conjure a scholiast, a shape-shifting spirit familiar who can take the form of a bird as well as a human. Your scholiast can travel and operate semi-independently from you, taking its own turns.'"

"Are you asking if I can shape-shift? Because the answer is no."

"Yeah, that isn't what I was going for. It's this next bit: 'It typically remains within one hundred feet of you in order to maintain telepathic communications, but it can operate at greater distances and/or travel with another player character for short periods of time by means of a reliquary.'" He looked up. "Tell me about reliquaries."

"A reliquary is a container for relics," Meddy said. "A harbinger needs one in order to summon a scholiast in the first place. Then there's a separate exploit called Spooky Action at a Distance where you can take a relic from the scholiast—a feather or whatever—and put it in the reliquary. You can give the reliquary to another player character to carry, and when you and that player split up, the scholiast can travel with the other person, but you and the scholiast can still interact with each other."

"Exactly," Milo said triumphantly. "So what if we thought about you as . . . I don't know, a scholiast tied to this house rather than to a harbinger? Maybe I could carry you with me if we used a reliquary." He took the red lacquer box out, opened it, and produced the gold vial. "Maybe something like this."

Meddy gave him a disbelieving look. "You do understand that I'm not *really* a scholiast, right? That's not a thing you're confused about, is it?" She whacked the book with the back of one hand. "I mean, that stuff is *made up,* Milo."

"Yes, I know all that," Milo said patiently. "But it made me wonder. I mean — well, you *are* still a supernatural being, right? Technically?"

"I suppose."

"And a lot of the stuff in Odd Trails is based on folklore, right?"

"Some," Meddy allowed. "But, Milo, if I was tied to a place based on where my . . . my physical remains are, I'd be tied to that garden outside. The one where I'm . . ." *Buried.* She didn't have to say the word for Milo to know what she meant. "I mean, what other relics do I have?"

Milo pointed at her pocket. "You have the Sirin owl."

Meddy took the figurine from her pocket and looked from it to the vial. "It might fit in there. But why the owl? I didn't even know it existed until last year."

"Yeah, but it's tied to you, and to Greenglass House, and to your dad. It represents a part of who you are in the house — the character you built for yourself here. The character your dad knew you always wanted to play. How is that not a relic?"

She eyed the figurine for a long time, thinking. "I don't see how it's even remotely possible that this would work," she said slowly. "But . . . I also don't see any reason not to try." Then she took a deep breath and blew it out. "Okay. Fine. But I want you to know I'm not getting my hopes up." Her voice was a little shaky. She *looked* hopeful, though.

"Whatever," Milo said with a smile. "Come on."

"Going somewhere?" Mrs. Pine asked as Milo pulled on his coat.

"Just outside for a minute. We're going to try and get Meddy to her dad."

"It's not going to work," Meddy added. "But no stone left unturned and all."

"Quit being negative." Milo led the way through the kitchen, and they all went out the back door into the frigid night: first him, then Meddy, then Mr. and Mrs. Pine.

Meddy stood on the step, the farthest point to which she could go without dissolving into the ether. She stood in silence for a moment, then turned and faced a stretch of woods to the left. "It was somewhere over there," she said quietly. "Where I saw him before. I'm sure I'm right." They stood there for another moment, waiting.

Nothing happened.

They waited some more. Still nothing happened.

Meddy glanced back at Milo. Tears bubbled up in her eyes. "What do I have to do?" she said brokenly. "Why won't he show himself to me?"

Milo's heart sank. He scratched his head. "Try calling him." It was all he could think of.

He squeezed her hand, then let go and stood behind her as she screwed up her courage. "Dad?" she called at last, in a voice that shook like a windblown fir. Now everyone held their breath. And as his name echoed across the lawn, it happened.

Doc Holystone appeared at the edge of the trees—the *real* Michael Whitcher, the one who had come to Milo's rescue along with the phantom hobby horse only hours earlier. Just as he had years before, he lifted a hand to wave at his daughter.

Milo's mother gasped. His dad said, "Whoa."

Meddy made a strange sound, something midway between a gasp, a sob, and a laugh. Milo reached for her hand. "You ready?"

She took a deep breath. "No. But let's try. Milo, if this doesn't work—"

"If this doesn't work, we'll think of something else." He held up the vial and took out the cork. "Your reliquary awaits."

Meddy slid the owl figurine carefully into it. "Now what?"

Milo put the vial in his pocket and held out his hand. Meddy took it. Together they stepped off the porch and onto the dead, frosty grass. As one, they looked down at their joined hands.

"You're still here."

"Don't jinx it, Milo."

They walked across the lawn, moving slowly. With every step, Milo was sure Meddy would flicker out like an extinguished candle flame and he would be left holding a handful of empty air. But she didn't. Every step was just another step closer to the trees and her watchful father.

One step at a time. Meddy clutched his hand tighter.

One step at a time. Milo forgot to breathe for a few minutes.

And then, miraculously, they were there, and Meddy fell into her father's arms. "Daddy."

Captain Whitcher laughed in pure joy. "Addie."

"I missed you so much." Her words were muffled, almost inaudible, but the words themselves didn't matter, not really. Not in that moment.

Milo took the reliquary vial from his pocket and slipped it into the pocket of Meddy's robe. Then he edged away, praying that he was right about this exploit they'd pulled: that she was tied to the owl in its reliquary, and that Milo himself didn't matter. He wanted to give them some privacy. And he figured if Meddy suddenly vanished, he'd know that for some reason, he was part of the equation, and he'd just go back.

He glanced over his shoulder as he walked away, but Meddy didn't vanish. She also didn't look back at him. He didn't blame her. She had more important things on her mind. Captain Whitcher, however, did glance up. He beamed at Milo over the top of Meddy's head, raised his hand once again, and mouthed the words *Thank you.*

Milo climbed up the porch stairs to where his parents stood, arms around each other. They reached out with their free arms and pulled him into their embrace.

A press of emotion engulfed Milo as he stood there with his parents, gazing across the lawn to where his friend stood with her father. "You did good, kiddo," Mrs. Pine said, leaning down to kiss the top of his head.

Mr. Pine gave him an extra squeeze. "Really proud of you."

Milo knew if he didn't do something, he would cry. He sniffled and blinked hard, trying to will away the tears. And then he realized he didn't want to will them away. They were good tears, with happiness in them — and sadness, too, because he had no way of knowing how long Meddy would stay this time, and he had missed her so desperately over the last year. There was just too much feeling to keep in. So Milo let the tears fall, and his parents held him silently while he cried.

And then: "Will you look at that?" Mr. Pine reached into the night with the arm that had been around Milo's mom. He held his hand out. "Finally! I was starting to think we were going to be stuck with nothing but this stupid frost."

Milo wiped his eyes and blinked them into focus. His face broke into a wide smile. He reached out a hand, too, and watched the flakes fall into his palm.

Snow, at last.

Author's Note

A couple things I did not make up that I should mention: The lyrics to "Good King Wenceslas" were written by John Mason Neale in the mid-nineteenth century and set to a much older melody. I included the song here as a sort of homage to a scene I love in *The Dark Is Rising*, where Will Stanton and Merriman Lyon sing it together as they walk through winter, and time. "The Holly and the Ivy" is a traditional folk carol I have always loved. (At one point my sister and I also had a pair of birds named Holly and Ivy, but the less said about those birds, the better.) "Jackanory" is an old English nursery rhyme that I learned as a child from my father, who told it as a bedtime story much as Mr. Larven does. Dad's usual rotation was some combination of "Jackanory," "Waltzing Matilda," and "Sam Hall" (another English folk song, this one written from the point of view of a very bitter murderer about to hang for his crimes. Ah, childhood.). Also, readers with an interest in winter folklore are invited to dig in to the names, costumes, and props of the Waits. Some Nagspeake traditions have very old roots.

Acknowledgments

This story came as a bit of a surprise to me. It happened in November of 2015, when the idea of Georgie and Clem pulling a heist-gone-wrong occurred to me out of the blue on the drive home to Brooklyn after Thanksgiving with my folks. After that, to my very great shock, the whole story came together in a matter of about a week, and I wrote the first outline I have ever done voluntarily. I'm telling you this because I really hate outlines and I'm terrible at them, so I'm inordinately proud of having done one without being made to do it by one of the more responsible adults who facilitate my writing career. Still, without those responsible adults, you wouldn't be reading this now, so thank you to Barry Goldblatt and Lynne Polvino for believing in the story, and to Jaime Zollars and Sharismar Rodriguez for once again making the book itself more beautiful than I could have imagined.

Milo and his friends had some very specific concerns this time around that I didn't feel confident I could address on my own. Fortunately, a group of truly exceptional readers had my back, and through their questions, guidance, insight, and generosity, every single one of them made this story better. I am so grateful to you, my friends, both to those who helped me navigate tricky waters by putting me in touch with better navigators than myself, and to those who read and proceeded to dedicate your time and trust to making sure the story didn't fetch up on any shoals. So thank you with love to MeeJin Annan-Brady, Karen Bao, Dhonielle Clayton, Catherine Gulotta, Mike Lewis, Grace Lin, Jon Slomka, and Kat Yeh, as well as to everyone at Spence-Chapin Services to Families and Children (who in addition to being tremendously helpful during the revision of this book have also been a critical support network during my family's own adoption journey). On behalf of Milo, Meddy, Marzana, Owen, and all the others, thank you for giving me the gift of your time and trust.

As ever, Emma Humphrey was the first reader of the first draft; Emma, never change, because this process just wouldn't be the same without you. Many thanks to Jason Milford and Colleen AF Venable, who helped me puzzle out the problem of how to keep Georgie busy during this book, and to Kristi Hayes and all the folks at Otherworld—I blatantly cribbed a line from Kristi and Company when I described Milo's alter-egos of Negret and Téngfēi as being more heroic versions of himself. It was too perfect not to use: thank you, Kristi, for your blessing on that one.

Once again, I owe Gus and the good folks at Emphasis Restaurant and the wonderful crew at Coffee RX in Bay Ridge, Brooklyn, a debt of gratitude for letting me camp out at their respective establishments and write, as well as to Chelsea Hesketh, Ray Rupelli, and Melissa Garvin, who make it possible to sneak away in the first place. To Sarah McNally, to my Saturday partner in crime, Cristin Stickles, and to everyone at McNally Jackson Books, thank you for everything you do, and for continuing to give me a place to restore my sanity through the simple act of being around you once a week. And of course, to Nathan, Griffin, and Tess, who are my best friends and my greatest loves — thank you for making room in all of our lives for me to keep writing. This is for you. It is always for you.

Last, but most of all, to everyone who read, loved, and shared *Greenglass House* — thank you, from the deepest depths of my heart. I had no idea what would happen when I started writing that first very sloppy proposal that would become Milo and Meddy's first adventure. You changed my life, and I will forever be grateful.